IRELAND

From the Act of Union • 1800
to the Death of Parnell • 1891

*Seventy-seven novels and collections
of shorter stories by twenty-two*
Irish and Anglo-Irish novelists

selected by
PROFESSOR ROBERT LEE WOLFF
Harvard University

A GARLAND SERIES

Stories of the Irish Peasantry

Anna Maria Hall

with an introduction by
Robert Lee Wolff

Garland Publishing, Inc., New York & London
1979

For a complete list of the titles in this series,
see the final pages of this volume.

Introduction copyright © 1979 by Robert Lee Wolff

All rights reserved

This facsimile has been made from a copy in
the British Library (1157.f.1).

The volumes in this series are printed on acid-free,
250-year-life paper.

Library of Congress Cataloging in Publication Data

Hall, Anna Maria Fielding, 1800–1881.
Stories of the Irish peasantry.

(Ireland, from the Act of Union, 1800,
to the death of Parnell, 1891)
Reprint of the 1850 ed. published by W. & R. Chambers, Edinburgh.
1. Peasantry—Ireland—Fiction.   I. Title.
II. Series.
PZ3.H14Sv   1979   [PR4735.H26]   823'.7   79-12010
ISBN 0-8240-3498-8

Printed in the United States of America

The Irish Fiction of
Anna Maria Hall (1800–1881)[1]

Somebody once remarked to William Carleton that his pictures of Irish peasant life were "really more reliable than those of Mrs. S.C. Hall," to which Carleton, quite typically, answered, "Why, of course they are! Did she ever live with the people as I did? Did she ever dance and fight with them as I did? *Did she ever get drunk with them as I did?*" Since Mrs. Hall was a fanatical advocate of temperance, which meant total abstinence from alcohol, and Carleton tended to err in the other direction, his question was doubly pointed.[2] Obviously Mrs. Hall did not know, could not have known, the peasantry as only Carleton did. Nonetheless, she does not deserve contemptuous dismissal. Her contemporaries and Carleton's regarded her as an authority on Ireland almost equal in weight to the Banims, Gerald Griffin, and Carleton, and a reading of her Irish fiction suggests that they were not wrong.

Born in Dublin as Anna Maria Fielding, her ancestors on her mother's side were Huguenots who had come to Ireland after the revocation of the Edict of Nantes in 1685. We know nothing of her father. When she was six weeks old, her mother took her to live at Graige, near Bannow, County Wexford, the home of George Carr, second husband of Mrs. Fielding's mother. Her stepgrandfather adopted her as his daughter. In this beautiful and relatively prosperous region, Anna Maria Fielding spent her girlhood until she was fifteen, when the family moved to London. At twenty-four, she married Samuel Carter Hall, a young man of antiquarian interests ambitious for a career in literature. He too had been born in Ireland, where his father in the late 1790's was commanding officer of the "Devon and Cornwall Fencibles" and later experimented with copper-mining. From 1824 on, for almost sixty years, the Halls led a busy life of editing, writing, traveling. They were deeply pious Evangelicals; he was certainly sanctimonious and is supposed to have been the original of Dickens' Pecksniff in *Martin Chuzzlewit.*

Yet it is hard to believe that he was as thundering a hypocritical villain as Pecksniff. He and Mrs. Hall had many friends and were apparently extremely happy together. They published several travel books jointly, including the handsome *Ireland, Its Scenery, Character, etc.,*[3] richly illustrated with steel engravings and woodcuts especially commissioned from the best contemporary artists. In addition to temperance, Mrs. Hall's causes included opposition to the women's rights movement, which she was convinced would undermine the family and unsex the human female. She and her husband were also ardent spiritualists, attending séances and propagandizing widely for the scientific truth of the phenomena they witnessed.

Mrs. Hall wrote nine novels, many books for children, books of travel, and religious tracts. She wrote so easily that at least once she later reread (and liked) one of her own early stories without remembering that she had written it. If none of this in itself inspires the reader to look at her Irish fiction, he will be all the more surprised at the level of its excellence. Ireland was the subject of her first book, remained a central interest throughout her life, sincerely involved her emotions, and inspired her best work.

Sketches of Irish Character (2 vols., 1829; No. 46 in this series) Mrs. Hall dedicated to Mary Russell Mitford, whose famous book, *Our Village*, was in the course of publication at the time. Two of Miss Mitford's five volumes had so far appeared and had won wide critical applause. Mrs. Hall expressed the hope that her readers would feel as familiar with Bannow, "my native village . . . justly the pride of the county of Wexford," as they had become with Miss Mitford's "sunny Berkshire." In Bannow, not far from the historic "Bag-and-Bun"—site of the twelfth-century Anglo-Norman victory over the Irish, "where Ireland was lost and won"—the landowners were not absentees but resident; the "people know little, and care less about politics; and the Protestant Clergyman and the Catholic Priest (at least it was so in my time), conceive that each has sufficient employment in attending to the moral and physical wants of his flock."[4]

This seems too idyllic to be altogether true, since Mrs. Hall's girlhood memories of Bannow began only half a dozen years after the rebellion of 1798, which had been more violent and more violently repressed in County Wexford than anywhere else in the south of Ireland. Between 1798 and 1829, when *Sketches* appeared, barely a generation had passed. Michael Banim's novel *The Croppy* (3 vols., 1828; No. 19), faithfully recording the horrors of 1798 in Wexford, had been published only the year before. And in Mrs. Hall's "Captain Andy" and "Black Dennis" the memories surface:

> "Black Dennis" had been an United Irishman, and one of the most violent order: the projector of more burnings, murders, and robberies, than any chief of them all; and when at last he found that he could no longer carry on the system of rebellion and plunder, into which he had drawn so many unfortunate victims, he turned king's evidence; many were the men, either transported or executed, on his evidence, all less guilty than himself.[5]

His return to Bannow produces a drama not unworthy of Carleton. If the blissful quality of Bannow life, then, as suggested in the introduction, proves to be an exaggeration, that is only because Mrs. Hall's stories are thoroughly honest. And her aim—to make her readers know and like the people of Bannow—she certainly achieves.

Lights and Shadows of Irish Life (3 vols., 1838; No. 47) is a composite work. Volume I contains *The Groves of Blarney,* a novel whose dramatic version opened at the Adelphi Theatre in London on the sixteenth of April, 1838, and had a successful run.[6] The novel itself retains its highly dramatic quality, its most memorable character being a wandering peddler-woman, a sinister female who smashes the hero's treasured ancestral drinking glass and does not stop at kidnapping and murder, having efficiently smothered one of her husbands in a trunkful of theatrical props. In her introduction Mrs. Hall reports that people have reproached her with neglecting the gentry in her writings. She replies that it is only among the peasantry that "we must look for original character." Irish gentlemen have since the mid-eighteenth century altogether changed their ways and are now indistinguishable from English gentlemen, and "with respect to Irish ladies, my readers do not require to be told of their beauty, goodness, and virtue."[7]

The same can hardly be said of the villainess: when she throws the half-crown across the room and breaks the goblet ("the most precious relic Connor possessed of all his family's former wealth and station," which "would have formed the glory of an Irish antiquarian"), she cries out,

> "May every one be so kilt, and spilt, and smashed, that turns their tongue on the Griffin; and may the seed, breed, and generation of Connor O'Gorman be in smithereens upon Ireland's ground, like that meminto of his glory—Amin."

a curse that would have fit well into Carleton's "Essay on Irish Swearing" (*Traits and Stories, Second Series*; 3 vols., 1833; No. 35) and no doubt aroused the Adelphi Theatre audience when they heard it from the stage. Connor O'Gorman remembers how his grandfather had "presented that glass, full to the brim of scalding punch, to the priest, or any other honoured guest" and how he himself had listened with "exultation . . . to the tales . . . recounted of those who, of high rank in ancient times, had drunk the stirrup-cup of gratulation and good-will at the castle gates of his ancestors, then the possessors of lands and rivers, where their descendant now could claim but a few poor acres."[8] To him the breaking of the glass has shattered his images of the past. Lady

Morgan herself never used more effectively the symbols of Irish antiquity, which with her were an ancient sword or an Irish wolf-dog or a skull of the Irish elk, the "moose-deer."[9] In the comic vein, the dialogue between Connor and the Cockney visitor, Peter, about the varieties of Irish potatoes, in which Connor's names for them grow more and more polysyllabically Irish and less and less comprehensible, is also a great success, ending as it does in a few genuine words of the mysterious Irish language, with the poor visitor besottedly ready to accept any yarn the Irishman wants to tell him.[10]

Volume II of *Lights and Shadows* consists of "Sketches on Irish Highways," written after Mrs. Hall revisited Ireland in 1834. She was shocked by the "misery which the poorer classes exhibit." The gilded memories of her youth, which predominated in her earlier book, were now tarnished; so that as she noted, these sketches have more of "shadows" than of "lights" in them.[11] They also include several excellent short stories suggested by the scenery she saw or the persons she met. Volume III has as its chief contents *Illustrations of Irish Pride*, which "differs in no respect from the proper dignity which calls upon nations and individuals to respect themselves."[12] Here Mrs. Hall comes to grips with Irish problems more directly than she had yet done.

Would a "judiciously-arranged code of poor-laws" help to eliminate beggary? Not if the laws were administered as they are in England, said Mrs. Hall, agreeing here with Harriet Martineau writing six years earlier (*Ireland*, 1832; No. 45). The trouble is that Ireland is a century behind England in civilization, and "in addition to its poverty, it has a host of prejudices and superstitions to overcome" which hold it back. Here one awaits resignedly an Evangelical attack on Catholicism. Not at all; Mrs. Hall proceeds to discuss Irish family feeling: the poorest peasant's determination to care for his most aged and helpless relatives, and the improbability that he would ever willingly consent to abandon them to the Workhouses scheduled to be built under the New Poor Law, just introduced into Ireland in the same year (1838). And instantly she illustrates her conclusion by an interview in a peasant hovel near Kilkenny, in which the aged grandmother of the family proudly affirms her memory of the time when the land belonged to them and scorns charity from those who have wrongfully seized it.[13] Carleton's "Tubber Dearg" and "The Poor Scholar" and "The Station" all include similar episodes.

Perhaps the most remarkable feature of Mrs. Hall's first two books about Ireland, in view of her strongly Evangelical leanings, is her open-minded attitude towards the Irish Catholic clergy. Only once in the five volumes does she introduce a cunning grasping priest and then it is with a word of apologetic explanation,

> It has been my lot to know, esteem, and love, true and loyal members of the Catholic Church. I have looked upon many priests and friars with veneration and respect—I have delighted in observing their kindness, their gentleness, and their honest discharge of what they considered duty; I have known them to make great sacrifices, and endure much patiently; and, I say it to their credit, that I have never met but one among them in any way

> resembling the person whom I have endeavoured to describe.

Carleton, in his moods of apology for his offensive anti-clerical fiction, never went as far as this.

Father Cormack's vituperative outburst[14] should be compared with that of the priest in Carleton's "Shane Fadh's Wedding" (*Traits and Stories, First Series*, 2 vols., 1830; No. 34). The "crime of conveying the daughters of respectable farmers from their own homes and forcing them to marry" which Mrs. Hall refers to in the same story is one that Carleton several times treated in his own fiction. Perhaps she had read his *Traits and Stories*; there would have been ample time between their appearance in 1830 and 1833, and 1838, when her *Lights and Shadows* was published. The chivalrous behavior of the young peasant lad in love, the decency and charm of the peasant girl: these things too Mrs. Hall has affectionately noted and set down.

And in her last book of Irish short tales, *Stories of the Irish Peasantry* (1850, No. 49), she kept the formula pretty much as it had been in her two earlier collections. But by 1850, with the dreadful Famine years just coming to a close, the English reading public was thoroughly tired of Ireland, and one senses that perhaps Mrs. Hall to a degree shared their fatigue. For the first time she manifests impatience with Irish conditions and lectures her peasant characters on their faults. Her moralistic tendencies, astonishingly suppressed in all her earlier Irish writings, emerge now. She still clings firmly to her conviction that much blame rests upon the landlords, but even this is weakened.

Well before this swan song, however, Mrs. Hall published *The Whiteboy* (2 vols., 1845; No. 48), her most complex, most distinguished, and least appreciated novel. Her hero, Edward Spencer, an English landowner, comes to Ireland to reside on his estates, just like the hero of Maria Edgeworth's *Ennui* (1809; No. 3). Having already wrought marvels of reform on the English properties he has inherited from his mother, he is full of Edgeworthian high principles and good intentions. Spencer Court, in the mountainous region between County Cork and County Kerry, he has inherited from a childless uncle, who had married an Ulster Presbyterian, a violent anti-Catholic. The wife's younger sister had fallen in love with a young Macarthy, Catholic descendant of the great Munster family, now in possession only of a ruined tower of their former castle. Privately married by a priest, this couple had had a child, young Lawrence Macarthy, but Mrs. Spencer had forced a separation between his parents. An alert reader will recognize overtones from Lady Morgan's *Florence Macarthy* (4 vols., 1818; No. 8). Mrs. Spencer has taken as her protégé a certain Abel Richards, converted to Evangelical Protestantism in his youth as a necessary step in his career as land-agent, loathed by the local peasantry, a counterpart to Carleton's Valentine M'Clutchy (who could not, however, have served as inspiration, since that book—No. 40—was published only a few months earlier).

As Edward's ship approaches Ireland in the prologue to the main action, he is still "peculiarly unfitted to comprehend the bickerings and bitternesses, the petty malignant nothings which form the superstructure of Irish discontent, frequently to the exclusion of thought for actual and positive grievances." He is "aware of the real miseries of the country," is steeped in "the romance of Irish history," and idolizes "Irish heroism, without distinction of party." Angry at "the long past cruelty," he is busily planning:

> His imagination erected cottages and covered them with roses; at one end of his smiling village arose the spire of a [Protestant] church, and at the other the cross of a [Catholic] chapel; the village green was in the centre and fronted the school, from which issued children of "all denominations," well clothed, noisy with joy, and full of spirits as of health.

It is like the vision that Glenthorne in *Ennui* had before he had begun to learn his lessons. Aboard ship, Edward meets a wise Anglican Dean, who warns him that "all knowledge of Ireland, acquired only by hearsay, leads to dreams." Sympathy and capital are of course needed, but most of all men "with MEMORIES, capable of tracing back the various causes of the people's discontent to by-gone times and by-gone events." England forgets these things, but in Ireland they are not only remembered but "continually revived, not only by agitators of the moment" but by national feeling. Ireland is two nations, a Catholic nation and a Protestant nation; but the poor peasantry have no party and are steeped in misery.[15] Edward soon receives a rugged initiation into the facts of Irish life. He is forced to face the fact of violence and is drawn into great personal danger.

The reader follows every step of the villainous Abel Richards' career. A steward's son, he is a hypocrite who toadies the rich and buffets the poor. Always looking after his own interests, he divides and redivides his own few original acres, turning them into "a place of poverty and potato-gardens." At the right moment he changes his faith, and blames all his unpopularity on that. He frequents Dublin Protestant drawing rooms, distributes tracts, and sexually persecutes young women when he can. As Mrs. Hall makes one of the Catholic peasants say, about the Methodists,

> "Is it Swaddlers, Sir? Well, I have no objection in life to a good sound Protestant; but the back of my hand to the Swaddlers, all the world over.... though you had no religion before Luther, still the Protestant faith is ould enough to be respectable; but the Swaddlers set up for themselves, without bell, book, or candle, and strike at us both. Why even Abel Richards grew worse when he took to Swaddling."[16]

Mrs. Hall waxes properly indignant over the troubles of 1822 and their repression: the government had allowed disorders to proceed and famine to drive the people to distraction. Then

> At last, the higher members of the community, the magistrates and "the castle," conceived it neces-

sary to do "something," . . . and the "something" done in 1822, was just the "something" done during the whole period of English rule over Ireland . . . placing the country under martial law, burning, and hanging, and shooting those whom fever and starvation had spared. And, doubtless, when the hunt was closed . . . the judges were wearied with passing sentence, and the ships heavy with convicts; when there were many widows and orphans in the disturbed districts—then "the troubles" as in former days, would be pompously announced as "over;" the country reported as "tranquillised;" no effort made to employ and pay those who were growing up to manhood with no other occupation than the memory of their sires' wrongs; no hope beyond hunger, revolt, and death.[17]

The Whiteboy was published in the first year of the new Famine. Mrs. Hall was both eloquent and prescient.

And after the violence of 1822 is over, and Spencer's education is complete and his own life disentangled from the exciting plot in which Mrs. Hall had involved him, and Catholic Emancipation has been won, he says, at the end,

I consider . . . Catholic Emancipation as only the first of a series of boons, or rather, the earliest demonstration of justice—wisely given; yet, if they had not agitated for it, it would never have been obtained. . . . my only fear is, that the malcontents of a party will continue the agitation for what may be unattainable, not for what all wise, as well as all just, Englishmen earnestly desire to give the Irish—*perfect equality.*[18]

Here one sees the limitations as well as the generosity of Mrs. Hall's thinking about Ireland. She has not understood that equality will not be enough; that what O'Connell and his successors now are agitating for (the "unattainable"), namely, liberation from England by the dissolution of the Act of Union and actual national independence, will in the long run not be negotiable. It would be another three-quarters of a century, however, before the English would learn that it was no longer a question of "giving the Irish" concessions. Mrs. Hall, then, emerges as an unexpectedly enlightened and eloquent member of her own generation, whose Irish stories deserve to be remembered.

Robert Lee Wolff

Notes

1. *The New Cambridge Bibliography of English Literature*, III, 2nd edition (Cambridge: University Press, 1969) has an entry on Mrs. Hall, incomplete and with some errors. She appears in the *DNB*. A memoir by her husband, Samuel Carter Hall, *Recollections of a Long Life* (New York: Appleton, 1883), includes (pp. 548–583) a section on his recently deceased wife, which is likely to remain the chief source of information about her life. Except for the entry in Stephen J. Brown, S.J., *Ireland in Fiction* (Shannon: Irish Universities Press, 1969, reprint of the second edition of 1919), pp. 125–126, I know of no criticism of her books on Ireland. Father Brown's book must be used with great care: of Mrs. Hall's *The Whiteboy* (2 vols., 1845; No. 48), for example, he says that it deals with the period 1761–1764, whereas in fact it deals with the year 1822.

2. David J. O'Donoghue, *The Life of William Carleton: Being His Autobiography and Letters; and an Account of his Life and Writings, from the Point at which the Autobiography Breaks Off* (London: Downey and Co., 1896; No. 44), II, 182, note 1. For Carleton, see my prefatory volume to those of his works reprinted in this series, Nos. 33–44.

3. 3 vols. (London: How and Parsons, 1841, 1842; and Jeremiah How, 1843).

4. *Sketches*, I, v-vii.

5. *Ibid.*, I, 189. For 1798, in addition to my introduction to *The Croppy* in this series, see Thomas Pakenham, *The Year of Liberty. The Great Irish Rebellion of 1798* (London: Hodder and Stoughton, 1969).

6. Allardyce Nicoll, *Early Nineteenth-Century Drama* (Cambridge: University Press, 1930), II, 313.

7. *Lights and Shadows,* I, vi-vii.

8. *Ibid.,* I, 52–53.

9. See the introduction to Lady Morgan's novels as republished in this series.

10. *Lights and Shadows,* I, 86–89.

11. *Ibid.,* II, unnumbered preliminary leaf, between title page and table of contents.

12. *Ibid.,* III, 24.

13. *Ibid.,* III, 24–29.

14. *Ibid.,* III, 265–266, 270.

15. *The Whiteboy,* I, 21–23, 24–28.

16. *Ibid.,* I, 125; II, 104.

17. *Ibid.,* II, 8.

18. *Ibid.,* II, 299–300.

STORIES

OF

THE IRISH PEASANTRY.

STORIES

OF

THE IRISH PEASANTRY.

BY MRS S. C. HALL.

'MIND NOT HIGH THINGS; BUT CONDESCEND TO MEN OF LOW ESTATE.'
—*St Paul.*

EDINBURGH:
PUBLISHED BY WILLIAM AND ROBERT CHAMBERS.

1850.

EDINBURGH:
PRINTED BY W. AND R. CHAMBERS.

TO

THE LANDLORDS AND TENANTS OF IRELAND,

I DEDICATE this volume, in the humble but earnest hope that I may benefit both, by showing that the interests of both are mutual and inseparable.

I trust I may not be over sanguine in expecting that I shall be aided in my heartfelt desire to serve my humbler countrymen and countrywomen, and that the Cheap Publication now submitted to them may be placed by the higher class within reach of the lower.

I shall indeed heartily rejoice if I have contributed to the social and moral improvement of those for whom my 'Stories' are chiefly intended. My design was to exhibit and illustrate those peculiarities in the Irish character which appear to be the root of evils in their condition—habits, many of which, though not in themselves vicious, commonly lead to vice; prejudices, from which nothing but injurious results can be expected; or ideas and pursuits, which are not considered dishonourable or dangerous, but which are unquestionably both; and at the same time to show the brighter as well as the darker side of the picture, by delineating the virtues which are, to say the least, as prominent and distinguishing parts of Irish nature.

ANNA MARIA HALL.

The Rosery, Old Brompton, May 20, 1840.

CONTENTS.

	PAGE
TOO EARLY WED!	7
'TIME ENOUGH,'	18
'IT'S ONLY A DROP!'	33
'DO YOU THINK I'D INFORM!'	42
THE LANDLORD ABROAD,	65
THE LANDLORD AT HOME,	82
'IT'S ONLY A BIT OF A STRETCH!'	95
'SURE IT WAS ALWAYS SO!'	102
'IT'S ONLY THE BIT AND THE SUP,'	114
THE FOLLOWER OF THE FAMILY. PART THE FIRST,	126
PART THE SECOND,	133
PART THE THIRD,	146
REDDY RYLAND,	160
THE CROCK OF GOLD,	169
THE WRECKER, A SEA-SIDE STORY,	181
'IT'S ONLY MY TIME,'	194
GOING TO LAW! PART THE FIRST—SHOWING HOW JOHN LEAHY, COMMONLY CALLED JOHNNY THE GIANT, WOULD GO TO LAW,	201
PART THE SECOND—SHOWING WHAT JOHN LEAHY, COMMONLY CALLED JOHNNY THE GIANT, GOT BY GOING TO LAW,	214
'UNION IS STRENGTH,'	233
FAMILY UNION,	237
GOING TO SERVICE,	244
DEBT AND DANGER,	258
THE TENANT-RIGHT,	282

STORIES

OF THE

IRISH PEASANTRY.

TOO EARLY WED!

'It's what I wanted to spake to your honour about,' said Sandy Donovan, who had entered my cousin's breakfast-room, and made her his best bow; 'it's what I wanted, my lady, is the lend of a loan of two-and-sixpence, if it would be plasing to ye; and I'll work it out in any way convenient—either in going messages to the squire, or anywhere else in the three kingdoms at a moment's notice; or taking a hand at the knives, whin Misther Langan, or Mike, or the footboy himself, has no mind to be dirting their hands wid their work, and yer honour wanting them to be clane before the quality; or driving the cows home, if the ould cowboy would be sick, or "overtaken," which will happen to any, let alone a boy of his years; or—but to be sure,' added Sandy, after a pause, as if to give weight to some peculiarly onerous service he was about to proffer—'to be sure, yer honour nor the masther are never in trouble that way, like yer neighbours—if you war, bedad! there isn't a boy in the barony would bate the bailiffs wid greater joy than myself!'—and Sandy's eyes brightened, and his hand grasped more firmly the handle of his good shillala; he looked what he really was, a fine handsome gay-hearted 'boy' of about nineteen—certainly not twenty.

'Well, Sandy,' replied my cousin, smiling, 'I will lend you the half-crown; and you shall repay it me, not in labour—for I require my servants to do their own work—but in money.'

'Och, ma'am dear, that's hard upon me intirely. I'd rather work it out.'

'But isn't your time your money? Cannot you sell that time to some other person, and discharge your debt out of the produce?'

'I'm no scholar, my lady,' he replied, twisting his shoulders; 'but I'd rather work it out.'

'We will speak of that by and by,' said my cousin; 'you must pay me twopence a-week, and tell me what you want with a half-crown.'

'Well, God bless you, my lady, I'm a made man; I'll pay it at the twopence, though I'd rather work it out, supposing even it came to double.'

My cousin smiled, and looked at me significantly, for we had often talked of the impossibility of making an Irishman consider time as a commodity of value; and then she asked him, 'Well, Sandy, and now tell me what you want with it.'

Sandy Donovan twirled his hat between his thumbs, looked down upon the carpet, and hemmed twice. I perceived at once the state of the case, for he blushed deeply. With the natural quickness of an Irishman he saw I understood the matter; and turning to me, said, 'If you plase, my lady, tell the misthress, for I see you're insensed into it already.'

'Sandy's in love!'

'I have known that for some time,' answered my cousin, 'and with the gatekeeper's daughter. But what has that to do with the half-crown?'

My cousin is one of those amiable, excellent persons, who, born, though not brought up, in the country, loving it also with the warmth of Irish love, can no more comprehend an Irishman's nature than can those who, having paid a visit of two weeks to Dublin, and the county Wicklow, return with a self-satisfied conviction that they are fully acquainted with the habits, manners, and feelings of the Irish nation.

'Is it what has it to do with the half-crown, my lady?' repeated poor Sandy to my infinite amusement; 'why, thin, just everything in life, sure; it's to help to pay Father Garratty for marrying us, my lady! We've made up the money all to that, misthress dear; and we didn't—that's I didn't—know what to do at all about it, until I thought I'd make bould with you, ma'am, that—can feel for us.'

'Me feel for you!' exclaimed my cousin indignantly; 'how could you fancy that?'

'Just, ma'am, the remimbrance of your own young days; that to be sure you don't look past yet, long life to you, and the masther's too, when, as I have heard tell, you thought the great battle of Waterloo put betwixt you both for ever, and he kilt at it, though he's so hearty now; and sure if the want of the half-crown put betwixt me and Lucy Hackett, it would be as bad to us as the battle of Waterloo.'

I never asked my cousin which of the two topics Sandy touched upon had softened her most—the sly compliment to her youthful looks, or the allusion to the 'great battle' where her beloved husband had played a distinguished part. Certainly her after observation had lost all asperity.

'Well, but, Sandy, what provision have you made for this new state of matrimony?'

'Provision is it, my lady?' answered Sandy with another turn of his hat; 'we've got lots of love, misthress dear; it'll hould out till the grave shuts over us, I'll go bail for that.'

'But, Sandy, you can't live on love?'

'It's cruel poor living without it—that I know, ma'am, any way,' he replied right readily.

'But there will be two to feed instead of one at your father's; for Lucy cannot continue at the lodge.'

'Nor doesn't want, ma'am—I've built her a cabin off the corner of my father's three acres, and there's a few sticks in it already. She's no great eater, and the pratees are cheap enough, thank God!'

'But by and by, you will have more than two to feed.'

'Plase God,' was Sandy's quiet reply.

'Sandy,' I said, 'I am sure your choice is a good one; Lucy is a pretty, cheerful, industrious girl, not yet eighteen, I think—too young to take the heavy cares of peasant life upon her. I will not say she will change, because that is what Irish women seldom do; but I must say you are laying the foundation of certain misery, both for her and yourself, by *not* waiting until you have something to begin life with.'

'Ah, thin, ma'am dear, it's a shame for ye to be evenin' sorrow to a bridegroom.'

'You even it, as you call it, to yourself, Sandy: look there!' I pointed from the window to a beggar woman who was coming up the lawn, followed by a troop of children. 'Look there! how would you like to bring the light-hearted fond girl you love to a fate like that? And yet such are the effects of very early marriages, combined with, or rather the first step to, imprudence. You are both young; labour in your several vocations for five or six years; you have an object to love and labour for; and at the end of that period, by God's blessing on your own industry, you'll have something to begin with—enough to furnish a cabin comfortably, and a short purse to defray first expenses.'

'But, ma'am dear, sure we can work as well together, and get the comfortable cabin and the short purse afther.'

'No—you will not have the same motive; circumstances will bend you down. If Lucy becomes the mother of children at so early an age, her exertions will be cramped.'

'She'd work the betther,' interrupted Sandy.

'She would be, as all Irish women are, the most affectionate mother in the world; but marrying so young, old age will come upon her prematurely. Her eyes will grow dim, and her hair turn gray before her time; her bodily strength must fail; and what woman can knit, or spin, or sew for hire, with a tribe of little half-starved children round her feet? It is not too late to change your resolution. I will see Lucy; I will reason with her; I know she will wait for you. Work on singly a little longer. She will be your reward; and, believe me, such a prudential course will render your future life prosperous and happy.'

'What can a young man save out of *tin*pence or a shilling a-day, my lady?' said Sandy.

'What could he spare at that rate for the support of a wife? what for the support of a family of children?'

'Bedad!' answered Sandy, twisting his shoulders—his invariable practice when in a hobble—'Bedad! I don't know; only they all does the same, and sure we'll be no worse off than our neighbours.'

'But Lucy, poor pretty Lucy, who has been more tenderly brought up than *her* neighbours; surely, Sandy, you would not wish to bring her into trouble?'

'Poverty I may bring her to—God help us, ma'am, there's none of us made up against that; but I'll work my fingers to the bone to keep her from trouble. I'll own she's too good for me; though that's not her own thought. But I'll say this: sorra a boy in the townland will make a better husband, let the other be who he may. Sure, ma'am, there's nothing in the poverty you think of to frighten us. We've been looking at it ever since we war born, more or less. We get used to it in these parts.'

'You bring it on yourselves. Nothing keeps down either young man or woman so much as a tribe of infants before there is anything to give them.'

'Bedad! so it does,' replied the young man with the most perfect composure; 'but how can we help it?—the craythurs ax nothing but pratees and salt, and grow up fine men and women on it, that bate the world for beauty.'

In fact, in no shape could we place poverty so as to render her aspect more hideous than he knew it to be; but his naturally gay spirit rose against the idea that either Lucy or he was doomed to encounter it; or if they were, he laid his thoughts upon the favourite phrase of those who are not able to help themselves— 'We'll get over it, by the help of God!' or, 'We'll not be worse off than our neighbours,' or, 'Something 'ill turn up for good.' Sometimes he would parry my argument by wit, sometimes by laughter—always respectful, yet merry laughter; and so, seeing he was determined upon an early marriage, and consequent poverty, I resolved to appeal to Lucy.

'She's a great fool,' said her grandmother at the lodge, who had brought her up; 'but if the worst come to the worst, she'll be no worse off than her neighbours.' Here was a pretty argument in favour of misery, by one who was old enough to have known better. 'She'll sup sorrow for it, I daresay, but we all have our taste of it one way or other.' Lucy was all smiles and tears. Sandy and she had learnt out of the same 'Read-a-made-aisy' at school; they had gone to their 'duty' together. She had been promised to him, and no thought of any one else had ever come across her heart. She was willing to wait for him till the day of her death; only, maybe, for anything she could tell, it would be the same thing in five years as it was then; there was nothing to make it better—and the ould loved each other the more who spent their sunny days together. I knew full well that comparatively little misery is produced among the lower classes in Ireland by the absence of connubial affection. Cottage trouble has its sweet consoling drop of love in the bottom of every cup of sorrow. Lucy seemed prepared for both. She did not attempt to deny that she loved Sandy; it 'was so natural to love him; she never had a brother, and he had been more than a brother to her since she was the height of a rose-bush.' I could not look on the young beauty—so fair, so truthful, so earnest, so bright—without a feeling of deep grief, for I anticipated what was sure to follow. She had not even the ambition which characterises the young English bride in the same sphere of life; she knew that poverty would be her dower, but she had made up her mind to encounter it with him she loved. 'Her uncle,' she said, 'had promised them half an acre, or maybe more, by and by, and then they'd do "bravely."' 'Why not wait for it?' 'And sure we must wait for it,' she replied with great naïveté, 'for he wont give it to us now.' In her quiet modest way, Lucy was as firm as Sandy. 'You perceive,' said my cousin, 'persons who seek to intimidate them, by pointing out the miseries of poverty, fail; they see it so often, that they yield to it rather than withstand it, or sometimes rather than avoid it, if the means of avoiding it disturbs their preconceived opinions.'

'They are always acting from impulse rather than reason; they run into danger, and then ask you how they might have kept out of it,' said I, sadly provoked with these foolish young persons.

'It is easy to see how it will end,' observed my cousin.

'Can't you give them a little land to begin on?'

'My dear friend, if we were to give land to all the silly youths who marry without the prospect of even potato food from one day to another, we should not have an acre left for ourselves. These early marriages are sources of the great evils of Ireland, and can never be prevented, as long as the peasantry have no ambition to elevate themselves in the scale of society, by means of better clothes and better dwellings than they generally possess. A man who is satisfied that his wife should beg while he reaps the English harvests, and that his children should go barefoot, cannot raise himself.'

'But he is not so satisfied,' I said; 'necessity compels it.'

'A necessity induced,' observed my quiet cousin, 'BY BEING TOO EARLY WED.' She was quite right. I have heard of cases where absolute boys and girls have been wedded parents; and it is no uncommon thing to meet a grandfather in the very prime of life. I would not be thought an advocate for restraining, except to very reasonable bounds, the greatest blessing which the Almighty bestows upon his creatures—the power to be happy by making another happy; but I would have my humble fellow-countrymen and countrywomen more duly reflect before they adopt a course upon which nearly all, if not all, the comfort, and, I may add, integrity, of their after-lives must depend. If marriage has its consolations in adversity, and its endearments in prosperity, courtship also has both, besides a greater proportion of that which is the strongest and truest stimulus to exertion—HOPE! It excites also to economy, prudence, and sobriety, by a continual manifestation of their utility in bringing nearer the consummation of a dearly-cherished purpose; money will be saved, when an object is directly to be achieved by saving; labour will be undertaken with cheerfulness, when its recompense is clearly and distinctly seen; and, in short, the FUTURE will be perpetually in the eye, in the mind, and in the heart. On the other hand, poverty—too often the parent of sin—is always an effectual barrier against social improvement: prudence is shut out, when its beneficial influence is only remotely anticipated; and those who find it difficult to procure the necessities, never think of searching out the comforts of life. My design, however, is to exhibit and illustrate evils less by precept than example: many will listen to a story who slumber over a sermon; and a picture may be made to speak more eloquently than words.

Five years had elapsed between the scene I have endeavoured to describe and my again visiting my native land; and greatly rejoiced was I once more to feel its bright green grass beneath my footsteps, to hear the music of its birds and rivers, and meet the welcome of bright eyes and warm hearts of many who had known me in childhood. During even so short a period, England had been gallopping onwards to perfection; Ireland, I saw, had been creeping—and that is something—towards it also. Schools had been established where education had never before been heard of; gardens had expanded around many cottages; the Sabbath day was more respected and hallowed than of old; and the dress both of men and women was neater and in better order. I certainly fancied beggars were on the increase, but this must have been only fancy. I came from a land where they are comparatively unknown, and had almost forgotten how crowded my poor country always was with poverty-stricken creatures, who are unable to provide for themselves the commonest food or the coarsest apparel. Dublin is a solitary-looking city. The magnificence of its noble buildings badly accords with the emptiness of the broad streets. There is an air of desolation in its highways, a loneliness in its most public places—

' 'Tis Greece, but *living* Greece no more.'

You can hear the echo of your own footsteps in its noble squares; and the beggars know a stranger's face in the most crowded places. This beautiful city is almost a wilderness; and the occasional bursts of laughter that resound from the neighbourhood of College Green towards midnight, as the young men hasten to their apartments, have seemed to me strange and unnatural—out of keeping with the silence of the queenly yet solitary capital. We seek in vain for the trappings of its ancient state; few above the rank of gentlemen are to be encountered in its paths; and the palaces of its departed nobility—departed in a worse sense than that of death—ring to the sounds of the money-changers. You perceive, indeed, signs of traffic along the noble quays; corn and cattle may be seen there in abundance, but both are on their way to England: they pay no duty; the enormous and splendid Custom-house is therefore an assemblage of unfurnished apartments. The returns of exports fill many a page in the quaymaster's book; that for the entry of imports has but the single word—*nil*. The corn and cattle are to be exchanged in British markets for money which the Irish farmer is not to see; it passes from the hands of the 'driver' into those of the banker, to my Lord This and my Lord That, who learn twice a year that they have tenants upon their hereditary estates in a place called Ireland, and who bestow upon the country just two thoughts—one upon each of the two occasions to which we make reference. My readers will find no politics in my sketches; but the topic on which I now write would give a pigeon gall. The absentees, who draw wealth out of Ireland, and impart no single blessing in return, are responsible to God, and ought to be held responsible to man, for much of the misery and crime of which unhappily the country is so fertile. But this subject is one that requires greater space and attention than it can at present have; ere long, I may be enabled to picture the system as I have seen it, and contrast the 'landlord at home' with the 'landlord abroad.' Now, I must intreat my readers to follow me with my story.

It was a fine moonlight evening, and we had spent it with some friends residing in that immense square called Stephen's Green. We were walking homewards; and whatever cheerfulness we had imbibed under the hospitable roof of our host, was effectually dispersed by the shivering and half-starved creatures who asked our charity with an importunity which only their civility prevented from being offensive. One slight creature—a child clinging to her cloak, another slung at her back, and one resting on her bosom—had followed us nearly to the corner of Grafton Street, not begging with her tongue, but appealing to our feelings by many outward tokens of misery.

'If you want charity,' said I, 'why do you not ask it?'

'We are all dying for want of food,' was the reply; and the voice, though I did not immediately remember to whom it belonged, thrilled through me like a strain of long-forgotten music.

'I have not tasted food all day,' she continued, leaning against a projecting shopshutter, 'nor wet my lips except with water: have mercy on me, for I am very young, and not used to begging.'

'I believe you,' I replied, for I had by that time recognised her voice; 'I believe you: your name is Lucy Donovan.' Poor, poor Lucy! She threw the hood back from her wasted features; she would have fallen on her knees at my feet, if I had not prevented her: her soft hair was matted across her brows; tears coursed each other down her cheeks; her nose was pinched by starvation; her lips, blue and trembling, could hardly give forth her thoughts —her prayers, I should rather say, for she appeared for a time to have forgotten her misery in the joy occasioned by the sight of a friend.

'To think, my lady, of my seeing you here!—and I conning over in my own mind yours and the misthress's warning about being too early married. It was the ruin of us all out, sure enough; the childre came so fast, and nothing to give 'em. This is little Sandy, ma'am, the moral of his father; only you can't see him, the moonbames are so pale. And the one at my back, little Thomas, afther my poor father. An't I thankful that he never lived to see me in this trouble! And this little hungry girl is Anty, after my grandmother; sure I'm glad she's in Heaven too. Ah, ma'am honey, a young loving heart must suffer a dale of sorrow before it blesses the grave for closing over, and the red worm for destroying, the things it loved more than life.'

'Come to me to-morrow morning, Lucy,' I said, 'and we will see what can be done for you.' I pressed a small donation and my address into her hand.

'I can't be out in daylight,' she whispered; 'I'll come at night —I've no clothes—nothing but the cloak left.'

My English readers may believe this tale: it is no fiction; it is perfectly true; true, without an atom of exaggeration. The young mother had parted with every article of clothing she possessed in the world, except the thin blue hooded cloak in which she enshrouded her misery and starvation: under its feeble protection she begged at night. When I mentioned the circumstance to the lady at whose house we were residing, she assured me it was a fact of no uncommon occurrence.

The next night Lucy came with her children. We had provided something for her in the way of clothes. 'Wont you put on those shoes, Lucy?' 'I thank you, my lady,' she replied, while one of her old smiles brightened up her face; 'I'll take them, since ye're so good; but it's a bad fashion to be tendering my feet up with shoes: they're used to the stones now, poor things. And so best——'

'Where is Sandy, Lucy?—I cannot believe he has deserted you.'

'God bless you for that right thought, my lady. He has not: he was forced to lave me, but *that* wasn't desarting me. You see, ma'am, afther we married, we got on very well for a bit; and the earnest true-hearted love we ever and always had for each other, held out wonderful, and I wasn't over strong, and poor Sandy took to working afther-hours, which everybody knew he need not have done had he been single. But, anyway, *that* brought on the fever. The fever, my lady, and this little Sandy, came together, before, indeed,' she added with her usual simplicity, 'we were ready for either—to say ready; and then, between nursing the husband and nursing the child, when I got up I had my hands full, and we both so young, and no experience. To be sure the poor neighbours helped us. They gave us a share of all they had, even to a handful of meal or a stone of potatoes; and the hardest word they ever spoke was, "God direct you, ye poor young craythurs; ye married too soon." Your cousin, ma'am, is a fine lady, and a good lady; but *she* put me ever and always in mind of how much better I might have been off had I remained single, which was true enough; and while my poor husband lay so bad intirely, the bitter taste of my folly was never off my lips. But when it plased God, he grew better; and when I saw him once more able to raise his head to the sun, and to notice the baby, I forgot a dale of the bitterness, and thought it might pass away altogether. But it never did. If a young bird gets a hurt, my lady, in the nest, it never rightly recovers it. It was so with us. We began poor—we bargained for *that;* but the sickness that's born of poverty came on the top of it, and they both together crushed us. Well, ma'am dear, the gentleman where he worked when he got up again, took great pleasure in foreign parts, and couldn't affoord to pay so many labourers, and Sandy was discharged. It's a poor case, ma'am, when the money scraped up in one country is taken clane away to spend in another. Sandy could have made out life alone, but another poor little babe had a mind to come into the world; so I could do nothing to help him. My grandmother (Heaven be her bed!) was called from us, and she left me what she had to lave. Your cousin, my lady, said it would have been a fine thing to have had it if we war beginning life; but coming in the middle of our trouble, when we war over and over in debt, it did us but little good, and melted away, like salt in rain, before we knew where it was. I've no blame to give to any: the neighbours war wonderful kind. My husband's father did all he could; but what could he do? My husband was the eldest of eleven, who had to be reared on three acres of land, one of which wasn't good enough for goose-grazing. I could have got plenty of knitting, and spinning, and sewing, and straw-bonnet making; but my hands war tied with the two childre; and it plased God to take the second in smallpox. It was a heart-trouble to us then; and I though'; the father would have broke his heart afther it. The neighbours said it was well for us it was called; but somehow it's lonesome to want a baby's smile, or laugh, or even its cry, when ye're used to it, and have little else to comfort you; and despite her misery, the mother's eyes filled with tears, and little Sandy saw them, and he lifted up his dirty face to kiss her: the never exhausted well-spring of Irish affection was already at work in the boy's heart. 'We struggled on, and this babe was born. We had been put above the world, in regard of debt, by my grandmother's death; and one morning Sandy said, "It's no use slaving on and starving as we're doing, Lucy. I had an offer yesterday when I was driving Aby Leary's creels; and if you've the heart to hear it, I'll tell it ye." And I clenched my hands, and set my teeth, as if it war death I expected, for I guessed that his mind was set on foreign parts. But I didn't gainsay him, though I was right. He promised to send me word, and money to bring me and the childre out to him, and I waited at home; and three months after he went, this last craythur was born.'

'To add to your trouble,' I said.

'No,' she answered, pressing it to her bosom; 'it helped me to put the trouble over: *it has the very eyes and smile of my poor Sandy.*'

How foolish, I thought, to attempt to sound the depth of woman's love! What fine feelings there were beneath that cloak—crushed by circumstances that must ever crush those who, without any provision, *too early wed!* 'At last,' she continued, 'I grew ashamed to stay longer in my own place: I couldn't beg there; I couldn't go *there*, from door to door, or stop those I met to ask for food or halfpence. I locked up the door of the cabin, put the key in the thatch, left word with a neighbouring woman that they could send to his uncle near Dublin any letter that came from HIM, and begged my way here. The poor always helped me on my journey, and I was easier moving from place to place—it seemed as though I was getting nearer Sandy; but I've had no letter: those more used to this life than me get more than

I do—I pray instead of beg. Bit by bit I lost every screed of clothes. But my worst trouble is, that my early marriage has brought these darlints into a world of trouble from which I have no power to deliver them; and though I have loved to look at them, yet often, dear my lady, when I have seen them staggering with hunger, I could have knelt in the cowld snow and cursed my folly. Wicked thoughts have come into my head then, and I have had no peace until I prayed to God to cool my poor burning brow, and clane the badness from my heart. I have one hope still—HE *may* DIE—but he will never forget us. If we can live over the present time, a letter may come; but the weakness is upon my heart when I think either of fresh joy or more sorrow. I walked the length of Stephen's Green afther yer honours last night, but the dryness of my parched throat hindered me from spaking. Since yer ladyship spoke to me last night, I have had fresh hope; but somehow I'm afeard to hope, for afther it trouble comes stronger. I've not been able to go afther a letter to his uncle's; I've been ashamed; but, plase God, there's no need of that now, the Lord reward ye all! though it's more than we deserve. Who knows!—there may be comfort for us yet.' She smiled, but there was a ghastliness in the smile that made me shudder: it was the smile of a corse rather than of a living woman. The poor infants devoured the food we gave them; and when they were satisfied, she ate, but not till then. Nothing could exceed her gratitude; the past seemed almost forgotten, after her story was told—a story of simple suffering, with no strong incident to rivet the attention, no powerful event to work upon the imagination—nothing but a tale of Irish misery, brought on, not by misconduct, but by a want of that carefulness, that 'long-headedness,' which makes the Irish peasant a beggar, and the simple possession of which lays the foundation of Scotch and English independence.

My story, if so it may be called, is not finished.

Lucy had been worn to a skeleton by anxiety and starvation. I saw she could not live; our succour came too late; she was dying—dying at the very age when, if she had followed our advice, she might have married in sure anticipation of happiness, and with a reasonable prospect of prosperity. I went to see her; for little Sandy had told me, with tearful eyes, 'that though mammy had plenty to eat, and new milk to drink, she was too sick to come out.' She was lingering in that hectic fever which scorches up, by slow degrees, the moisture of existence; the baby, too, was dying. 'I am sure,' she said, 'there is a letter from Sandy at his uncle's.' I found out the place; she was right. How she screamed, and how her skeleton fingers quivered, when she saw it! 'I knew if he was in life he would not forget us,' she said.

The poor fellow was full of hope; and though his feelings were roughly expressed, they were *there*, warm from his affectionate but imprudent heart: the next letter was to bring money—but a little, yet some; and the one after would bring them out to him. And she heard all this; and at first, while I read, the flush was bright on her cheek, and then it faded; and she called little Sandy, and said, 'You hear—it is from your own daddy, my boy;' and then I thought a slight convulsion moved her features. She grasped the poor soiled paper, the record of his affection; pressed it to her lips; another convulsion; her fingers stiffened round it —SHE WAS DEAD!

'TIME ENOUGH.'

ONE of the most amusing and acute persons I remember—and in my very early days I knew him well—was a white-headed lame old man known in the neighbourhood of Kilbaggin by the name of BURNT EAGLE, or, as the Irish peasants called him, 'Burnt *Aigle.*' His accent proclaimed him an Irishman, but some of his habits were not characteristic of the country, for he understood the value of money, and that which makes money—TIME. He certainly was not of the neighbourhood in which he resided, for he had no 'people,' no uncles, aunts, or cousins. What his real name was I never heard; but I remember him since I was a very little girl, just old enough to be placed by my nurse on the back of Burnt Eagle's donkey. At that time he lived in a neat pretty little cottage about a mile from our house: it contained two rooms; they were not only clean, but well furnished—that is to say, well furnished for an Irish cottage. During the latter years of his life, these rooms were kept in order by two sisters; what relationship they bore to my old friend I will tell at the conclusion of my tale. They, too, always called him 'Burnt Aigle;' all his neighbours knew about them—and the old man would not be questioned—was, that he once left home suddenly, and after a prolonged absence, returned, sitting as usual between the panniers on a gray pony, which was young then, and instead of his usual merchandise, the panniers contained these two little girls, one of whom could walk, the other could not: he called them Bess and Bell; and till they were in a great degree able to take care of themselves, Burnt Eagle remained entirely at home, paying great attention to his young charges, and exciting a great deal of astonishment as to 'how he managed to keep so comfortable, and rear the children;' his neighbours had no idea what a valuable freehold the old man possessed—in his time. When Burnt Eagle first came to Kilbaggin, he came with a load of fresh heather brooms, in a little cart drawn by a donkey; but besides the brooms, he carried a store of sally switches, a good many short planks of wood, hoops large and small, beehives, and the tools which are used by coopers and carpenters. These were few, and of the commonest kind, yet Burnt Eagle would sit on a sort of driving box, which raised him a great deal above the level of the car, into which he elevated himself by the aid of a long crutch that always rested on his knees : there he would sit ; and as the donkey jogged quietly, as donkeys always do, through the wild and picturesque scenery of hill and dale, the old man's hands were busily employed either in weaving kishes or baskets, or forming noggins or little tubs, and his voice would at times break into snatches of songs, half English, half Irish ; for though sharp-mannered, and of a sallow complexion that tells of melancholy, he was naturally cheerful-hearted, and his voice, strong and clear, woke the echoes of the hills, though his melodies were generally sad or serious.

I never heard what attached him to our particular neighbourhood, but I have since thought he chose it for its seclusion. He took a fancy to a cottage which, seated between two sand-hills covered by soft green grass and moss, was well sheltered from the sea-breeze that swept along the cockle strand, and had been the habitation of Corney the crab-catcher, who, poor fellow, was overtaken by a spring tide one windy evening in March, and drowned. For a long time 'Crab Hall,' as it was jestingly called, was untenanted ; and when Burnt Eagle fell in love with it, it was nearly in ruins. Some said Corney's ghost walked at nights over the sand-hills ; but my old friend entered the dwelling, together with the donkey and a gray cat, and certainly were never disturbed by anything worse than their neighbours or a high storm. It did not, however, suit Burnt Eagle's ideas of propriety to suffer the donkey to inhabit any portion of his cottage dwelling ; and accordingly, after repairing it, he built him a stable, and wove a door for it out of the sally switches. His neighbours looked upon this as a work of supererogation, and wondered what Burnt Eagle could be thinking of to go on slaving himself for nothing. What would ail a lone man to live in our town !—wasn't that enough for him ? It would be 'time enough' to be building a house when he had some one to live in it. But he went on his own way, replying to their remonstrances with a low chuckling laugh, and darting one glance of his keen piercing eyes upon them, in return for the stare of lazy astonishment with which they regarded his proceedings.

Burnt Eagle was, as I have said, an admirable economist of time : when he took his little car about the neighbourhood with brooms, or noggins, or baskets, or cockles, or anything else, in fact, that might be wanted, he never brought it home empty;

when he had disposed of all his small merchandise, he would fill it with manure or straw, which the gentry or farmers gave him, or he gathered on the roads. If he could bring nothing else, he would bring earth or weeds, suffering the latter to decay, preparatory to the formation of a garden, with which he proposed to beautify his dwelling: the neighbours said it would be 'time enough' to think of getting the enrichment for the ground when the place was laid out for it. But Burnt Eagle would not be stayed in his progress by want of materials. So, not until he had everything ready, even a sty built for the pig, and a fence placed round the sty to prevent the pig from destroying his bit of land when it was made and cropped—not until then did he commence; and though the neighbours again said 'it would be "time enough" to deprive the pig, the craythur, of his liberty when the garden was to the fore,' Burnt Eagle went on his own way, and then every one in the parish was astonished at what he had accomplished.

The little patch of ground this industrious old man had, after incredible labour, succeeded in forming over the coat of sward that covered the sand, was in front of Crab Hall. The donkey had done his best to assist a master who had never given him an unjust blow: the fence round the little enclosure was formed of gray granite, which some convulsion of nature had strewn abundantly on the strand; these stones the donkey drew up when his day's work was ended, three or four at a time. Even this enclosure was perfected, and a very neat gate of basket-work, with a latch outside and a bolt in, hung opposite the cottage door before Burnt Eagle had laid down either the earth or manure on his plot of ground.

'Why, thin, Burnt Aigle dear,' said Mrs Radford, the netmaker's wife, as, followed by seven lazy, dirty, healthy children, she strolled over the sand-hills one evening to see what the poor *bocher** was doing at the place, 'that was good enough for Corney the crab-catcher without alteration, dacent man! for twenty years. Why, thin, Burnt Aigle dear, what are you slaving and fencing at?'

'Why, I thought I tould ye, Mrs Radford, whin I taught ye the *tight* stitch for a shrimp-net, that I meant to make a garden here; I understand flowers, and the gentry's ready to buy them; and sure, when once the flowers are set, they'll grow of themselves, while I'm doing something else. Isn't it a beautiful thing to think of that!—how the Lord helps us to a great deal if we only do a *little* towards it!'

'How do you make that out?' inquired the netmaker's wife.

Burnt Eagle pulled a seed-pod from a tuft of beautiful sea-pink. 'All that's wanted of us,' he said, 'is to put such as this in the earth at first, and doesn't God's goodness do all the rest?'

* A lame man.

'But it would be "time enough," sure, to make the fence whin the ground was ready,' said his neighbour, reverting to the first part of her conversation.

'And have all the neighbours' pigs right through it the next morning?' retorted the old man laughing: 'no, no, that's not *my* way, Mrs Radford.'

'Fair and aisy goes far in a day, Masther Aigle,' said the gossip, lounging against the fence, and taking her pipe out of her pocket.

'Do you want a coal for your pipe, ma'am?' inquired Burnt Eagle.

'No, I thank ye kindly; it's not out, I see,' she replied, stirring it up with a bit of stick previous to commencing the smoking with which she solaced her laziness.

'That's a bad plan,' observed our friend, who continued his labour as diligently as if the sun was rising instead of setting.

'What is, Aigle dear?'

'Keeping the pipe a-light in yer pocket, ma'am; it might chance to burn ye, and it's sure to waste the tobacco.'

'Augh!' exclaimed the wife, 'what long heads some people have! God grant we may never want the bit o' tobacco! Sure it would be hard if we did; we're bad enough off without that.'

'But if ye *did*, ye know, ma'am, ye'd be sorry ye wasted it —wouldn't ye?'

'Och, Aigle dear, the poverty is bad enough when it comes, not to be looking out for it.'

'If you expected an inimy to come and burn yer house' ('Lord defend us!' ejaculated the woman), 'what would you do?'

'Is it what would I do? Bedad, that's a quare question. I'd pervint him, to be sure.'

'And *that's* what I want to do with the poverty,' he answered, sticking his spade firmly into the earth; and leaning on it with folded arms, he rested for a moment on his perfect limb, and looked earnestly in her face, 'Ye see every one on *the sod*—green though it is, God bless it—is somehow or other born to some sort of poverty. Now, the thing is to go past it, or undermine it, or get rid of it, or prevent it.'

'Ah, thin, how?' said Mrs Radford.

'By forethought, prudence; never to let a farthing's worth go to waste, or spend a penny if ye can do with a halfpenny. Time makes the most of us—we ought to make the most of him; so I'll go on with my work, ma'am, if you please; I can work and talk at the same time.'

Mrs Radford looked a little affronted, but she thought better of it, and repeated her favourite maxim, 'Fair and aisy goes far in a day.'

'So it does, ma'am; nothing like it; it's wonderful what a dale can be got on with by it, keeping on, on, and on, always at something. When I'm tired at the baskets, I take a turn at the tubs; and when I'm wearied with them, I tie up the heath—and sweet it is, sure enough; it makes one envy the bees to smell the heather! And when I've had enough of that, I get on with the garden, or knock bits of furniture out of the timber the sea drifts up after those terrible storms.'

'We burn that,' said Mrs Radford.

'There's plenty of turf and furze to be had for the cutting; it's a sin, where there's so much furniture wanting, to burn any timber —barring chips,' replied Eagle.

'Bedad, I don't know what ill luck sea timber might bring,' said the woman.

'Augh! augh! the worst luck that ever came into a house is idleness, except, maybe, extravagance.'

'Well, thin, Aigle dear!' exclaimed Mrs Radford, 'what's come to ye to talk of extravagance?—what in the world have poor craythurs like us to be extravagant with?'

'Yer time,' replied Burnt Eagle with particular emphasis; 'yer time.'

'Ah, thin, man, sure it's "time enough" for us to be thinking of that whin we can *get anything for it*.'

'*Make anything of it*, ye mean, ma'am; the only work it 'ill ever do of itself, if it's let alone, will be destruction.'

'Well!' exclaimed Mrs Radford indignantly, 'it's a purty pass we're come to, if what we do in our own place is to be *comed* over by a stranger who has no call to the country. I'd like to know who you are, upsetting the ways of the place, and making something out of nothing like a fairy man! If my husband *did* go to the whisky shop, I'll pay him off for it myself; it's no business of yours; and maybe we'll be as well off in the long-run as them that are so mean and thoughtful, and turning their hand to every man's trade, and making gentlemen's houses out of mud-cabins, and fine gardens in the sand-hills; doing what nobody ever did before! It wont have a blessing—mark my words! Ye're an unfriendly man, so ye are. After my wearing out my bones, and bringing the children to see ye, never to notice them, or ask a poor woman to sit down, or offer her a bit of tobacco, when it's rolls upon rolls of it ye might have *unknownst*, without duty, if ye liked, and ye here on the sea-coast.'

'I have nothing that doesn't pay duty,' replied Burnt Eagle, smiling at her bitterness. 'I don't go to deny that the excise is hard upon a man, but I can get my bit of bread without breaking the law, and I'd rather have no call to what I don't rightly understand. I'm sure ye're heartily welcome to anything I have to give. I offered to make a gate for yer sty, to keep yer pig out of the cabbages, and I'm sure——'

Again Mrs Radford, who was none of the gentlest, interrupted him.

'We are ould residenters in the place, and don't want any of your improvements, Misther Burnt Aigle, thank you, sir,' she said, drawing herself up with great dignity, thrusting her pipe into her pocket, and summoning her stray flock, some of whom had entered Crab Hall without any ceremony, while others wandered at their ' own sweet will' in places of dirt and danger—' I daresay we shall get on very well without improvement. We're not for setting ourselves above our neighbours; we're not giving up every bit of innocent divarsion for slavery, and thin having no one to lave for what we make—no chick nor child!'

'Woman!' exclaimed Burnt Eagle fiercely, and he shook his crutch at the virago, who, astonished at the generally placid man's change, drew back in terror, ' go home to yer own piggery, follow yer own plan, waste the time the Almighty gives to the poorest in the land, gossip and complain, and make mischief; what advice and help I had to give, I gave to ye and to others ever since I came to the place; follow yer own way, but lave me to follow mine—time will tell who's right and who's wrong.'

'Well, I'm sure!' said Mrs Radford, quailing beneath his bright and flashing eye, ' to taink of that now! How he turns on us, like a wild baste, out of his sand-hole, and we in all friendship! Well, to be sure—sure there was " time enough"——'

'Mammy, mammy!' shouted one of the seven ' hopes' of the Radford family, ' ye're smoking behind, ye're smoking behind!'

'Oh, the marcy of Heaven about me!' she exclaimed; ' Burnt Aigle's a witch; it's he has set fire to me with a wink of his eye, to make his words good about the coal and the pipe in my pocket. Oh, thin, to see how I'm murdered intirely through the likes of him! I've carried a live coal in my pocket many's the day, and it never sarved me so before! Oh, it's thrue, I'm afeared, what's said of ye, that ye gave the use of one of yer legs to the devil— mother of marcy purtect me!—to the devil for knowledge and luck; and me that always denied it to be sarved so. Don't come near me—I'll put it out meself! Oh to think of the beautiful *gownd*, bran new it was last Christmas was a year! Am I out now, children dear? Oh, it's yer mother's made a show of before the country to plase him! What would come over the coal to do me such a turn as that *now*, and never to think of it afore! Oh, sorra was in me to come near yer improvements!'

'Mammy,' interrupted the eldest boy, ' don't be hard upon Burnt Aigle; there's the coal that dropt out of the pipe red-hot still—see, here where ye stood—and the priest tould ye the danger of it long ago.'

'Oh, sure it's not going to put the holy man's advice ye are on a level with Burnt Aigle's! Come, we'll be off. I meant to take off my beautiful *gownd* before I came out, but thought it would be " time enough" whin I'd go back. And to see what a *bocher* has brought ye to, Judith Radford!' And away she went, fuming and fretting over the sand-hills, stopping every moment to look back at the devastation which her own carelessness had occasioned her solitary dress. Burnt Eagle imagined he was alone, and kept his eyes fixed upon the foolish woman as she departed, but his attention was arrested by Mrs Radford's second daughter, who stole round the lame man, and touched his hard hand with her little fingers.

'Ye're not a witch, are ye, daddy?' she said, while looking up smilingly, but with an expression of awe, in his face.

'No, darlint.'

''Twas the coal done it—wasn't it?'

'It was.'

'Well, good-night, Burnt Aigle; kiss little Ailey—there. Mother will forget it all, or have it all out—the same thing you know. I hav'n't forgot the purty noggin you gave me; only it hurts mother to see how you get on with a little, and father blames her, and gets tipsy; so just go on yer own way, and don't heed *us*. Mother wants *that the sun should shine only on one side of the blackberries;* but I'll larn of ye, Daddy Aigle, if ye'll tache me; only don't bother the mother with what she has no heart to, and sets the back of her hand against.' And after asking for another kiss, the little barefooted pretty girl—whose heart was warm, and who would have been a credit to any country if she had been well managed—darted over the banks like a fawn, her small lissom figure graceful as a Greek statue, her matted yellow hair streaming behind her, and her voice raised to the tune of 'Peggy Bawn.'

'It's truth she says—God's truth, anyway,' said Burnt Eagle, as he turned to enter his cottage. 'It's truth; they set the back of their hand and the back of their mind against improvement; they'd be ready to tear my eyes out if I tould them what keeps them back. Why, their own dislike to improvement part; and the carelessness of their landlords part; the want of sufficient employment a great part; and, above all, their being *satisfied with what they get, and not trying to get better*. As long as they're content with salt and potato, they try for nothing else. Set John Bull down to salt and potato, and see how he'll look; and why shouldn't you get as good, Paddy agrah? But no, you wont; a little more method, a little more capital employed amongst you, and plenty of steadiness, would make you equal to anything the world produced since it was a world. But no: ye keep on at yer ould ways, and yer ould sayings, and all things ould, and ye let others that hav'n't the quarter of yer brains get the start of ye. Yet where, Paddy, upon the face of the earth, is a finer man or a brighter head than your own?' The old man shut his door, and lit his lamp, which was made of a large scallop shell, the wick floating in oil he had extracted from the blubber of a grampus that otherwise would have decayed unnoticed on the shore.

I have told all I heard as to Burnt Eagle's first settlement in what I still call 'my neighbourhood.' I will now tell what I know, and what occurred some time after. I very well remember being taken by my mother, who was a sort of domestic doctor to the poor, to see Judy Radford, who, plunged into the depths of Irish misery, was mourning the loss of her husband, drowned because of the practice of the principle that it was 'time enough' to mend the boat; 'it had taken the boys often, and why not now!' But the boat went down, and the poor, over-worked, good-natured father and his eldest son were lost! We could hardly get to the door for the slough and abominations that surrounded it. 'Judy,' said my mother, 'if this was collected and put at the back of the house, you need not have come begging to the steward for manure.'

'Och, ma'am, wont it be "time enough" to gather it when we have the seed potatoes? Sure it *was always there, and the young ducks would be lost without it.*'

'Such a heap of impurity must be unhealthy.'

'We has the health finely, thank God! if we had everything else;' and then followed a string of petitions, and lamentations, and complaints of her neighbours, all uttered with the whine of discontent which those who *deserve* poverty indulge in, while those who are struggling against it seek to conceal, from a spirit of decency, the extent of their wants. 'Indeed, ma'am,' she continued, 'the ill luck is after us; my second boy has, as all the country knows, the best of characters, and would have got the half acre at the Well corner, if he had gone to his honour in time for it, and that would have been the help to us sure enough; but we thought there was "time enough," and Bill Deasy, who's put up to all sorts of sharpness by Burnt Aigle, got the promise.'

'Well, did Ailey get the flax wheel I told her she could have from Lucy Green until she was able to buy one?'

'Oh, ma'am, there it is again; I kep her at home just that *one* day on account of a hurt I got in my thumb, and thought it would be "time enough" to be throubling yer honour for a plaster if it got worse—which it did, praise be to God!—and never did a hand's turn with it since; and whin she went after it, Miss Lucy had lint it, and was stiffer about it than was needful. My girl tould her she thought *she'd* be "time enough;" and she hurt her feelings, saying "she thought we'd had enough of 'time enough' among us before." It was very sharp of her; people can't help their throubles, though that ould thriving *bocher* that's made all he has out of the gintry, never scruples to tell me that I brought them on myself.'

'I must say a word for Burnt Eagle,' said my mother; 'he has made all he has out of himself, not out of the gentry; all we did was to buy what we wanted from him—one of his principles being, never to take a penny he did not earn.'

'And very impudent of him to say that, whin the gintry war so kind as to offer him money—setting himself up to do without help!' said Mrs Radford, whom we were fain to leave in the midst of her querulous complainings.

We now proceeded along the cliffs to the *bocher's* dwelling. To visit him was always a treat to me; but childhood's ready tears had been some time previously excited by the detail of his sorrow for his companion and friend, for such the poor donkey had been to him.

The struggle which took place between his habit of making the best and most of everything, was in this particular instance at war with the affection he had borne his dead favourite: he knew her skin was valuable, and he did not see why he ought not to use it. One of our friends had called accidentally at the cottage, and found Burnt Eagle standing beside a deep pit he had excavated in the sand-hill, intended for the donkey's grave; he had a knife in his hand, and had attempted the first incision in its skin.

'It can't be any hurt to a dead animal, sir,' he said; 'and yet I can't do it! It seems like taring off my own flesh. The poor baste had such a knowledge of me—such a feeling for me—up hill and down dale—it *knew all my poverty, and was through the world with me, in throuble that was harder to bear than poverty*—and if ever I struck it a hasty blow, it would look in my face like a Christian. It was neither giddy, nor greedy, nor wilful, *though it was a she;* and the low whining it would give me of a morning, was like the voice of a dear friend. I know the skin would be useful, and the times are hard; but I can't, sir—I can't: *it would be like skinning a blood relation*,' and he threw the knife from him. The finest sea-pinks of the banks grow on the donkey's grave!

We found our humble friend surrounded by business, and indeed we jested with Mrs Radford's daughter Ailey, who met us at the gate, for visiting her old sweetheart. The yellow-headed child had grown into a fine young woman; the old man's precept and example had been of use to her; whatever she had learnt of good, she had learnt from him. She had been tying up some flowers for her friend, and hastened to tell us that Burnt Eagle had been making her a flax wheel, and she was to *knit out* the money for it in stockings; but her mother knew nothing of it, and we mustn't tell. I was lifted, for the first time, on the gray pony, the poor donkey's successor, and gallopped it, to Burnt Eagle's delight, over a sand-hill. There was something to love and respect in the old man's countenance. I remember him so well that day, leaning on the top of his staff at the gate of his little garden, which had become celebrated for beautiful flowers: there he stood—I can close my eyes and see him now!—his small figure bent over his stick; his thick, long, gray hair curling on the white collar of his shirt; his eyes rendered more brilliant by the healthy complexion that glowed upon his cheeks; his jacket of gray frieze girded with a leathern belt, that was garnished by such tools as he was constantly requiring; the outline of his form, thrown forward by the clear sky; the roll of the distant waves, the scream of the sea-gull; the cottage, so picturesque— its white smoke curling up, up, up, till it mingled with the air; I can hear the warning voice of my dear mother, intreating me not to canter; the admonishing yet pleased tone in which the old man spoke to his new purchase; the sleepy look of his dog Blarney, as he half wagged his tail, and opened one eye to observe what passed:—in the distance, the old ruined church of Kilbaggin, standing so bravely against sea and land storms; my own heart echoing the music of the pony's feet, as, despite all warning, he cantered right merrily over the sward: happy, happy was I then as any crowned queen! how fresh the breeze! how clear the air! Faster, good pony; don't lag on my account—well done!— there's metal in you, that there is! Oh, memory!——I open my eyes. It was indeed but memory, for here is my desk, and there my books and town-bred flowers, and my pretty quiet greyhound —and the sea, the ruins, the cottage, those lofty hills and toppling cliffs, are now far, far from me, yet near my heart as ever. And poor Burnt Eagle!——But I must not anticipate, and will only say that, if we endeavour to improve our generation with as much zeal and sincerity as did that old man, we shall owe Time nothing.

I have seen lately in Ireland as well-built and as well-kept cottages as I ever saw in England. They are not common—would to God they were!—yet I *have* seen them, and in my own county too, where, I trust, they will increase. But when I was a very little girl, they were far less numerous, and Burnt Eagle's was visited as a curiosity; the old man was so neat and particular; the windows—there were two—looked out, one on his little garden, the other commanded the vista that opened between the sand-hills; and when the tide was in, the cockle strand presented a sheet of silver water; the rafters of the kitchen were hung with kishes and baskets, lobster pots, bird-cages, strings of noggins, bunches of skewers, little stools, all his own workmanship; and the cabbage and shrimp nets seemed beyond number; then brooms were piled in a corner, and the handles of spades and rude articles of husbandry were ready for use: there was a grinding-stone, and some attempt at a lathe; and the dresser, upon which were placed a few articles of earthenware, was white and clean ; a cat, which Burnt Eagle had not only removed, but, in defiance of an old Irish superstition, carried over water, was seated on the hearthstone, and the old man amused us with many anecdotes of her sagacity. One beautiful trait in his character was, that he never spoke ill of any one : he had his own ideas, his own opinions, his own rules of right, but he never indulged in gossip or backbiting. 'As to Mrs Radford,' he said, when complimented on the superior appearance of his own cottage, 'the hand of the Lord has been heavy on her to point out the folly of her ways, and *that* ought to tache her. Those who cast the grace of God from them are very much to be pitied ; for if it's a grace to the rich, it is surely a grace to the poor. But the people are greatly improved, madam, even in my time : the Agricultural Societies do good, and the Loan Societies do good, and there's a dale of good done up and down through the counthry, particularly here, where the landlords—God bless them !—*stick to the sod ;* and the cottages are whitewashed, and ye can walk dry and clane into many of the doors ; and some that used to turn me into ridicule, come to me for advice ; and I'm welcome to high and low—not looked on, as when I came first, with suspicion ; indeed there are not many now like poor Mrs Radford : but Ailey will do well, poor girleen—she always took to dacency.'

'You certainly worked wonders both for yourself and others. I think you might do me a great deal of good, Burnt Eagle, by telling me how you managed,' said my mother.

'Thank you, my lady, for the compliment ; but indeed the principal rule I had was, "NEVER TO THINK THERE WAS TIME ENOUGH TO DO ANYTHING THAT WANTED DOING." I've a great respect for time, madam ; it's a wonderful thing to say it was before the world, and yet every day of our lives is both new and ould—ould in its greatness, yet new to thousands ; it's God's natural riches to the world ; it never has done with us, till it turns us over to Eternity ; it's the only true tacher of wisdom—it's the interpreter of all things—it's the miracle of life—it's flying in God's face to ill use it, or abuse it ; it's too precious to waste, too dear to buy ; it can make a poor man rich, and a rich one richer ! Oh, my lady, time is a fine thing, and I hope little miss will think so too. Do, dear, remember poor Burnt Aigle's words, never to think it " TIME ENOUGH TO DO ANYTHING THAT IT'S TIME TO DO." '

'I wish,' said my mother, 'that you had a child to whom to teach so valuable a precept.' The old man's lips (they were always colourless) grew whiter, and he grasped the top of his crutch more firmly ; his eyes were rivetted as by a spell ; they looked on nothing, yet remained fixed ; his mouth twitched as by a sudden bitter pain ; and by degrees tears swam round his eyelids. I could not help gazing on him, and yet, child though I was, I felt that his emotion was sacred; that he should be alone; and though I continued to gaze, I moved towards the door, awe-struck, stepping back, yet looking still.

'Stay, stay, miss,' he muttered.

'Sit down; you are not well,' said my mother.

'Look at that child,' he continued, without heeding her observation; 'she is your only one, the only darlint ye have; pray to the Lord this night, lady, this very night, on yer bended knees, to strike her with death by the morning before she should be to you what mine has been to me.' He staggered into his bedroom without saying another word. My mother laid upon the table a parcel containing some biscuits I had brought him, and we left the cottage, I clinging closely to her side, and she regretting she had touched a string which jarred so painfully. I remember I wept bitterly. I had been so happy with the pony, which I fancied worth all the horses at our house; and the revulsion was so sudden, that my little heart ached with sorrow. I wanted to know if Burnt Eagle's daughter had been 'very naughty,' but my mother had never heard of his daughter before.

What I have now to tell has little to do with the *character* of my story, but is remarkable as one of the romances of real life, which distance all the efforts of invention, and was well calculated to make an impression on a youthful mind. The next morning, soon after breakfast, my cousin came to my mother to inquire if she knew anything of the destruction of a provincial paper, the half of which he held in his hand. 'I wanted it,' he said, 'to see the termination of the trial of that desperate villain, Ralph Blundel, at the Cork assizes.' 'I think I wrapt it round the biscuits Maria took to Burnt Eagle,' said mamma; 'but I can tell you the termination of the tragedy. Blundel is executed by this time; but the sad part of the story is, that a young woman, who is supposed to have been his wife, visited him in prison, accompanied by two children; he would not speak to her, and the miserable creature flung herself into the river the same night.'

'And the two children?'

'They were both girls, one a mere baby; there was nothing more said about them.'

Tales of sorrow seldom make a lasting impression even on the most sensitive, unless they know something of the parties. We thought little, and talked less, of Ralph Blundel; but we were much astonished to hear the next morning that Burnt Eagle had set off without anything in his creels. This was in itself remarkable; and it was added, that he appeared almost in a state of distraction, yet gave his cottage and all things contained therein in charge to his friend Ailey. Time passed on, and no tidings arrived of the old man, though we were all anxious about him.

Some said one thing, some another. Mrs Radford hinted, 'the good people had got him at last,' and began to speculate on the chance of his never returning, in which case she hoped Ailey would keep Crab Hall. He had been absent nearly six weeks, but was not forgotten, at all events by me. I was playing one summer evening at the end of the avenue with our great dog, when I saw Burnt Eagle jogging along on his pony. The animal seemed very weary. I ran to him with childish glee, forgetting our last interview in the joy of the present. I thought he looked very old and very sad, but I was delighted to see him notwithstanding. 'Oh, Burnt Eagle!' I exclaimed, 'Gray Fan staved in Peggy's best milk-pail, and cook wants some new cabbage-nets; and I've got two young magpies, and want a cage; and grandmamma wants a netting pin; and—— But what have you got in your panniers?' and I stood on tiptoe to peep in; but instead of nets or noggins, or cockles, or wooden ware, there was a pretty rosy child as fast asleep in the sweet hay as if she had been pillowed on down.

I was just going to say, 'Is that your little girl?' but I remembered our last meeting.

'That's little Bell, miss,' he said, and his voice was low and mournful. 'Now, look in the other, and you will see little Bess,' and his smile was as sad as any other person's tears would have been.

I did look, and there was another! How astonished I was!— I did not know what to say. That child was awake—wide awake —looking up at my face with eyes as bright, as blue, as deep, as Burnt Eagle's own. He wished me good-by, and jogged on. I watched him a long way, and then returned, full of all the importance which the first knowledge of a singular event bestows. The circumstance created a great sensation in the country. The gentry came from far to visit Burnt Eagle's cottage. Civil he always was, but nothing could be extracted from him relative to the history of his little protégées: the priest knew of course, but that availed nothing to the curious; and at last, even in our quiet nook, where an event was worn threadbare before it was done with, the excitement passed away, and my mother and myself were the only two who remembered the coincidence of the old man's emotion, the torn newspaper, and Burnt Eagle's sudden disappearance.

Bess and Bell grew in beauty and in favour with the country. They were called by various names—'Bess and Bell of Crab Hall,' or 'Bess and Bell Burnt Aigle,' or 'Bess and Bell of the sand-hills.'

For a long time after the old man's return, he was more retired than he had been. He was melancholy too, at times, and his prime favourite Ailey declared 'there was no plasing him.' By degrees, however, that moroseness softened down into his old, gentle, and kindly habits. He would not accept gifts of money or food from any of us, thanking us, but declining such favours firmly. 'I can work for the girleens still,' he would say; 'and by the time I can't, plase God they'll be able to work for themselves; there's many wants help worse than me.' It was a beautiful example to the country to see how those children were brought up; they would net, and spin, and weave baskets, and peel osiers, and sing like larks, and weed flowers, and tie up nosegays, and milk the goats, and gather shell-fish, and knit gloves and stockings, emulating the very bees (of which their protector had grown a large proprietor) in industry; and in the evenings the old man would teach them to read, and the nearest schoolmaster would come in and set them a copy, for which Burnt Eagle, scrupulously exact, would pay night by night, although the teacher always said 'it would be "time enough" another time;' and the old man would reply, while taking the pence out of his stocking-purse, 'that there was no time like the present; and that if folks could not pay a halfpenny to-day, they would not be likely to be able to pay a penny to-morrow.' The neighbours laughed at his oddity. But prosperity excites curiosity and imitation; and his simple road to distinction was frequently traversed. Solitary as were his habits, his advice and humble assistance were often asked, and always given.

When we left our old home, we went to bid him farewell. He was full of a project for establishing a fishery, and said 'some one had told him that the Irish seas were as productive as the Irish soil, that there was a new harvest every season, free of rent, tithe, or taxes, and needing only boats, nets, and hardy hands, to reap the ocean crop which Providence had sown. I've spoke to the gentry about it,' he said, 'but they say "they'll see about it," and it 'ill be "time enough." *If my grave could overlook a little set of boats,*' he added, 'going out from our own place, I'd rest as comfortable in it as on a bed of down; but if they stick to "time enough," the time will never come!'

'Burnt Aigle,' said Bell, who was growing a very tall girl—girls do grow so fast!—'you said "time enough" to Bess yerself yesterday.'

'When, avourneen?'

'When she asked you when she might begin to think about—about—oh, you know what.'

'I can't think of anything but the fishery—what was it, a chora?'

'Oh, thin, it was a sweetheart,' said the merry maid, covering her blushing face with her hands, and running away.

'See that now, how they *turn on me!*' he exclaimed, while his eyes followed her. 'Well, Miss Bell, maybe I wont be even with you "time enough." God bless her, the gay light-hearted girleen!—the life is in her heart and the joy in her eye!—only she's too like *them that's gone!* But, sure, out of the deep pit of throuble rose up the joy and pace to me in the end, though at first it drove me for ever from my own people, and I've done my best for *her* that's gone; and poor Ailey is married to a dacent boy, and will do well. *An empty heart's a lonely thing in a man's bosom*—but the counthry and the girls has filled mine— God be praised for his goodness! I knew ye mistrusted how it was—on account—but it's all over, my lady; *and for a poor ould sinner like me, I've had a dale of happiness!* I never ill-treated Time, and he has never ill-treated me. Maybe I'll never see either of you again; but oh, miss dear, don't forget yer counthry, and don't think there'll be "time enough" to do it a good turn, but do it at *onct*—do—and God bless you! It's to manage time rightly—that's a fine knowledge—it's a great knowledge, and would make a poor man's fortune, and tache a rich one to keep it. You'll do a good turn for the counthry, and think always there's no time like the present.'

I saw the old man no more, but the last time I visited Kilbaggin I stood by his grave. It was a fine moonlight evening in July; and Bess and Bell, the former being not only a wife, but a mother, had come to show me his last resting-place: they had profited well by his example, and Bess made her little boy kneel upon the green sward that covered his remains. 'He died beloved and respected by rich and poor,' said Bell (Bess could not speak for weeping), 'and had as grand a funeral as if he was a born gentleman, and the priest and minister both at it; and the Killbarries and Mulvaneys met it without wheeling one shillala, and they sworn foes, only out of regard to his memory for the fine example he set the counthry, and the love he bore it.'

The old ruined church of Kilbaggin overlooks the entrance to its pretty silver-sanded bay, and the voices of the fishermen, who were at that time putting out to sea, availing themselves of the beauty and stillness of the night, arose to where we stood. I shall never forget the feelings that crowded on me; the ocean was so calm, the moonlight so bright: the picture of the good old man who lay beneath, where the innocent baby was still kneeling, came before me; I remembered the useful and virtuous tenor of his life, the heroism with which he withstood envy, and persevered in the right way: the white sails of the fishing-boats glimmered in the moonlight; it was Burnt Eagle who had stirred up the hearts of the people to the enterprise, which now brought plenty from the teeming ocean to many a cottage home.

'I mind, when you war going to England first,' said Bell, 'his saying that if his grave could overlook a little fleet of boats going out from our own bay, he'd be as happy as on down; sure he may be happy now!—his good thoughts and quiet good actions *blossom over his grave.* I remember how delighted he was with the first regular boat that went; it was built by Bess's husband. What a happy man he was, to be sure! and how he sat on the cliff, shading his eyes with his hand from the sun, though he had lost sight of the sail long before; and then he knelt down, and raised his ould hands to Heaven, and blessed us both.'

'That's enough,' said Bess; 'sure the lady knew the good that was in the *ould pathriot*, who asked her—if ever she could—never to think it "time enough" to do a good turn for the country, but to believe *there's no time like the present for doing that and everything else.*'

~~~~~~~~~~~~~

'IT'S ONLY A DROP!'

IT was a cold winter's night, and though the cottage where Ellen and Michael, the two surviving children of old Ben Murphy, lived, was always neat and comfortable, still there was a cloud over the brow of both brother and sister, as they sat before the cheerful fire; it had obviously been spread not by anger, but by sorrow. The silence had continued long, though it was not bitter. At last Michael drew away from his sister's eyes the checked apron she had applied to them, and taking her hand affectionately within his own, said, 'It isn't for my own sake, Ellen, though the Lord knows I shall be lonesome enough the long winter nights and the long summer days without your wise saying, and your sweet song, and your merry laugh, that I can so well remember—ay, since the time when our poor mother used to seat us on the new rick, and then, in the innocent pride of her heart, call our father to look at us, and preach to us against being conceited, at the very time she was making us as proud as peacocks by calling us her blossoms of beauty, and her heart's blood, and her king and queen.'

'God and the blessed Virgin make her bed in heaven now and for evermore, amen,' said Ellen, at the same time drawing out her beads, and repeating an avé with inconceivable rapidity. 'Ah, Mike,' she added, 'that *was* the mother, and the father too, full of grace and godliness.'

'True for ye, Ellen; but *that's* not what I'm afther now, as you well know, you blushing little rogue of the world; and sorra a word I'll say against it in the end, though its lonesome I'll be on my own hearthstone, with no one to keep me company but the ould black cat, that can't see, let alone hear, the craythur!'

'Now,' said Ellen, wiping her eyes, and smiling her own bright smile, 'lave off; ye're just like all the men, purtending to one thing whin they mane another; there's a dale of desate about them—all—every one of them—and so my mother often said. Now, you'd better have done, or maybe I'll say something that will bring, if not the colour to your brown cheek, a dale more warmth to yer warm heart than would be convanient, just by the mention of one Mary—Mary! What a purty name Mary it is, isn't it?—it's a common name too, and yet you like it none the worse for that. Do you mind the ould rhyme?—

"Mary, Mary, quite contrary."

Well, I'm not going to say she is contrary—I'm sure she's anything but *that* to you, anyway, brother Mike. Can't you sit still, and don't be pulling the hairs out of Pusheen cat's tail; it isn't many there's in it; and I'd thank you not to unravel the beautiful English cotton stocking I'm knitting; lave off your tricks, or I'll make common talk of it, I will, and be more than even with you, my fine fellow! Indeed, poor ould Pusheen,' she continued, addressing the cat with great gravity, 'never heed what he says to you; he has no notion to make *you* either head or tail to the house—not he; he wont let you be without a misthress to give you yer sup of milk or yer bit of sop; he wont let you be lonesome, my poor puss; he's glad enough to swop an Ellen for a Mary, so he is; but that's a sacret, avourneen; don't tell it to any one.'

'Anything for your happiness,' replied the brother somewhat sulkily; 'but your bachelor has a worse fault than ever I had, notwithstanding all the lecturing you kept on to me: he has a turn for the drop, Ellen; you know he has.'

'How spitefully you said that!' replied Ellen; 'and it isn't generous to spake of it when he's not here to defend himself.'

'You'll not let a word go against him,' said Michael.

'No,' she said, 'I will never let ill be spoken of an absent friend. I know he has a turn for the drop, but I'll cure him.'

'After he's married,' observed Michael not very good-naturedly.

'No,' she answered, '*before*. I think a girl's chance of happiness is not worth much who trusts to *after*-marriage reformation. *I wont.* Didn't I reform you, Mike, of the shocking habit you had of putting everything off to the last? and after reforming a brother, who knows what I may do with a lover! Do you think that Larry's heart is harder than *yours*, Mike? Look what fine vegetables we have in our garden now, all planted by yer own hands when you come home from work—planted during the very time which you used to spend in leaning against the door-cheek, or smoking your pipe, or sleeping over the fire. Look at the money you got from the Agricultural Society.'

'That's yours, Ellen,' said the generous-hearted Mike; 'I'll never touch a penny of it; but for you, I never should have had it; I'll never touch it.'

'You never shall,' she answered; 'I've laid it every penny out, so that when the young bride comes home, she'll have such a house of comforts as are not to be found in the parish—white tablecloths for Sunday, a little store of tay and sugar, soap, candles, starch, everything good, and plenty of it.'

'My own dear generous sister!' exclaimed the young man.

'I shall ever be your sister,' she replied, 'and hers too. She's a good *colleen*, and worthy my own Mike, and that's more than I would say to 'ere another in the parish. I wasn't in earnest when I said you'd be glad to get rid of me; so put the pouch, every bit of it, off yer handsome face. And hush!—whisht! will ye! there's the sound of Larry's footstep in the bawn—hand me the needles, Mike.' She braided back her hair with both hands, arranged the red ribbon that confined its luxuriance in the little glass that hung upon a nail on the dresser, and after composing her arch laughing features into an expression of great gravity, sat down, and applied herself with singular industry to take up the stitches her brother had dropped, and put on a look of right maidenly astonishment when the door opened, and Larry's good-humoured face entered with the salutation of 'God save all here!' He 'popped' his head in first, and after gazing round, presented his goodly person to their view; and a pleasant view it was, for he was of genuine Irish bearing and beauty—frank, and manly, and fearless-looking. Ellen, the wicked one, looked up with well-feigned astonishment, and exclaimed, 'Oh, Larry, is it you; and who would have thought of seeing you this blessed night! Ye're lucky—just in time for a bit of supper afther your walk across the moor. I cannot think what in the world makes you walk over that moor so often; you'll get wet feet, and yer mother 'ill be forced to nurse you. Of all the walks in the county, the walk across that moor's the dreariest, and yet ye're always going it! I wonder ye haven't better sense; ye're not such a chicken now.'

'Well,' interrupted Mike, 'it's the women that bates the world for desaving. Sure she heard yer step when nobody else could; its echo struck on her heart, Larry—let her deny it; she'll make a shove off if she can; she'll twist you, and twirl you, and turn you about, so that you wont know whether it's on your head or your heels ye're standing. She'll tossicate yer brains in no time, and be as composed herself as a dove on her nest in a storm. But ask her, Larry, the straightforward question, whether she heard you or not. She'll tell no lie—she never does.'

Ellen shook her head at her brother and laughed. And immediately after the happy trio sat down to a cheerful supper.

Larry was a good tradesman, blithe, and 'well to do' in the world; and had it not been for the one great fault—an inclination to take the 'least taste in life more' when he had already taken quite enough—there could not have been found a better match for good, excellent Ellen Murphy, in the whole kingdom of Ireland. When supper was finished, the everlasting whisky bottle was produced, and Ellen resumed her knitting. After a time, Larry pressed his suit to Michael for the industrious hand of his sister, thinking, doubtless, with the natural self-conceit of all *man*kind, that he was perfectly secure with Ellen; but though Ellen loved, like all my fair countrywomen, *well*, she loved, I am compelled to say, *un*like the generality of my fair countrywomen, *wisely*, and reminded her lover that she had seen him intoxicated at the last fair of Rathcoolin.

'Dear Ellen!' he exclaimed, 'it was "only a drop," the least taste in life that overcame me. It overtook me unknownst, quite against my will.'

'Who poured it down yer throat, **Larry**?'

'Who poured it down my throat is it! why, myself, to be sure; but are you going to put me to a three months' penance for that?'

'Larry, will you listen to me, and remember that the man I marry must be converted before we stand before the priest. I have no faith whatever in conversions after——'

'Oh, Ellen!' interrupted her lover.

'It's no use oh Ellen—ing me,' she answered quickly; 'I have made my resolution, and I'll stick to it.'

'She's as obstinate as ten women!' said her brother. 'There's no use in attempting to contradict her; she always has had her own way.'

'It's very cruel of you, Ellen, not to listen to raison. I tell you a tablespoonful will often upset me.'

'If you know that, Larry, why do you take the tablespoonful!'

Larry could not reply to this question. He could only plead that the drop got the better of him, and the *temptation* and the *overcomingness* of the thing, and it was very hard to be at him so about a trifle.

'I can never think a thing a trifle,' she observed, 'that makes you so unlike yourself. I should wish to respect you always, Larry, and in my heart I believe no woman ever could respect a drunkard. I don't want to make you angry; God forbid you should ever be one, and I *know* you are not one yet; but sin grows mighty strong upon us without our knowledge. And no matter what indulgence leads to bad; we've a right to think anything that *does* lead to it sinful in the prospect, if not at the present.'

'You'd have made a fine priest, Ellen,' said the young man, determined, if he could not reason, to laugh her out of her resolve.

'I don't think,' she replied archly, 'if I was a priest, that either of you would have liked to come to me to confession.'

'But Ellen, dear Ellen, sure it's not in positive downright *earnest* you are : you can't think of putting me off on account of that unlucky drop, *the least taste in life* I took at the fair—you could not find it in your heart. Speak for me, Michael ; speak for me. But I see it's joking you are. Why, Lent 'ill be on us in no time, and then we must wait till Easter—it's easy talking——'

'Larry,' interrupted Ellen, 'do not you talk yourself into a passion ; it will do no good ; none in the world. I am sure you love me, and I confess before my brother it will be the delight of my heart to return that love, and make myself worthy of you, if you will only break yourself of that one habit, which you qualify to your own undoing, by fancying, because it is the *least taste in life* makes you what you ought not to be, that you may still take it.'

'I'll take an oath against the whisky, if that will plase ye, till Christmas.'

'And when Christmas comes, get twice as tipsy as ever, with joy to think your oath is out. No !'

'I'll swear anything you plase.'

'I don't want you to swear at all ; there is no use in a man's taking an oath he is anxious to have a chance of breaking. I want your reason to be convinced.'

'My darling Ellen, all the reason I ever had in my life is convinced.'

'Prove it by abstaining from taking even a drop, even *the least drop* in life, if that drop can make you ashamed to look your poor Ellen in the face.'

'I'll give it up altogether.'

'I hope you will one of these days, from a conviction that it is really bad in every way ; but not from cowardice, not because you dar'n't trust yourself.'

'Ellen, I'm sure ye've some English blood in yer veins, ye're such a raisoner. Irish women don't often throw a boy off because of a drop ; if they did, it's not many marriage dues his Reverence would have, winter or summer.'

'Listen to me, Larry, and believe that, though I spake this way, I regard you truly ; and if I did not, I'd not take the throuble to tell you my mind.'

'Like Mick Brady's wife, who, whenever she thrashed him, cried over the blows, and said they were all for his good,' observed her brother slyly.

'Nonsense !—listen to me, I say, and I'll tell you why I am so resolute. It's many a long day since, going to school, I used to meet—Michael minds her too, I'm sure—an old bent woman ; they used to call her the Witch of Ballaghton. Stacy was, as I have said, very old intirely, withered and white-headed, bent nearly double with age, and she used to be ever and always muddling about the strames and ditches, gathering herbs and plants, the girls said to work charms with; and at first they used to watch, rather far off, and if they thought they had a good chance of escaping her tongue, and the stones she flung at them, they'd call her an ill name or two; and sometimes, old as she was, she'd make a spring at them sideways like a crab, and howl, and hoot, and scrame, and then they'd be off like a flock of pigeons from a hawk, and she'd go on disturbing the green-coated waters with her crooked stick, and muttering words which none, if they heard, could understand. Stacy had been a well-rared woman, and knew a dale more than any of us: when not tormented by the children, she was mighty well spoken, and the gentry thought a dale about her more than she did about them; for she'd say there was not one in the country fit to tie her shoe, and tell them so, too, if they'd call her anything but Lady Stacy, which the *rale* gentry of the place all humoured her in; but the upstarts, who think every civil word to an inferior is a pulling down of their own dignity, would turn up their noses as they passed her; and maybe she didn't bless them for it!

'One day Mike had gone home before me, and coming down the back bohreen, who should I see moving along it but Lady Stacy; and on she came muttering and mumbling to herself till she got near me, and as she did, I heard Master Nixon (the dog man*)'s hound in full cry, and seen him at her heels, and he over the hedge encouraging the baste to tear her in pieces. The dog soon was up with her, and then she kept him off as well as she could with her crutch, cursing the entire time; and I was very frightened; but I darted to her side, and with a wattle I pulled out of the hedge, did my best to keep him off her.

'Master Nixon cursed at me with all his heart; but I wasn't to be turned off that way. Stacy herself laid about with her staff, but the ugly brute would have finished her, only for me. I don't suppose Nixon meant that; but the dog was savage, and some men, like him, delight in cruelty. Well, I bate the dog off; and then I had to help the poor fainting woman, for she was both faint and hurt. I didn't much like bringing her here, for the people said she wasn't lucky; however, she wanted help, and I gave it. When I got her on the floor,† I thought a drop of whisky would revive her, and accordingly I offered her a glass. I shall never forget the venom with which she dashed it on the ground.

"Do you want to poison me," she shouted, "afther saving my life?" When she came to herself a little, she made me sit down

---

* Tax-gatherers were so called some time ago in Ireland, because they collected the duty on dogs.

† In the house.

by her side, and fixing her large gray eyes upon my face, she kept rocking her body backwards and forwards while she spoke, as well as I can remember—what I'll try to tell you—but I can't tell it as she did—that wouldn't be in nature. "Ellen," she said, and her eyes fixed in my face, "I wasn't always a poor lone creature, that every ruffian who walks the country dare set his cur at. There was full and plenty in my father's house when I was young, but before I grew to womanly estate, its walls were bare and roofless. What made them so ? Drink !—whisky ! My father was in debt; to kill thought, he tried to keep himself so that he could not think; he wanted the courage of a man to look his danger and difficulty in the face, and overcome it; for, Ellen, mind my words—the man that will look debt and danger steadily in the face, and resolve to overcome them, *can do so.* He had not means, he said, to educate his children as became them: he grew not to have means to find them or their poor patient mother the proper necessaries of life; yet he found the means to keep the whisky cask flowing, and to answer the bailiffs' knocks for admission by the loud roar of drunkenness— mad, as it was wicked. They got in at last, in spite of the care taken to keep them out, and there was much fighting, ay, and blood spilt, but not to death; and while the riot was a-foot, and we were crying round the deathbed of a dying mother, where was he !—they had raised a ten-gallon cask of whisky on the table in the parlour, and astride on it sat my father, flourishing the huge pewter funnel in one hand, and the black jack streaming with whisky in the other; and amid the fumes of hot punch that flowed over the room, and the cries and oaths of the fighting drunken company, his voice was heard swearing 'he had lived like a king, and WOULD die like a king !'"

"And your poor mother ?" I asked.

"Thank God ! she died that night—she died before worse came ; she died on the bed that, before her corpse was cold, was dragged from under her—through the strong drink—through the badness of him who ought to have saved her ; not that he was a bad man either, when the whisky had no power over him, but he could not bear his own reflections. And his end soon came. He didn't die like a king ; he died smothered in a ditch, where he fell ; he died, and was in the presence of God—how ? Oh, there are things that have had whisky as their beginning and their end, that make me as mad as ever it made him ! The man takes a drop, and forgets his starving family; the woman takes it, and forgets she is a mother and a wife. It's the curse of Ireland—a bitterer, blacker, deeper curse than ever was put on it by foreign power or hard-made laws !'"

'God bless us !' was Larry's half-breathed ejaculation.

'I only repeat ould Stacy's words,' said Ellen ; 'you see I

never forgot them. "You might think," she continued, "that I had had warning enough to keep me from having anything to say to those who war too fond of drink; and I thought I had; but somehow Edward Lambert got round me with his sweet words, and I was lone and unprotected. I knew he had a little fondness for the drop; but in him, young, handsome, and gay-hearted, with bright eyes and sunny hair, it did not seem like the horrid thing which *had made me shed no tear over my father's grave.* Think of that, young girl: the drink doesn't make a man a beast *at first*, but it will do so before it's done with him—it will do so before it's done with him. I had enough power over Edward, and enough memory of the past, to make him swear against it, except so much at such and such a time; and for a while he was very particular; but one used to entice him, and another used to entice him, and I am not going to say but I might have managed him differently: I might have got him off it—gently, maybe; but the pride got the better of me, and I thought of the line I came of, and how I had married him who wasn't my equal, and such nonsense, which always breeds disturbance betwixt married people; and I used to rave, when, maybe, it would have been wiser if I had reasoned. Anyway, things didn't go smooth: not that he neglected his employment: he was industrious, and sorry enough when the fault was done; still he would come home often the worse for drink—and now that he's dead and gone, and no finger is stretched to me but in scorn or hatred, I think maybe I might have done better; but, God defend me, the *last* was hard to bear." Oh, boys !' said Ellen, 'if you had only heard her voice when she said *that*, and seen her face: poor ould Lady Stacy, no wonder she hated the drop—no wonder she dashed down the whisky !'

'You kept this mighty close, Ellen,' said Mike; 'I never heard it before.'

'I did not like coming over it,' she replied; 'the last is hard to tell.' The girl turned pale while she spoke, and Lawrence gave her a cup of water. 'It must be told,' she said; 'the death of her father proved the effects of deliberate drunkenness. What I have to say, shows what may happen from being even once unable to think or act.

"I had one child," said Stacy; "one—a darlint, blue-eyed laughing child. I never saw any so handsome, never knew any so good. She was almost three years ould, and he was fond of her— he said he was, but it's a quare fondness that destroys what it ought to save. It was the Pattern of Lady-day, and well I knew that Edward would not return as he went: he said he would; he *almost* swore he would; but the promise of a man given to drink has no more strength in it than a rope of sand. I took sulky, and wouldn't go; if I had, maybe it would not have ended so.

The evening came on, and I thought my baby breathed hard in her cradle; I took the candle, and went over to look at her: her little face was red; and when I laid my cheek close to her lips so as not to touch them, but to feel her breath, it was hot—very hot; she tossed her arms, and they were dry and burning. The measles were about the country, and I was frightened for my child. It was only half a mile to the doctor's; I knew every foot of the road; and so, leaving the door on the latch, I resolved to tell him how my darlint was, and thought I should be back before my husband's return. Grass, you may be sure, didn't grow under my feet. I ran with all speed, and wasn't kept long, the doctor said, though it seemed long to me. The moon was down when I came home, though the night was fine. The cabin we lived in was in a hollow; but when I was on the hill, and looked down where I knew it stood a dark mass, I thought I saw a white light fog coming out of it; I rubbed my eyes, and darted forward as a wild bird flies to its nest when it hears the scream of the hawk in the heavens. When I reached the door, I saw it was open; the fume cloud came out of it, sure enough, white and thick. Blind with that and terror together, I rushed to my child's cradle. I found my way to *that*, in spite of the burning and the smothering. But, Ellen—Ellen Murphy, my child, the rosy child whose breath had been hot on my cheek only a little while before, she was nothing but a cinder. Mad as I felt, I saw how it was in a minute. The father had come home, as I expected; he had gone to the cradle to look at his child, had dropt the candle into the straw, and, unable to speak or stand, had fallen down and asleep on the floor not two yards from my child. Oh how I flew to the doctor's with *what* had been my baby; I tore across the country like a banshee; I laid it in his arms; I told him if he didn't put life in it I'd destroy him in his house. He thought me mad; for there was no breath, either cowld or hot, coming from its lips *then*. I couldn't kiss it in death; *there was nothing left of my child to kiss*—think of that! I snatched it from where the doctor had laid it; I cursed him, for he looked with disgust at my purty child. The whole night long I wandered in the woods of Newtownbarry with that burden at my heart."'

'But her husband, her husband!' inquired Larry in accents of horror; 'what became of him; did she leave him in the burning without calling him to himself?'

'No,' answered Ellen; 'I asked her, and she told me that her shrieks, she supposed, roused him from the suffocation in which he must, but for them, have perished. He staggered out of the place, and was found soon after by the neighbours, and lived long after, but only to be a poor heartbroken man, for she was mad for years through the country; and many a day after she told me that story, my heart trembled like a willow leaf. "And now,

Ellen Murphy," she added, when the end was come, "do ye wonder I threw from yer hand as poison the glass you offered me! And do you know why I have tould you what tares my heart to come over? Because I wish to save you, who showed me kindness, from what I have gone through. It's the only good I can do ye, and indeed it's long since I cared to do good. Never trust a drinking man; he has no guard on his words, and will say that of his nearest friend that would destroy him soul and body. His breath is hot as the breath of the plague; his tongue is a foolish, as well as a fiery serpent. Ellen, let no drunkard become your lover, and don't trust to promises; try them, prove them all, before you marry."'

'Ellen, that's enough,' interrupted Larry. 'I have heard enough —the two proofs are enough without words. Now hear me. What length of punishment am I to have? I wont say that, for, Nelly, there's a tear in your eye that says more than words. Look—I'll make no promises—but you shall see; I'll wait yer time; name it; I'll stand the trial.'

And I am happy to say, for the honour and credit of the country, that Larry did stand the trial—his resolve was fixed; he never so much as tasted whisky from that time, and Ellen had the proud satisfaction of knowing she had saved him from destruction. They were not, however, married till *after* Easter. I wish all Irish maidens would follow Ellen's example. Women could do a great deal to prove that '*the least taste in life*' is a great taste too much!—that 'ONLY A DROP' is a temptation fatal if unresisted.

'DO YOU THINK I'D INFORM!'

JAMES HARRAGAN was as fine a specimen of an Irishman as could be met with in our own dear country, where the 'human form divine,' if not famous for very delicate, is at least celebrated for very strong proportions: he was, moreover, a well-educated, intelligent person; that is to say, he could read and write, keep correct accounts of his buying and selling, and managed his farm, consisting of ten good acres of the best land in a part of Ireland where all is good (the Barony of Forth), so as to secure the approbation of an excellent landlord, and his own prosperity. It was a pleasant sight to see the honest farmer bring out the well-fed horse and the neatly-appointed car every Saturday morning, whereon his pretty daughter Sydney journeyed into Wexford, to dispose of the eggs, butter, and poultry, the sale of which aided her father's exertions.

Sydney was rather an unusual name for a young Irish girl; but her mother had been housekeeper to a noble lady, who selected it for her, though it assimilated strangely with Harragan. The maiden herself was lithe, cheerful, industrious, and of a gentle, loving nature; her brown affectionate eyes betokened, as brown eyes always do, more of feeling than of intellect; and her red lips, white teeth, and rich dark hair, entitled her to the claim of rustic beauty. Her mother had been dead about two years; and Sydney, who, during her lifetime, was somewhat inclined to be vain and thoughtless, had, as her father expressed it, 'taken altogether a turn for good,' and discharged her duties admirably as mistress of James Harragan's household. She had five brothers, all younger than herself; the two elder were able and willing to assist in the farm, the juniors went regularly to school.

Sorrow for the loss of his wife had both softened and humbled James Harragan's spirit; and when Sydney, disdaining any assistance, sprang lightly into the car, and seated herself in the midst of her rural treasures, her father's customary prayer, 'Good luck to you, Sydney, my darling,' was increased by the prayer of 'May the Lord bless you, and keep you to me, now, and till the day of my death!'

The car went on, Sydney laughing and nodding to her father, while he smiled and returned her salutation; though, when she was fairly out of sight, he passed the back of his rough hand across his eyes, and murmured, 'I almost wish she was not so like her mother!' When James entered his cottage, he sat by the fire, and taking down a slate that hung above the settle, began to make thereupon sundry calculations, which I do not profess to understand. How long he might have continued so occupied I cannot determine, for his cogitations were interrupted by the entrance of a gentleman, who was by his side ere he noticed his approach. The usual salutations were exchanged; the best chair dusted, and presented to the stranger; everything in the house was tendered for his acceptance. 'His honour had a long walk, would he have an egg or a rasher for a snack? Sydney was out, but Bessy her cousin was above in the loft, and would get it or anything else in a minute; or maybe he'd have a glass of ale: good it was—Cherry's ale—no better in the kingdom.' All Irishmen—and particularly so fine and manly a fellow as James—to be seen to advantage, should be seen in their own houses—CABINS I cannot call such as are tenanted by the warm farmers of this well-cultivated district.

Mr Herrick, however, could not be tempted; he would not suffer the rasher to be cut, nor the ale to be drawn, and James looked sad because his visitor declined accepting his humble but cheerful hospitality.

'James,' said Mr Herrick, 'I am glad I found you at home, and alone, for I wanted to speak with you. I have long considered you superior to your neighbours. I do not mean as a farmer—though you have twice received the highest prizes which the Agricultural Society bestow—but as a man.'

James looked gratified, and said he was so.

'I have found you, James, the first to see improvement, and to adopt it, however much popular prejudice might be against it; you have been ever ready to listen to and act upon the advice of those your reason told you were qualified to give it; and you have not been irritated or annoyed when faults, national or individual, have been pointed out to you which can be and ought to be remedied.'

'I believe what your honour says is true; but sure it's proud and happy we ought to be to have the truth told of us—it is what does not always happen; if it did, poor Ireland would have had more justice done her long ago than ever came to her share yet.'

'And that, James, is also true,' said Mr Herrick; 'the Irish character has not only its individual differences, which always must be the case, but it has its provincial, its baronial distinctions.'

'Indeed, sir,' replied Harragan, 'there can be no doubt about that; we should be sorry, civilised as we are here, to be compared to the wild rangers of Connaught, or to the staid, quiet, tradesman-like people of the north.'

'The northerns are a fine prudent people,' said Mr Herrick, 'notwithstanding your prejudice; but what you have said is only another proof that persons may write very correctly about the north of Ireland, and yet, unless they see the south, form a very limited, or, it may be, erroneous idea of the character of the southerns. The Irish are more difficult to understand than people imagine. You are a very unmanageable people, James,' added the gentleman good-humouredly.

'Bedad, sir, I suppose ye're right; some of us are, I daresay. And now, sir, I suppose there is a raison for that.'

'There is,' answered his friend. 'You are an unmanageable people, *because of your prejudices.*'

'That's your old story against us, Mr Herrick,' said James; 'and yet you can't deny but I've been often led by your honour, and for my good, I'll own to that.'

'James,' continued his friend, 'will you answer me one question? Were you, or were you not, at Gerald Casey's on Monday week?'

James's countenance fell, it positively elongated, at the question. So great was the change, that those who did not know the man, might have imagined he had committed a crime, and anticipated immediate punishment. 'At Gerald Casey's?' he repeated.

Mr Herrick drew a letter—a soiled, dirty-looking letter—from his pocket, and slowly repeated the question.

'I was, sir,' he answered, resting his back against the dresser, and pressing his open palms upon the board, as if the action gave him strength.

'Who was there, James?'

'Is it who was in it, sir? Why, there was—— Bedad, sir, there was—— Oh, thin, it's the bad head I have at remimbering—— I forget who was there.' And the countenance of James assumed, despite his exertions, a lying expression that was totally unworthy his honest nature.

'James,' observed Mr Herrick, 'you used not to have a bad memory. I have heard you speak of many trifling acts of kindness my father showed you when you were a boy of twelve years old.'

The farmer's face was in a moment suffused with crimson, and he interrupted him with the grateful warmth of an affectionate Irish heart. 'Oh, sir, sure you don't think I'm worse than the poor dog that follows night and day at my foot? You don't think I've no heart in my body?'

'I was talking of your memory,' said Mr Herrick quietly; 'and I ask you again to tell me who were at Gerald Casey's on Monday week?'

'I left Gerald Casey's before dusk, sir; and it's what took me in it was——'

'I don't ask you when you left it, or what took you there. I only ask you who were present?'

James saw there was no use in equivocating, for that Mr Herrick would be answered. He was, as I have said, an excellent fellow; yet he had, in common with his countrymen, a very provoking way of evading a question; but anxious as he was to evade this, he could not manage it now. Mr Herrick looked him so steadfastly in the face, that he slowly answered, 'I'd rather not say one way or other who was there or who was not there. I've an idea, from something I heard this morning, before the little girl went into Wexford, that I know now what your honour's driving at. And sure'—and his face deepened in colour as he continued—'and sure, Mr Herrick, "do you think I'd inform?"'

Mr Herrick was not astonished at the answer he received. On the contrary, he was quite prepared for it, and prepared also to combat a principle that militates so strongly against the comfort and security of all who reside in Ireland.

'Will you,' he inquired, 'tell me what you mean by the word "inform?"'

'It's a mean dirty practice, sir,' replied Harragan, 'to be repeating every word one hears in a neighbour's house.'

'So it is,' answered the gentleman; 'an evil, mean practice, to repeat what is said merely from a love of gossip. But suppose a person, being accidentally one of a party, heard a plot formed against your character, perhaps your life, and not only concealed the circumstance, but absolutely refused to afford any clue by which such a conspiracy could be detected——'

'Oh, sir,' interrupted Harragan, 'that's nothing here nor there. I couldn't tell in the gray of the evening who went in or out of the place; I had no call to any one, and I don't want any one to have any call to me.'

'You must know perfectly well who was there,' said Mr Herrick. 'The case is simply this: a gentleman in this neighbourhood has received two anonymous letters, attacking the character of a person who has been confidentially employed by him for some years. James Harragan, *you know who wrote those letters;* and I ask you how, as an *honest man*, you can lay your head upon your pillow and *sleep*, knowing that an equally honest man may be deprived of the means to support his young family, and be turned adrift upon the world, through the positive malice of those who are envious of his prosperity and good name.'

James looked very uncomfortable, but did not trust himself to speak.

'I repeat, you know by whom those letters were written.'

'As I hope to be saved!' exclaimed James, 'I saw no writing —not the scratch of a pen!'

'Harragan,' continued Mr Herrick, 'it would be well for our country if many of its inhabitants were not so quick at invention.'

'I have not told a lie, sir.'

'No, but you have done worse—you have equivocated. Though you did not see the letter written, *you knew it was written;* and an equivocation is so cowardly, that I wonder an Irishman would resort to it: a lie is in itself cowardly, but an equivocation is more cowardly still.'

Harragan for a moment looked shillalas and crab-thorns at his friend, for such he had frequently proved himself to be, but made no further observation, simply confining himself to the change and repetition of the sentences—'Do you think I'd inform!' 'Not one belonging to me ever turned informer.'

'Am I then,' said Mr Herrick, rising, 'to go away with the conviction that you know an injury has been done to an innocent person, and yet will not do anything to convict a man guilty of a moral assassination?'

'A what, sir?'

'A moral murder.'

'Look here, sir; one can't fly in the face of the country. If I was to tell, my life would not be safe either in or out of my own house; you ought to know this. Besides, there is something very mean in an *informer.*'

'It is very sad,' replied Mr Herrick, 'that a spirit of combination for *evil* more than for *good* destroys the confidence which otherwise the gentry and strangers would be disposed to place in the peasantry of Ireland. As long as a man fears to speak and act like a man, so long as he dare not hear the proud and happy sound of his own voice in condemnation of the wicked, and in praise of the upright—so long, in fact, as an Irishman dare not speak what he knows—so long, *and no longer*, will Ireland be insecure, and its people scorned as cowards!'

'As cowards!' repeated James indignantly.

'Ay,' said Mr Herrick; 'there is a moral as well as a physical courage. The man who, in the heat of battle, faces a cannon ball, or who, in the hurry and excitement of a fair or pattern, exposes his bare head to the rattle of shillalas and clan-alpines without shrinking from punishment or death, is much inferior to the man who has the superior moral bravery to act in accordance with the dictates of his own conscience, and does right while those around him do wrong.'

'I daresay that's all very true, sir,' said James, scratching his head; adding, while most anxious to change the subject, 'it's a pity yer honour wasn't a councillor or a magistrate, a priest, minister, or friar itself, then you'd have great sway intirely with your words and your learning.'

'Not more than I have at present. Do you think it is a wicked thing to take away the character of an honest man?'

'To be sure I do, sir.'

'And yet you become a party to the act!'

'How so, sir?'

'By refusing to bring, or assist in bringing to justice, those who have endeavoured to ruin the father of a large family. Do you believe so many murders and burnings would take place if the truth was spoken?'

'No, sir.'

'That's a direct answer from an Irishman for once. If the evil-disposed, the disturbers of the country, knew that truth would be spoken, disturbances would soon cease; you believe this, and yet, by your silence, you shield those whom you *know* to be bad, and despise with all your heart and soul.'

'I don't want to have any call to them one way or other, good, bad, or indifferent,' answered James.

'Very well,' said Mr Herrick, thoroughly provoked at the man's obstinacy, and rising to leave the cottage; 'you say you wish to have no call to them. But mark *me*, James Harragan: when the spirit of anonymous letter-writing gets into a neighbourhood—when wicked-minded persons can destroy either a man's reputation or his life with equal impunity—there is no knowing where the evil may stop, or who shall escape its influence. The knowledge of the extent to which these secret conspiracies are carried, deters capitalists from settling amongst us: they may have security for their money, but they have none for their lives; if they offend by taking land, or offering opposition to received opinions, their doom may be fixed; those whom they have trusted will know of that doom, and yet no one will come forward to save them from destruction.'

'Sir,' said Harragan, '*secret* information is sometimes given.'

'I would accept no man's secret information,' answered Mr Herrick; for he was an upright man, perhaps too uncompromising for the persons with whom he had to deal; 'justice should not only be *even*-handed, but *open*-handed: it is a reproach to a country when the law finds it necessary to offer rewards for *secret* information. I wish I could convince you, James, of the difference which exists between a person who devotes his time to peeping and prying for the purpose of conveying information to *serve himself*, and him who speaks the truth from the upright and honourable motive of seeing justice done to his fellow-creatures.'

'I see the *differ* clear enough, sir,' replied the farmer; 'but none of my people ever turned informers. I'll have no call to it, and it's no use saying any more about the matter: there are plenty of people in the country can tell who was there as well as I—I'll have no call to it. When I went in the place, I little thought of who I'd meet there, and I'll go bail it's long before I'll trouble it again. There's enough said and done now.'

'A good deal *said*, certainly,' rejoined Mr Herrick, 'but nothing *done*. There are parts of the country where I know that my entering into this investigation would endanger my life, but, thank God, that is not the case here. I will pursue my investigation to the uttermost, and do not despair of discovering the delinquent.'

'I hope you may, with all my heart and soul, sir,' replied the farmer.

'Then why not aid me? If you are sincere, why not assist?'

And again James Harragan muttered, 'Do you think I'd inform?'

'I declare before Heaven!' exclaimed Mr Herrick, 'you are the most provoking people under the sun to deal with.'

'I ask your honour's pardon,' said James slyly; 'but you have not lived long enough in foreign parts to know that.'

'Your readiness will not drive me from my purpose. I repeat, you are the most provoking people in the world to deal with. Convince an Englishman or a Scotchman, and having convinced his reason, you may be certain he will act upon that conviction; but you, however convinced *your* reason may be, continue to act from the dictates of *your* prejudice. Remember this, however, James Harragan: you have refused to pluck out the arrow which an unseen hand has planted in the bosom of an excellent and industrious man—take care that the same invisible power *does not aim a shaft against yourself.*'

Mr Herrick quitted the cottage more in sorrow than in anger; and after he was gone, James Harragan thought over what he had said: he was quite ready to confess its truth, but prejudice still maintained its ascendancy. 'Aim a shaft against myself,' he repeated; 'I don't think any of them would do that, though I'm sorry to say many as good and better than I have been forced to fly the country through secret malice: it is a bad thing, but times 'll mend, I hope.'

Alas! James Hárragan is not the only man in my beloved country who satisfies himself with *hoping* that times will mend, without *endeavouring* to mend them. 'Aim a shaft against myself!' he again repeated. 'Well, I'm sure what Mr Herrick said is true; but for all that, I couldn't inform!'

The fact was, that, reason as he would, James could not get rid of his prejudice; he could not make the distinction between the man who turns the faults and vices of his fellow-creatures to his own account, and he who, *for the good of others*, simply and unselfishly speaks the truth.

Time passed on: Mr Herrick of course failed in his efforts to discover the author of the anonymous letter; the person against whom it was directed, although protected by his landlord, was ultimately obliged to relinquish his employment, and seek in other lands the peace and security he could not find in his own: he might, to be sure, have weathered the storm, for his enemies, as will be seen by the following anecdote, had no immediate intention of persecuting him to the death. A stranger, who bore a great resemblance to the person so obnoxious to those who met at the smith's forge, was attacked while travelling on an outside car in the evening, and in the immediate neighbourhood, and beaten most severely, before his assailants discovered they had ill used the wrong man! Nothing could exceed their regret when they discovered their mistake.

'Ah, thin, who are ye at all at all?' inquired one fellow, after having made him stand up that they might again knock him down more to their satisfaction; 'sure ye're not within a foot as tall as the boy we're afther. Is it crooked in the back ye are on purpose? Well, now, think o' that! What call had ye to be on Barney Brian's car, that so often carries *him*, and with the same surtoo? And why didn't ye say ye wasn't another! Well, it's heart sorry we are for the *mistake*, and hope it'll never happen to ye again, to be like another man, and he an *out-lawyer*, as a body may say, having received enough notice to quit long ago, if he'd only heed it, which we'll make him do, or have his life, after we admonish him onct more, as we've done you by mistake, with a taste of a bating, which we'd ask ye to tell him, if you know him.

There, we'll lay you on the car as aisy as if you war in yer mother's lap, and ask ye to forgive us, which we hope you'll do, as it was all a *mistake !* and no help for it!'

The victim of 'the mistake,' however, who was an Englishman, suffered for more than three months, and cannot comprehend to this day why those who attacked him so furiously were not sought out and brought to justice. He never could understand why an honest man should refuse to criminate a villain. The poor fellow for whom the beating was intended was not slow to discover the fact, and with a heavy heartache bade adieu to his native land, which, but for the sake of his young children, he would hardly have quitted even to preserve his own life.

James Harragan did not note these occurrences without much sorrow; he saw his daughter Sydney's eyes red for three entire days from weeping the departure of the exile's wife, whom she loved with the affection of a sister; and he had the mortification to see his beloved barony distinguished in the papers as a 'disturbed district,' from the *mistake* to which we have alluded, at the very time when many of the gentry were sleeping with their doors unfastened. James Harragan knew perfectly well that if he had spoken the truth, all this could have been prevented. Still time passed on. Mr Herrick seldom visited James; and though he admired his crops, and spoke kindly to his children, the farmer felt he had lost a large portion of the esteem he so highly valued.

But when a man goes on in the full tide of worldly prosperity, he does not continue long in trouble upon minor matters. Sydney's eyes were no longer red; nay, they were more sparkling than ever, for they were brightened by a passion to which she had been hitherto a stranger. And Sydney, though gifted with as much constancy as most people, if she did not forget, certainly did not think as frequently as before of her absent friend. Sydney, in fact, was what is called—in love; which, I believe, is acknowledged by all who have been in a similar dilemma to be a very confusing, perplexing situation. That poor Sydney found it so, was evident, for she became subject to certain flushings of the cheek, and beatings of the heart, accompanied by a confusion of the intellectual faculties, which puzzled her father for a time quite as much as herself. She would call rabbits chickens, and chickens rabbits, in the public market; and was known to have given forty-two new-laid eggs for a shilling, when she ought only to have given thirty-six.

Then in her garden, her own pet garden, she sowed mignionette and hollyoaks together, and wondered how it was that what she fancied sweet pea, had come up 'love-lies-bleeding.' Dear, warm, affectionate Sydney Harragan! She was a model of all that is excellent in simple guileless woman; and when Ralph Furlong drew from her a frank but most modest confession that his love was returned, and that 'if her father did not put against it,' she would gladly share his cottage and his fortunes, there was not a young disengaged farmer in the county that would not have envied him his 'good luck.'

Soon after James Harragan's consent had been obtained to a union which he believed would secure the happiness of his darling child, the farmer was returning from the fair of New Ross, where he had been to dispose of some spare farming-stock; and as he trotted briskly homeward, passing the well-known mountain, or, as it is called, 'Rock,' of Carrickburn, he was overtaken by a man to whom he had seldom spoken since the evening when he had seen him and some others at Gerald Casey's forge. Many, many months had elapsed since then. And truth to say, as the young man had removed to a cottage somewhere on the banks of the blue and gentle river Slaney, James had often hoped that he might never see him again.

'I'm glad I overtook you, Mr Harragan,' he said, urging his long lean narrow mare close to the stout well-fed cob of the comfortable farmer. 'It's a fine bright evening for the time of year. I intended coming to you next week, having something particular to talk about.'

'Nothing that concerns me, I fancy!' replied Harragan stiffly.

'I hope it does, and that it will: times are changed since we met last—with me particularly.' Harragan made no reply, and they rode on together in silence for some time longer.

'Mr Harragan, though you are a trustworthy man as ever stept in shoe leather, I am afraid you hav'n't a good opinion of me!'

'Whatever opinion I may have, you know I kept it to myself,' replied the farmer.

'Thank you for nothing,' was the characteristic reply.

'Ye're welcome,' rejoined James as dryly. Again they trotted silently on their way, until the stranger suddenly exclaimed, reining up his mare at the same moment, 'I'll tell you what my business would be with you; there's nothing like spaking out of the face at onct.'

'You did not always think so,' said the farmer.

'Oh, sir, aisy now; let bygones *be* bygones; the country's none the worse of getting rid of one who was ever and always minding other people's business; and you yerself, Mr Harragan, are none the worse for not having high-bred people ever poking their noses in yer place!'

'Say what you have to say at onct,' observed James; 'the evening will soon close in, and the little girl I have at home thinks it long till I return.'

'It's about her I want to spake,' said the stranger. 'If you'll take the trouble some fine morning early to ride over to where the dark green woods of Castle Boro dip their boughs in the

Slaney, ye'd see that I have as tidy a place, as well filled a *haggard*, and as well managed fields, as any houlder of ten acres of land in the county; besides that, I have my eye on another farm that's out of lase, and if all goes right, I'll have it. Now, ye see my sister's married, and my mother's dead, and I've no one to look after things; and for every pound ye'd tell down with yer daughter, I'd show a pound's worth. And so, Mr Harragan, I thought that of all the girls in the country, I'd prefer Sydney; and if we kept company for a while'—he turned his handsome but sinister and impudent countenance towards the astonished farmer, adding, 'I don't think she'd refuse me.'

'You might be mistaken for all that,' replied James, grasping his stout stick still more tightly in his hand, from a very evident desire to knock the fellow down.

'Well, now, I don't think I should,' he replied with vulgar confidence; 'it's the aisiest thing in life to manage a purty girl, if one has the knack, and I've managed so many.'

'Ride on!' interrupted the farmer indignantly. 'Ride on, before I am tempted to knock ye off the poor starved baste that ye hav'n't the heart to feed! *You* marry my Sydney—*you!*—a rascal like *you!* Why, Stephen Murphy, you must be gone mad—Sydney married with a cowardly backbiter! I'd rather dress her shroud with my own hands. A—a—ride on, I tell you,' he continued, almost choked with passion; 'there is nothing, I believe, that you would think too bad to do. And hark ye, take it for your comfort that she is going to be married to one worthy of her, and I her father say so.'

'Oh, very well! very well!' said the bravo; 'as you plase, Mr Harragan; as you plase; I meant to pay yer family a compliment —a compliment for yer silence; ye understand me; not that I hould myself over and above obleeged for that either. Ye like to take care of yerself for the sake of yer little girl, I suppose; and the counthry might grow too hot for you, as well as for others, if ye made free with yer tongue. No harm done; but if I had spaking with the girl for one hour, I'd put any sweetheart in the county, barring myself, out of her head. I'll find out the happy young man, and wish him joy. Oh, maybe I *wont* wish joy to the boy for whom I'm insulted,' he added, inflicting a blow upon the bare ribs of the poor animal he rode, that made her start; 'maybe I wont wish him joy, and give him Steve Murphy's blessing! Starved as ye call my baste, there's twice the blood in her that creeps through the flesh of yer overfed cob;' and sticking the long solitary iron spur which he wore on his right heel into the mare, he flew past James Harragan, flourishing his stick with a whirl, and shouting so loud, that the mountain echoes of the wild rocks of Carrickburn repeated the words 'joy! joy!' as if they had been thrown into their caverns by the fiend of mockery himself.

Instantly James urged his stout horse forward, crying at the top of his voice to Murphy to stop; but either the animal was tired, or the mare was endowed with supernatural swiftness, for he soon lost sight even of the skirts of Murphy's coat, which floated loosely behind him. 'The scoundrel!' he muttered to himself, while the gallop of his steed subsided into a heavy but tolerably rapid trot; 'I wanted to tell him to take care how he meddled with me or mine. Sydney! Sydney indeed! And the rascal's assurance!—he never spoke three words to my girl in his life! It's a good thing we're rid of him here anyway. I hope he's not a near neighbour of any of Furlong's people, that's all: his impudence—to me who knew him so well! Sarve me right,' he thought within himself, when his mutterings had subsided; 'sarve me right, to keep the secret of such a fellow. I suffered those who war innocent to leave the country—and he to talk paying of my family a compliment! Mr Herrick said it would come home to me; and so it has. I'm sure Murphy must have been *overtaken*,* or he'd never dare to propose such a thing. But then, if he was, why, the devil takes the weight off a tipsy man's tongue, and then all's out.'

It was night before Harragan arrived at his farm, and there the warm smiles and bright eyes of his Sydney were ready to greet his descent from the back of his stout steed; and the bridegroom elect was ready to hold the horse; and his sons, now growing up rapidly to manhood, crowded round him; and his dog, far more respectable in appearance than the generality of Irish cottage dogs, leaped to lick his hand; and the cat, with tail erect, purred at the door; the very magpie that Sydney loved for its love of mischief, stretched its neck through its prison bars to greet the farmer's return to his cottage home.

'There's no use in talking,' said James Harragan, after the conclusion of a meal which few small farmers are able to indulge in—I mean supper. 'There's no use in talking, Sydney—but I can't spare you—it's a certain fact, I cannot spare you. Furlong must find a farm near us, and live here: why, wanting my little girl, I should be like a sky without a sun.'

'Farms are not to be had here—they are too valuable to be easily obtained, as you well know,' replied the young man; 'but sure she'll not be a day's ride from you, sir, unless, indeed, my brother should have the luck to get a farm for me that he's afther by the Slaney, a little on the other side of the ferry of Mount Garrett; but that is such a bit of ground as is hard to be met with.' The father hardly noticed Furlong's reply, for his eyes and thoughts were fixed upon his child, until the word 'Slaney' struck upon his ear, and brought back Murphy,

---

* Tipsy.

his proposal, his threat, and his flying horse, at once to his remembrance.

'What did you say of a farm on the Slaney?' he inquired hastily.

'That I have the chance, the more than chance, of as purty a bit of land with a house, a slated house upon it, on the banks of the silver Slaney, as ever was turned for wheat or barley—to say nothing of green crops, that would bate the world for quality or quantity. My brother has known the cows there yield fourteen or sixteen quarts. I did not like to say anything about it before, for I was afraid I should never have the luck of it; but he wrote me to-day to say that he was almost sure of it, though some black-hearted villain had written letters without a name to the landlord, and agent, and steward, against us. Think of that now! We that never did a hard turn to man, woman, or child in the country.'

James Harragan absolutely shuddered; and passing his arm round Sydney's neck, drew her towards him with a sort of instinctive affection, like a bird that shelters its nestling beneath its wing when it hears the wild hawk's scream upon the breeze.

'Sydney shall never go there!' said Harragan.

'Not go to the banks of the Slaney!' exclaimed her eldest brother. 'Why, father, you don't know what a place it is—you don't know what you say. Besides, an hour and a half would take you quite aisy to where Furlong means. You make a great deal too much fuss about the girl.' And having so said, he stooped down and kissed her cheek, adding, 'Never mind, father; I'll bring you home a daughter that 'll be twice as good as Sydney. I'll just take one more summer out of myself, that's all, and then I'll marry; maybe I wont show a pattern wife to the country!' And then the youth was rated on the subject of bachelors' wives. And he retaliated; and then his sister threatened to box his ears, and was not slow in putting the threat into execution; and soon afterwards Furlong rose to return home; and Sydney remembered she had forgotten to see to the health and comforts of a delicate calf; and though the servant and her brothers all offered to go, she would attend to it herself; and five minutes after, her father went to the door, heard her light laugh and low murmuring voice, and saw her standing with her lover in the moonlight—he outside, and she inside the garden-gate, her hand clasped within his, and resting on the little pier that was clustered round with woodbine. She looked so lovely in that clear pure light, that her father's heart ached from very anguish at the possibility of any harm happening to one so dear. He longed to ask Furlong if he knew Murphy, but a choking sensation in his throat prevented him. And when Sydney returned, he caught her to his bosom, and burst into a flood of such violent tears as strong men seldom shed.

The poisoned chalice was approaching his own lips. What would he not have given at that moment that he had acceded to Mr Herrick's proposal! for had Murphy's villany become public, he must have quitted the country. How did he, even then, repent that he had not yielded to his reason instead of his prejudice!

Young Furlong was at a loss to account for the steady determination with which, at their next meeting, his intended father-in-law opposed his taking a farm in everyway so advantageous; James hardly dared acknowledge to himself, much less impart to another, the dread he entertained of Steve Murphy's machinations; this was increased tenfold when he found he was the person who not only desired, but had offered for that identical farm a heavier rent than he would ever have been able to pay for it. The landlord, well aware of this fact, and knowing that a rack-rent destroys first the land, secondly the tenant, and ultimately the landlord's property, had decided on bestowing his pet farm as a reward to the superior skill and industry of a young man whose enemies were too cowardly to attempt to substantiate their base charges against him.

I can only repeat my often-expressed desire, that every other Irish landlord acted in the same manner.

It would be impossible to convey an idea of how continually James Harragan's mind dwelt upon Steve Murphy's threat: at first he tried if Sydney's love towards Furlong was to be shaken; but that he found impossible.

'If you withdraw your consent, father,' she said, 'after having given it, and been perfectly unable to find a single fault with him, I can only say I will not disobey you; but, father, I will never marry—I will never take to any as I took to him, nor you need not expect it. You shall not make me disobedient, father, but you may break my heart.' Sydney, resigned and suffering, pained her father more than Sydney remonstrating against injustice. She had before shown him how hard it was, not only after encouraging, but actually accepting Furlong, to dismiss him *without reason*, and had reproached him in an agony of bitter feeling for his inconsistency. When this did not produce the desired effect, her cheek grew pale, her step languid, her eyes lost their gentle brightness, and her eldest brother ventured to tell his father 'that he was digging his daughter's grave!' The disappointment of the young man beggars description; he declared he would enlist, go to sea, 'quit the country,' break his heart, shoot any who put 'betwixt them,' and after many prayers, used every possible and impossible threat—except the one which the Irish so rarely either threaten or execute, that of self-destruction—to induce James to alter his resolution. James, unable to stand against this domestic storm, did of course retract; and the consequence was, that he lost by this changing mood the confidence of his children, who had ever till then regarded him with the deepest affection. He dared not communicate the reason of his first change, for doing so would have betrayed the foolish and unfortunate secret he had persevered in keeping, in opposition to common sense, and the estrangement of an old and valuable friend; he could not witness the returned happiness of his children without foreboding that something was to occur that would completely destroy it: and the joyous laughter of his daughter, at one time the sweet music of his household, was sure to send him forth with an aching heart.

Nor was young Furlong without his anxieties: he received more than one anonymous letter, threatening that if he did not immediately give up all thoughts of the farm, he would suffer for it : the notices were couched in the usual terms, which, in truth, I care not to repeat ; it is quite enough to say that they differed in no respect from others of a similar kind, and with a like intention. However inclined the young man might feel to despise such hints, the experience of the country unfortunately proved that they ought not to be disregarded: but his brother, stronger of heart and spirit, argued that their faction was too powerful, their friends too numerous, to leave room for fear ; that their own county was (as it really is) particularly quiet; and that as Mr Harragan was 'so humorsome,' the best way would be to say nothing at all about it; that it was evident those who had tried to set the landlord against them, having failed in their design, resolved to try the effect of personal intimidation; concluding by observing, 'that it was the best way to go on easy,' and 'never heeding,' until after the lease was signed and the wedding over, and then they'd 'see about it!' However consistent this mode of reasoning might be with Irish feeling, it was very sad to perceive how ready the Furlongs were to trust to the strong arm of the people, instead of appealing to the strong arm of the law. I wish the peasantry and their friends could perceive how they degrade themselves in the scale of civilised society by such a course ; it is this perpetual taking of all laws, but particularly the law of revenge, into their own hands, that keeps up the hue and cry against them throughout England. I confess time has been when there was one law for the rich and another for the poor ; but it is so no longer ; and humane lawgivers, and administrators of law, grow sick at heart when they perceive that they labour in vain for the domestic peace of Ireland.

A few days before the appointed time for Sydney Harragan to become Sydney Furlong, she received a written declaration of love, combined with an offer of marriage, from Murphy. He watched secretly about the neighbourhood until an opportunity arrived for him to deliver it himself. Sydney, to whom he was almost unknown, at first gave a civil yet firm refusal; but when he persevered, she became indignant, and said one or two bitter words, which he swore never to forget. She hardly knew why she concealed from her father the circumstance, which, upon consideration, she was almost tempted to believe a jest; but she did not even mention it to her brothers, fearing it might cause a quarrel, and every Irish woman knows how much easier it is commenced than quelled. Moreover, one mystery is sure to beget another.

At last the eventful day arrived—Sydney all hopes and blushes, her brothers full of frolic and fun, the bride's-maids arrayed in their best, and busied in setting the house in order for the ceremony, which, according to ancient Catholic custom, was to take place in the afternoon at the dwelling of the bride.

'Did ye ever see such a frown over the face of a man in yer born days!' whispered Essy Hays to her sister-maid. 'Do but just look at the masther, and see how his eyes are set on his daughter, and she reading her prayers like a good Christian, one eye out of the window, and the other on her book. Well, *she is* a purty girl, and it's no wonder so few chances were going for others, and she to the fore.'

'Speak for yourself!' exclaimed Jane Temple, tossing her fair ringlets back from her blue eyes. 'She is purty for a dark-skinned girl, there's no denying it.'

'Dark-haired, not dark-skinned!' said Essy indignantly; 'the darlint! She's the very moral of an angel. I wish to my heart the masther would not look at her so melancholy. *Maybe he's thinking how like her poor dead mother she is!* My! if here isn't his reverence (I know the cut of the gray mare, so fat and so smoothly jogging over the hill), and Misthur Furlong not come! He went to his brother across Ferry Carrig yesterday, and was to sleep at his aunt's in Wexford last night: I think he might have been here by this! Well, if it was me, I would be affronted: it is not very late, to be sure—only for a bridegroom!'

'Whisht, Essy, will you,' returned Jane, 'for fear she'd hear you; I never saw so young a bride take so early to the prayers; it seems as if something hung over her and her father for trouble.'

'I wonder ye're not ashamed of yerself, Jane!' exclaimed the warm-hearted Essy, 'to be raising trouble at such a time. Whisht! if there isn't the bridegroom's brother trotting up to the priest. What a handsome bow he makes his reverence, his hat right off his head with the flourish of a new shillala; but, good luck to us all! what ails the masther now?'

James Harragan also had seen the bridegroom's brother as he rode up the hill which fronted their dwelling, and sprang to his feet in an instant. When the heart is fully and entirely occupied by a beloved object, and that object is absent, alarm for its safety is like an electric shock, commencing one hardly knows how, but startling in its effects. Sydney looked in her father's face and screamed; while he, dreading that she had read the half-formed thoughts which were born of fear within his bosom at the sight of the bridesman without the bridegroom, uttered an imperfect assurance that 'all was well—all must be well: Ralph had waited for his aunt—old ladies required attention—and no doubt they would arrive together.' With this assurance he hastened to the door to meet the priest and his companion, and his heart resumed its usual beatings when he observed the jovial expression of the old priest's face, and the *rollicking* air with which the bridesman bowed to the bride, who crouched behind her father, anxious to hear the earliest news, and yet held back by that sweet modesty which enshrines the hearts of my gentle countrywomen.

'Where's Ralph?' inquired the farmer, while holding the stirrup for his reverence to dismount.

'That's a *nate* question to be sure,' answered his brother. 'Where would he be? And so, Miss Sydney, *you* asked Mr Herrick to come to the wedding, and never tould any one of it, by way of a surprise to us—that *was* very purty of you—and that's the top of his new beaver coming along the hedge. Well, it's quite time Ralph showed himself, I think, and we in waiting.'

'Don't be foolish, Harry Furlong!' exclaimed the farmer hastily. 'You know very well that Ralph is not here.'

'Well, that's done to the life,' said the light-hearted fellow; 'that's not bad for a very big—— I mustn't say it before the bride: but it's as bould-faced a story as ever I heard. Not here! Then where is he?'

'With his aunt, I daresay, if you don't know,' answered Essy.

'Oh, ye're in the mischief too, are ye, bright-eyed one? Why, ye know he's hid here on the sly to surprise us. Aunt, indeed! To be sure he's with his ould aunt Bell and his bride alone! What a mighty quare Irishman he must be! I'll advise *him* not to come to you for a character, whatever I may do; eh, Essy?'

'Will you give over bothering?' she said. 'Look at the colour Sydney's turned, and see to the masther—the Lord be betwixt us and harm!—none of your nonsense, but tell us *where* is Ralph?'

The aspect of things changed in an instant. Harry *saw* that his brother was not there—concealed, as he had supposed him to be, in mere playfulness—and *knew* that he was not with his aunt Bell. He knew, moreover, that he had parted from him the night before at the other side of Ferry Carrig; that he was *then* on his way to Wexford, where he had promised to meet him in the morning; that he had been to their aunt's to keep his tryst, but that he had felt no uneasiness on finding Ralph not there, concluding that, instead of going to the town, he had gone to his bride's house in the country, for which he had intended mirthfully to reproach him when they met. Now seriously alarmed, his anxiety to prevent Sydney from partaking of his feelings almost deprived him of the power of speech; but he had said enough, and just as Mr Herrick crossed the threshold, the bride fainted at his feet.

Nothing could be more appalling than the change effected in a few moments in the expression of the farmer's face. While each was engaged in imparting to the other hopes for the bridegroom's reappearance, and reasons for his delay, Harragan, having put forth every other assistance, was bending over his insensible child, on the very bed from which she had that morning risen in the fulness of almost certain happiness for years to come. Alas! how little can we tell upon what of all we cherish in this changing world each rising sun may set!

'If she's not dead,' he muttered to himself, 'she will die soon. May the Lord deliver me!—the Lord deliver me!' he continued, while chafing her temples: 'I saw it all along, like a shroud above me to fall round her—I did, I did. Who's that?' he inquired fiercely, as the door gently opened, and Mr Herrick entered within its sanctuary. 'Oh, it's you, sir, is it? You may come in. I thought it was some of them light-hearted who don't know trouble. Shut them out: my trouble's heavy, sir: look at her, Mr Herrick: and this was the wedding my little girl asked you to, out of friendliness to her father. *Her* father! why, the Holy Father who is above us all knows that, as sure as the beams of the blessed sun are shining on her deathy cheek, so sure am I Ralph Furlong's murderer! You need not draw back, Mr Herrick. I *know* he's murdered; I felt struck with the knowledge of his death—*and I could not help it*—the minute his brother (God help him!) laughed in my face. Don't raise up her head, sir; she'll come to soon enough—too soon—like a spirit that comes to the earth but to leave it. I'm not mad, Mr Herrick, though maybe I look so. Be it by fire or water, or steel or bullet, Ralph Furlong's a corpse, and *I'll inform this time.* I've heard tell the man that betrayed Christ wept afther. What good war *his* tears! What good my informing now? But I will—I will. I'll make a clean breast for onct. I'll do the right thing now, if all the devils of hell tear me into pieces! I tell you, sir, Steve Murphy did it!—black-hearted, cunning-headed, and bloody-handed he was, from the time his mother begged with him from door to door for what she did not want, and taught him lies by every hedgerow and green bank through the country. I'm punished, Mr Herrick—I'm punished. If I'd informed—but I'll not call it informing—if *I'd told the truth*, when you wanted me, about the letters at the forge, he would not have been in the country to commit murder. She's coming to now, sir; she's coming to.'

Gradually poor Sydney revived, but only to suffer more than she had previously gone through. The people were greatly astonished at the conviction which rested on the farmer's mind that the young man had been murdered, a belief which extended itself to his daughter; for, from the moment she heard that Ralph was not with his aunt, it appeared as if every vestige of hope had vanished from her mind. The men of the company set forward an immediate inquiry; every cottage was emptied of its inmates—the women flocking to the farmer's house to pour consolation and hope into the bosom of the bereaved bride, and the men to assist in a search which, at the noonday hour, was a very uncommon occurrence. It is rarely, indeed, that the Irish peasantry seek assistance either from the police or military force; though they are fond of going to law, they detest those connected with the law. But Mr Herrick promptly rode into Wexford, and having made the necessary inquiries, and ascertained that young Furlong had not been seen at the town, he informed the proper authorities of his mysterious disappearance, and then turned his horse towards Ferry Carrig, to ascertain from the gatekeeper who had passed over the bridge the preceding evening.

Ferry Carrig is one of the picturesque spots which are so frequently seen by those who journey through my native county. On one side of the Slaney—here a river of glorious width—rises, boldly and wildly, a conical hill, upon the summit of which stands out, in frowning ruins, one of the boldest of the square towers of which so many were erected by the enterprising Fitz-Stephen. The opposite side of the bridge is guarded by a rock, not so steep or so magnificent as its neighbour, but not less striking, though its character is different: the one is absolutely garlanded with heaths, wild-flowers, and the golden-blossoming furze; while the other, affording barely a spot for vegetation, seems planted for eternity—so stern, and fixed, and rugged, that one could imagine nothing save the destruction of the universe capable of shaking its foundation.

The bridge erected across this beautiful water is of singular construction, and partakes of the wildness of the scene; the planks are not fastened at either end, and the noise and motion has a startling effect to one not accustomed to such modes of transit.

When Mr Herrick arrived at the toll-house, he learned that many inquiries had been already made, and all the toll-keeper could say was, 'that positively Ralph Furlong, whom he knew as well as his own son, had not crossed the bridge the preceding evening, although he had been on the look-out for him.' The elder Furlong had accompanied his brother to within a mile of the Eniscorthy side of the bridge, so his disappearance must have occurred between the spot where they separated and the bridge of Ferry

Carrig. Nothing could exceed the energy and exertion to discover the lost bridegroom—every inquiry was made, every brake explored, the rivers even were dragged—but no trace of Ralph Furlong was obtained. Mr Herrick returned to the farm, and it was heartbreaking to observe the totally hopeless expression of Sydney's beautiful face.

'There is no knowing,' said the kind gentleman, with a cheerfulness that he but imperfectly assumed; 'there is no knowing—he *may* have left the country.'

'No,' was her reply; '*he would never have deserted me!*' Thus did her trust in her lover's fidelity outlive all hope of meeting him alive in this changing world.

In the meantime, James Harragan had proceeded alone to Steve Murphy's cottage. The sun had set, when he found him sitting by his fire, not alone, for his sister was seated on the opposite side.

Harragan entered with the determined air of a desperate man, and neither gave salutation, nor returned that which was given.

'I come,' said he, 'to ask you where you have hid Ralph Furlong.' The man started, and changed colour; and then assuming a bold and determined air of defiance, hesitated not to inquire what the farmer meant, who, in reply, as boldly taxed him with the murder. Hard and desperate words succeeded; and the screams of the accused man's sister most likely prevented death; for the farmer, a tall powerful man, had grasped Murphy so tightly by the throat, that a few minutes must have terminated his existence. Although by no means a weakling, he was as a green willow-wand in the hands of his assailant.

In vain did his terrified sister declare that her brother was at home early in the evening, and went to bed before she did. Harragan persisted in his charge; and had it not been for the force of superior numbers, he would have succeeded in dragging him to the next police station; but Irish assistance is much more easily procured *against* the law than for it, though I confess in this instance it was hard for those who did not know all the circumstances to determine whose part to take; for Harragan was under the influence of such strong excitement, that he acted more like a maniac than a man in the possession of his senses.

Having failed in his first object, that of dragging Steve Murphy to justice himself, he mounted his horse, and laid before the nearest magistrate sufficient reason why Steve should be arrested and detained until further inquiries were made; but when the police force sought for him, he was gone!—vanished! as delinquents vanish in Ireland, where hundreds of sober honest men will absolutely *know* where a villain is concealed, and yet suffer him to escape and commit more crimes, because their prejudices will not suffer them *to inform.*

Great was the excitement throughout the country, occasioned

by this mysterious event. James Harragan lived but for one object—that of bringing the murderer to justice. This all-engrossing desire seemed to have absorbed even his affection for his child; that is to say, he would stroke her hair, or press her now colourless cheek to his bosom, and then turning away with a deep sigh, go on laying down some new plan for the discovery of poor Ralph's murderer. Everybody said that Sydney was dying; but her father did not seem to observe that *her* summer had ceased, when its sun was at the hottest, and its days at the longest, and that the rose was dropping leaf by leaf to the earth. Once Sydney attempted to take to market the produce of her dairy, which her kind friend Essy tended with more care than her own.

'If they don't notice me,' she said, 'I'll do bravely; you'll tell them, Essy, to never heed me.' And so Essy did; but it would not do. No prudential motive yet was ever sufficiently strong to restrain the sympathy of the genuine Irish. When her car stopped at the corner of the market-place, twenty stout arms now were extended to lift the pale girl off. There was not a woman in the square who did not leave her standing to crowd round the *widowed* bride. It would have been as easy to turn the fertilising waters of the Nile as that torrent of affection. The young girls sobbed, and could not speak for tears; but those tears fell upon Sydney's hands, and moistened her cheeks; it was refreshing to them, for she herself had long ceased to weep; hers were the only dry eyes in the crowd. The mothers prayed that God might bless her, and 'raise her up again to be the flower of the country.'

'Never heed, Sydney, darlint; sure you've the prayers of the country.'

'And the double prayers of the poor,' exclaimed a knot of beggars, who had abated their vocation to put up their petitions in her favour.

Sydney could have borne coldness or neglect, but kindness overpowered her, and she was obliged to return, leaving her small merchandise to Essy's care.

Every one said that Sydney was hastening to her grave, but still her father heeded it not; no bloodhound ever toiled or panted more eagerly to recover the scent which he had lost, than did the farmer to trace Steve Murphy's flight; it was still his absorbing idea both by day and night. Had it not been for the exertions of his sons, his well-cultivated farm would have gone to ruin. His health was suffering from this monomania; the flesh shrank daily from his bones, and the healthy jocund farmer was changing into a gigantic skeleton. The priest talked to him; Mr Herrick reasoned with him; but all to no purpose.

Time passed, and James Harragan entered his cottage as the sun was setting. He had stood for the last hour leaning against the post of his gate, apparently engaged in watching the sparrows flying in and out of their old dwelling-places in the thatch. His sons had prepared his supper, and he sat down to it mechanically; the two lads whispered for some time together at the window, when suddenly Harragan inquired 'what they muttered for?' The youths hesitated to reply.

'Let me know what it was!' he exclaimed. 'I'll have no whispering, no *cochering*, no hiding-and-seeking in my house. Boys, there's a hell at this moment burning in yer father's breast! Look, I never could kill one of them small birds that destroy the roof above our heads, without feeling I took from the innocent thing the life I could not give; and yet, what does that signify? Isn't *my* hand *red* at this time of speaking with that boy's blood! Red—it's red hot—hissing red with the blood of Ralph Furlong! It is as much so as if I did it! And why? Because I held on at the mystery that shades the guilty, and hurries on the innocent to destruction—*because I wouldn't inform!* Now, mind me, boys, I'll have nothing but *out* speaking; no whispering; where there's that sort of secrecy, there's sin and the curse. What war you whispering?' he added in a voice of thunder.

'We war only saying, sir,' replied the elder, 'that we wonder Sydney and Essy ain't back.'

'Back! Why, where is my little girl?'

'She took a thought this morning, sir,' he answered, 'and we don't like to say against her, that she'd walk from Ferry Carrig Bridge to where HE parted from his brother, and took Essy with her on the car as far as the bridge: it's a notion she had.'

'My colleen!—my pride!—my darlint!' he ejaculated, much moved; 'and I not to know this! Yer mother little thought, when she made ye over to *me* before death made *her* over to the holy angels, what would happen. And ye didn't tell me, because ye thought I didn't care! Well, I forgive ye—I forgive ye, boys! I didn't neglect her though, for all that; my heart was set on another matter. There is but one thing she can spake on, one thing I can spake on—and it is better we shouldn't—*but* when she does *look* at me, though my little girl strives to keep it under, there is in her eyes what says, "If ye'd spoken the truth long ago, it's a happy wife I'd be now, instead of——" Oh, God!—oh, God!' he exclaimed passionately, 'that I should have suffered such a snake to fatten on the land, when I could have crushed him under my heel! I'd have rest in my grave if I could see him in his. I'll go meet her, boys. You should have gone before.' And the farmer stalked forth, and silently mounting his cob, proceeded on the road to Ferry Carrig.

There are mysteries around us, both night and day, for which it would be difficult indeed to account: the impulse that drew Sydney that morning to the banks of the Slaney was, and ever must be, unaccountable.

'Nurses,' she said to her faithful friend Essy, after they crossed the bridge, and quitting the coach-road, made unto themselves a path along the bank—'nurses like you, Essy, may be called the brides'-maids of death, and you have been my nurse all through this sickness.' Essy afterwards said she did not know what there was in those words to make her cry, but she could not answer for weeping. The two girls wandered on, Sydney stopping every now and then to look into the depths and shallows of the river, and prying beneath every broad green leaf and clump of trees that overhung its banks. More than once they sat down, and more than once did Essy propose their return; but Sydney went on, as if she had not spoken. At last they came to a species of deep drain, almost overgrown with strong, tall, leafy water-plants, that was always filled when the tide was full in. Essy sprang lightly over it, and then turning a little way up to where it was narrower, she extended her hand to her feeble friend. Although the gulf was narrow, it was very deep; the root of a tree had formed a natural dam across it, so that much water was retained. As Sydney was about to cross, she cast her eyes beneath, started, and held back. She did not speak, but with her hand pointed downwards, Essy's shriek rang through the air—the face of Ralph Furlong stared at them from the bottom of the silent pool!

Had she not removed the broad leaves of a huge dock that shaded the water, so that Sydney's footing might be sure, the unconscious girl would have stept, without knowing it, over her lover's liquid grave. Essy was so overwhelmed with horror, that she ran shrieking towards the highway; several minutes elapsed before she returned with assistance; and then where was Sydney! The faithful girl, in endeavouring to draw his body from the waters, had fallen in; her head was literally resting on his bosom, and her long beautiful hair floating like a pall above them!

They were buried in the same grave!

When Murphy's cottage was searched by the police, the only weapon, if so it could be called, which they discovered, was a broken reaping-hook; this James Harragan had taken to his own house, and under the folds of poor Ralph's coat, those who prepared him for his earthy grave discovered the missing portion. The farmer was seen to shed no tear over his daughter, but registered an oath in Heaven that he would never take rest upon his bed until he had brought the murderer to justice. Within a week after, he relinquished his farm to his sons, and it is believed he journeyed to foreign lands in pursuit of one who, in the first instance, escaped justice through James Harragan's own weak and almost wicked perseverance in a wrong cause. Years have passed since the melancholy event occurred, and no tidings have ever reached the country relative to Harragan or the murderer.

Well, indeed, might he have remembered Mr Herrick's warning. The farmer had, by withholding his information, refused to pluck out the arrow which an unseen hand had planted in the bosom of an excellent and industrious man, and the same power had been employed to overthrow his happiness for ever!

THE LANDLORD ABROAD.

IT was a bright, yet a weeping morning—the sun was shining, but thick heavy clouds flitted across the sky, sometimes softening, sometimes altogether obscuring its rays; the birds were singing cheerfully in the hedges, whose leaves bent beneath the rain-drops; and the poultry in Widow Clement's little yard were shaking the moisture off their wings.

'Look at that beautiful Norah,' said the widow to her daughter Peggy, Norah being a favourite hen of snowy plumage; 'she's just as fretted at the feathers being wet upon her, as you'd be if Paul Kinsala saw a dirty handkerchief'——

'Lave off, mother,' interrupted the daughter, blushing, and turning her wheel with such increased velocity, that the thread snapped; 'lave off—what's Paul Kinsala to me?'

'Och, Peggy, for shame, to be throwing sand in yer mother's eyes!' exclaimed the widow.

'Throwing sand in yer eyes, mother darlint, eh!—then the girl's not born yet that could do *that*, I'm thinking. Well, mother, if I *have* a kindness to him, sure he's well to do.'

'He *was* well to do, Peggy mavourneen; but the lase of his farm, little as it is, and high as the rint was, is out.'

'But sure the agent, Mr Crumbie, heard my lord promise him a renewal, and a taking off of three pounds in the year, on account of the improvements he made.'

The widow shook her head—those who grow old in the country learn to understand human nature as well as those who read the more varied page of town life. 'He never said he *wouldn't* grant the renewal,' continued Peggy, looking anxiously in her mother's face.

'He never said he *would*,' was the reply. There was a long silence. Widow Clement sighed, and continued her knitting. Peggy did not sigh, but she went on spinning, as if nothing had been said to give her pain; but her mother noted the heaving of her bosom. Twice she rose under pretence of seeing if the gray hen which was seated upon her eggs in a corner was covering them as she ought; her mother knew she moved to conceal her tears.

'Peggeen gra, never heed the hen; the nature's in her to manage her eggs herself, and looking at her only disturbs her; *it's an insult to her, Peggy, and we mustn't hurt her feelings.* Sorra a finer hen in the parish afther a brood than that same Gray-malkin, as the darlint young misthress used to call her. Why, thin, Peggy, I often think I'd like to see Lady Ellen in the court at London, forenint the king and queen, and all the grandees looking at her. I'll go bail she takes the shine out of them all!'

'I daresay she does,' replied Peggy; 'I don't doubt that; but sure it would be fitter for his lordship to come and stay among his people, in the counthry *where his forefathers' bones makes part of the soil,* and where the grass grows, the corn ears, the water flows, the cattle dies, all for him, than to be laving those that's bred, born, and reared under him and his, for I don't know how many thousand or hundred years, to the *bitter wrath* of an agent, and all belonging to him. And what's the upshot of it all?'

'Heart throuble, a-lannan; and discontent even when there's no raison; like all the mimbers fighting one another for want of a head—that's what it is!' replied the widow sorrowfully. 'The nature of man and beast is not to be put upon by its equals, and the landlord could do more with us than another, for he's the protector placed over the land to see justice done to his dependents.' The widow paused; her reasoning was the reasoning of a class more numerous formerly than at present—a class of well-disposed affectionate persons, who looked up to their landlord as a friend and counsellor in all trouble: it is a pity such confidence should ever be misplaced. The absentee landlord knows but little of the affections or feelings of his tenants, and, it is much to be feared, cares less. After a moment, Widow Clement resumed—
'And yet, sure, when we pay our rint, and are honest, we can stand as straight before God as the landlord himself.'

'And straighter,' added Peggy smiling.

'That's a bright girl, Peggy; it joys my heart to see the smile in yer eye, my own girl! Sure when the Almighty gave me you and your brother, He let fall a blessing from each hand; praise be to His holy name! It's little we have to complain of ourselves, though the family is in furrin parts. Mark, being my lord's groom, is on the spot to take care of us—but it's for the neighbours my heart bleeds. The cottages that in the ould lady's lifetime war the admiration of the counthry, are falling to decay; the pigs that used to be kept to themselves, are free on the roads again; many have turned their face from their *people's graves,* who couldn't pay the rack-rint; the sorra a thing thrives in the place, Peggeen gra, but the whisky shops; and boys,* that I re-

---

* This term means *all* unmarried men, no matter what their ages.

mimber quiet and industrious whin the lord was in it, and kept the improvements going on, and more than a hundred men at them winter and summer; them very boys, that never handled a shillala, barring at a fair, or for a bit of sport at Shrove or Martinmas, are in constant practice with it now, wheeling through the counthry by day, and not trusting to sticks only at night.'

'Hush, mother!' exclaimed Peggy; 'least said soonest mended. Only I wish Lady Ellen was in it again, like a sweet moss-rose as she always was. It's not the same place since the people war turned over to strangers;' and Peggy sighed bitterly as she spoke.

This was true; the old Lady Killbally died, leaving no heir to the property, and but one fair daughter, the 'Lady Ellen' whom Peggy sighed for. Lady Killbally had been a blessing to her tenantry; but after her death, his lordship imagined he required change of scene for a longer period than usual—indeed he had generally spent one or two months of every year in England, and returned with new ideas and new plans for the improvement of his hereditary estate. Alas! and alas! he did not mourn long. Before the twelvemonth was expired, he had married a woman of fashion, who had no idea of reciprocal duties between landlord and tenant; and though she visited Killbally, it was evident she had no thought of residing there.

Lord Killbally made a speech at the county town, previous to quitting the country to 'winter' in London, full of the most sublime sentiments of patriotism; he had never *talked* about it before: he recommended his new agent, a stranger, to the friendship of the gentry; as if friendship, even in warm-hearted Ireland, grew on the furze bushes, and could be pulled off and appropriated at pleasure; and he begged of his tenants to respect the laws: as yet, they had never been violated in his neighbourhood.

'Where's the good of behaving as we have done?' said the Killbally smith, and a party of loose-coated Irishmen gathered round him as he spoke; 'where's the good of behaving as we have done? We never gainsaid him; we never riz a ruction at fair or pattern, for fear we'd displase him. We paid our rint, when we had it, regular; and when we didn't, why, he was never cruel on us. We never voted agin him; we sent all our children to get the larning at his or Lady Ellen's schools; we planted trees; we kept up our pigs; we made back-doors to our houses; we took oaths against the whisky—and all to plase him. *Our prayers were heavy on him*, yet he'll go from us, boys—he'll go from *us*, and lave us a *black-a-viced* agent, a stranger to our hearts and homes, who doesn't understand us, nor we him—he'll go from us, as the good, the dear ould, and the purty young, lady did. He'll melt off like snow in summer; he'll go from us, and *keep* from us; he'll be an absentee; he'll forget to feel for us.

Mark my words: for all this fine talk, in three months the workmen will be discharged; there'll be no traffic in the place. God help poor Ireland! She's ever and always trated as Barney Barret trated his cow—fed on thraneens, and then abused for giving poor milk. "How can I help it," says the cow, "with the usage I get?" "Bad scram to ye," says Barnaby; "sure the strength is in ye; and it's a compliment I pay you, you ignorant baste, to expect more from you, though you *are* fed on thraneens, than from any other cow that would be fed on clover."' The thoughtless laughed at the simile, but the thoughtful shook their heads, and returned in silence and solitude to cottages which, if doomed to live under an absentee landlord, they might soon be despoiled of.

The agent was certainly an unfit person to have been placed over such a tenantry; he was full of new systems, and if they did not immediately work well, he became harsh and impatient. Paddy likes to go on the old way; if his father had a dunghill at the door, it is a difficult matter to convince him that it could be more advantageously disposed of elsewhere; and he has a most provoking habit of saying, that whatever he does in the way of improvement, is done to 'plase' the landlord, or the 'clargy,' or any one but himself, though all the time it is for his own benefit those who have his interest at heart have persuaded him to change his plans. Then Paddy is so full of humour, real genuine humour, that he will lean his back against the door-post, between which and the wall a deed of separation, by mutual consent, has taken place; put one foot over the other, take his 'dudeen' out of his mouth, fold his arms across his ample chest, and beguile you from the intention of giving him a good lecture both on the management and mismanagement of his farm, until you wish him good evening, enjoying the remembrance of the raciness and humour of his stories, and the mirthfulness that shakes his rags with laughter. It is not till after you sit down to your reading table that you think how completely you were beguiled of your wisdom! An Irishman loves a jest, and likes to laugh—and Mr Crumbie the agent never laughed: he had a long, business-like face. He had served three years in an attorney's office, and never regarded anything as binding that was not binding *in law*. It is to be hoped, for the sake of sweet charity, that he *meant* well; but certainly he *acted* ill. His wife was a rigid sectarian, believing in her heart of hearts that all who did not think exactly as she did must be in error. She made hard bargains, and gave low wages; in short, she was a very unfit person to preside over the people in the place of the 'ould misthress.' A spirit of discontent of the most alarming kind was abroad. Lord Killbally had managed, with a skill peculiarly Irish, to 'spend half-a-crown out of sixpence a-day;' that is to say, he was deeply in debt; he had overstepped his income, and wrote constantly to the agent to obtain fresh supplies, when, in fact, there were none to obtain.

Matters had arrived at this crisis—the landlord driving the agent, and the agent the tenant—when my story commences. The widow and her daughter continued their conversation a little longer, and would have talked till evening, had not the sight of the postman, on his old gray pony, wending round the distant hill, and then entering the bohreen that led to their cottage, sent both mother and daughter to meet him, on the chance of receiving a letter from the hope of the family—Mark Clement.

The expected letter was instantly produced ; the postman took his departure ; and Peggy, being what is called a 'fine scholar,' was able to peruse it for her mother's benefit. It was a curiosity in its way, remarkable for acute and affectionate feeling.

'DEAR MOTHER AND SISTER—My love goes with this paper, and my blessing, and all my prayers, which you're never out of, nor never will be—why should you !—Amin ! It's long ago I'd have written again to you all, but indeed I hav'n't much heart to the pen, let alone the time, which bewilders me the way it flies, and no good of it. It's four years three-quarters, my blessed mother, since I saw you ; and often in the night, or rayther the morning— for morning's night here—often do I think you are at my bedside ; often do I hear yer voice in my dreams ; and when I wake, it isn't your voice at all, but little Anty Maguire, the milk girl, calling "milk *below*" down the airees, when it's milk *above* she means ; and very quare milk it is ; but that's not Anty's fault, for it's ready watered before she gets it.

'Well, the only real pleasure I have almost is, when Lady Ellen of a day she rides out with my lord, says, " Oh, Mark, when did you hear from your mother ? and is Peggy quite well ? and how is Gray-malkin ?" ['Think of that !' interrupted the widow ; 'think of her remimbering the hen !'] But, mother, Lady Ellen doesn't ride as often in the Park as she used, on account that the mare stumbled, and I *know* the masther didn't find it convanient to buy her another, though she lets on to her maid she's tired of the exercise. Ah, poor lady ! that's not the only throuble she puts up with. Ye see, when first we came over, and had lashins o' money, and the masther, poor gentleman, thought, because his wife was young, he was young too ; it was all very fine ; and my Lady Killbally here, and my Lady Killbally there, and my Lady Ellen everywhere, and an acknowledged beauty, only even then, a taste of pulling to pieces on account of her brogue, or being Irish. ['Think of that !' exclaimed the widow indignantly.] And offers she had, as I tould you before ; but the *money* stood in the way, or rather it was out of the way, *for it wasn't in it*, on account that the property is entailed on the heir-male, master's nephew, and poor Lady Ellen will have hardly anything, barring master's blessing, and that she earns hard enough, for of late he bates Bannaghar with the crossness; and small blame to him, poor gentleman, to see the way he's looked down upon, now that it's known he's only an Irish peer in embarrassment, which means debt and danger. There's no dacent Irish property could stand up to cut a figure here. With the Irish it's all going out, and too proud to do anything to bring in; but with the English, why, if they give out with one hand, they grapple in with the other; very few, indeed, to say above their business, only work all, work all, and tradesmen worth tens o' thousands. I can't but think it's the best plan—which you wont, I know—only you don't know anything of the hardship of wanting to appear grand and show off whin you've nothing to do it with—like the girl we remimber who turned her cotton to make the neighbours believe she'd two gowns, when she was trusting to one. Well, that's the way we've been many a long day, making the one thing appear two, and my mistress without a head, or, what's worse in a woman, without a heart; and, och, murdher intirely! to hear the sneers and the slurs that's put upon them—tradesmen's bills unpaid, and bills having been passed to them over due, and then money borrowed by the lawyers to the tune of fifty per cint. ['What tune's that!' inquired the widow. 'Roguery, I daresay,' answered Peggy; 'isn't the lawyer in it']; and then a flash in the pan that whirls away the cash, and the misthress so *sonsy* while it lasts; and that's the time to ask a favour from the masther, for he never thinks of to-morrow, and the creditors then give a little more credit, and my lady pays half for the opera box ['What's that, a-lannan?' inquired the widow again. 'Oh,' said Peggy, who liked to appear wise, 'it's a snuff-box, I daresay, though she's raythur young to take to it'], and gets the carriage new painted, and four horses on job. ['Och, my bitther throuble!' exclaimed Mrs Clement, bursting into tears, 'to think of the ould ancient family of the Killballys being drawn by job horses, and the agent's horses and coults thrampling down all the young trees in his lordship's plantations!'] And we're as gay as sarvants can be that don't get their wages. ['That's mean of Mark,' said Peggy; 'sure he ought to be proud to sarve the family without wages— that's part of his English breeding.'] And all this is talked over in the sarvants' hall, for they've no respect for the family, and no feeling at all for the masther or misthress, nor even Lady Ellen. ['They are no better than heathens,' interrupted the widow; 'and if I was Mark, I'd manage to let the masther know what vipers he has about him.' 'Why couldn't he stay in his own counthry, where he was honoured and respected, and in those times had the ball at his foot?' replied the angry Peggy, and then resumed the perusal of the letter.] The gintleman that'll have the estate, by all accounts wont value it a thraneen, because he doesn't want it, but has full and plenty in the Western Indies, or some other part, I hardly know where, but somewhere it is—flashins of money, and to spare; so, in coorse, he'll not have a heart to the sod no more than others.'

['God help us!' exclaimed Peggy, changing colour a little, and letting the open letter rest upon her knees, 'this is a poor look-out for here and hereafter!'

'It must only tache us to *look up* the more,' said the widow, raising her eyes. 'God help us!—we're a nation of castaways!'

'We are not!' exclaimed Peggy, and her eye kindled. 'We are not, mother; and it's our thinking ourselves so, and putting up with the usage we get, that makes us be looked down upon.'

'No, Peggy, darlint, that's not it,' replied her mother; 'we've a dale of heart and spirit; but, as I heard a gentleman say once, *we want* the wisdom; and that's the cruel want at this time o' day, when the world's going mad about it. Poor Paddy's head gets hard enough with blows, but not with wisdom. Go on with the letther, dear.'

'There's not much more in it, mother, and what there is, isn't much good.']

'Indeed don't be surprised if there's a change for the worse before long. I'm sure the masther will be forced to rack-rent every perch that isn't rack-rented already, and then maybe sell the green acres that war so long the pride and glory of the family. I *can't* think what comes over the gentry; I'm sure in Ireland a pound goes as far as three here, and the *somebody there* is a *nobody here*—so that either in regard of the saving or the grandeur, "ould Ireland for ever!"'

'The country's warm about his heart still,' said the widow, wiping her eyes; 'it isn't out of sight out of mind. Is there much more in the letther?'

'Not much,' answered Peggy, blushing; 'only a few words to Paul Kinsala, which I trust he doesn't need. Mother, did ye ever doubt that Paul had a laning to any wild ways?'

'Wild ways, a-lannan! Sure I never see even the corner of his eye turned on any girl except yerself.'

'It's not in regard of the girls!' exclaimed the rustic beauty, tossing her head with as much pride as if she had been bred at St James's. 'It's not *that*—I don't thank him for constancy—he can't help *that*, mother, so no thanks to him; but in respect of the doings they say some are at—the swearing-in, and things of the kind. Any wildness that way, mother?'

'No, darlint, not exactly. I can't say I ever did. I hope he has better sense; he has seen enough of examples to keep him from *that*, I hope. No good ever came yet from such doings. Even suppose one man is got out of the counthry that has behaved badly to the poor, sure another will be put in worse; and if we drive the gentry away, they take their money with them. The law has a kinder eye on the poor now than it ever had before, and it's by showing obedience to the law, *particular when it's in a good-humour*, that we prove to the world that we deserve the protection we receive, and not the bad name we've got in England; we have enough to bear in the way of poverty still; but, plase God, times will mend. What do such disturbances lead to but shame? Wasn't one of those who war forced to fly from the other side the counthry on account of—you know what—at hide-and-seek through the rocks and bushes of Knocklatrim for as good as three months, and his wife forced to beg? and wasn't he at last forced to die without benefit of clargy, down in the Black Cave of the fever, and nothing handed him except on the end of a stick? and I remimber him *once*, bright as the sun—— But here *is* Paul Kinsala, Peggy, coming over the hedge. Ah, girl machree! you saw him before *I did;* and I might as well have talked to Gray-malkin as to you, for you never heeded me. There, your hair's as smooth and shining as satin.' And as the old woman advanced to meet her intended son-in-law, she laid her hand on her daughter's head, and signing the sign of the cross on her brow, kissed it affectionately.

When Paul entered, *his* brow was darkened, and there was an unnatural expression about his face which startled both mother and daughter; he hardly waited to return the warm salutation, met in every peasant's cottage, of 'God save ye,' with the meet reply of 'God save ye kindly,' but inquired 'if they had had a letther from Mark?' Peggy replied in the affirmative, and placed it in his hands. After he had read it, he folded it up with great deliberation, saying, 'There is nothing in this half so bad as what we know already.'

'And what is it you know, Paul *avic?*' said Widow Clement, laying her hand upon his arm; while Peggy, unable to speak, gazed earnestly and tenderly in his face.

'What is it I know?' he repeated; 'I know *this*, that there's to be levying of fines, and every species of wickedness; every lase that can be broke will be broke; and the agent himself this blessed holy Thursday stood before me—me, Paul Kinsala—and tould me there was no good in my promise—that I must quit— the land—quit the house my father and myself war born in—for —that the place was let to a better tenant than I could be, who had money and stock. What do you think of *that?*' he said, fixing his eyes on the widow, for he could not tell such tidings, and gaze on the face of her he so dearly loved. 'What do you think of *that?* Now, the truth is, that the farm *wants* no stocking; the crops are in: he said I should be allowed for them—allowed for the grain my own two hands sowed, with a prayer to the Almighty that we—that Peggy and I—might reap it together. Money! he said I had no money to give for the premises on a new lase, or to carry on the farming. And what did I say?—that I had not, because every penny, every farthing had been spent on that land. He has the law on his side—and I—who never let a gale run on to another, but paid—like an English tenant——I—am to starve!'

The young man covered his face with his hands, to conceal his emotion; how long he might have endeavoured to do so, it is impossible to say, for his attention was roused by a cry from the widow—the light-hearted, and, generally speaking, strong-headed Peggy, had fainted.

When she recovered, there was too much feeling excited to admit of many words; the poor girl laid her head on her lover's shoulder and wept bitterly; the widow stood at the other side, and with more affection than worldly prudence, said, 'My dear Paul, never heed it. I'll tell you what: we have a snug house here, and as good as two acres of land, and a bigger penny saved than you might think of, for I had no mind to let my daughter be beholden to you all out, and laid by what I could. So I'll tell you what, Paul: I'll spake myself to the priest, and *get the words said** as soon as may be; and then, instead of Peggy's going home to you, *avic*, why, you'll come home to *us*. Where's the great differ, Paul? Don't I know the girl's heart is in ye? It's no time to be denying it *now, when ye're in throuble;* and sure ye're the same as my own son this many a day. Maybe it's a showing of God's mercy after all. I'm not as light either on the foot or in the heart as I used to be, and would be lonely many a time if she was away; but now I'll have a son, instead of losing a daughter; and Mark has my lord's ear; and if that wouldn't do, I'm not too ould to go to London myself, and get spaking to him; and sure, with my *two* birds in my cage, though it is but a *dawshy* one,' sobbed the kind woman, looking round cheerfully through her tears, 'I'll be a proud and a happy woman, and no need to hire a labourer now, or be beholden to the neighbours, who never let a lone woman hire, if they can help her. Sure you'll do a hand's turn for Peggy's mother for sake's sake? Or,' she continued, after a pause, with a generosity that would have done honour to a heroine—' or, if it would be more agreeable to you, Paul, I'd settle the bit of land and the place on the both of you, for it was given me by the lord for myself, to do what I pleased with, at a peppercorn rent. And that would ease the proud spirit that you ever had, Paul, darlint; and small blame to you, for your people war far above us, and yet you never looked down on us, nor on her.'

'Look down on *you*—on *her!*' he exclaimed, pressing his bo-

* Get married.

trothed to his bosom ; 'who ever looked down on Peggy Clement ?
But no, mother, no ; by all that's holy, I'll be revenged—I'll be
revenged—justice I'll have. If I can't have it by law, I'll have it
—see that, now !' he continued ; and for a moment forgetting the
presence of the two women he loved best on earth, he stamped
his foot violently on the ground, and suddenly dropping on his
knees, threw his arms upwards, and clenching his hands, swore a
deep and bitter oath, that unless his farm was given back, he
would '*water* the earth with the blood of agent or landlord.' This
was very frightful ; and while the widow and her daughter looked
on him, they clung together, unable to restrain his words, yet
trembling at their import.

'I didn't desarve this from you,' said the gentle old woman,
weeping; 'I thought to turn the throuble from you, and you have
turned black bittherness on me.'

'No, mother—no, Peggy !' he exclaimed, the warm and affectionate current of Irish feeling rushing back to his heart, now that
he had given vent to his fury—'no, no ; you'll be proud of me yet.
I'll do no meanness—nothing to call a colour to your cheek ; nothing—though I'm not to be trod like a worm in the dust.——No
money to pay for a new lase ! I might have had full and plenty to
spend for a new lase, if it had not been that I spent it on the land
—and now for it to be taken from me ! I'm not the only one in
the place that cries shame ; not the only one that will have revenge. Go through the townland, into the villages, along the
high roads, and ye'll hear the same thing from every lip ; ye'll
see the same purpose in every eye. Didn't Macmurray himself
say '——

'Don't name Macmurray,' interrupted Peggy, speaking for the
first time ; 'he's bad, egg and bird, and no fit companion for you
at all, at all, Paul ; his character's blasted this many a day, and
he always had a spite to the family. Have nothing to do with
him ; for Godsake have nothing to do with *him*. Keep yerself
to yerself, Paul ; no harm can ever come of that.'

'She speaks the truth, *avic,*' added the old woman. 'Take
patience, and it will come round—it will all come round ; ye're of
a good stock, Paul, with fine health—praise be to God !—and a
good character ; and with that, no need of fear for any boy of
five-and-twenty ; think of what I said, Paul.'

'God bless you, dear mother ; it is not because I'm not down
on my knees to thank you, and bless you, that I don't feel your
goodness. And, come bad or good, in the presence of the Almighty
I swear there's no girl on the face of the green earth will ever
have my heart but Peggy Clement ; though, as things are—I
mean from what I know, I—I—can have no claim on yer promise,
Peggy—I '——

He could not finish his sentence, and Peggy looked upon her

lover in stupified astonishment. It never occurred to her—indeed it very seldom occurs to Irish women of her class—that poverty should offer any barrier to a union. And the poor girl's feelings were torn by the love-beatings of her own heart, and the dread that Paul's 'heart' was changed towards her. What was the cause of this sudden declaration, neither mother nor daughter had time to inquire; for suddenly he invoked a blessing on the widow, and kissing the maiden's lips, burst from the cottage. When he was gone, strange as his conduct appeared, no word of reproach escaped his friends. Peggy, after a genuine flood of tears, communed with her mother for a long time.

Nothing could exceed the agitation of the neighbourhood. Wild rumours were afloat; positive injustice had been already done to more than to Paul Kinsala; and the fine old trees—trees that had been the pride and glory of the neighbourhood for years—were doomed to the woodman's axe; in truth, the beautiful valley of Killbally, that during the landlord's residence had been gemmed with cottages, and adorned by happy smiling faces, might now be called a valley of tears. Great as the change had been, it needed this to complete it; and the sighs and moans of, in this instance, a decidedly ill-used peasantry, mingled with the free air and bright sunshine that poured upon the landscape! The bitterest curses were heaped upon the agent's head, who, notwithstanding his desperate injustice to Paul, had not exceeded the instructions he received from *the landlord abroad*, whose difficulties had dictated the heartless order—that he was to rack and drive, and get money by humane means if he could, but get it by *any means* sooner than *not* get it. His very nature seemed changed by his necessities. There was evidence of a movement in the country to resist this oppression, and plenty of persons (who having forfeited their own claim on society, had become lawless) were sufficiently anxious to induce others to follow their example, and spread the spirit of discontent far and wide. Peggy Clement, with the assistance of the village schoolmaster, indited a letter not only to her brother, but to Lady Ellen, stating the rights of the case, and pleading, if *not elegantly, eloquently*, for her lover, and indeed for all those who had been honest, faithful, and true in their callings. These letters were, to the schoolmaster's astonishment and her own, not only written, but despatched that very day; while the widow was 'questing' through the neighbourhood picking up every bit of news, not from a love of idle gossip, but from the deepest anxiety to discover if the machinations of others, or his own impetuosity, were likely to lead Paul into serious mischief. The Widow Clement, though not young, was both clear and quick-sighted. She knew that if Paul was led to do anything rash, his life would pay the forfeit, for he was too fearless and too frank to have a villain's caution; and, moreover, she knew that the happiness, the very existence, of her child depended upon him. These were strong incentives to the curiosity of a woman and a mother, and a strong feeling of respect for 'the family' mingled with her sympathy for the distrained and ruined tenants, who were breathing vengeance at every whisky house in the neighbourhood; for mischief is never undertaken in Ireland without its having been first planned over the burning fluid, which stimulates them to the destruction of themselves and others.

'There's enough work now for day labourers anyway,' said Larry Toole to Andy Smith.

'And what will they get for it? Eightpence a-day, and the nagur that offers it saying "that if the neighbours don't take it, he'll get plenty of the mountaineers that will." Think of that!—bringing starving strangers down upon us, whose boast it used to be to keep our own poor from begging! Let them come and take what they get—that's all! I'll never work in it for eightpence a-day! We never were offered less than tinpence before! However, let 'em go on their own way; there's one comfort, it wont last for ever.'

'Sure, the agent says the common's my lord's, and that no cattle, not even a pig, is to go on it now without payment, and the marsh beyont it too—think o' that! And the turf we had for cutting off the bog is to be paid for! I wonder does the lord know that?'

'There is a Lord knows it!' answered Andy again, who had always been dissatisfied; 'but never heed; it wont be always so, I'll go bail.'

Many such hints did the widow hear, but she and her daughter had been unable that evening to determine what course to pursue as regarded Paul Kinsala. That night passed, the next day, and the next. The spirit of discontent increased more and more. Some said Paul had refused to yield possession; others, that he had gone to London to appeal against the agent's decision. The first, nay even the second day, Peggy had borne herself bravely. She had restrung her nerves, and waited the result with many and many an earnest and deeply-breathed prayer to those in whom she trusted, that she might be spared more suffering, or taught to bear it. Her wheel, or knitting needles, pursued their wonted motions, and she moved about the house as usual, save that a restless gaze was ever directed to the door or window.

The agent had been pelted and hooted through the village, and had thought it wise to station a police force in the castle that had once been guarded by the hearts of an affectionate people. There were other disturbances; more than one act of wild excess had been committed, at once absurd and unjustifiable; and Peggy's cheek grew pale, and her step feeble, in the course of one little week.

'I shall die, mother, and soon,' said the poor girl; 'there's a weakness about my heart, and a mist, *like the film of a winding-sheet*, over my eyes, that means no good. If Paul wasn't afther something bad, he'd have been here before this; and afther all you said to him. But maybe so best. I had two hopes in the world, mother—you—my hope for you was, that I might be a blessing and a comfort to you hereafter; and when the Lord thought fit, that I might close yer eyes: my hope in him!—— But it's all gone, it's all gone, like the bloom of that thorn-tree which the last wind shook to the earth.' The widow did not overwhelm her beloved child with consolation. She said few words, but she said them wisely, and endeavoured, by every simple means in her power, to vary her employments. She knew that though she might suffer greatly, she had really a strong and active mind, and that those who have such, seldom die, as it is called, for love.

The Widow Clement felt all this; yet while her trust in the Almighty schooled her to patience and obedience, it did not cramp her exertions; and with a firm resolve to find out if things were as bad as she suspected, and how Paul was engaged, she contrived some new occupation for her daughter, and set off, determined to fathom the troubled waters; and be it remembered, it was the troubled waters of a disturbed Irish district this solitary, unprotected woman resolved to fathom. She left the cottage soon after daybreak, and about one o'clock, Peggy, whose eyes, despite her employment, were seldom off the undulating line that showed how the road wound round the mountain, perceived the approach of the letter-carrier. She flew to meet him.

'It's bad for the townland,' he said, 'when even you, Miss Peggy, have a serious face. There's nothing else going now; the boys at the castle have turned out for higher wages in regard of the trees they're felling, and the place is so shut up, that they wont let me pass the lodge, though I have English letters. They say there's a despatch gone off for more police. God help us if that's thrue, for they're ripe for a ruction through the whole townland. Some say the agent's not in the house, some say he is, some say the property's sold; but, God be with ye, Peggeen gra, ye're not minding a word I'm saying,' and the old man retraced his path.

No painting could convey an idea of the rapid changes of colour and expression that passed over the cheeks and brow of Peggy Clement as she stood at her cottage door, the sunlight resting on her hair, which fell in heavy masses on her neck and bosom. She held the letter before her with both hands; her bosom heaved convulsively; and though her very arms trembled, still she grasped the paper so tightly, that there was no danger of its falling. Her very soul seemed drinking in the contents; but whether the draught was of joy or sorrow, it would have been impossible to tell. She gasped for breath, pressed her hands upon her bosom, turned to the cottage, and twice ejaculated 'mother!' Then remembering that her mother was not there, that she had no one near to whom she could disclose her emotions, she dropped upon her knees, and throwing her head back, as if she wished her thoughts and feelings to wing their way to Heaven, she uttered a few broken exclamations of joy and gratitude; then hastily throwing on her cloak, and drawing the hood forward so as to conceal her agitation, she followed in the path pursued by the old postman. At first my heroine walked with great rapidity, but then she suddenly paused, and said within herself, 'But I'm not to tell it except to my mother and Paul. Mother will be part sorry—and Paul!—where shall I find Paul?—but, anyway, I'll find *her*.' She had not proceeded very far, when she saw her mother coming towards her, and before she could communicate her news, the old woman burst into tears. A few words can describe their cause: she had received information—*how*, it does not matter—that the agent had left the castle; that, finding the country so outrageously disturbed, he had taken refuge, as secretly as he could, at the house of a neighbouring gentleman, resolving to proceed to Dublin that night; that he believed his intention was unknown, perfectly unknown, but that it had transpired; and that several persons had determined he should never reach his destination. The widow had every reason to believe that Paul Kinsala was of the number. To give the doomed man information of what was intended, would have been to draw down the vengeance of the party upon their own heads. Much as Peggy had suffered, she saw not only the wickedness, but the impolicy of the fearful crime they meditated. The best and bravest sink beneath small trials, and many great minds are incapable of small sacrifices; but present an object of sufficient magnitude before them, and their courage and fidelity stand forth boldly and at once to encounter and overcome. So it was with this simple peasant girl. She told her mother what she intended. The old woman would have accompanied her, but time pressed. She was already worn out with walking and anxiety, and no third person could share their confidence. But she looked on her daughter; and the bright flashing of her eye, the proud and determined carriage, that, as it were, bespoke, while it enshrined, her purpose, assured the mother that her daughter was determined. As long as she was by her, she felt assured of her success; when, however, she was out of sight, her spirits sunk, and she could only weep and pray, sitting on the hill-side, from whence she still saw Peggy's receding figure. The day was on the wane, and yet she felt as if the sun would never set. Then, again, she fancied he set too quickly. The crescent moon hung its silver bow in the clouds before the fading away of daylight. The widow could not return to her cottage; she fancied she should see her child sooner where she was; she would not, could not stir. At last she took out her beads; one by one the silent tellers of her devotion dropped from her fingers, while her lips mechanically repeated her prayers. Still Peggy came not. The firmament was glittering with those jewels of immortality—types, beautiful and mysterious, of Him who is the same 'to-day, yesterday, and for ever.' Still her daughter came not: there was no bell to tell the passing world of passing hours, but hill and valley, mountain and river, were dark beneath the sky; the grasshopper had folded his wings under the shamrock, and Heaven's own minstrel nestled with her young in the deep corn-furrow; the vanguard of the rooks had swept towards the woods of Killbally, where they were soon to be despoiled of their homes—their last caw! caw! had sounded in the widow's ear. She was sorry they were all past— crows are good company on a mountain's brow. The shrill whistle of the curlew suddenly darted like an arrow through the air. She started to her feet, as if it had been the warning whistle of a Whiteboy, and the humming beetle, that had rested on her cloak, whizzed away, wondering why the mountain moved. Presently, as she looked around (for still her daughter came not), she saw a large bird flying heavily, heavily, between her and the now risen moon, upon which she had unconsciously fixed her eyes. It came nearer—then turned and hooted—again and again. Widow Clement was a strong-nerved woman, yet the hoot of that wild owl sent the blood curdling to her heart. She could support the silence no longer; the solitude became frightful to her. She walked with rapid strides, not towards her own home, but along the path her daughter had pursued.

The destination of Peggy Clement was a hut about three miles from where she had met her mother. It was ruined and desolate, save when peopled by those who wished concealment. It could not be distinguished from the high road along which Mr Crumbie was to pass, and still it was close to it. My tale is already too long; I must hasten its conclusion. Her hand, girl though she was, did not tremble when she knocked at the door, that was fastened on the inside; nor, when she had done so, was there the least noise or reply. The inmates were evidently on their guard against intrusion. Again she knocked. No answer. At last she knelt down by the door, and placing her mouth to the latch-hole, she said, 'Paul Kinsala, Peggy Clement is here, and will stay here until the time comes when, for a reason you have, you will all lave it.' There was a murmur within—a whispering; the door was silently unfastened; a hand, whose touch sent the blood thrilling from her arm through her whole frame, led her in, where all, except the light of her own brave virtuous spirit, was dark; and a voice she would have given worlds to hear anywhere but there, whispered, 'You are mad!'

'*You* are all mad!' she said aloud, and the tones of her clear fearless voice made music in the darkness. 'Strike a light, see me, and hear what I have to tell you! Strike a light—a gun-flint will do it, and ye're not wanting *that*.' She was obeyed; but the light emitted from the small candle was hardly enough to render visible the countenances of five men, who peered at her where she stood, close to Paul Kinsala, who trembled by her side as if he were the aspen, she the oak. 'I don't ask ye why ye are here—I know why; but I will tell ye why I came. Ye want vengeance on the agent! Boys, boys, it's a poor vengeance that returns evil, as it would here, fivefold on yerselves; for, sooner or later, such it would be. I thought to have been here before, though there's plenty of time; and, boys, what d'ye think I've brought ye!— VENGEANCE!' There was a movement in the hovel; and Paul, who had shrunk from her side, from that feeling which prevents a high mind from coming in contact with a high mind, when it knows it has been guilty of an unworthy action, advanced again.

'Indeed, it's truth I'm telling; and I hope ye'll remimber me in yer prayers, for, by God's mercy, I'll keep the stain of blood from yer souls this night. Listen to me, thin, and here's my *credentials*.' She took from her bosom the letter she had received from the postman. 'Here's news—*the ould lord's dead!*'

Various ejaculations followed this announcement. 'The letter is from my brother Mark. The ould lord is dead of a suddent; and whin he was still in it, before the breath was out of his body, he gave his consint to the heir's marriage with Lady Ellen. Ye all know how rich the heir was, and how my lord couldn't abide the name of him in the house. But somehow, under some false name, he knew Lady Ellen, and won her heart; and the last thing my lord did was to give them his blessing. And Lady Ellen wouldn't hear to the love, Mark says, until the heir promised to redeem Killbally from debt and agents, and reside six months of the year at the ould castle!'

When Peggy entered, not one of the party could have been called sober; all were more or less intoxicated, and all were labouring under unnatural excitement. This unexpected announcement sobered them, and a shout of triumph burst from four of the number. The fifth would have preferred murder to gold or prosperity; so he waited, with the cold-blooded determination of a villain, to hear what would follow.

'Where's the proof of this?' he inquired.

'Here,' said Peggy, triumphantly showing the letter. 'And more—my lord acknowledged the promise of a new lase to you, Paul, and the heir promised it—promised it before Mark.' It was only in saying this that her voice faltered.

'And because *you* get a new lase, I suppose we all may go to the *douil*,' retorted Shawn Glyne; 'but if ye forget yer oaths, boys, I don't forget mine. I swore I'd have the heart's blood of Crumbie, and I will; before all the holy saints of Heaven, and by this blessed book, I will!' He sank on his knees, and kissed a small prayer-book which he drew from his vest. Nothing could be more picturesque than the appearance of the interior of the hut at that moment; the light of the candle fell full upon Shawn's face, darkened and distorted by every bad and violent passion, and the erect form and bright animated countenance of Peggy Clement was also distinctly visible. As she stood a little in advance of her lover, every other object seemed clouded and misty; but these two, so different, yet so expressive of their several characters, were finely contrasted—the one so like an angel, in all the pure and holy semblance of good and firm intent; the other composed of great and powerful elements, yet blighted by sin—converted from a man into a demon.

The party were perplexed by the determination of their comrade; they hated the agent with a bitter hatred; but Peggy's clear statement of what had occurred, convinced them at once that they would have justice without taking the law into their own hands; thus their personal safety was secured, and their purpose effected. But Shawn had already passed the pale, and his hatred to the agent was mingled with a fiendish desire to see others steeped in crime as deeply as himself.

'You hear him, Paul?' said Peggy, and her voice sounded sweetly, as a voice from Heaven. 'You hear him—what do you say?'

'I swore I'd have justice,' replied the young man, 'and I saw but one way: the Lord, in his mercy, has seen another; and it wont be the first time I've had reason to bless your step and your voice. You have saved me from destruction.'

Shawn advanced towards him while he spoke, but Peggy stood between them. 'Thank God!' she exclaimed; 'thank God, Paul, I've heard yer words; I've blest ye for them. My heart's lighter, for I knew *yours* could never be rightly in it. I'm satisfied of that. I see, Shawn—I see that ye're determined to have the agent's life; and there are others whose minds are not made up. But your opportunity is past.' Again there was a movement amongst the men more decided than before. They pressed towards the girl, as if uncertain what she had done, or what they must do; her lover would have drawn her towards him, but she stood firm.

'Your opportunity is past, I say. *I* told the agent he would be murdered if he quitted where he is. *I* sent to hasten the soldiers that now, ay, at this minute, protect the house. No one suspects you—*that will tell*. And bless God, every one of ye—if ye don't now, ye will yet, and on your bended knees—that the little wisdom of a simple girl saved ye from a crime that would have brought disgrace on yer counthry, and sin to yer souls for ever!'

THE LANDLORD AT HOME.

In the prosperous county of Wexford—my own dear county—may be seen much that will rejoice the hearts of all who desire the improvement and happiness of Ireland. It can boast of but little natural beauty. We have certainly one or two fine rivers, and besides a number of hills, ONE mountain—a genuine mountain—'the Mountain of Forth,' the great magician of my youthful imaginings. I remember when I used to climb the flowery ascent at the back of my home, turn my eyes towards that time-honoured mountain, and, with childish sagacity, foretell, by the clouds either hanging above, or resting on its summit, whether the day would be foul or fair.

No sea, to me, ever looked so beautiful as that which bounds the county Wexford—that portion of it more especially which extends from the long thin tower of Hook to the capacious harbour, where the shifting sands are as variable as a lady's humour. The Saltee and Keerogue islands are set like emeralds in its crystal waters, which chafe and fret against the dark rocks that in winter frown to scorn the mariner's craft, and send his treasures 'full fathom five' to mingle with the silver sands of their creeks and foaming bays. The fine sea scenery is beheld to great advantage from the mountain I have mentioned—that dark rocky mountain, behind whose crags, and in whose crevices, shelter scores of hardy mountaineers; fine specimens of the animal creation, but rather fond of having their own way, and not inclined to render obedience to any code of laws that would at all interfere with 'their own sweet will.' Still they are brave, honest, and hospitable, and look quite as picturesque, to my fancy, on that noble mountain as brigands on the finest Italian crags that were ever painted. I remember once having achieved the highest peak of Forth; I do not think I ever beheld a landscape that delighted me so much as on that day. In the immediate valley to the right, the fertile barony of Bargy, as remarkable for its agricultural as its antiquarian riches, spreads its corn-fields and verdant meadows, and innumerable castles in various stages of decay, showing that it must have been both valuable and debateable ground in the 'good old times,' and giving the scene an air of feudal grandeur and magnificence that filled me with dreams of the past. The park, superb woods, and turrets of Johnstown Castle, told their true and happy tale of present good, for the flag streamed gaily from the highest tower, giving token that the landlord was—where a patriot ought to be—AT HOME, dwelling on his own land—the fountain of blessings to his people. Many other abodes, of small extent in comparison to Johnstown, are also inhabited by the landlords of the soil, and to this I attribute the county's prosperity and peace. The silver sea that bounded the land on the right was speckled with fishing-boats; occasionally, the broad sails of a stately merchant ship would float along like a sea-queen, and the soft, white, cloud-like streak of an arriving or departing steamer tell of that rapid commerce which the good folk of the barony know how to turn to advantage. I was enchanted with the scene, and expressed my admiration warmly; when suddenly a bold, brown, ragged fellow, with the frame of a Hercules and the grace of an Apollo, came up to us, and, evidently delighting in my delight at the glorious expanse of land and water, flung off his coat at my feet, and said, 'The rock is damp and cowld, my lady; ah, thin, stand upon that: sure it would be bad manners of the mountain to do ye any harm, and you so plased with the fine old craythur.'

I vowed in my heart of hearts never to say a word against the mountaineers—and all for the sake of Dan'nel Devereux, who, with many others, had built his hut of the mountain granite, and paid to no one rent for that or his mountain garden: thanks to his gallantry, I would not, even if the law gave me the right, ask either Dan'nel or any of Dan'nel's people for rent or tithe. I should very much like to transport certain of my friends to the peak of the mountain of Forth, where I lingered from noon till evening; and after admiring the glory of the sea, and the fertility of the land-view, descend with me into the valley, and there behold, on the estate of one particular LANDLORD AT HOME, as much peace, safety, and comfort, as are to be met with in any part of England.

I hear dozens of persons exclaiming against Irish dirt! Irish mismanagement! Irish this and that! and I exclaim against these things myself. I know they exist to a frightful degree, and to a frightful extent; but my heart beats high and proudly at the knowledge of what good and *patient* management can effect with the Irish peasant. I say *patient* management: without patience and temper, no system of improvement will work well in Ireland. Paddy would worry the angels with his prejudices, and unless you laugh with him, he is apt to become mulish. But *get at his heart;* convince him by deeds, not words, that you seek his good, and he will show his gratitude by trying to please you. Here is my proof:—An estate unincumbered, bringing in to the possessor several thousands a-year, spent by himself in the country, the money, as it were, returned to the tenant, with the rich interest of protection and kindness. Three hundred labourers constantly employed on this estate. A school-house, beautiful to look at, and useful in its construction, built and supported without any regard to expense, at the gate leading to the princely domain; the master, a man qualified in every respect for his occupation;

no religious distinction made, and none thought of, either by the learning or the learner. Cottages built in the midst of flourishing gardens; roses and woodbines clustering round their windows; the landlord doubling the amount of whatever prizes his tenants receive from agricultural societies, as encouragements to good conduct. No wild pigs, no beggars, no dunghills, no fear, few whisky shops, little quarrelling, very little idleness; clean, healthy, well-dressed children; the prettiest girls and 'neatest boys' in Ireland. You ask of the landlord's and landlady's religion; both are members of the Church of England; some of their servants are Catholics, some Protestants. I never heard the sound of religious difference in their household, where I have spent some of the happiest days of my life. The Catholic priest seconds all their plans for the improvement of the country; and by night and by day their house is open to relieve either sorrow or sickness: there are no traces of extravagance in their arrangements, though the park is full of deer, and the merry horn frequently calls forth the stag-hounds to the chase; but little is spent in vain entertainment, though great is the outlay of actual benevolence: every new improvement is tried at home before it is adapted to cottage use, and Paddy *sees* the good with his own eyes before he is called on to adopt it: this is especially necessary, for my countrymen love 'ould ways;' and I doubt much if my beneficent friends would be as honoured as they are, were it not that the people know 'they are come of a good ould stock— none of yer musharoon gentry.' This is not an Irish Utopia; it is, to use an Irish phrase, 'to the fore.' Any one sceptical as to the possibility of Irish civilisation, may go to Wexford, and drive in half an hour to Johnstown Castle, where he can see what I have described; and more—for the proprietors have introduced amongst the mechanics, as well as the agriculturists, a hitherto unknown taste, by fitting up certain rooms in the castle with oak carvings after the antique, which would do no discredit to our best artists in that way, and prove what *can be* done not only *in* the country, *but by the countrymen themselves,* when there is a kind and liberal spirit to draw forth and foster their abilities. How trite is the observation that 'Rome was not built in a day!' Neither are the Irish to be won round to neatness, and order, and comfort, and 'all that sort of thing,' in a day.

A few years ago, a *posse comitatus* of the peasantry were sitting and lounging and idling away some fine hours of a sunny Sunday round the door of a public-house near one of the entrances to the deer-park in the neighbourhood I have mentioned: there was Michael Gabbett the smith; Jeremiah Mackay, his wife, and daughters; Gerald Murphy, Phil Dwyer, and a certain Anty O'Toole, the belle and beauty not only of the parish of Rathaspeck, but of a much larger district. Some were sitting on the stone fence, others were shouldering the old piers, that, truth to tell, looked as if they could not bear a great deal of rough usage, though they had stood many a storm. Abel Connor, a handsome, fine-looking fellow, half mason half farmer, was evidently bent on making himself agreeable to the pretty Anty, who, to do her justice, seldom flirted more than a very pretty cheerful-hearted girl might flirt in all propriety. She did not think there was a great deal of harm in teasing Aby, because Aby not only was handsome, but thought himself so—a piece of impertinence which women are bound to punish as an encroachment on woman's prerogative. The truth was, he thought no girl in the county could or would refuse him—a delusion by no means confined to *handsome* men. Anty O'Toole had a great deal of good practical sense, and a taste and desire, not beyond her means, but beyond, or what was called beyond, her station. This taste had grown upon her, and had originated in one or two causes; the principal one being, that she had resided a good deal in the houses of the resident gentry, and had learnt to contrast the thoughtless and reckless extravagance of some with the prudence and good conduct of others.

'I'll tell ye what it is,' said Michael Gabbett, who was a regular whisky-shop orator—and, by the way, as the greater number of my readers do not know what a whisky-shop orator is, I will pause a moment in my tale to describe him. Be it remembered, that while beer stupifies its ordinary consumers, whisky renders them emaciated; and, accordingly, our orator has a lean, yellow, haggard look; his lips are thin, his teeth discoloured; and even when he declaims coolly, which is seldom the case, there is a tremor and twitching about his mouth that speaks of habitual intoxication, though the fever may not then be in its strength. His eye at such times has nothing in it; it is not sober, but dull and bleared; its natural fires have been long extinguished, and it is only after strong libations that those *spirit-lamps* blaze up, with a fierce and unearthly light, that renders the cadaverous aspect of his countenance still more fearful. His brows are shaggy and loose; his hair prematurely gray; his beard unshaven, for his hand is so unsteady, that it cannot perform the necessary task; and as he has lost credit even with an Irish barber, he cannot always pay for the operation. His stockings sit loosely on his shrunk legs—for the grass is not yet green on the grave of his broken-hearted wife, and his little shoeless girl is unable to knit him new ones; his blue long-tailed coat hangs awkwardly from his shoulders, and one of the skirts bears the mark of having been nearly torn off; the tie of his faded neckerchief is never straight; his waistcoat has been green, but now it is greasy, and the buttons are almost all departed; the strings at his knees are either knotted or vanished; and his hat leans more to one side than the other; the binding is worn off the edge, and the band has been replaced by a piece of cord, in which his pipe is stuck jauntily, and, it may be, one or two speeches he has cut from a worn-out newspaper are also folded under it. When he reads, he sits on the table of the shebeen shop, while his auditors lounge (an Irish peasant seldom stands erect) or crouch around him; his legs dangle from the table, though sometimes, animated by his energy, he makes them emulate the action of his arms; and what he reads now, having often read before, he interpolates with various passages of his own. After this he declaims much too long upon subjects which are forbidden in my pages, and which I think it would be better were less thought of elsewhere. Such was Michael Gabbett—such was *not* Abel Connor; and when Anty O'Toole looked at the contrast, she vowed in her heart of hearts, that if there was any chance of Abel's ever being such a man, why, she'd die before she'd marry.

This particular evening Michael was not very tipsy; he was only half so, and was sitting on the step of a stile leading into the park. He had just put up a tattered newspaper, and commenced —'I'll tell ye what it is: there has been what is called a long minority on this estate, and there is a noble, a very great fortune intirely; but, ye see, the masther and the misthress have been to furrin parts; and though they stayed away a very little while, yet it's very sartin they are full of new improvements. There's a fine flash-my-eye school-house building: I—don't—like—that.'

'Why don't you like it?' inquired the pretty Anty with dancing eyes; 'why don't you like it, Michael?'

'I've my rasons, Miss Anty O'Toole; miss, I've my rasons; and, having my rasons, Miss Anty, I'm rasonable; and, being rasonable, Miss Anty, I don't feel bound to talk rason to a woman who's always unrasonable. That's logic; aint it, boys?'

'It's a sin you warn't a schoolmaster instead of a smith,' said old Molly Mackay, for Michael had a great reputation amongst old people for wisdom.

'It was indeed, Mrs Molly Mackay, ma'am, a great pity and a sin. I never took right to the smithy.'

'That's the rason ye're so seldom in it, I suppose, Misther Gabbett,' said the saucy Anty.

The lazy smith rolled his lack-lustre eyes on the bright girl.

'Why do you say that hard word, Miss Anty?'

'Because it's talked of through the country that you might have had a chance of the work of an iron gate for the mistress's school, if you could be depended on; but you couldn't.'

'The country talks folly; I wouldn't do the gate. I'm a pathriot and an honest man, and I've my rasons for—not—liking —the—school.'

'And what's in the rasons you have, sir, if a poor uninstructed girl like myself might make bould to ask, Mr Gabbett ? What's in them ? Sure the children are to be educated, and have tickets given them, which, at the end of the quarter, if they are well conducted, will gain them clothes; and learning is a fine thing. Why, I am told that even if the boys have a talent for *mathewmaticks*, they are to be let learn them.' And Anty looked round triumphantly.

'And who's Matthew Matticks, to set up for a taicher?' inquired Michael Gabbett contemptuously.

'It's not a man, but a—a—learning,' answered Anty; 'a learning of great advantage to such as can get round it. A thing to make people think; and, for anything I know to the contrary, get them both in, and through, and out of, the College of Dublin.'

'Oh, ye get great larning, ov coorse, at the big houses, miss; but I wonder what Father Sinnott will say to it. Do you go to your duty, Miss Anastasia?'

'Thank ye for nothing, Misther Michael. Ye're not my father confessor anyway; and I hope I'm not content with only GOING to my duty; I try to *do* my duty. And as to Father Sinnott, he's as glad of the school as ourselves.'

Michael Gabbett made a very peculiarly ugly face, accompanied by an expressive twist of his mouth, and comical blink of his eye, which always assisted his eloquence, because every one laughed at it. But Anty did not laugh; she grew angry.

'Father Sinnott *is* glad of it,' she said with dignity; 'and if you don't believe me, here he comes himself: ask him.'

As soon as the priest appeared, every one rose; Michael Gabbett even stood up: the little children needed no bidding, but curtseyed to 'his reverence,' and drawing near their mothers, looked at him with silent respect.

That good old priest is now in his grave, and I am sorry for it, though I hear his successor is a kind man also. If so, Rathaspeck has been greatly favoured—a good priest and a good landlord; good clergymen, too; a good school, and all manner of good examples. No wonder the people prosper! But to return to that good old man and his flock. After the usual interchange of prayers and blessings, Anty, curtseying and blushing, approached the priest.

'Well, Miss Anastasia, and when am I to say *the words* for you, eh? But it's Abel that ought to make the bargain, Anty, not you. I wont bargain with you; you'd be trying to come over the priest with your bright eyes and sweet smiles to get a bargain, you deluder!' The assembly laughed, and exclamations of 'Long life to him; what a hearty* man he is! God bless him; he's a fine gay† ould gentleman!' were heard among the crowd.

---

* Cheerful.   † Happy.

'It isn't *that*, yer reverence, at all,' blushed Anty still more deeply; 'only, if you please, I said that yer reverence would be glad of the school our landlady's building on a corner of the park, and Michael Gabbett said you would not.'

'Without wanting to fight Abel Connor, on account of contradicting his sweetheart,' answered the orator, 'that's not thrue, yer reverence; I appeal to the people!'

'If you did not say it, Michael, you made an ugly face,' said Anty, 'and that was worse. You made a face at his reverence.'

'Oh fie, Anty! Oh—oh—oh! Anty!' echoed around and about.

'Never mind,' laughed the good-natured priest, taking a huge pinch of snuff, one-half of which settled itself in the folds of his ample waistcoat; 'I appeal to all here if my friend Michael could make an uglier face than the one he's forced to put up with working-day and Sunday.'

'But the school, father, if you please, sir?' persisted Anty, like a cat or a woman, sticking to her point.

'My good people, I'm sure the school, in the hands it's in, will be a blessing to the country. The gentry that's doing it are of a good old stock.'

'I beg yer reverence's pardon, but an ould stock doesn't like grafting,' said young Mackay, who was following, at a humble distance, in the steps of the public-house orator.

'Oh, then, look at his manners,' exclaimed the ready Anty, 'to interrupt a priest!'

'Where would he get manners,' answered Father Sinnott, 'or grace? I haven't seen him at my foot for many a day; and I'll tell you what, my nate boy, *you'd* be the better for grafting, that you would; only, Peter, I'm afraid what would be in the old stock would poison the graft.' This raised a laugh at Mackay's expense, who shrunk behind the group; but Connor, who was exceedingly out of temper at something Anty had whispered him, exclaimed, 'Aint we to complain at not being allowed to till the ground our own way? I do think it's cruel hard that we're obliged to pay for the land, and yet must farm it exactly in the way that the master or mistress pleases.'

'And cows stall-fed, and shupervisors appointed to see what we have, and do, in our own houses, reporting everything at the castle!' exclaimed the orator.

'As to the land, Abel,' answered Father Sinnott, 'throw up the bit you have when you please: you knew the conditions when you took it, and there's scores will be glad to get it. I don't understand the house-feeding, or the green crops, Michael, but you'll find them spoken of in Mister Martin Doyle's books; and as to the gentlemen employed by the mistress to look at the cabins, you know that where misery exists, it is relieved; and where industry and cleanliness are found, they are rewarded. I'm glad,' added the priest laughing, 'they have not visited me. No one would think there was a smith in the neighbourhood, and the priest's gate wanting a latch ; no one would think, Abel Connor, there was a mason nearer Wexford, and the step to the priest's door rooted into marbles by the pigs.' After these, and a few more priestly admonishings, mingled with excellent advice, the venerable man intimated to his sleek fat mare that she was to proceed, which she did at a pace something between a shuffle and a walk.

Anty O'Toole knew that the priest's words would make their impression, and wishing a kindly good-evening to 'the neighbours,' she set out by a short cut across the park on her way home. Abel Connor had walked a little way down the road with young Mackay, and the first intimation he received of her flight, was from seeing her crossing the hill in the distance with a swiftness which emulated that of the fawn. Abel sprang over the fence, and was soon out of hearing of the laughter of his companions. He did not overtake the runaway until she was by the bank of one of those enchanting streams where the water is so pure, the grass so soft and green, the trees so luxuriant, that it might be imagined the chosen spot for the revels of fairies that haunt the sylvan spring. It was bewildering in its extreme of loveliness ; the most beautiful spot in this most beautiful park— the *most* beautiful, at all events, but one, towards which Anty was hastening.

'Is it going up to the ould church of St Kevin you are, Anty ! Well, it's I that am glad of it, for I'll be the longer in yer company. Oh, you wild deer, to run me such a race !' said the panting lover.

'I never asked you either to come or run,' replied Anty ; 'and, indeed, maybe you had better not come, for you will hear what will not please you. God be good to us ! but the ancient ruin does look beautiful ! and the shine and glitter of the setting sun, how bright it is, coming through the trees upon the ivy and the gray ould stones, and turning it all into fairy gold and silver, just the way youth, and hope, and all that, shines everything to their own colour for a while, until it turns ! It is doing it now; you see the colour is fading while I speak : there—there—and now the ivy is green, and the stones are gray, and the brightness of the gold and silver is gone ; and by and by the moon will rise, and then that will be like the case, and silence, and quiet of the sleeping graves.'

'What's over ye, Anty ?' exclaimed Connor, seizing her hand. 'I never heard ye talk this way before. Sure ye're not angry with me for the trifle of temper I showed above there ! I did not mean it, only your people are all for improvements, and that like, and the Connors stick to the ould ways.'

'I'm not angry with you, Abel, but I'm sorry for you, that's all. I wonder a knowledgeable boy like you would *set the back of yer hand** against improvements, and ye seeing the good of it. There isn't a thing the master or mistress proposes, that has not been tried and known to prosper in their own place ; but that *you* should turn against me with a set of such poor craythurs, ignorant both of the laws of God and man ! Oh, Abel, I did not expect it from you, and you that know so much better.'

'Anty !'

'Now don't talk so fast, Aby ; you always have the talk to yourself. But it's no use now, none in the wide world. I've made up my mind'——

'Darling, Anty'——

'It's no use, Abel ; none in the world. I'll never be tied to a boy that wont be convinced ; nor I wont be tied to a boy that consorts or *comrades* with Michael Gabbett, or any of those lounging people that we left there below. Leave me now, for I'm going to say a prayer at my poor mother's grave, and tell her I haven't forgot the promise I made her.'

'And what was that, Anty ?'

'To see what a man was made of before I married him. And now once for all, Abel, let everything be over betwixt us, or make up yer mind to wait two years.'

'What !'

'Two years, Abel—no less. By that time maybe I might have some chance of seeing what *you* are made of ; by that time we shall know whether the changes are improving or not; they've been going on some time already: if we come together now, we'd do nothing but quarrel about them. Be easy now ; there's no use in running into contention or poverty. I'll see what you are by that time, anyway, and you'll see what I am ; and as to living with a man, and not agreeing with him, like Poll Shea and her husband, I'll never do it—so that's enough. Ye're free of yer promise from this moment ; as to me, I never gave you one.'

Abel stormed and prayed, and I suppose swore ; but Anty was determined, and the lovers parted, not exactly understanding whether or not they were lovers any longer.

It was evident to all who wished the improvements in progress to prosper, that the peace, comfort, and prosperity of the neighbourhood were greatly increased by the fact of Michael Gabbett's having been suffocated in a pool of stagnant water outside his own door. He had wound up an oration that very Sunday evening touching the advantages of old times and old customs, until, owing to the combined influences of strong whisky and weak reasoning, the company, at first admiring, became uproarious, then very tipsy,

---

* Set your face against.

and finally, so really intoxicated, that he, after blinking home in the moonlight that shone so peaceably on the ruined church, stumbled over some stones, and his face sank in the stagnant pool. It is worthy of record, as connected with this unfortunate man, that the last words he said when leaving his companions were—' I'll have my own way; I'll have no new improvements; I'll—never let—an improvement near me—or mine!' He had resisted all advice to remove the pool, that, like a treacherous and unworthy friend, destroyed him at the last. What rendered it still more remarkable was, that the typhus fever broke out amongst the poor parentless children of this bad man, and spread only in those cottages which had withstood all attempts at purification in the way of whitewashing and cleanliness. This was so practical an evidence of the effects of neglect, and its consequent ruin, that the greatest murmurers were silenced; and the excellent agent, who had ever gone hand in hand with his excellent friends in improvement, seized upon every little occurrence to work out the great object of showing the peasants not only how they could be benefited, but how they could benefit themselves. Instead of shrinking from the 'inspection' of the state of their cottages, and its subsequent report, when rewards of merit were bestowed by the hands of their 'own' mistress, if the report was favourable, they learnt gradually—some of them so gradually, that it would try the patience of a saint; but still they *did* learn—to look forward to these rewards with pride and pleasure, and to feel the approbation of 'the landlord at home' a reward of as much value as the 'shining siller,' or sometimes 'gold,' which they received. Mrs Mackay herself was heard to confess 'that it was a fine thing to see her bits of grandsons getting genteel learning and purty bits of clothes now and again out of the school, and to have the masther on the spot, without any pride in him, to ask a favour of, which was sure to be granted, God bless him! And the misthress, so active, and kind, and good, only mighty fond of having everything done regular; but somehow, when things war done as she ordered, they turned out best.' This was a great deal from Mrs Mackay, who was a professed grumbler.

But still the way was by no means clear for our perseveringly domestic landlord. One morning the lady visited one of those pretty cottages whose building she had herself planned, and whose flowers and culinary plants had been supplied from her own garden; the cottage consisted of four rooms,* two below, and two above, the floor of the lower rooms composed of strong lime cement. Now, it had occurred to the sapient occupier of the cottage that he would rather thrash his corn in that room than in

* My friends have, however, found that the peasants are more comfortable in *two-roomed* cottages, with sheds, &c. at the back, than in four-roomed ones, which seem almost too much for them to attend to.

the shed; and as the ceiling interfered with the action of the flail, and Paddy could not conveniently *remove* it, why, according to ancient practice, he scratched a wise thought out of his 'coolan,' and *dug a deep hole in the floor;* and in this hole was he thrashing away right merrily, to the tune of 'The Rakes of Mallow,' when his fair young landlady entered! This is only one of scores of similar little annoyances which landlords, bent on *home Irish improvements,* meet with—the Irish are so fond of making a thing serve any purpose but the one it was intended for; fond of giving their pigs, poultry, and cattle, abundance of air and exercise at their neighbour's expense; an almost unconquerable aversion to plant trees, though the landlord offers to register them in the planter's name, by which means they become his property. Fortunately for the Johnstown peasantry, their bad habits are firmly resisted, but resisted with the most inconceivably good temper, which certainly is as a halo round the inhabitants of that fine old castle: the reward to such benevolent hearts, even now, is great.

'We know,' said an old farmer to me one day, 'that it's for our good; for *sure they're in it themselves,* to see and understand the difference.'

To return to Abel Connor: he declared loudly and strongly his determination not to be put upon by any woman; and for what?—just because he would not farm according to other people's fancies, and liked a bit of fun: that was the worst any one could say of him. And this was certainly true: he made love to half a dozen girls at least, and all at the same time. This was very shocking, at least so all the girls said, except *the* particular one to whom he chanced to be making love at the time it was declared 'shocking' by the others; but somehow, though he talked every fine Sunday evening as much nonsense to the fair sex as an Irishman *can* talk—and that, truly, is a great deal—still he made no direct offer of his hand and heart to any. Anty continued to improve and earn money—earn money and improve; and many said they believed, after all, that Abel Connor would do more at the new farming than at his trade. Despite his gaiety and self-confidence, the death of the orator had made a great impression on him, although the mortification occasioned by Anty's conduct rendered him for a time susceptible of little else than what he called her injustice; but frequently the fact stared him in the face, that Michael Gabbett had scorned improvement, and lost his life in consequence of his attachment to the stagnant pool at his own door. Whenever he felt himself inclined to grumble at the new change, the vision of the suffocated whisky shop orator would rise before him; and somehow or other, he had so sobered down before the expiration of eighteen months, that he felt half inclined to forsake all others, and return to his first affection; but *pride* prevented him. Anty's good conduct had recommended her to the favour of the lady of the castle; and though he longed most ardently for one of the pretty new houses he was assisting in building, and had saved enough to stock and plenish, being, moreover, convinced that plans which worked so well for others must work well for him, still he was obstinate.

Now, I confess that my friend Anty was to the full as obstinate as her old lover; and so they went on, she peeping at him through the pearl edge of her straw-bonnet whenever she saw him at mass, and *he* peeping at her through the great trees of the park, or through the battlements of the *new old* castle that flank the beautiful lake; there and everywhere did Abel wander to see if Anty 'would speak first:' his heart, poor fellow, had returned to its first affection: it was asserted that he flirted *less* than any other young tradesman or farmer in the neighbourhood, and very likely that was true, for *they* flirt a great deal; but still, though the two years were expired within a day or two, the '*first* word' had not been spoken. Abel was hardly called upon to give up idle acquaintances, for the very *idle* were no longer tolerated by the peasants, who were now able to enjoy the sweets of industry; and certainly everything that had been fairly tried had fairly succeeded.

It was again a fine sunny Sunday evening; and a young woman, after decking a grave in the old park churchyard with the sweet tribute of flowers, and having said the necessary number of prayers, was sitting upon the green mound, her head against the gray gravestone, and her tearful eyes were bent upon the simple inscription and rude cross engraved thereon.

'I have tried him, that is, he has tried me, mother dear,' she said, holding that soothing though imaginary converse with the dead which is so sweet a consolation to the living. 'I have tried to see what he was made of, and sure he's mighty like the rest of the boys, only maybe better, and turned to your heart's content to the improvements; and sure I thought the heart would burst in my bosom when my mistress asked me only on Thursday last if I had any thoughts of marrying; for if I had, there was a new house ready for me.'

'And what did you answer, Anty?' inquired a voice seldom heard, but well remembered.

* * * * *

Abel and Anty did not separate that night in anger; they knelt together, and exchanged promises, and walked lovingly by the mill-pond stream towards the domain.

'I'd rather,' said the lover, as, after much explanation and love-talk, they paused to look at the noble pile to which wings and towers in admirable taste have been added—'I'd rather that castle was on the top of the Mountain of Forth, as an example to the country, than sunk down in a valley.'

'Sure it is as well where it is; has as fine a *moral* influence—the people, I mean, that's in it,' answered Anty, who, with all her goodness, if she had been 'a lady,' was fond enough of hard words to merit the distinction of a 'blue-stocking.'

'MORAL INFLUENCE!' repeated Abel; 'I daresay that's the right sort of thing; but I'd have the advantage of every sort of influence given to such people. The castle, I tell you, should be on the top of the mountain in its glory.'

'The glory of their good deeds will go higher than that,' said Anty.

'I know—to Heaven!' replied the young man. *'But for all that, I'd have him a lord on earth.'*

'They'll be saints in heaven,' said the girl.

'I tell you, Anty *avourneen*, I know nothing can make them holier nor happier, barring it was seeing the whole country as prosperous as their own estates; but for the sake of the example, you know—*the example*, don't you see?'

'The example—that converted you: it wasn't love of me, you know, Aby—there's Judy'——

'Now hush, Anty! By the powers, I'll go to the priest to-night to get the blessed words said at onct. I've passed my vocation, and'——

'You ought to go the first six months over again: you behaved badly at first, Abel.'

'Ah, whisht, *cora machree!* sure I knew the obstinacy was in you, and that you would not give in. Now, Anty, I see the good of everything you used to say; and if you'll only, in a humble way, take pattern of the mistress'——

'Oh, Abel! but I'll try, in a humble way, as the wren said, when she tried to fly after the eagle, if you will take pattern by the "Landlord at Home."'

Note.

It has been often and truly said, that the best feelings are the most difficult to express, and I believe I must confess myself more at home with fiction than with facts: perhaps this is the reason why these stories have cost me more time and more anxiety than all my others put together. The CAUSE has kept my heart beating as long as the pen was in my hand. In this story I have failed the most; failed to express the deep and earnest sense I entertain of my friends' virtues—failed to depict their usefulness—failed to do justice to their *practical patriotism*. I would, with Abel, that they enjoyed all earthly distinction; not because it would gratify them—they are above such wants and wishes—but because of the example which, the more it is known, the more it will be imitated. In the story I refrained from mentioning their name, lest I should wound that sensitive delicacy which confines them almost too closely within their own domain; but I saw only this morning that other travellers have named Mr and Mrs Grogan Morgan as examples of all that could be desired in *landlords at home*. I have often looked on the grim old portrait of one of their ancestors, and could almost fancy the stern features smiled in approbation of their good deeds. Hamilton Knox Grogan Morgan is a lineal descendant of the great Scottish Reformer.

A. M. H.

'IT'S ONLY A BIT OF A STRETCH!'

'AND were there many at the race, Pierce?'

'Many—is it many, aunt? Faith, I believe ye; thousands upon thousands!'

'And did many horses run, Pierce?'

'Ay, hundreds!'

'Oh, Pierce, how could that be?—there would not be room; and, besides, I'm astonished at the people's coming out in the teams of rain.'

'Och, aunt, ye're such a bother! Warn't there hundreds of tents to shelter them?'

'Is it to shelter *thousands*, Pierce?' said his Aunt Kitty, laying down her knitting, and looking with her pale blue eyes steadfastly in his face.

'Lord! aunt, how can ye go on believing every word a fellow says?'

'That's true, my dear, when *you* are "the fellow,"' answered Aunt Kitty in her usual placid way.

'Sure,' he continued, 'there were plenty of people on the racecourse, and that's all as one as thousands; and there were plenty of horses, and a good sprinkling of tents; but, aunt, you drive all the spirit out of a man with your regulation questions. I tell you, you drive all the spirit out of me.'

'Then I do very wrong,' replied Aunt Kitty smiling. 'I only want to exchange spirits—the spirit of truth for the spirit of falsehood.'

'Falsehood, aunt?'

'Lying—whether black or white—if it pleases you better.'

'By the powers!—and they're a large family—I wouldn't let a man say that of me.'

'You could not prevent his thinking it.'

'No man should dare tell me I was a liar!'

'I daresay not, Mr Pierce Scanlan. You quarrelled last week with Miles Pendergast for repeating, as if it had been truth, what you *afterwards* said was a jest; and then you quarrelled with him for saying that something else was falsehood which you wished to be understood was truth. You said on both occasions you'd blow his brains out; but you have stated your intention of doing so towards so many, that I suppose my friend Miles still has his brains. I hope he will keep them cool.'

'I wish,' exclaimed the young farmer, 'I wish my mother had been anything but an English woman.'

'Why, Pierce?'

'Why, because then I should not have had an English aunt to fuss about nothing. Now, don't look angry; no, not angry; you never look angry, that's the d—l of it: nor don't blow me up: but no, that's as bad, you never blow me up; if you did, there would be some comfort in it; but you wont do either. You wont do anything but reason with me: it is really enough to make a fellow mad!'

'To be reasoned with?'

'Ay, to be reasoned with. My father used to say it was one of the privileges of an Irish husband that he was never expected to listen to reason.'

'Irish husbands,' said Aunt Kitty very solemnly, while preparing to take up a stitch she had just dropped, 'are, generally speaking, great tyrants: they have the most tender affectionate wives in the world, and they bluster their lives out. Storm!—storm!—fly! —fly!—and then (as was the case with my poor sister), when the trembling spirit has found refuge in the grave, they cry over her! Irish fathers are bad fathers!'

'Oh, Kitty, Kitty, if you warn't my aunt!'

'But I *am* your aunt. I left my home and my country, when the Almighty took your parents, to share what I had with my sister's children. All I want is for you to *hear* me.'

'Aunt, you want us to *heed* you too.'

'Not unless your reason is convinced, Pierce.'

'Bother the reason, aunt! I want to have no call to it; and I hope you wont be coming over what you said just now to Eliza Byrne about Irish husbands.'

'Irish husbands are generally bad, and Irish fathers are even worse.'

'Oh, aunt!—why, their *love* for their children goes beyond everything.'

'And their care for their comfort and prosperity amounts to nothing. Peer and peasant live up to what they have, and leave their children the Irish heritage of beggary. How did your own father leave you and your three little sisters? It breaks my heart when I think of it! You're a good boy, Pierce; a kind-hearted boy, if you'd give up *stretching*. Only stick to the truth, the bright ornament, Pierce. I do think if you would, you'd be almost as good a husband as an Englishman, as wise a one as a Scotch.'

'Will you say that to Eliza Byrne, aunt? Do, aunt, like a darling, and I wont *give a stretch* for a week!'

'Talking of Eliza Byrne,' said his kind but peculiar Aunt Kitty—'now I think of it, Eliza heard something you had said of Lucy Flynn that has cut her up very much.'

'Of Lucy Flynn?'

'Yes; either of Lucy or to Lucy, I am not sure which, so do not run away my story *into a stretch*. And, Pierce, what did you mean by saying that Brady owed Garrett more gold than his mare could carry, and that he'd be broke horse and foot if he could not pay?'

'Oh, by the powers!' replied Pierce, colouring deeply, 'I never said such a word—not that I remember; or if I did, *'twas only a bit of a stretch*, just to taze ould Mother Brady, that thought to haul me over the coals about a bit of fun concerning her son and Ellen Graves. I meant no harm at the time. Anyhow, he does owe Garrett a matter of ten pounds.'

'*Is that more than his mare could carry?*'

'Oh, Aunt Kitty, be aisy; ye're too bad intirely; faith, the townland's turning English upon us, observing every *stretch* a boy makes for diversion.'

'There is plenty of diversion on the subject, I assure you,' said his aunt. 'Every lie in the parish *is called a Pierce Scanlan.*'

'By the powers!' he exclaimed; 'any man that says that, I'll break every bone in his body.'

'Wouldn't it be easier to break yourself off the habit of *stretching*, as you call it?' inquired his aunt.

'Bad cess to the people that can't see a joke; and ye're enough, aunt, so you are, to set a body mad.'

The interview had proceeded to this particular point, when Pierce's sisters—Jane, and Anne, and little Mary—entered together; they had taken a half holiday, and crossed the hill to spend it at Eliza Byrne's, and now returned, not laughing and talking as usual, but with sober steady countenances and quiet footsteps. Each entered without speaking, and there were traces of tears on little Mary's cheeks.

'Holloa, girls!' exclaimed their really good-tempered brother, 'have you been to a funeral?'

'Be aisy with yer nonsense,' said Jane.

'Too much of one thing is good for nothing,' muttered Anne.

'I wonder at you, so I do, brother Pierce, to say what you did of Eliza Byrne,' added little Mary.

'And your life isn't safe in the country, I can tell you,' recommenced Jane; 'for every one of the Bradys' people are up as high as the Hill of Howth.'

'And will have you as low down as the towers in Lough Neagh,' added Anne.

'And Ellen Graves's father has been all the way to Newtownmountchallagharshane to see 'Torney Driscoll, to take the law of you for taking away his daughter's character.'

'Aisy, girls, for the love of the holy saints ! Aisy, I say,' said Pierce, looking, as well he might, bewildered ; 'you open upon me for all the world like a pack of hounds. Aisy—one at a time !' exclaimed the brother ; '*aisy with the hay, avourneen, and insense* me into it—quietly.'

'Quietly !' repeated little Mary, who was the pet and the beauty of the family ; 'it's mighty aisy to *say* quiet to the waves of the sea, and the storm whirling them about.'

'A joke's a joke,' said Jane ; 'but what right had ye to touch the girl's character ?'

'And crying up Lucy Flynn before Eliza Byrne's brother's face. *She'll* have nothing more to say to you, I can tell you that,' continued Anne.

'And meddling with the Bradys—the *quarrelsomest* people in the five parishes ; we'll have the house burned over our heads through you,' sobbed little Mary.

'And be brought before judge and jury, if that 'Torney Driscoll smells out the yellow guineas Ellen Graves's father keeps hid in the ould stocking in the thatch of his house : and oh ! on the raceground—I forgot that—how could you say the councillor's *cowlt* Conn was all head and tail like his owner ? The councillor will be down on ye, ye misfortunate boy, as well as the 'torney !' said Jane.

'And that's not the worst of it. But oh, Pierce, the *stretch* you made'——

'Whisht, Anne,' interrupted Mary : 'what was it all to compare to little Matty O'Hay's turning up his nose when I said my aunt could fine-plait better than the lady's-maid at the castle ? he turns up and round his ugly nose, that looks for all the world like a stray root of mangold-wortsel, and says " he supposes *that* must be put down as another *Pierce Scanlan*."'

'Did he say that ?' exclaimed Pierce, jumping upwards to where three or four exceedingly well-looking, well-organised shillalas were 'seasoning'—up the chimney ; and bringing down his favourite at a spring, he weighed it carefully in his hand.

There is something particularly national and characteristic in the manner of an Irishman's weighing a shillala ; the grasp he gives it is at once firm and tender ; he poises it on his open palm, glancing his eye along its fair proportions ; then his hand gently undulates ; again he regards it with a look of intense and friendly admiration, grasps his fingers round it, so as to assure himself of its solidity, until the knuckles of his muscular hand become white, and the veins purple ; then, in an ecstasy of enjoyment, he cuts a caper ; and while his eyes sparkle, and a deep and glowing crimson colours his cheeks, he wheels his national weapon round his head, and the wild 'whoop!' of the wild Irish rings through the air. So did Pierce; and 'the whoop,' intended as a sort of war-challenge to the faction of the O'Hays, compelled his Aunt Kitty to speak.

'My dear,' said the good, quiet English soul, fairly letting her knitting drop, and placing her fingers on her ears—'my dear Pierce, put down that dirty stick; don't make such a noise, but sit down and *listen to reason!*' Now, let any one who can understand what an Irishman is in a state of excitement, imagine how Pierce received this well-intended but ill-timed admonition. Never had he been so 'badgered' before; for a moment the stick was poised above his head, as if the good woman had been a sorceress, and had fixed it there; and then uttering a deep oath, he rushed towards the door with something like a determination of 'cracking the pate' of the first man he met, merely to get his hand into practice for what was to come. It is not, however, easy for a man to escape from four women; and they hung round him with such tenacity of grasp, that he was literally dragged to the 'settle.'

'Now, my dear Pierce,' said his aunt, when the cries and 'ah, do's' and 'ah, don't's' of the sisters had subsided, 'will you listen to reason?'

'No!' roared Pierce with the voice of a Stentor.

'Ah, do, Aunt Kitty, let him alone for a minute or two,' whispered little Mary; 'it's no use now, and he foaming mad alive with the passion; let him come to a bit; or put,' she added judiciously, 'an ould crock or something in his way for him to break: that always *softens* his temper.'

Now though Aunt Kitty knew that little Mary was right in both cases, she loved her 'crocks' too well to attend to the second admonition. She could not help thinking, very truly, what an immensity of harm is done by the *gaggish* and mean kind of wit which springs from falsehood: like the weeds growing upon rank and unwholesome soil, their fruit is poison; the innocent and playful mirth sparkling in the sunbeams of a warm imagination, and both giving and receiving pleasure, is healthful and inspiring; but in Ireland, all classes are more or less cursed with the spirit of exaggeration, that, to my sober senses, is nothing more nor less than unredeemable falsehood: there are several persons of my acquaintance who have many good qualities, but I cannot respect them; they are perpetually lying. If they have walked a mile, they will tell you they have walked six; and if there is a crowd, it is magnified into thousands, like poor Pierce's people on the race-course. You must be, like Michael Cassio, 'a good arithmetician' to *deduct* the item of truth from the million of falsehood. If you believe them, they are rude enough to laugh at you; and if you do *not* believe them, they are inclined to quarrel with you. Although I have in this instance made exaggeration a *peasant*-failing, I think the middle class are the most addicted to the vice of what I must call by its own vulgar name, 'humbugging'—saying what is not true, that they may have the pleasure of laughing at those who do *them* the injustice to believe they have spoken *truth*.

In England we have no understanding for this spurious wit. No country cherishes truth as it deserves to be cherished; it is a blessed and a holy thing, but we do not in England *profess* to put truth to the blush. 'He's a fine gentleman,' said a cousin of Pierce Scanlan's to me, when speaking of his landlord—'he's a fine gentleman; the *very light of his eyes is truth*.'

To those unaccustomed to the contradictions of the Irish character, it is extraordinary, that in a neighbourhood where eight or nine young men live, all known to belong to the *humbugging* class, any should be found weak or foolish enough to credit a word they say; and yet those very 'boys' will go on telling falsehoods of each other, at which they will laugh one moment, and about which (as in Pierce Scanlan's case) they will quarrel the next. It is very painful to associate with those who never reflect that they sacrifice the moral dignity of manhood when they desecrate the temple of truth.

Pierce Scanlan's imagination was very vivid, and he loved a laugh; he had given himself the habit of speaking without consideration; and as the jollity of the many stifled the annoyances and pains of the few, he had gone on until even those who confessed 'he meant no harm' became annoyed at his practical jokes. Eliza Byrne had loved him, but not as well as he loved her; and the match was effectually broken off, at least for a time, by her brother, who declared, after what Pierce had said of Lucy, his sister should have nothing to say to him.

Now Pierce had said this *for a stretch*, a sort of desire to *cut a dash*, by showing that he had two strings to his bow; but Eliza's feelings were wounded, and though she had known that Pierce was a '*stretcher*,' she did not seem to care for the fault, until it *reached herself*. This is the way in general—we laugh at the jest until it cuts home!

But to return to the cottage.

Pierce, although not wrought up to the pitch of being able to reason, was brought about by his sisters to *think*, though but little time was given either for that or any other consideration; for the Brady faction had mustered strong, and, stimulated by strong drink, entered the farmhouse, to the terror of his sisters, and almost the death of his aunt; and taking the law, as they are too fond of doing, in their own hands, beat the unfortunate Pierce in a way that rendered him dumb for a long time on the subject of whatever debts the Bradys might have contracted. He had only done it *for a stretch;* but what of that?—it had come home to the Bradys; and although, one and all, they were rather sorry the next day for 'being so hard on Pierce, pleasant boy!' still that was but a poor salvo for his aching bones and insulted pride.

Aunt Kitty undertook to talk over old Jem Graves, and Mary accompanied her aunt to prevent her 'giving him too much English.' I really think that Mary's bright eyes had more to do with the withdrawal of 'Torney Driscoll's instructions touching '*the bit of a stretch*' which the honest old man imagined affected his daughter's fame, than all Aunt Kitty's reasons. Pierce made him an earnest and ample apology, and thus prevented further trouble on that score. The councillor had taken umbrage at the license Pierce had given to his imagination when speaking of 'the colt.' Words wound more deeply than swords; and long after the desire for fun had prompted the folly, the councillor remembered the foolish 'jest' which Pierce had indulged in at the expense of him and his 'colt,' and refused Pierce a new lease of a couple of acres which he had much desired to retain, and which his father and grandfather had tilled. Aunt Kitty never could understand why it was that the Brady faction took the law into their own hands, and thrashed her nephew; nor how it was that, they having so done, her nephew did not take the law of them; but this want of comprehension was set down by her Irish neighbours to the score of English stupidity. The various rumours the disturbances gave rise to spread all over the country, and far and near, Pierce was always reminded of his fault by, 'Well, Pierce, what's the last? —have you got a new *stretcher?*' Pierce must have carried his art of exaggeration to great perfection, to have attained such note in a country where the practice is so largely indulged in; but circumstances had given him peculiar celebrity, and his aunt had so far succeeded in making him 'listen to reason,' as to convince *his* reason that the practice was wrong. The painful part of the matter was, that when he really and truly spoke truth, no one would believe him.

Eliza Byrne more than once was on the point of relenting; but though Pierce swore over and over again that he was an altered man, every exaggeration in the parish was fathered upon him, and poor Eliza did not know what to do for the best. Her brother is certainly Pierce's enemy in the matter, and but for him, I really think they would have been married. I wish it was a match, for Pierce Scanlan deserves a reward for fighting, as he has lately done, against a habit, the triumph of which is '*never to be believed!*' It may yet be a match. I saw them walking together the last time I was at Artfinne—Eliza listening, and Pierce, with very little exaggeration either in his look or manner, making love earnestly yet soberly; the worst symptom I perceived was, that Eliza Byrne shook her head frequently.

'Well, Pierce,' I said, as we passed them (they had paused for the purpose), 'I hope you are weighing your words?'

'Bedad! ma'am, I've been truer than standard weights and measures this many a day, but I get no thanks for it.'

'But you will, Pierce, in time. The priest, the minister, and Aunt Kitty, say you improve.'

'I am improved,' he said somewhat proudly, 'though Eliza wont believe it. Yet I know I'm improved.'

'Pierce, Pierce!' exclaimed Eliza with a very sly quiet smile, '*isn't that a bit of a stretch?*'

I think Eliza might venture!

'SURE IT WAS ALWAYS SO.'

THE incident I am about to relate occurred in a very picturesque but wild neighbourhood on the sea-shore—not in my own more civilised district, but where I spent a fortnight of mingled pleasure and pain, where I saw misery it was out of my power to relieve, and found the people so fond of assuring us things *were always so*, that it was no easy matter to convince them things might be better than they had been or were. The house in which we were domiciled commanded a wild and extensive sea view. Miserable and neglected cottages clung to the crumbling walls of a domain once of princely extent, and no fashionable lady ever laboured to *kill time* more zealously than the amphibious occupants of those huts. Amphibious I may well call them: the men were fishers by profession—that is, they went to sea when compelled to do so by the want of that simple food which is all they desire. They were (the younger portions of the community especially) very independent of clothing. The women—what did they do? Why, they married, and nursed children, and sat in the sun in summer, and over their turf or drift-wood fire in the winter, carried the fish their husbands caught to the farmers' houses, or the dwellings of the gentry; *made* nets, and knit stockings, although they seldom *mended* either the one or the other. The children (what healthy, ruddy-brown, handsome young things they were!) ran about and over the rocks and sands at low water, gathered the pretty conical periwinkle, or knocked the green striped limpets off the rocks, watched cunningly for the rising of the observant razor-fish, or waded through the rippling waves to catch the springing shrimps. Women and men both gathered delisk, and what they call *slewk*, or *slewkawn* (I cannot spell it, but so it sounds), here called *laver;* they were indolent as the Neapolitan lazzaroni, and quite as picturesque; very sensible of kindness, as the Irish peasant always is; superstitious, as dwellers by the mighty waters commonly are; patient and cheerful, willing to do anything in the world for 'the quality,' and as little as possible for themselves; honest as truth itself. There we were, in the midst of what in England is branded with the degrading term of '*pauper population*'—poor, half-starved, half-dressed, ragged creatures— and yet neither lock nor bolt was ever used in the house. I tried once to turn the key in the great hall-door. I shall never forget the amused countenance of the good old master of the mansion, when he found me with both hands endeavouring to accomplish my intent.

'God bless you, my dear! let it alone. I give you my honour' (his pet declaration) 'the key has never been turned in that lock since the year of the rebellion; and though we had hardly any of it here, Pat Delaney and myself *fixed it for locking*, and the fishermen heard of it, and came up, women and all, roaring and crying to know what they had ever done to make me lock my doors.'

There never was a more benevolent man than our host, but he *said* he had nothing left to give to the poor except kind words, and had grown so accustomed to their misery, that he did not seem to mind it—it was a thing of course; in truth, he had deep sorrows of his own. One evening we were sitting in the ruined window of the gray old tower that overlooked a stony bridle-road, leading from the beach to a near mountain; the old gentleman had gone to the neighbouring town to consult his attorney about some five or six lawsuits that were coming on, or hanging over, and his daughter and myself were chatting and systemising—she, alive to every plan of improvement, but lacking patience to carry them into execution, mourning over her want of means, while I proved, at all events to my own satisfaction, that more improvement can be worked out in Ireland *without* money, than in any other country in the world *with* it. Nothing can be done in England without *capital*. Every hundred you possess is a step in public estimation; but there are many ways to an Irishman's heart—*wealth* being the last, the very last thing to raise you in *his* opinion. A person of small means, gifted with good temper, *patience*, and good sense, could work miracles in Ireland—*patience* being an indispensable requisite to every planner of Irish improvement.

Well, there we sat, and presently a woman, bearing in her hand a kettle, having lost its cover and the top of its nose, and balancing a pitcher in tolerably perfect condition, followed, of course, by a numerous progeny, strolled up the hill.

'Good evening to you, Molly,' said my friend.

'God bless you, miss, and give the masther great glory over his enemies! We know he's away to the lawyer's; and, Miss Machree, if I war to send up to the big house, maybe you wouldn't have a *bitteen* of plaster to take the sting out of little Sandy's foot—a burn the craythur got last night on his shin while I was away for the water. Oh, thin, it's weary to think we've so far to go for a *dropeen* of water. Oh, wisha! wisha! I often pray God to make the salt sea fresh, and then we'd have it ready to *bile* the paytees in at our own door. My husband says it's a sin for me to be going that way against *nature*, " for," says he (he's a knowledgeable man) " Molly," says he, " you ould fool, if the sea was *fresh* water, what would we do in the Lent for *salt* herrings!" Anyway, my heart's broke these *ten* years, *ever since I cum to the place*, for want of fresh water.'

Having been assured that Sandy should have a plaster, Molly went toiling and grumbling up the hill; and I learned for the first time that the want of 'fresh water' was a serious inconvenience to the fishers' village, as they had more than a mile to go for it.

Presently up came a party of young girls, laughing so that their white teeth glittered like pearl, balancing their pitchers on their heads with inimitable ease, while their bare feet passed over the stones without apparent annoyance; and their carriage, so free and graceful, as they placed their hands on the water-vessels, and dropt their curtsey beneath our window, would have made the fortune of a *danseuse*.

'Margaret,' said my friend, 'where's Norah?'

'Is it Norah, miss? She had a misfortune, miss, with Katty Magg's can. The sharp rock at the edge of the stream above there knocked the side out of it, and she's hiding for fear of Katty Magg; and sure that same stone has destroyed everything, sticking up so sharp at the most convenient place to draw the water.'

'Is it a big stone?'

'No, ma'am, but cruel sharp.'

'Why isn't it removed?'

'Oh, ma'am, *sure it was always so;* we must mind better, or there wont be a pitcher in the townland left alive with it!' And away tripped the maidens.

Many others, women, girls, and children, followed, all complaining of the want of water, all complaining of the distance, and all murmuring that they had nothing 'fit' to bring home 'a sup' of water in, which was perfectly true. Old women and thirsty men followed after a time, some pausing to lean against the gray stones that formed the *ditches*, others ascending the hill half way, and then lying down on the road, to await the water-carriers' return; and they, too, bewailed the want of water.

'It's the ruin of the women and girls this going to the hill-spring, miss,' said a crabbed-looking old sailor to my companion. 'I can't get my Nelly to mend a net, or put a hand to the boat, for going for water, and half the time spent in gossiping. I'm sure I wish some one would see if there's any truth in what ould Grizzle Burn used to say, of a well her mother drew water from, where the white thorn hangs over the cliff. To be sure the tree in my memory *was always so.*'

'And is it possible,' I exclaimed, 'that there is the remotest chance of your obtaining water so near home, and yet you have never sought it?'

'*It was always so,*' repeated the crabbed old sailor; '*my* mother— God be good to her!—*broke her leg and went a cripple to her grave,* through the manes of the sharp stone at the hill-spring's side; bad luck to it for a stone! *It was always so.*'

The very stone, I suppose, that completed the ruin of Katty Magg's can!

My friend was not a bit too well pleased that I had received another hint as to the injurious effects of 'we'll see about it;' the gentry are very apt to take offence if you notice an Irish fault; I am constantly obliged to remind them that

'I, too, am of Arcadia,'

and have an undoubted right to find fault with my own. God help them! if they all loved the land with the affection I bear to every blade of its green grass, it would have a more peaceable and prosperous peasantry. Why have they not found out that an Irishman must be actively employed, to be either peaceable or happy! But to my story. Those who arrived first from the hill-spring had to return there again, for the thirsty waiters drank the water, with the certainty that it was cheerfully bestowed.

'Take another drink, Andy, poor man!' said one of the slight girls to the crabbed sailor. 'Wisha! I wish it was potteen, or whisky itself, for your sake, if I have to go back every step of the way for more. God refresh you with it, and don't be cross to the wife, Andy! She has an *impression** about her heart with the weakness, and I tould her not to hurry. I'll put the paytees down for you before she comes, if you like, for shrimping's hungry work.'

'Granny, I brought your share and my own this time,' exclaimed another, addressing an old woman, 'and didn't feel it much; only I think I'll bring yours in the morning, and our own in the evening.'

'Let us go,' said my friend.

I paused to look one moment at the beautiful sunset, which steeped the roofs of the fishers' huts as they lay crouching and crowded together—in molten gold; beyond lay the sea, as I have shown in Burnt Eagle's history, a liquid, rolling, living mine of

---

* Oppression.

wealth, and yet those poor creatures could hardly subsist; there was no one to teach *them* how to husband the treasures the mighty deep almost cast upon the shore; they possessed heart and feeling, the drink of water was given with a good will, that to *my fancy* converted it to nectar, and that girl had managed the crabbed sailor so well, that he positively smiled upon his wife, and offered to take her pitcher; and yet those *feeling* creatures could go day after day, year after year, to the hill-spring, and never take the trouble to discover if really the gushing waters of a well were buried beneath the thorn-tree.

Which is most necessary, I inquired of myself, to the welldoing of a community—reason or feeling? It cannot prosper without the exercise of both.

'It is the worst case,' I said aloud at last. 'This "*it was always so*" is decidedly the worst case I have met with in Ireland. Why did not your father excavate this well?'

'Oh, my father has something else to think about—"*it was always so.*"'

I could not help smiling at my friend's unconscious repetition of the to me obnoxious sentence, and sighed when I thought how much the character indicated by these four little words ran through the country.

I slept, and dreamed of bright bubbling springs, and awoke before sunrise. I looked out of the window, and saw two crows; everybody in the world knows it is lucky to see two crows, *particularly before* sunrise; indeed those who have a great deal to do will find it 'lucky' to see anything *before* sunrise, either a single crow or a single magpie; but having seen *two* crows, I felt bound, as an Irishwoman, to be exceedingly rejoiced at the good omen, and therefore summoned the only allies I could depend on, my own maid, and an old man, who, according to his own account, knew and respected 'my people' before I was born. Having succeeded in rousing them from their slumbers, we proceeded to the old thorn-tree, but unfortunately there was only one fisherman on the beach, and my inquiries touching the well were not likely to be very successful.

'Did you never hear there was a well near that tree?'

'A well, is it?'

'Yes, a well.'

'Oh, sure they fetch every sup of water from the hill-spring.'

'I know they do; but there is a well, or there was a well somewhere hereabouts.'

'Myself don't know.'

'Did you never hear that there was a well long ago under that thorn-tree?'

'Myself has no call to the tree; it's on Nancy Cahill's ground, and nobody meddles with Nance; the tree "*was always so.*"'

I was not pushed from my purpose by this hint of Nancy's quarrelsome propensities. There were a number of cottage gardens, or what should have been gardens, grown into one, for the divisions were not even perceptible, and the thorn-tree grew, or hung, at the bottom of the one that appertained to Nancy Cahill. My ally could give me no information; 'sure my honour knew he came from another country.' At last we discovered a very old white-headed man asleep on some lobster pots in an almost bottomless boat; the lobster pots ought to have been set over the night, but the old man and his son had a very successful 'haul' two nights before; and why they should be at the trouble to set and haul the pots, except when they wanted, did not enter into their calculations. However, he half arose and set me at rest as to the spot; close to the left of the thorn-tree the well had certainly existed—at least so his Aunt Biddy had said.

'Did no one ever endeavour to open the well?'

'Bedad I don't know; *it had no luck.*'

'How no luck?—was the water bad?'

'Is it the water? Bedad I don't know, I never heard tell; but I believe the stones or something gave way, and thin the water was choked. "*Sure it was always so;*" they fetch all the water from the hill-spring; many a good tide I've lost, waiting for the women to fetch it.'

'We are going to try and find the well.'

'A yarra wisha! Sure it's a long way down, and on Nancy Cahill's field.'

'Will you come and help us to try?—we will provide you a pick-axe.'

'Oh, God bless your honour, I was never used to that sort of work; I'm a fisherman!' and he laid himself down with an air of such lazy determination, that I saw nothing more could be done with him. The sun had risen before *my* old man James got to work, and the brightness of the grass over the spot the fisherman had pointed out, would have convinced any one in the habit of watching the indications of nature that water was at no very great distance beneath.

I must say WE worked very hard, and the signs and ejaculations of my English maid were not the least amusing part of the exhibition. We soon found the clay clammy, then positively wet; anon, and little unwashed, undressed children came running forth, to look and wonder. Presently Nancy herself, with drapery floating on the fresh sea-breeze, made her way over a heap of mingled shells of oyster, periwinkle, limpet, and all the shells of the sea, and then through a stagnant pool, of anything but sweet savour, and stood before me with a very sour expression of countenance.

'Well, Mrs Cahill, what will you give me for finding a well on your estate?'

'Plase yer honour, I never *get* anything; how can I give?'

'Don't say that; you'll have fresh water to give to all your neighbours.'

'Oh, sure I knew it was in it.'

'And why did you not get it out of it? How old are you, Mrs Cahill?' This was an unfortunate question; I ought to have known better than to have asked it; her lowering brow soon showed me my mistake. 'Well, you are five-and-thirty, I suppose?' Mrs Cahill smiled. She was certainly fifty; so upon thirty and the odd five being named, she smiled, satisfied that I intended no discourtesy.

'How old were you when you began to draw water at the hill-spring?'

'Oh, yarra! maybe five, not more.'

'And since then you have spent two hours every day drawing water?'

'Is it two hours? Yarra wisha! nearer upon three, or maybe four, of a time I'd have a bit of washing or cleaning to do. Not often'——

'Well, say two; two hours a day are fourteen hours a week; that is 56 hours a month, 168 hours a quarter, 672 hours a year! See all the time you have wasted—no fewer than 840 days in the course of thirty years!'

'See that now!' she exclaimed with an air of provoking wonder, which, if she had not been an Irish woman, I should have called stupid.

'Two hours a day, properly managed, goes a long way towards making a house comfortable.'

'Anan!' exclaimed Mrs Cahill, sitting down upon her heels to watch our progress. When seated, as she would call it, comfortably, she said, 'Ye're kindly welcome, my lady, to *divart yerself* as long as ye plase at the well, since it's a well ye'll have it; but take care of the *ould tree*. My great-grandfather planted it, I've heard tell, *for a shelter to the well*, and I'd be sorry it was hurt, out of respect to his memory!' Now, was it not provoking that this woman knew of the existence of that well, had its tradition from her great-grandfather, and yet had spent so many of the best hours of her life going to the hill-spring? I liked her, however, for reverencing the *old tree*. In a little time the whole population of the village turned out to watch our operations; old James plied his axe and shovel right well; the English girl plucked away the roots, and flung aside the stones; young and old men, young and old women, looked on—some listlessly, some with anxiety; *none* offered to assist. 'Come, will you not help?' I said at last.

'Yes, my lady, only we must go now to the hill-spring, or the fathers 'ill have no paytees in time for breakfast. God send you good luck, my lady!'——and three or four girls went off.

'But you—you, young man—poor James is tired; take the pick or the spade; it is for the comfort of you and yours *we* are thinking and working.'

'God save ye, my lady, ye have a tender heart, and we'll go from this to Jericho to sarve *you;* but in regard of labouring work, I was never used to it, ma'am. I'm a fisherman, my lady.'

'And do you think *I'm used* to it?' said the maid petulantly.

'Oh no, bedad!' was the reply. 'We never thought you war used to any useful thing. Why, it's a pity you should trouble yerself, miss!'

'To think,' she muttered, 'that they will not help themselves.'

'*We* must teach them *patiently*.'

Still, it was very provoking to see them lounging and loitering about. At last the water began to ooze forth.

'See that now!' exclaimed Nancy. 'Who'd ha' thought it, and it all so covered up!'

'*Sure it was always so,*' observed another. 'In rainy times the water would shine through the grass; only, Mrs Cahill, ma'am, as the well was on your land, it wasn't our *business* to look to it.'

'That's thrue for ye,' said the crabbed-faced sailor; 'sure I know myself it's not pace and quietness meddling with Nancy Cahill.'

'What's that you say, you'—— And Nancy seized a stone, which she would certainly have hurled at the last speaker, but that her arm was held down, while all exclaimed, 'Oh, Nancy, for shame!—before the quality! Oh, Nancy!'

'Look,' said the termagant, rising, and standing with her arms akimbo, 'I'm a quiet woman, and a God-fearing, peace-loving woman; but by all the books that ever war shut and opened, if ye don't every one, barring the lady and her helps, quit my bit o' land, see if I don't'—— I never shall forget the fierce expression of her countenance, as men, women, and children withdrew, muttering, '*Sure it was always so,*' and left her in undisturbed possession of her estate.

'It's only a bit of a breeze,' muttered James; 'when it blows over, there's worse hearted women in the world than Nancy Cahill.' She watched progress for another hour.

'There's water, sure enough, and I suppose *it was always so;* but look at the throuble yer honour has had, and not sure that the earth wont fall in again as it did before; think of that now!'

'The earth will certainly fall in again, if it is not prevented,' I replied; 'but I hope you are convinced that if a thousandth part of the time and labour had been spent in excavating the well that was expended in fetching water from the hill-spring, the well would have been useful to this day.'

'That's thrue,' said Nancy.

The sun was high and fervent, so I went to my home for the

time being, proud of my achievement, and amused at the observations of my English servant.

'I never saw such people, spending an hour upon what could be done in a minute; I wonder will they do anything to the well while we are away—it would not be believed in England.'

'And there really is a well?' said my friend. 'I have heard so; but I remember papa saying it must all be a story, because, if it was not, surely they would have found it out. There is some legend, too, about it, at least I think so; I almost forget what it is—something about the first person who pulled the grass up over its mouth dying before morning.'

'Surely,' I replied, laughing, 'not if they saw *two* crows the first thing after sunrise.'

'There was, there is, such a legend,' she repeated. 'I suppose they would not like to tell it you, lest you should laugh at them; but I really think the superstition had a great deal to do in the way of strengthening the "it was *always* so" that you complain of.'

We agreed to go down in the evening, and see if any of the people had continued what was so pleasantly commenced.

When the evening came, we rambled there: it was a fine night. From some particular cause, the arrival, I believe, of visitors in the neighbourhood, there was a demand for fish, and the men had set forth in their cobles, but there were many women and children round the well. I was in great hopes that they had triumphed over their evil habit; I forgot, for a moment, that the habits of years are not often overcome in a few hours. One point was achieved: they were convinced of the existence of water, for they had turned down saucers, little dishes, or whatever utensils of the kind they could collect, over the plashy soil, and were dipping up the water so collected, and filling their kettles as fast as they could. Nancy was in capital humour: if the well really turned out to be a well, she had become a person of importance; but I thought she looked rather sadly at me.

'I ax yer honour's pardon,' she said, as, after talking and advising, we were going away; 'but, lady dear, which of *yez* was it *pulled up the first grass?*'

'I did, Mrs Cahill. Why do you ask?'

'Just out o' curiosity, my lady—a way I have.' She crossed her hands over her bosom, and added in a solemn tone, 'God mark ye to grace!'

This question and observation confirmed me in the belief I had gathered from the kind and anxious looks they bent upon me, that the foolish superstition had in a great degree cramped their exertions, and that a fear, peculiarly Irish, of being laughed at, prevented their telling me the fact.

I did not rise so early the next morning; and when coming down stairs, I saw Nancy's head thrust in through the hall door,

'SURE IT WAS ALWAYS SO.'

which had a great dislike to close, partly perhaps from a feeling of hospitality, which even Irish hall doors seem to participate in, and partly from a certain awkwardness about the hinges, which, owing to their advanced age, were unwilling to move rapidly, if at all.

'Well, Nancy,' I said, 'I hope the well gave you plenty of fresh water this morning?'

'Y'a, then, it's myself is glad to see yer face so cheerful-like this morning, lady dear—thanks be to the Almighty for his marcy. Amen!' And once more she crossed her hands over her bosom.

'And pray, Nancy, why should my face not be cheerful?' I inquired.

'Yarra! it's myself doesn't know, so I don't; only the gentry sometimes do be putting long faces on themselves for nothing. And are ye *brave and hearty** this morning, plase yer honour?'

'That I am, Nancy, thank you—never was better. I am always better in Ireland than anywhere else in the world.'

'Why, thin, my lady,' answered Nancy quaintly enough, 'if that's the way, *it's a pity* ye should ever lave it. Myself thinks there's some *charrum*† about ye; but maybe, my lady, like the rest of the English *furriners*, you don't believe in the *charrums*.'

'Oh yes, Nancy, I believe in a great many charms.' Nancy advanced fairly into the hall, and throwing her gray hair back from her eyes with both hands, looked steadily in my face, exclaiming, 'See that now!' 'Yes, Nancy, there is a great charm in the kindness and good-nature of my poor Irish friends.'

Nancy looked disappointed, and yet pleased.

'There is a great charm in industry, a great charm in patience, a great charm in perseverance. If we had not persevered with the well, you would have been journeying to the hill-spring to the end of your days, but I will see *that* trouble prevented before I leave you. And, Nancy, if you will find me a four-leaved shamrock, I will promise faithfully to exert all my powers of belief in *its* charms.'

'God bless you, my lady; sure I never had the luck of finding sich a thing as that! I wish I had. Oh my! but I'm glad to see you well, ma'am; and *sure we'll have heart now to go on with the well ourselves*, and God's blessing on ye!'

'And why had you *not heart* to go on with it before?'

'Oh, ma'am, there's no good in telling you; maybe you'd *be putting it in a book*.'

'Perhaps I might, Nancy.'

'Ah, my lady, I and my people *always kept out of disgrace*.'

'Well, but, Nancy, sure they put St Patrick in a book, and kings and queens, and they never consider it a disgrace. When

* Very well. † Spell.

there's nothing wrong done, what harm can there be in telling it?'

'Wisha, that's thrue; Morgan Regan has the Life of St Patrick.'

'Well, and there is nothing disgraceful to the saint in it.'

'Wisha, no! that's thrue!'

'Well, then, do you not see, what possible harm could there be in putting the well in a book?'

Nancy paused; and then, as if a sudden idea had struck her, she exclaimed, 'Maybe, as I know *the rights** of it myself, I may as well tell you, for others will. Ye see, ma'am, long ever ago, before I was born, and my mother nothing but a dawshy slip of a girl running about the rocks, like our own *childre*, one of the fisher boys picked a very swarthy-coloured child off a wreck, and by the same token the mast of the vessel was to be seen at low water, off Greystone Point, for many a long sunny summer day, and many a bitter short winter one. Well, the very night Michael Grime (that was the boy's name) brought the child to the shore, the very same night the well *fell in!*'

'But it might have done so if the poor dark child had *not* been saved. I daresay it had been in a bad state.'

'*Sure it was always so* in the memory of man; and what would ail it to *keep so*, as it had done for scores of years?'

'My good Nancy, is not that tower more likely to tumble down now than when it was built?'

Nancy was, however, too cunning to be trapped. She saw the analogy at a glance, and would not give in.

'Myself doesn't understand them things, but the well fell in anyway,' she said, with a twist of her shoulders, adding, 'and the people said it wasn't for luck.'

'That I believe. How can anything be considered for luck that does harm?'

'Ay, indeed. Well, the swarthy child—it was a girl—delighted in sitting by where the well fell in, in the hot sun, or under the bames of the ould pale-faced moon—it was all one—picking up bits of grass or stones, and throwing them among the plashing wather that hissed up out of the ground; and the roll of her great black eyes wasn't pleasant—and'——

I interrupted the narration by the question of 'How did she live?'

'Is it how did she live? Oh, thin, I suppose up and down just with the neighbours; only, to be sure, the best bit and sup was saved for *her who had no one to look to her*—God help us! Well, ma'am, the people observed, as I heard tell, that the well filled up wonderful; and at morning dawn and rising moon the swarthy child

* The truth.

was there—nor would she suffer any to meddle with her or her doings—only sit and sing her *song like the sighing of a breaking heart*, and would stay whispering about the houses even in the people's sleep. Nothing would she do but gather stones and grass to put in the well, and sing.'

'Do you remember hearing what were the words she sang?'

'Yarra, no; not all out. She sang with a *furrin* tongue. Only this much I do mind hearing; a *wise woman* intarparted part of it, and the sense was this, that she would die on the grass planted by herself over the well, *and leave her curse to the first hand that* pulled the grass she sowed, and the *curse she left was full and heavy—that the hand that did pull it might be cowld before morning.*'

I smiled, and held out my hand to Nancy; and with the feeling of an Irishwoman, no matter how rude or untutored, she pressed it to her lips.

'It isn't *cowld*, God be praised,' she said, 'but it's not *as warm as yer heart.*' I am free to confess that the pretty compliment softened the expression of Nancy's features wonderfully in my opinion.

'And what became of the girl?' I inquired.

'She pined, and pined, and pined, as a bird might that left too soon its mother's nest; and at last I heard tell she grew a shadow, and used to wrap the ould red shawl round her head, and her eyes would glare out from it like bonfires of a St John's night— and at last she was found dead by the well!'

'Poor thing! And you never heard who she was?'

'Yarra, no! how should we? Some said one thing, some another. Many thought she was something of a mermaid, others—— But anyhow, there was no doubt of her being'——

'What, Nancy?'

'*Something not right,*' answered Nancy, turning away.

'Stay, Nancy; is it possible that this circumstance gave rise to the superstition which prevented your opening the well?'

'Shooperstition!' repeated Nancy, greatly offended. 'Yarra, ma'am! how can you call it shooperstition? Didn't my grandmother know the well to fall in.'

'Granted.'

'And the swarthy craythur, whatever she was, to leave her skin and bones over it?'

'Granted.'

'And her curse, that the first hand that removed the grass might be cowild before morning?'

'Granted.'

'Sure, then, that's not *shooperstition;* it's real truth.'

'My hand is not cold, and I pulled away finely at the grass.'

'God save us! sure ye did!'

'Believe me, the Almighty loves his creatures too well to permit the foolish words of sinful people to act against those who love and trust Him.'

'Maybe so,' said Nancy; '*but was it always so?*'

'Indeed it was. When you are in a passion, you wish a great deal of harm to your neighbours, and yet it does not come to pass.'

'God forbid!' she exclaimed, crossing herself.

'Amen to that, good Nancy; and now, as I hope you are satisfied that *I am* alive and well this morning, go down to your house, stir up those lazy men and boys; you *know*, Nancy, they *will* work if you order them! And bring me a pitcher of well water for my dinner.'

'Yarra, ma'am, clear water is very cowld in the stomach.'

'Now, Nancy, don't begin to undervalue the water the moment you have obtained it; but I will promise you all something stronger if you work hard. Good porter!'

We never suffered 'it will do' to rest until we had achieved *it is done!* And the well *was* done, a comfort bestowed, and a superstition overcome, at a very small expense of time and trouble. Nancy to this day is quite lady patroness of the well, and, like all lady patronesses, a trifle capricious and tyrannical at times; but the pure fresh water is there with its thousand blessings, and the 'neighbours' are practically convinced that even if a thing has been '*always so*,' there is no reason it should continue to be 'ALWAYS SO.'

'IT'S ONLY THE BIT AND THE SUP.'

A FRIEND who resides in the neighbourhood of Dublin related to me the following anecdote:—A man had lived with him for some years, a man of the name of Laurence Cassidy, who was exceedingly fond of doing as little as he could, and taking as much time as possible about that little.

'Larry,' said our friend to him one morning—'Larry, you cost me a great deal of money during the year; and you are not worth the third part of what you cost.'

'The Lord save us!' ejaculated Larry, casting up his eyes, 'what has put the likes of that into yer honour's head?'

'Your laziness, Larry.'

'Oh, my law! and I working myself to an oil every day and night of my life; and to say that to me! Well, I did not expect it from yer honour; but, in regard of the *cost*, yer honour, I wonder ye'd be throwing *that* in my face; I'm sure the thrifle I gets isn't worth the thinking of such a gentleman as yer honour.'

'Trifle!' repeated Mr H——; 'you may consider thirty pounds a year a trifle, if you please; but I do not so consider it, I assure you.'

'Bedad, sir, I believe you; I don't know who would; but sure all I ever got from yer honour, night or day, fresh or fasting, was a bare ten pounds—a year, I mane.'

'Ay, wages; but you cost me *more* than thirty pounds a year for all that.'

'Ya, then! sure it isn't the thrifle of ould clothes you throw to your fosterers that ye're rising against *me*, sir, is it!'

'Not at all: what I give, I give; I should be ashamed of myself to calculate the old clothes.'

'See that now! Why, thin, your honour's great in the rule of addition anyway. Will ye be plased to insense us into it?'

'Ten pounds a year wages,' said my friend.

'Well, your honour, I own to that.'

'Twenty pounds, at the very least, your board.'

Laurence opened his large eyes very wide, and looking steadfastly at his master, exclaimed, ' Boord twenty pounds ! Twenty pounds for the aiting and the drinking! Oh, *yarra machree!* whin a gintleman thinks of the *bit and the sup*, and it *only the bit and the sup!* it's all up with us! Oh, my grief! *is it the bit and the sup?* Well, afther that! that bates Bannaghar! the masther counting out the *bit and the sup!*'

Nothing could exceed Larry Cassidy's astonishment and horror that Mr H—— should *demean* himself to think of the *eating and the drinking*, '*the bit and the sup.*' 'And it is always so,' he said. Larry's case is by no means uncommon; they cannot comprehend the possibility of what they eat and drink being an expense. I have never found them able or willing to understand it.

I confess that my reason and my feelings have been always at war with each other on this very subject; it is impossible not to admire the frank and hearty welcome, given with the fresh warmth of Irish hospitality, the *caith mille a faultha*, that breathes from every lip, and sparkles in every eye. A sincere welcome to the stranger is always one of the dear and sweet remembrances we bring from Ireland, but it has a bitter alloy when we remember that the hospitality exercised towards us, and towards others, is, strictly speaking, evidence of wrong thinking. If a man has a shilling, and owes a shilling, there can be no question as to the fact that he has no RIGHT to spend that shilling, save in the discharge of his debt; and yet I know persons who have been hospitably entertained, drank claret, and rode hunters, in houses where the dispenser of hospitality should have eaten his humble fare in solitude, though not in sorrow, and paid his debts. This class of persons cannot, in their career of reckless extravagance, lay the flattering unction to their souls that they hope to mend their circumstances either by industry or exertion. They do, indeed, exist in the hope that somebody may die, and leave them—one knows not how much; or they may have had promises of places under government; upon such promises I have known dozens of young men fish and shoot, and lounge away the best hours of lives which, in industrious England, would have been laden like bees with the honey of wealth. But the principle of this is so deceptive, so bad, so destructive to high and low, that I am tempted to write in stronger terms upon it than many will like—I cannot help it. I confess, while exposing what I may not but stigmatise as *dishonest* hospitality, that there is a decided difference in the *manner* of display between the two countries; *here*, when the love of display beyond its means takes possession of a family, it invariably affects the possession of *great* riches: this is lowering the moral standard of excellence in a piteous degree; an Englishman cannot bear it to be supposed there is anything which he cannot afford. The Irishman laughs at his poverty; scorns it; he is a man of family, he has something better than wealth to be proud of. He will rejoice with his friends amid the ruins of his house— ruins which the too lavish gift of the '*bit and the sup*' has occasioned.

The English love of display is *dishonest*, if the tradesman suffer by it. The Irish hospitality is *dishonest*, if the host cannot pay his debts. There is one great difference between them—the Irish give with *both* hands; the English with *one*.

'Sure the welcome is all we have to give,' said a peasant to me. 'Sure it's only a potato, a lock of straw, and a seat by the sod of turf,' said another. 'Sure it's only my time,' exclaims a third; 'and, lady dear, don't be talking to us as ye would to the quality. Sure they're in debt in many parts of the country, and have the lashings of eating, and drinking, and company intirely; it's them yer honour ought to talk to.' These last words were addressed to me by Mary Flanagan, who, with a family of five children, a blind grandmother, and a lame husband, had done her and hers the injustice of bringing in a piper, his wife and child, during a cold long winter's month, and giving them share of what they had; but the piper and his wife would be always in want, because they had acquired idle and extravagant habits, knew they were certain of support from the cottagers, and spent their money upon whisky. 'I am glad to find you so rich, Mary, as to be able to keep your friends as well as your family.' 'Rich! oh, bedad! yer honour's always laughing at us.' 'Why, if you were not rich, you could not support Jim Lacy, his dirty wife, and lazy boy.' 'Lord! yer honour, do you call *that* supporting, just the bare *bit and the sup!*' 'Have you anything besides for yourselves?'

'Augh, no; sure in decency we'd give the best bit we had to the stranger.' 'They have been with you just a month; and now remember that you have spent on them what would keep your husband, mother, and child a month; so that if, at the end of the *year*, you come asking for a month's potatoes, or a month's milk, I shall put you in mind that you reduced yourself to the disgrace of begging, and just tell you of Jim, his wife, and son. We have no right to give what God has given us to hold in charge for *others;* to deny *ourselves* is right and righteous, but we are not given the goods of others, be it a potato or be it a pound, to bestow on whom we will.' I pursued my argument still farther with Mary. 'If you wanted to support the piper and his wife, Mary, you should have made them live upon the half of your own potato dinner, and not have given what was hardly sufficient for your family during the year; the consequence will be, that we shall have not only you, but the piper and his family wanting potatoes by and by.'

'Sure the craythurs could not live on the half of my potatoes.'

'But, Mary, with the prospect of your little ones starving before the expiration of the year, you *had no right* to give away.'

'Oh,' says Mary, 'who knows what may turn up before the end of the year?—sure it was *only the bit and the sup.*' Nothing, however, *did* turn up before the end of the year, except starvation, and Mary was obliged to ask, as we anticipated, both potatoes and milk. What made it more provoking was, that the money the piper and his wife, and even their boy, had spent in whisky, would have insured them more comfortable fare than poor Mary Flanagan could bestow.

Floyd of Castle Floyd—I mean the last of his house, who died in C—— jail about twelve years ago—inherited what had been a fine property, and was still a good one. He was a cheerful, generous, warm-hearted fellow, full of good intentions, which somehow he forgot to perform. When he came of age, an old, and, by some miracle, an honest lawyer, who had been his guardian, laid before him a statement of his affairs, pointing out the course by which (selling a part of his estate) he might effectually redeem and preserve the other; this would have left him about nine hundred a year. He intended to do it. The arrangements were talked of, but not made; the advertisement for the sale of the land was absolutely written out, but not sent to the papers; when one of the hangers-on of Castle Floyd brought the young man's mind to the belief that it would be better to secure Miss Gubbins of Fort Gubbins *before* the sale, as her father might demur; and poor Frank Floyd had fallen desperately in love with Fanny Gubbins at an assize ball; and, moreover, she had (so said the county) great, very great—expectations. His mentor, the old lawyer, was ill in Dublin, and the young man thought there could be no harm done by putting off the business for a little time.

He did so—was beguiled into returning to the open-house system until, only until, after the wedding. The lady, who had

> 'Brothers and sisters by dozens,
> And all charming people they say,'

fond of profusion, and either too young or too uneducated to understand its danger, persuaded her husband to wait till somebody died, for then she was sure money enough would come to pay off incumbrances. After the wedding, open house was of course kept, for the joint honour of the houses of Floyd and Gubbins; and then, somehow, Frank's prudence evaporated, and the old lawyer died, having commenced a letter to his ward, beginning, '*Beware of the bit and the sup.*'

Never did relations so multiply—full-grown, ready-made relations; and when there were not beds enough to accommodate the visitors, why, they very good-naturedly put up with 'shakedowns,' and any shake, except the shake off. Frank had his moments of reflection, and saw this would not do; but how could he change now? After a little time, all the Floyds and all the Gubbinses were talking of the probability of there soon being an heir to Castle Floyd; and all the relations came to wish him joy of the probability of such an event. Great preparations were made for it, and at last it came, and the pretty Fanny and her still-born child occupied the same coffin. This melancholy change removed but few of the household visitors; they all felt too much for 'the poor fellow,'

> 'To leave him alone with his sorrow.'

Not having any particular faith to keep up his spirits, he took first to claret, and finding that not strong enough to quench grief, strengthened it with whisky. Hours of intense anguish succeeded to frightful fever fits. Those who really kept open house on his means, declared society was necessary to his existence, and he believed it—believe anything he would, rather than bring his follies and extravagances to the stern test of thought. The foxhunters' club always breakfasted and dined at Castle Floyd. Embarrassment was heaped on embarrassment, custodium on custodium. Everything that could be done to raise money he did—except rack-rent his tenants.

Still, the household expenditure continued unabated, until the crash came; and even then, a few were not wanting to partake of his prison fare. Many circumstances, of too elaborate a nature to be unravelled in a short story, tended to hasten this catastrophe; and the eaters and the drinkers, shaken off by the strong arm of the law from their prey, set forth to strike down another quarry. This is one of the disgraceful systems so prevalent in Ireland—so totally at war with noble exertion, with the high feeling of *self-*dependence—that, if I had a thousand voices, I would raise them all against those who would rather eat at another's board than labour to supply their own. Poor Floyd died before he had numbered two-and-thirty years, debased in mind and prostrated in body by dissipation. Two or three only of his once numerous retinue were with him at the last. 'Boys!' he said, while the hectic fever, that was soon to yield to a deathlike paleness, gave an unnatural light to his eyes, and a contraction of the throat prevented his swallowing even liquids—'boys! I never refused "*the bit and the sup*," did I?'

'Oh, never,' was the true reply.

'And yet it refuses me. Ah, ah! it refuses me;' and with this miserable attempt at jest and laughter, he turned on the other side, and died!

Mrs Dennis Shannon kept a hosier's shop in Dame Street, Dublin; but widow though she was, and having five daughters to bring up, she loved to entertain her friends. 'Sure the drawing-room was there—a beautiful room as any in the city; and the furniture—beautiful furniture; and a party was quite easy to give. She was so used to it; it was only sperm instead of mutton candles; and "*the bit and the sup*," and who'd be mane enough to grudge that, and the chance in it of getting the girls off her hands?'

'The girls,' however, did not 'get off,' but debts 'came on.' The cheapness of articles of provision is a great excuse for recklessness in that same city of Dublin; profuse housekeeping people seem to forget that if things are cheaper, incomes are smaller in proportion; the '*bit and the sup*' given in such prodigality soon rendered Mrs Dennis Shannon not only *minus* her drawing-room, but *minus* her shop; and Betty, the last of her servants, clapped her hands and exclaimed—while tradesmen remained unpaid, and 'the girls,' brought up in thoughtless extravagance, were billetted upon every Shannon that had a house—'Augh, then, more's the pity!—she never begrudged the "*bit or the sup*."' These are extreme cases, but no one acquainted with Ireland can say that such are of rare occurrence. Thoughtless and fond of amusement—fond of giving, fond of all things liberal—the silent, unobtrusive, even stream of justice is overleaped; and unfortunately, when a person above the very poorest class falls, he does not fall alone.

'I have been visiting your country,' said an English gentleman to me the other morning. 'I have spent three months at Ballyray in the most delightful manner. Capital snipe-shooting, capital trout-fishing, and lots of good things.'

I was greatly astonished, for I knew the proprietor of Ballyray owed the Englishman a sum of money which I suspected he could never *pay*.

'Indeed! Well, and did you succeed in your mission?'

'No, I cannot say I did,' he answered laughing. 'Myself, and horse, and servant, I believe all my family, could have lived board and lodging free all the time of our lives at Ballyray; but as to money, they have none to give. They are talking of levying fines; so I suppose I shall have some chance, as it is really a noble property. I could not press the matter. Besides,' he added, after a little hesitation, ' the gentleman's eldest son always calls any one out who asks for money in real earnest—that is, if the debt is considerable.'

' And if it is not considerable ?'

' Why, then, I believe *the servants drag the creditor through the lake*—the little lake, not the great one.'

God forbid that I should wish people not to help each other; it is one of the privileges of our existence to do so; but the helper should not be expected both to set the machine in motion and keep it going. We all can do something in the great and ennobling labour of independence.

I could fill volumes with the effects of the reckless generosity of those even within a limited sphere whom I have known and loved. The experience of a few years has shown me so much of the ruin of this system, or rather no system, that I have been severe as regards both my precepts and examples. I wish to be true in this matter, but unfortunately truth says even more than I have ventured to repeat.

There are many Irish persons of good sense who have argued with me, that if a rich relation *can afford* to support a poor one, he ought to do so: granted, if the *poor* relation be incapacitated, by mental or bodily indisposition, from labour; but otherwise, he does him a severe moral injury to support him without calling his energies into action. The wise man (I hate the word patron; there should be no such words as patron or pauper in an English vocabulary)—the wise man will, if he has the means, place his poor relations on the high road to independence, cheer and comfort them on their way, and give them occasionally a helping hand; *but he will not doom his own flesh and blood to the degradation of dependence.*

The person who, in a higher grade of society, distributes the 'bit and the sup' till he has not a ' bit or a sup' left for himself, wrongs those who furnish his supplies. The poor cottager must not persuade himself, that if he gives his own and his children's food to the poor traveller, he wrongs none *but his own.* Society is so constituted, that we cannot wrong *only ourselves ;* 'those who give all, give none.' When Mary Flanagan supported the piper, his wife, and child for a month, having barely enough to feed her own family until the potatoes came in, she *created beggary.* It is not for me to point out to the legislature how this system might be changed as regards the peasantry. Something will, I trust, be done, and soon ; but *I want the peasantry to help themselves.* I have seen amongst the Irish peasants instances of self-sacrifice, devoted attachment, elevated and generous affection, that would add laurels to any wreath of national glory. It is because I love them dearly that I would remove the incrustations of the diamond; I want to make them think and reason.

I said all this, and more, about three years ago, to Jenny Jeffers, who loved to hear her country praised; pretty Jenny Jeffers, who had had twenty pounds and a cottage, a little land, three acres, well stocked, left her by her Uncle Bob, who died just when I think he ought to have lived; for poor Jenny was in love with her cousin, 'Jumping Jeffers,' as he was called, of Ballinmote; and her Uncle Bob had resolved that 'Jumping Jeffers' should never have a farthing of his money. But what are a dead man's resolves against a living woman's love!

'Sorra a wildness in him that I know of, except that he'd give the last *bit and sup* he had in the world to a neighbour,' she said; 'and that was what turned my Uncle Bob against him; "for," says he, "Jenny, avourneen, he has no head." But he has a heart anyhow, my lady.'

'An Irishman's heart may be as stout as a shillala, Jenny; but, after all, it's a poor stock in trade for the wants of the world.'

'Oh, sure, I've the twenty pounds a'most to the good; to say nothing of the house and farm.'

'And your cousin?'

'Oh, sure, he has'—— Jenny paused.

'What, Jenny?'

'Himself, then, and what he stands upright in, sorra more!' said Jenny, stooping to look for a 'lucky pin' she said she had dropped.

'That's not a great deal, Jenny.'

'But sure, my lady, I have a good share of everything. Praise be to God for it.'

'Well, so you have, Jenny, an excellent commencement, and good to keep on with also; but my great objection to Jeffers is, the quantity of poor relations that besiege him—folk that are not your *blood* relations at all.'

'His mother's people,' said Jenny; 'and that's thrue for ye, my lady. He has, God help him! a round score, neither able nor willing to do a hand's turn for themselves. More's the shame and the pity! Wild, rollicking craythurs they are, getting into scrapes; but sorra more harm than that in them.'

It was of no use for me to argue with Jenny. When a woman, and an Irishwoman especially, takes it into her head to walk deliberately into love's quagmire, why, you may talk to her, and reason with her, but she will not change her mind. If she falls into a passion, you have some chance from the reaction; but if she reasons with you, as Jenny did with me, she is resolved.

'Jumping Jeffers' was married to Jenny, and the sweets of an imprudent honeymoon left their usual proportion of bitterness. A good deal of the twenty pounds was spent in distributing the *bit and the sup* to 'his mother's people;' under the generosity of such profusion, there frequently runs an under-current of *love of praise*, which stimulates persons not high-minded enough for liberality to a reckless extravagance. This was the case with Jeffers; he liked to be thought a slashing, liberal, careless fellow; and he certainly had his desire amongst his own class; his superiors considered him in a different and dangerous light. Time passed on; there was not a Sunday that the '*bit and the sup*' was not dispensed with a too liberal hand; 'the drop,' also, was too frequent and too strong; and the consequence was, that the pretty quiet cottage of poor Jenny had become occasionally the scene of midnight outrage. This was very distressing to her. She saw the little she had squandered by a thoughtless, unfeeling husband, and the property melting, as it were, away from them. She was too Irish to refuse the '*bit and the sup;*' and she was likely to be left without a home.

There is no country in the world where retrenchment is so difficult as in Ireland; they sacrifice not only their future means of giving, but their future means of living, to the desire of affording *present* enjoyment to each other. Jenny, urged by her respectable friends, tried to stem the torrent, but she ought to have avoided entering the stream.

'It's only Bill Casey and the two boys of the Ban, Jenny,' her husband would say to her remonstrance. ' You can't refuse them the "*bit and the sup*," and they come so far! Don't let us disgrace ourselves before dacent people by having nothing to give, Jenny; bring out the long bottle, *achora!* Do.'

'I cannot—I cannot; it's no use now; lave me alone; just say you haven't got it. Sure you know our last guinea's upon the go, and not a seed in the ground yet. My goodness! how can you behave so? It's no use, I tell you again! Now be quiet—we'll be ruined all out; you haven't done a hand's turn at the farm, and there'll be nothing to pay the *rint*, small as it is, the way you're going!'

This difference of opinion ended as usual; the husband had his way: and truly, when '*gale-day*'* came, there *was* nothing to pay the rent. The neighbours said how it would be; but Jeffers had still '*the bit and the sup*' to give, though Jenny went without stockings during the week, and her pleasant, cheerful voice was now seldom heard in song or laughter. The next rent day arrived, and the same story was told to a landlord who had hitherto been just and kind. Landlords are too often the contrary, but this man was poor, and could not do without his money. When

---

* Rent-day.

tenants refuse to pay rent for the advantages they enjoy, they ought to consider how utterly impossible it is for their landlords to exist without money, and remember that they themselves expect to be paid for the butter, fowls, eggs, and corn they take to market. Jeffers, however, could not pay: his wife's money had been squandered, and he had neglected their little crops for the sake of amusement; his landlord's expostulations were, in his wife's absence, returned by insolence; the landlord threatened, what the tenant dared him to perform. When Jenny entered, she found her husband half mad with whisky and rage: he had good reason to believe his landlord would distrain, and had sent for Bill Casey and his companions to prevent it. Poor Jenny, finding she could not turn her husband's purpose, and knowing how he had exasperated his landlord, resolved, in this time of peril, to appeal to the generosity of an aunt who lived at some distance, and set forth in a state of agitation better imagined than described, having first prevailed upon a female friend to remain in the house during her absence, to prevent everything in it from being destroyed. 'He'll give the "*bit and sup*" to the last,' she said, as distinctly as she could speak for tears; 'and if you don't watch, Aileen, the dresser from the wall, and the bedstead from under us, will be sould for that same.'

Poor Jenny intreated them all to be patient till her return, but she might as well have expected patience from a March whirlwind; they had been so long accustomed to lawless deeds, that they were much better pleased with the prospect of the landlord's putting his threat into execution, than with the hope of his forbearing altogether.

Jenny, poor Jenny, had a long and weary journey. She had endeavoured, before she set out, to see her landlord, but he was from home, and perhaps for the first time in her life she did not squander her time. Her aunt was old, and cross, and fractious; yet she obtained her desire, and turned towards home with an anxious heart, but many good resolves in case of her husband's persisting in his ill conduct. She had been offered a home with her aunt; but, in truth, the constant-hearted woman prayed more earnestly for his reform than for her own release. She had journeyed the greater part of the night, but when she arrived at the end of the *bohreen* that led to her cottage, although it was the very earliest morning, sounds of tumult struck upon her ear, and she flew rather than ran towards her cottage. When she came in sight of 'the bawn,' she beheld a scene of confusion too frequently witnessed in Ireland—the landlord was attempting to fulfil his threat, and had been resisted.

One violence brought on another; the police had, it would appear, seized a couple of pigs. A scuffle had ensued; her husband was struggling on the ground with two of the men; and her friend, whom she had left to keep peace and preserve order, was whirling stones from her apron upon the assailants, in a way that left no doubt of her intention.

The half-suffocated screams of her husband urged her to frenzy. Impelled by an impulse she had no time to reason with, or strength to resist, she flew to his rescue, seized a wattle that lay in her path, and succeeded in drawing off the attention of one of the men from her husband. Jeffers took immediate advantage of this rescue, and rallied with his friends, so as to be able to make a retreat, which ended in flight; but one of the bailiffs was so severely injured, that his life was despaired of. Poor Jenny and her friend were carried to the county jail, amid the tears of her acquaintances, who, but for her earnest and well-managed intreaties that they would keep the peace, and commit no second outrage, would most certainly have rescued her. The man who had been so severely beaten by Jeffers died, but his companions bore testimony to his having received the injuries which caused his death before the women interfered in the least with the fray, and certainly before Jenny's arrival at the scene of contest. The verdict returned was one of murder against Jeffers and Bill Casey. Poor Jenny endeavoured to support her friend's spirits and her own. The latter were considerably relieved by the information, secretly given, that her unfortunate husband had escaped from the country, though the bitterness of heart she experienced in the knowledge that he had left her without one love *token*, one kind message, after all she had done and suffered for his sake, was hard to bear. If it had only been 'a God be with you, agra, or a lock of his hair; and he gone for ever from the sight of my eyes; though I pray that God may pity him as I do. And he may be at this moment tossing on the wide ocean, with the fresh air of heaven about his head, and the free waters of the Almighty rolling him to a free country; while I'm here, my heart crushed in my body, between the hard walls of a jail. Och! it's hard to bear—it's hard to bear; sure I couldn't stand to see him murdering, and he my husband. I couldn't stand *that*, anyhow; and how 'ill my people ever stand the disgrace?—and all that *he*, poor fellow, gave the "*bit and the sup*" to with both hands, scattered by the law and their own devilment. Och, my grief! But keep a good heart, *avourneen; you* shan't be worse off than me, that you shan't, and the day will soon come, and be soon gone too. God tache us the right way!'

There was something in Jenny's uniform good intentions, though she had failed to carry them into action, in her fond yet foolish attachment to her worthless husband, that interested us all in her behalf; and greatly pleased were we to hear that a fine of a few pounds, with the alternative of three months' imprisonment, had been named as her punishment, for we knew she could easily contrive to raise the money. A morning or two after the termination of the assizes, we accompanied some friends to visit the jail, and to our great astonishment, there, in the female ward, was Jenny, spinning away, her black hair braided back neatly as usual, and her aspect more composed, more calm, than we had seen it for months.

'Why, Jenny, how is this? We thought you had gone to your aunt's?'

'Thank ye, madam,' she answered; 'but my people's very angry with me—very angry with me intirely; and when my time's up here, I'm thinking I'll have to go to sarvice, for indeed I shouldn't be able to go begging for the "*bit and the sup*," though many begged it from me. I might have kept it, to be sure; *but all we can do with spilt milk is to cry over it*, my lady.'

'*And not spill it again*, Jenny.'

'Bedad, ma'am,' said Jenny, smiling, 'it's great luck intirely we must have to win the chance of spilling it *twice!*'

'But, Jenny, how came you here now? Surely if you could not raise enough to pay the fine on your own place, your friends would do it for you?'

'As to my poor little place, it's altogether gone to the bad; and sure my people did raise it—God bless them!'

'And why are you here?'

'Ah, ma'am, that's a bird of fresh feathers. You see, my lady, that misfortunate morning I warned poor Ailey to take care of the dresser and the bits of things; and that drew her into the ruction, poor craythur; and sure, ever since she's been here, on my account, as a body may say, there's been no child's hand to give a drink of water to her ould mother, or look after anything in their little house; so, my lady, *I paid her ransom instead of my own.* She's gone free to her mother, God be praised! and though my aunt's mad with me, I have their blessing, and the knowledge that I did right—to *strengthen me against the trouble.*'

The noble-hearted woman deserved the strength her self-sacrifice created; and though, before our converso had finished, she bowed down her head and wept bitterly, as she said herself, over the 'spilt milk,' and, above all, at the remembrance of her husband's heartless conduct, still her tears were not those of despair, though her own folly will oblige her to trust to that charity which she squandered. If she had learnt the wise lesson of withholding judiciously she might still have had the 'BIT AND THE SUP' to share with those who really needed them.

THE FOLLOWER OF THE FAMILY.
PART THE FIRST.

MARGARET SHEIL had been born on the estate of the O'Dwyers; and the truth of the legend, which asserted that her father's grandfather or great-grandfather was killed at some famous battle defending the life of Gerald O'Dwyer, a 'great man intirely,' was never for a moment doubted either by the gentry or ' the people.' Margaret was not likely to question its authenticity, for she lived amid the wreck and remnants of the 'big house,' which had fallen into wretched decay: a sort of authorised *follower of the family*, tending the lady, a poor, weak, delicate woman, and cherishing, beyond every earthly thing, a wild, careless, thoughtless youth, the last of a race remarkable (if such a character, being Irish, could be considered remarkable some fifty years ago) for its profuseness and extravagance. The O'Dwyer family had fallen in consequence of this heedless expenditure of a pound, where prudence, with a *shilling*, could have done as much—fallen to the very depths of embarrassment and poverty; and the young man's mother, sickly in mind and body, worn out with the whirling cares and distracting anxieties which a year before had buried her husband beneath their ruins, was not able to think or act. In Ireland, if misfortune visits a portion of a respectable house, the distressed too frequently live upon the wealthy, thinking it derogatory to exert themselves; this brings down, sooner or later, the prop whereon they rested, and is, moreover, both mean and cruel. But poor Mrs O'Dwyer had no prop to lean on; her husband's family having been long before levelled in the dust, from the habits to which I have alluded. They had kept open house for years past telling. Poor O'Dwyer, her husband, died in jail; and the mercy of a creditor left the widow and her son the ruined walls of their ancestors, their only shelter against the pelting of the pitiless storm. What had been the garden to the ruined mansion, was, by the positive charity of the tenants who had passed with the land to other landlords, cultivated for her benefit; they managed to find hours or days to sow potatoes and cut turf for ' her honour,' and treated the wild, buoyant, boisterous lad, who was as free and frank in his bearing as if he were master of the soil, with the respect and attention which, they said, 'they owed the family.' It was very touching to witness the various little attentions—small in service, but rich in love—that were heaped upon the widow by the untiring hand of Irish gratitude; and no one was more devoted to her service than was Margaret Sheil. Margaret was a small, active, neat little body; fair and blue-eyed—eyes so bright and blue, that they seemed to dart into futurity; and Margaret's character was in keeping with her eyes, for she looked forward with a longheadedness very *unIrish*. She was gifted with a much greater degree of worldly knowledge than her mistress. She would even take upon herself to lecture her favourite Garrett O'Dwyer himself whenever he did anything she considered it wrong for an O'Dwyer to do. This was not often, for he appeared to her as near perfection as man could be. Garrett had attained the age of nineteen; could fight like—like an Irishman; sing—like an Irishman; dance—like an Irishman; was thoughtless—as an Irishman; generous—as an Irishman; proud—as an Irishman; poor—as an Irishman! His mother, when he was about six years old, had refused the offer of a relative to take and educate the child, partly because he was the only O'Dwyer who had ever been in trade, but more because her heart clung, as mothers' hearts will cling, to their solace, their hope, their all!

Garrett had been long engaged in both open and covert rebellion against petticoat government; wished to go abroad, to enlist, to do anything rather than remain at home; but when the scoldings and repinings of the mother failed, her tears always triumphed, and Garrett would lay down his gun and take up his flute, the only two luxuries he enjoyed.

His coat was of frieze, and his hat of straw; and yet there was not a handsomer fellow in the county; he rode admirably; the neighbouring gentry would always lend him a horse, which he was always anxious to borrow, and would have given him as many dinners as he could eat, and, in those claret days, as much claret as he could drink; but he declined dinners almost invariably.

'Misther Garrett, dear,' said Margaret to him one afternoon, 'Misther Grace has sent a gorsoon over the mountain to ask ye to dine with him to-day. Go, *avick machree;* ye're all as one as a man now, and ought to go.'

'No, Margaret, I'll not go; the food, the meat, would poison me, when I thought of my mother striving to swallow potatoes— dry potatoes—here in these ruins.'

'That's kind of ye too, Masther Garrett, dear; but, darlint, sure it's better to have the paytees dry than wet anyway. Maybe the sand will turn!'

'When it's run, all run,' replied the lad; 'but I can't stay here much longer at all rates.'

'Nor wont be needed, Masther Garrett,' said Margaret; 'I wanted to break it to you, *avick*, and didn't know how rightly. *She'll not be in it* many weeks; so don't cross her by contrariness anyhow; don't.' The truth startled the youth; he was unprepared for it; he could not speak; and Margaret Sheil turned away muttering, 'The craythur! them menkind never likes to let each other or the women see their tears.'

She had said the truth: in another week, Garrett saw, and told her he saw, the fearful change; and yet, strange to say, he absented himself for days together from the place. This greatly perplexed and astonished Margaret, who knew how much he loved his mother, and how much he had been ready to sacrifice for her; the poor lady had become almost unconscious of passing events, and yet Garrett had not returned.

Now, Margaret was in agony lest she should die without leaving her son her blessing, and despatched many messengers to seek him; but in vain. Mrs O'Dwyer had passed some hours in that state of inanity which foreruns death; the heaving of the poor worn chest, the occasional sighs, the rattle in the throat, had increased as the night closed; the wind hissed through the crevices into the chamber of death, howled its mad revels in the dilapidated hall, and rushed furiously through the passages and up the chimneys. Margaret had taken off her apron to prevent the light from being extinguished, and pinning one end of it to the bed-post, fastened the other to a chair. The priest had given her the last sacrament; and Margaret, ever and anon, when the body heaved with a convulsive movement, brought the crucifix to her lips and repeated a prayer. The neighbours, who had watched with her to near midnight, returned to their cabins, save one old woman who slept soundly in a corner on a chest. Again the lady heaved and moaned.

'Oh!' exclaimed Margaret, 'that the Lord would but send her her child. She'll never have an easy death till she sees him!'

'I am here,' whispered Garrett, stealing through the darkness; 'here I am!' The young man's face was pale and haggard; large drops stood upon his brow, his beautiful bright hair hung around his face. Margaret uttered an exclamation of surprise, and they conversed in an under tone for a moment or two; then, with strong emotion, the young man threw himself upon his mother's bed, calling to her, in the most piercing accents, to bless and forgive him. Nature was strong within him; he shed bitter and abundant tears over his dying parent.

The poor lady could not speak, but a faint smile irradiated her features for a moment; twice she smiled on him, and placed her hand upon his head: he felt her fingers rest upon his brow like icicles; he laid his cheek to hers; a breath, cold and chill, passing from her lips made him start; the fingers no longer pressed; they stiffened amid his hair.

'I knew,' said Margaret, while tears coursed each other down her cheeks—'I knew she'd never make an easy death till she saw ye.'

'Margaret, Margaret,' whispered Garrett when he could articulate, 'leave her for a few minutes with others, and come with me. Grace, and Stacey, and many of the neighbours, are watching about the ruins to be of use; I saw them as I stole past. Come with me, for God's sake, or I shall go mad!'

Garrett almost dragged Margaret Sheil from the chamber of death. *She* had stifled the cries which the poor Irish so usually send forth, and which often, in so unnatural a manner, disturb the quiet of the solemn scene where death is present; but when the watchers entered, *their* cries shook the old walls, and mingled with the howling wind.

'What call can I have to your room now!' said Margaret, as she climbed up the ruined stairs leading to a small turret chamber he called his own. 'Sure the bed has been made, and not touched for more than a week.'

Garrett made no answer, but strode to the bedside, paused, turned round, looked at Margaret, and then slowly moving down the coarse coverlet, Margaret, to her astonishment, saw a new-born sleeping infant.

'Mother of mercy!' she exclaimed, 'whose is this?'

'MINE!' was the astounding reply. 'The child is MINE!'

'Yours, Masther Garrett—yours! The Lord be about us! Sure it isn't in earnest you are!'

'God help me, and keep me my senses,' he answered; 'I am in earnest; the child is mine.'

'And its mother?'

'Again,' replied the youth, 'God help us all! Its mother and its grandmother are both corpses this woful night. Its mother —so young—so—so——Oh, Moyna, Moyna, what you suffered for me!'

Margaret Sheil stepped back from gazing with that tenderness which only women feel towards the little undefined-looking heap of infant helplessness that seemed unconscious of its own existence, and repeated, 'Moyna—what Moyna? Not Moyna of Ferry Barrett, on whom shame has lain heavy for the last three months? Oh, not that young sweet girl? Oh, Masther Garrett, if you brought Moyna of Ferry Barrett to sin, and shame, and death, the Lord had need look down on ye, for your sin is black.'

'Listen to me, Margaret,' he said sadly; 'I did *not* bring her to sin or shame—we were married by Father Myles.'

'Father Myles!' repeated Margaret contemptuously; 'Father Myles indeed!—a runaway Roman! a half friar! a *couple-beggar!* nothing more or less. Father Myles's marriage isn't worth a *traneen*, that's what it's not; and sweet and purty as Moyna was, she was no match for an O'Dwyer!'

'I knew my mother would never consent. The poor girl sent for me when her trouble came on her; and oh, Margaret, but I have suffered—the abuse of her people—the agony of hearing she must die. And when die she did, after placing the baby in my arms, her father cursed us both, and turned me—me, Garrett O'Dwyer—as a dog from his door.'

Margaret clasped her hands.

'Think what I've gone through! I shed no tear for the bright-eyed girl I loved, and who loved me by stream, and hill, and valley, ever since we met, before we knew what love was, before it had marked us to break our hearts; to see her die, and she not all out seventeen—to be hunted like a wild dog from her corpse —to come here—to catch the last breath of my mother—oh, Moyna, Moyna, I could not cry for you! my sorrow was too deep for tears to soothe it. Her father would have murdered me, but her mother saved me, when I had not power to save myself; and then I would have my child. I can't tell you how I got off; I only know that I covered it close in my bosom, that I did not heed its cries, that I brought it to you, Margaret; and that I ask you, in the name of her whose eyes you have just closed, to look to that child, to be a mother to it. The blood of the O'Dwyers is in its veins, and you have been a faithful *"follower of the family"* since you were born.'

'May the Lord look down on me, as I am,' she replied, falling on her knees. 'Maybe it'll be for luck after all. Oh, why should I be talking of luck, and this heavy trouble in the house! Och, my grief, to think of it! Oh, Masther Garrett, you war desperate 'cute—but what has it done for ye? The baby's an O'Dwyer, sure enough—just the nose and the mouth; it's a noble fine baby. Oh, thin, Masther Garrett, I can thank God the misthress didn't live to know this last turn; you married by a couple-beggar to Moyna of Ferry Barrett, and her people—the likes o' them insulting an O'Dwyer; oh, that's what comes of young men wandering over the country! The poor misthress!'

Margaret, or, as she was usually called, Marg'ate, went on talking, forgetting for a moment the dead in the living. Garrett looked on his child for a little time, heedless of her words. There was an expression upon his countenance as if ten years of sad and harrowing trouble had been added to his young life. Earnestly did he look at the infant, as if anxious to impress its features on his memory, then turned away without another word, and left it to the care of the faithful follower. The little helpless stranger woke and cried: Margaret found that it was loosely wrapt in flannel and shawls: before she attempted to return to whence she came, she fed and warmed it, talking to it all the time, and determining that it should be called Evelyn, after the grand lady of the family. This arrangement passed rapidly through her mind, but the good creature was sadly perplexed between sorrow and anxiety. At last she determined to leave the sleeping babe, and return to perform the last duties towards the mistress.

'The neighbours'—that is, the poor—were scattered through the house, lingering till they should be admitted to take a 'last look at the misthress;' the women in the chamber were waiting till the *'follower of the family'* came to give the necessary directions —which, as there were no female relations, she was expected to do.

And Margaret performed her task with extraordinary command over the feelings which at any other time would have overpowered her; the frigid limbs were decently arranged, the drapery folded, the candles lit, the water sprinkled, and then Margaret began to wonder where the young master was. Daylight came on stealthily, as if unwilling to look on the destruction of the night; but it *did* come, and she sought him everywhere in vain. That Garrett should leave the house at such a time, was a matter of astonishment to all. The women said he had entered his mother's room, and one had seen him kneeling by the corpse, and another heard him weeping. It seemed very evident, however, that he was *gone;* and what increased the mystery was, that no one had seen him depart.

Margaret knew not what to do. There was something unnatural in permitting his mother's body to go unattended to the grave; something so shocking in the idea of his deserting his child, that the humble follower could only wring her hands in bitter sorrow. Another matter was also to be considered; there were no means to lay the remains decently in earth. The priest, Margaret knew, would go without his dues, for the sake of the family; the carpenter would make the coffin—not because he had ever been employed by Mrs O'Dwyer, but for the sake of the family—but then he could not give the timber, because he had none to give. This difficulty, however, was obviated by the suggestion that enough of planks could be raised from the flooring of the rooms; which was accordingly done. Some of the more wealthy of the humble class sent '*presents*' of the materials supposed at that period to constitute the respectability of an Irish wake; and the poor lady was followed to her grave not only by the followers of the family, but by many of the gentry, who at that time never neglected to keep up the credit of their *caste* at a funeral. The morning (the third after the poor lady's death) appointed for the ceremony was chill and dreary; the mist lay upon the mountains, and the scream of the eagle, and croak of the ancient raven, sounded through the filmy clouds. The procession was large—some on horseback, some on foot; two *keeners*, whose ancestors had keened the O'Dwyers time out of mind, attended *for the honour of the family;* they crouched by the side of the coffin, and ever and anon sent forth their lamentations that the 'lady had left her country,' spoke of that son who had deserted the last duty he could perform towards his mother, and recounted, in wild disjointed stanzas, the heroic deeds of gone-by times, when the O'Dwyers had 'more land of their own than the eagle could see from the top of Slievegranaugh,' when they had horses to carry their faction to battle, when their name flamed through the country like lightning, when every eye that saw blessed them, and their voice was as the sound of music to the country; but now, the wind rattled where the wine had flowed, the hard-headed and hard-hearted possessed their land, and there was no one to shed the *heart's tears* upon the grave of the poor lady but '*the follower of the family.*'

There was, however, one other of whom the keeners knew nothing—the little helpless infant whom Margaret had concealed beneath the folds of her cloak, so that the poor lady, her mistress, might have some one of her own blood to see her in her grave. Margaret Sheil having performed this last duty, as she had done all others, with zeal and fidelity, bethought her that in a day or two she must leave the ruin, which could hardly afford shelter to any but the wild owl or chattering jackdaw. The keeners at her lady's funeral had stigmatised as hard-headed and hard-hearted those who honestly possessed the land which the O'Dwyers had wasted; but Margaret knew they did not deserve the blame, and after removing what few things were left by the spoiler—Time— she prepared to depart to the house of a younger brother, where she was much needed, as the poor fellow had lost his wife. He lived in a neighbouring town, and it was with regret that Margaret exchanged the freshness of the air, and wild sweetness of the fields, for the noise and vapours of a congregation of ill-built, dirty houses. The night before she quitted the last seat of the O'Dwyers, the maternal grandmother of the little baby came stealthily to the ruins, to look upon her daughter's child. Her husband, she said, prayed that it might die; but she forgave her poor girl; she believed she had been a wife in the sight of God; and that was a comfort to her. She threw some light upon the disappearance of Garrett: he had become linked in his wanderings with some mountaineers, who plotted treason deeply and dangerously. Garrett's superior intelligence and address made him a sort of leader among them, and two of the party having been arrested some time before, the military were on the look-out for Garrett, who, she said, her husband believed had quitted the country. Margaret consoled herself with this intelligence. 'He did not desert us from choice; I knew he did not—I knew he did not,' she repeated to herself; and the secret and unworthy marriage, the reckless and imprudent daring which made him link with dangerous characters, seemed as nought in the eyes of '*the follower of the family*'—now convinced that Garrett had 'not deserted them from choice.' All his folly, all his thoughtlessness, were forgiven.

'I often tould the misthress,' she said, 'that she was trying to rein in a red deer of the hills with a rope of sand.'

The poor bereaved woman departed with many tears, which Margaret was particularly careful should not fall on Evelyn's face, deeming it not lucky, as she said, 'that the salt of a tear should fret its tender skin for the first three months.' Her brother, it must be remembered, was one of the same clan; and though he had two little ones of his own, he welcomed the infant brought by his sister with a humble affection most touching to witness.

'It has the blood in its veins of those who sheltered our forefathers, and we should not want if they were to the fore, as in ould times,' said the man; 'neither shall it want love, duty, or respect, while I have a bit to give my own. Tache them to sarve it, Margaret; sure its being with us doesn't make it like us; it's an O'Dwyer—God bless it.'

Murtogh Sheil avowed that 'the young lady,' as he always called her, 'brought a blessing to his " four walls" from the day she entered them—everything *thruv so*.'

This was true: the Almighty blesses us in this world for our good deeds; but Margaret's right-thinking, industry, and cleanliness, were also blessings of magnitude, and 'Murtogh's sixpence went as far as another person's shilling.' This was evident to all; and the little babe acquired the happy second name of 'Blessed' —the Blessed Evelyn—from her poor neighbours, whose affectionate attentions entitled them to the epithet of friends.

PART THE SECOND.

When little Evelyn, surnamed 'the Blessed,' was taken to dwell among the simple people of Tullygarrett, she was then a few weeks old. We must pass over some years of her history, and find her now a beautiful bright-haired child, singularly interesting and intelligent. As she grew older, her nurse imagined she perceived a thin film spreading over her eyes. Her feelings upon this painful subject resolved into *one* idea: if she should ever find 'Masther Garrett,' Evelyn perhaps would not be able to see her own '*father.*' The simple-minded affectionate woman imagined this the summit of human misery. She would bring up his child, and yet, if she should ever meet him, the pleasure of looking on him would be denied to her. She had often pictured the joy of such a meeting; but an Irishwoman's joy is always eloquent, and Margaret failed to fancy how Evelyn could express herself if she were denied the power of beholding her parent. She would move various colours before the child's eyes, and finding that the eyes remained motionless, she would turn away in the bitterness of her sorrow, and exclaim, 'He left her sightless, and he will find her so!' She would then add, 'But it's the will of God! it's the will of God! and sure His will is both justice and mercy.' This trusting in the justice and in the mercy of Divine Providence is a never-ceasing comfort to the poor Irish; no matter what their troubles are, such reliance never deserts them; and though Margaret used every probable and improbable means to restore sight to her darling, yet each disappointment was followed by the resigned expression of 'God's will be done,' even while tears of bitter sorrow and disappointment were coursing each other down her cheeks. It was pleasant to observe the delicacy and attention with which the poor treated this little object of their solicitude. Every peasant felt an interest in Evelyn, and this feeling of interest was mingled with one of respect. 'Sure she's of a good ould stock on one side anyway, and it wouldn't be right for the like of us to forget *that*. It's all in the hands of God! Who knows what will turn up for her yet, the craythur!' The little maid was always better dressed than Margaret's young relations, and no jealousy or discomfort was excited by the distinction; the most 'mealy' potatoes were chosen by their own hands for her, and 'the drop of sweet milk' placed in her little china mug on the top shelf of the dresser, while the young Sheils' noggin of sour milk waited their dinner, where it sometimes became the prey of the kitten or the 'bonneen.' * The rich may think these small attentions and sacrifices nothing, but those who have never wanted, are bad judges of what it is to bestow, not from multitude, but from misery. Margaret had found in Mrs O'Dwyer's trunks many of those shreds and patches, and even pieces of damask and chintz, lutestring and mode—'relics of ould dacency,' as she called them—which she had already begun to convert into 'coats' for Evelyn, and mounted a long feather or two in the wide-leaved straw-hat plaited by her own industrious fingers, to protect her favourite's delicate complexion from the sun. There was a wild common stretching at the back of the cottages, forming what was ostentatiously called the *town* of Tullygarrett; and day after day, little Evelyn, carefully watched by Mary or Essy Sheil, would wander through the heath, or nestle amid the fern to sleep when fatigued. A little incident will show that though Evelyn was *with* the cottage children, she had imbibed somehow or other a feeling of pride beyond them. The Cork mail crossed this heath once a day, and the children of the village used to watch its passing, and beg most vociferously of the passengers. It was wonderful how fast the little urchins used to run, and how loud they used to scream; run! ay, a mile and a half for a halfpenny, their two little dirty feet going as fast as the coach-horses' four. One day, however, an accident happened the coach; the guard had substi-

* Little pig.

tuted a kippeen* for a linch-pin, and, as might have been expected, the wheel rolled quietly off, and deposited the outside passengers in the soft earth of a bog. This was very unpleasant, but it might have been worse. Irishmen bluster and swear at an accident, but soon get over it; and after a little blustering, and a good deal of swearing, the passengers walked on, while the guard manufactured a linch-pin out of the handle of the door.

Little Evelyn had heard the bustle from a hillock at a distance, and was always much amused by the passing of the coach. She continued plaiting a rush basket, and when, attracted by her exceeding beauty, one of the passengers addressed her, she shook

'The golden treasures of her hair,'

and answered in her own sweet childish voice, still continuing her occupation. Little Essy Sheil came up, and in reply to a question addressed to Evelyn, dropt her curtsey, and observed, 'Sir, if you plase, she has no *light* at all at all.' Upon this Evelyn blushed, and tears fell from her sightless eyes.

'What! blind?' he inquired; 'sight is in her eyes for all that.'

'Ay,' said Essy, 'but no good; only aunt says maybe it wont be always so.'

'Is she your cousin?'

'Oh no, plase your honour; she's a born lady.'

The gentleman laughed, and presented the 'born lady' with a silver coin; but Evelyn, who had risen, flushed crimson, and returned him the coin with anything rather than a grateful manner.

'She's no beggar, yer honour,' said Essy, herself half offended; 'nor are we beggars either, sir; only we *takes* what we *gets*.'

'I daresay you do,' he replied, taking the hint, and transferring the coin; 'and now, take me to your aunt, and I will hear this child's history.'

It was soon related. The gentleman was a well-known oculist, and with much kind feeling told Margaret that if she liked to bring the child to his house in Dublin, he would see if anything could be done for her; and the coach being mended, departed, as visitors always do from the dwellings of the Irish poor—overwhelmed with blessings.

Margaret was not slow at perceiving and feeling 'the divided duty' which this proposal led to—her brother and his children on the one hand, little Evelyn and *her promise* to Garrett O'Dwyer on the other—and in the fulness and simplicity of her heart, she called her brother Murtogh to share its counsels.

'It's a poor case intirely to leave you, Murtogh, and Essy so wild, though Mary, to be sure, *is* a rock of sense, considering her years; but Essy's cruel wild, though Mary's head is long, and she

* Bit of wood.

can spin, sew, make, and, what's better, mend as well as myself; and sure it's proud I am to see you go to your work as clean as any gentleman, and the cabin, God be praised! as white as the priest's vestment (God bless us!); and all that's a comfort anyhow; and the dawshy craythur, poor little Evelyn—bird of beauty that she is!—has no one but me to look to her; and if the grace o' God would beam down on her, and restore her her sight, sure I could tache her many a thing against the time she'd see him.'

'True for ye, Marg'ate, it would be a comfort to me, let alone you; only don't say, sister, that the child has no one to look to her but you; I know ye're the best friend any one ever had, but if you wasn't in it, sure I'd guard her myself—I would, *for the honour of the family!* But go, sister; go to Dublin with her at onct, and what help I can raise for you I will, to send you comfortable on your journey. It's your duty, Marg'ate, *to the family,* that's what it is; and a proper duty to do, and God speed ye with it! And don't be fretting while ye're away, though it's a good step * to Dublin: only *take it aisy,* and I'll go bail Mary will mind the place and the pigs, and everything that way. And ye'll write to us, as *you've the larning,* and maybe my prayers wont be with ye! Only go, Marg'ate, *astore;* and sure, if she's restored, it's a bright † girl she'll be, as well as beautiful. If she's not, why, sure we must only do the best we can for her; and anyhow, the blessing has been in it ever since she set foot among us. I know you've a heart good enough to stay, but yer duty is to go amongst strangers, if it would do her good; we've been *followers of the family* for more than two hundred years, and it isn't now we'd give in at the heel of the hunt.'

This disinterested conduct on the part of poor Murtogh needs no comment, and Margaret prepared for her long and fatiguing journey with the same cheerfulness as though she were dressing in her best for mass on a sunny Sunday. Margaret was not one who saw no difficulties, no obstacles in her path. She perceived and understood them all; but she *was a follower of the family;* and the more the little offset stood in need of support, the more did she feel it her duty to protect and shelter it. The next Sunday the priest took occasion to address his congregation from 'the altar,' and to tell them that Margaret Sheil had resolved to go to Dublin to see if it would please the Almighty God to restore the sight of her eyes to the child she had promised to watch over. The priest was a kind-hearted man, and knew the character of the people he addressed; he first of all made his congregation laugh, by declaring what an advantage it would be to men if all women were blind to their faults anyway, and then aroused their sympathies in behalf of the heroic exertions of Evelyn's nurse.

* A long way.   † Clever—intelligent.

Nor was this all: when he saw his congregation wiping their eyes, and turning them towards where Margaret and Evelyn were, he urged them to give something even of the little they possessed to forward so good and pious an object. He told them that by so doing they would receive in this world the prayers and blessings of grateful hearts, and do a deed acceptable in the eyes of the Almighty. Whatever of superstition was mixed up with this kind-hearted man's discourse, I do not know; it was delivered long before I was born; but an old man who heard Father Roche's address on the occasion, told me there was not a dry eye in the chapel, and that a purse, long and heavy, with brave big and little money, was the result of his appeal. The times are bad, indeed, with Paddy when he has nothing to *give*.

Murtogh Sheil was unprepared for the priest's address, and in the chapel yard he thanked him from the overflowing of his heart, and assured his neighbours that one time or other he'd hope to make it up to them. Murtogh's tears evinced his sincerity; and when, a week afterwards, Margaret and Evelyn's preparations were completed, and they were about to depart, it would be impossible to imagine a more kindly crowd than waited to bid them farewell. Evelyn was kissed, and crossed, and blessed, and the best horse and car in Tullygarrett, with a feather bed, and a patch quilt spread over it, prepared to take them 'a piece of the way;' and every woman that had an old shoe on, threw it after them 'for good luck.' And it was hard to tell whether Margaret laughed or cried most; she did a good deal of both; but it was not till, having embraced her beloved brother for the last time, and called her niece Mary twice back to hear more 'last words' touching various cottage matters, and having from the brow of the hill on which she stood watched the car and its attendants descend into the last hollow, that she felt the utter loneliness of her situation; and pressing Evelyn, who understood and participated in her feelings, to her bosom, fairly burst into the passionate tears which a sense of her loneliness and the length of her journey called forth.

In this railway age, it is hard to imagine the toil and difficulty of a journey from Tullygarrett to Dublin; it was both tedious and painful, although safe, as travelling in Ireland always is. Margaret had more than eighty miles to walk. When Evelyn was fatigued, she carried her on her back, for the roads were then but little frequented, except by the country carmen at stated periods; and now and then a heavy lumbering coach, which seemed built for eternity, groaned past, heavily laden with luggage and passengers; and sometimes the guard would 'give her a lift,' which lightened her journey, and afforded her the opportunity of conversing with her fellow-beings. As yet, she had spent but little of the generous gifts she had received; and though very much fatigued one night in particular, that Evelyn had been faint and weary all day long, consoled herself with the information she had just obtained, that it was only fifteen miles to Dublin. The next morning her precious charge was weak and feverish; poor Margaret herself felt that she, too, was very unwell, but having said her prayers, she dressed herself as usual, and prepared for her departure. It was evident that Evelyn could not walk far, but her nurse longed with the impatience of a fervent spirit for the conclusion of their journey, and knew that every mile would diminish the distance. She therefore tied Evelyn on her back, in a way peculiarly Irish, and set forward.

She had not, however, journeyed more than three miles, when she felt her own strength sensibly diminishing. She was sick at heart, her head became dizzy, her limbs refused to perform their office, and the dreary landscape through which they were passing danced before her eyes. She unfastened the cloak, and sat down beneath the shade of a solitary tree, whose leaves rustled in the hot wind that swept the common, but whose breath was scorching, not refreshing. When her cloak was untied, little Evelyn crawled rather than walked from beneath its folds, and Margaret, as she pressed her own parched lips to her burning brow, muttered, 'Now the Lord, in his mercy, look down upon us, for it's the fever, or something worse, that's over her; and as to me, God help me! the hot and cowld *shivers* will shake the life out of me soon.' Evelyn laid her head on her nurse's shoulder, and moaned heavily; Margaret observed that her eyelids were swollen, her face red, and her hand dry and hot. She thought that the same illness had seized both: she was mistaken; the child was attacked only by measles, but she herself had been seized upon by the fearful fever whose ravages have from time to time rendered the cottage homes of Ireland desolate. Overwhelmed by a lassitude she could not overcome, she wound her arms round her charge, and fell into a deep but painful slumber.

When she awoke, Evelyn was still sleeping, and though in a species of half delirium, she had not altogether lost her consciousness. She attempted to rise, but her strength was prostrated; she could not even move; her lips were unable to convey to the air the incoherent but fervent prayers she framed to the Almighty for the bestowing of His care on the sleeping child. The sun had set, and she was not in sight even of a dwelling; the only thing upon the dreary waste that indicated her proximity to a human habitation was a lean, spectral-looking gray horse, which had limped towards them, and after gathering with his skinny lips a few leaves from off the young shoots of the thorn-tree, stared pitifully in her face, as if to say, 'Hail, fellow-sufferer!'

Before the evening closed, the owner of the horse, a poor man called Larry Twist, who lived by making mats of the rushes cut from the swamps, and manufacturing fern brooms, came to seek his poor gray horse, and soon saw that one, if not both, of those beneath the tree were affected by the pestilence which had been ravaging that part of the country for some time. In such cases the peasantry never totally desert each other; they dare not, of course, bring the infected parties to their houses; but before the next morning dawned, this good Samaritan had, with the assistance of a neighbour, erected a sort of shed over the sufferers, so as to protect them from the inclemency or heat of the weather, and placed a comfortable quantity of dried heath beneath them. Nor was this all: from time to time milk was begged for by the poor man 'for the travellers, God help them! who war struck by the way, and no one to see to them, only just the Almighty, and maybe a slave like himself, who had *nothing* to give.' This milk was pushed towards them with a long wattle; and Evelyn, whose childish disease lightened in a day or two, made a wonderful nurse in her turn, and well merited her name of 'the Blessed.' She would sit all day long, her sightless eyes bent towards her 'mammy nurse,' whose head she supported on her little lap, replying to the ravings which conjured the whole world to take care of her 'Blessed Evelyn,' with the assurance that 'sure she was taken care of;' an assurance which the poor patient could not comprehend. By degrees Evelyn learned to guide herself round the tree, and from under the shelter of the hut, and her quick ear could distinguish the barefooted and nimble tread of those who shared with her their poor food, and begged for her support from the 'big house.' Sightless as she was, poor child, the sweet tenderness of her nature was to her instead of sight; and she watched, without seeing, her fainting and fading friend— without being able to discern the frightful ravages which fever was making with the being she loved.

When the crisis came, and every faculty of life was suspended, when she could neither feel Margaret's heart beat, nor the breath from between her lips, then, indeed, Evelyn shrieked, and ran out upon the waste, clasping her little hands, while the tears gushed from her eyes, and the black crow rose heavily on the wing, croaking his displeasure at the disturbance. There was none but the crow to answer her cries of distress, for the mist of morning was heavy on every blade of grass; but as the day advanced, when the sun rose, the birds of the morass, and those which shelter amongst the gorse and furze, commenced the business and pleasure allotted to the span of their existence, Evelyn, exhausted by her cries, had sunk upon the heather, and prevented by the innate dread of death which makes the blood run cold when we grasp the damp heavy weight, *for the last time,* of the beloved hand which never was cold to us before—impelled, I say, by this untaught innate dread, poor Evelyn feared to return to the hut, when all at once a lark sprang from beside her, and soared, and soared into the very heavens, flinging its music with the prodigality of abundance, until it mingled with the fleeciness of the morning clouds; and the child's feelings, softened by the melody into a gentler sorrow, subsided. She loved the song of the sweet wild bird. She no longer screamed or sobbed, though the tears flowed on: she almost restrained her breath, and turned her face right upwards, that she might not lose the fragment of a sound! It was a picture to look upon. Gradually rising from the ground, she rested on her knees upon the wild heath, with nothing intimating the presence of humanity within reach save the crouching temporary hut, and a red cloak hanging with picturesque effect above it, from amid the green branches of the solitary tree, which stood out, in strong relief, against the clear firm-looking sky.

So absorbed were her senses and feelings, that she did not hear the approach of her constant friend Larry Twist, who, in addition to the half-filled noggin of milk, had brought her on this morning a fragment of barley bread, and three or four potatoes.

'And what ails ye, *avourneen*,' he said kindly, 'to be saying yer prayers on the wet grass? Get up, *alanna*, and take this to yer mammy.'

'She's stiff and cowld,' she replied, her tears and sobs recommencing as the knowledge of evil returned to her; 'and no beat in her heart, and she wont open her eyes: *I felt them.*'

Larry moved cautiously towards the hut, keeping, as he said, 'the wind between them;' and after peering over the cloak, assured Evelyn 'that it was only the *lull* of the fever,' which assurance, though she did not understand it, conveyed hope to the child's mind; the hope was increased by his adding, 'Eat yer breakfast, my *corra!* and thin take a turn at the prayers. God can raise her up still, if it is His blessed will to do so. And pray with all yer innocent heart and soul, *avourneen*—pray—do. The prayers of the innocent are sweeter to the Lord than the perfume of the flowers to us—God help us! Pray, my darlint, and God *will* hear you—poor blind lamb that ye are! I'll come back in the evening, *alanna;*' and he muttered to himself, while departing, 'by that time she'll be either dead or better.'

The child did as he desired. The day seems long to many a listless child of luxury, but Evelyn did not know what the word 'dull' meant. Many a petted girl would not have been suffered to arise from her bed after such an illness as she had endured, and yet there she was, abroad in the breeze and the sunbeam, gathering strength; and having repeated half-a-dozen times the prayers she knew, she crept to her 'mammy's' side, bathed her lips with milk, kissed her damp brow, then stole as noiselessly away, and plucking up long grass as if it had been long rushes, plaited them together, and forgetful, as blessed childhood always is, of the past agony when its hour *is* past, she warbled softly the most mournful of those beautiful melodies which the Irish children seem to imbibe with the air they breathe. The evening found her sitting by Margaret's side, and, watchful as a fawn, her benevolent friend did not approach this time unnoticed. She advanced to meet him.

'I'm sure it's near night, sur,' said the child; 'for the sun's gone to bed, and the birds are done singing. Tell me how mammy is now?'

The poor man looked at the woman with exceeding caution, for the humbler Irish think a fever more than usually infectious when it is, as they call it, 'on the turn.' Faded as she seemed, there was an aspect of returning life about the face; it was pale and wan, but its rigidity was gone; a certain degree of apparent warmth was over the features, and the long lank hair was moist.

'Cover her up careful, *avourneen*,' said the man; 'keep her warm, and sit as far from her as ye can. Maybe she'll spake to ye in the morning.'

'I can't sit far from her, sur, and she in it,' answered Evelyn. And the old man wept to see the tenderness evinced by the innocent child towards her protector.

Margaret lived. It would be impossible to describe, because, thank God, I can only imagine, the faintings and weakness that confined her for a long time to the shelter of that miserable hut. The weather continued astonishingly dry for that weeping country; and at last Larry Twist, having informed her that he was going a good piece of the way towards Dublin, and would give her and the 'girleen,' God bless her! a lift on the same gray mare that had stared so wofully at her the day she sat, in utter weariness of body and mind, beneath the old thorn-tree, she once more commended herself to the Almighty protection, and departed with, if it were possible, increased feelings of affection towards Evelyn. In due time, pale and emaciated, she arrived in Dublin, and presented herself at the door of the oculist. What was her dismay at being informed that, in consequence of severe ill health, he had quitted Dublin the day before—only the day before—for Bath!

This was indeed a blow the poor woman little expected. She calculated her small finances, and finding that they would afford her a deck passage to Bristol, and something more, she set forward, nothing dismayed at the idea of travelling in a strange country, but bent on the one great prospect of seeing her favourite restored to sight. She landed at Bristol, and, despite the weakness attendant upon sea-sickness, and her former illness, the following day found her at the door of the humane oculist in Bath. She knew enough of human nature, which it is the habit to call 'knowing the world,' to dress herself and Evelyn in their very best; and as Evelyn's best was somewhat grotesque, she attracted so much notice, which immediately, on looking at her beautiful face, deepened into admiration, that Margaret, though flattered, was somewhat alarmed at the number of persons who stopped and questioned her as to whom the child belonged to. The extreme delicacy of her features, the quantity and colour of her hair, the softness of her complexion, the length and darkness of the eyelashes that curtained her dim but beautifully-formed eyes, rendered her, when spoken to, an object of deep interest. And more than one lounger along the gossipping streets of Bath followed, and lingered near the door at which Margaret knocked. The servant told her—the servants of good kind people are always civil—the servant told her that his master was very ill, too ill to see any one, much less perform an operation, and that she need not call again. The blood that for a moment had mantled poor Margaret's cheek rushed back to her heart, and the domestic, fearing that she might faint, with great humanity permitted her to sit in the hall.

'Tell him—just tell him,' she said to the man—'just tell him, if ever ye hope to meet yer father and mother (God be good to them!) in paradise—tell him that it's the woman from the far Irish moor—she that lived in Tullygarrett—she, with the fair, purty child, Evelyn O'Dwyer, that never can see a glimpse of the blessed light of heaven until it plases God *and his honour* to grant it. I was seized by the fever on the road, and missed him on its account in Dublin, and now I shall miss him again, and the craythur may go stone blind to her grave, and never have the blessing to look in her father's face, if she should have the joy to meet him!' Many more were her prayers and words, and at last they prevailed. The servant told his master, who, kind as he had ever been, consented to receive the nurse and her charge in his bedroom. His days, however, were numbered; and he knew it; but he looked at Evelyn's eyes; and Margaret wept to observe how changed he was, for she well remembered the ruddy health of his countenance at their former meeting.

'I am sure it may be cured,' he said, 'and she could bear it; but I dare not venture on so delicate an operation now. I feel, my good woman, I shall never live to restore this child to sight; but *she may remain here until I can see her no longer*, and then I will leave you a letter to a London oculist, who, for my sake, will, with God's blessing, restore her sight.'

Every day, while the good man was able to sit up in bed, was little Evelyn placed by his bedside, and the child interested him greatly. The nature of the disease was peculiar, and her intelligence and beauty no less so. Margaret's industry, her devotion and affection for her charge, made a strong impression in her favour; and before the gentleman died, he placed ten guineas in her hand, together with a letter to his London friend. This appeared to Margaret a mine of inexhaustible wealth, but her tears were not the less sincere when she saw the remains of the excellent friend whom 'God had raised up to her' consigned to the tomb. It was indeed a bitter trial, and she left Bath with an aching heart. Everything was new and strange; she felt, as she said, 'going through a dale of grandeur without a heart, and in the midst of it all no tidings of *the boy*.' Margaret was too longheaded to travel in the heavy and expensive coaches of those days, or even in a wagon; she determined to 'walk it,' with an occasional 'lift' from a passing vehicle. But the English were not as ready to give the 'lift' as the Irish had been; they valued their time and the labour of their horses at a much higher rate than she had expected, and the refreshment and bed at the wayside inns were always to be paid for. She had journeyed considerably past Reading, when, overcome with fatigue, she stopped at a cottage which seemed far removed from a village, and requested a drink of milk for the child and one of water for herself. The woman answered the petition with a tolerable grace, and her husband, struck by the beauty of the child, added to the gift a second draught of milk.

The woman sneered; 'the rebellion in Ireland,' she said, 'had driven those away from the country who had made it too hot to hold them.'

It was the first time Margaret had heard of 'the rebellion,' which unhappily formed so terrible an epoch in Irish history. She inquired the meaning of the words, and the woman gave her a paper, saying, if she could read, that would inform her better. Margaret *could* and did read what made her heart both beat and bleed. The rebellion had raged in *her* part of the country; the cruelties of both parties had been great; and the little village of Tullygarrett had been the scene of frightful tumult. This was agony to poor Margaret, and little Evelyn threw her arms round her neck, exclaiming, 'I hear ye're in trouble, my own dear mammy nurse; oh, do tell yer darling what ails ye.' She could make no reply. Her brother probably murdered, her nieces without protection, in the fearful tumult of civil war, were before her! She considered, if she were to go back, what could she do for them?—where find them? Besides, if she were to turn from her duty *now*, Evelyn would go '*dark*' to her grave, and '*the follower of the family*' have lacked in duty. This decided her on proceeding, though with tearful eyes and a beating heart; and whenever she saw a group of men assembled together, she would stop and listen, and, if she dared venture, would ask a question as to 'what news from Ireland?' Alas! England has always news of tumult from that poor country; but at that period the execrations and bitterness heaped upon it knew no bounds. Now, indeed, it is not so; England understands the country better. Many were the trials of poor Margaret's fidelity: and when she entered the long straggling village of Hammersmith, she had already discovered that ten pounds was not the inexhaustible fund she had imagined—travelling *for the poor* in England and Ireland are two distinct things. She presented herself at the door of the fashionable oculist, and her letter of introduction—the letter, one of the last her good friend had written—gained her immediate admittance.

'Several weeks' must elapse, the doctor said, before the child could be couched, and he would perform the operation *for the sake of his old friend*. 'Several weeks!' thought Margaret; 'and how are we to live? This wont last for ever, and we so far from our own home, where the "hearty welcome" is in every hand and on every lip. Well, I must work anyway I can; and so best; it will keep me from thinking!'

But poor Margaret's work was not London work; spinning and knitting were despised; there were no potatoes to dig, no corn to bind, no turf to clamp. Margaret was for a time at a loss for labour; but it is marvellous to the idle how the industrious will make employment. She was always ready to do a 'hand's turn' for her landlady, who soon discovered she had an Irishwoman in her house, who, though awkward in 'her ways,' was clean, active, industrious, and not quarrelsome. This was new, and useful. Under other circumstances, Margaret would have been cheerful; but how could she be so now? The Irish disturbances were to be exterminated rather than extinguished; and though she had written to both 'priest and minister' concerning her brother—written in her own way, but so as to be intelligible to both—she had received no reply. She had also to bear the galling and ignorant taunts which the lower class of English, from want of knowing better, are too apt to heap upon the inhabitants of their sister kingdom, who work for less, and endure more, than they think right or proper that anybody should. But Margaret humbly and faithfully prayed to, and trusted in, God; and though her troubles were many, they were lessened, not increased, by time. She managed, by hard labour, to earn a few shillings each week, so that the remaining portion of the ten pounds remained untouched. 'It was intended for her, not me; and God knows what trial may be before her yet, besides the pain, in this strange country.' It is a mistake to suppose that the poor Irish set their faces, in those bygone days even, against education; persons who live and observe the peasant part of the community, cannot fail to observe that, on the contrary, they are an exceedingly curious and investigating people, anxious to obtain information in the quickest possible manner, the elders not persevering themselves, but wishful that their children should persevere in 'their schooling,' if they do so in nothing else. Margaret had a great desire that her blind charge, now nearly eight years old, should learn as much as possible; and when evening came, and her daily labours were terminated, the wash-tub deserted, and the scouring concluded, she would sit down and read to her, not perhaps the sort of books we should recommend now-a-days; but a book was a book to Margaret, no matter what was in it. She read on, until in general she read Evelyn to sleep. She had brought her own Prayer-book with her, a dilapidated 'Reading made Easy,' 'Valentine and Orson,' one or two fairy tales, an old 'Voster's Arithmetic,' and the 'Vicar of Wakefield,' that had belonged to 'Masther Garrett.' Moreover, there was a volume of O'Halloran's History of Ireland, which she regarded with great veneration, marked with the armorial bearings of the O'Dwyers.

Evelyn never went to sleep when her nurse read her the 'Vicar of Wakefield,' and she knew the poem of 'the Wanderer' by heart. This was a consolation to Margaret. At length the doctor intimated his intention of couching one eye, and Evelyn attended with Margaret at his house. This operation was performed to the oculist's satisfaction, who praised the child's extraordinary firmness, and called her nurse into another room to give her some private directions as to her treatment; having done so, he said in his usually abstracted way, 'O'Dwyer, O'Dwyer!—I met a very clever gentleman yesterday of that *name;* as handsome a young fellow as ever I saw in my life.'

'O'Dwyer—a gentleman—handsome, did you say, sir!' asked Margaret, breathless, for whom the whole world contained only *one* O'Dwyer. 'Ah, thin, will yer honour just be plased to tell me where he is!'

'Why, really, I believe he leaves London to-day, but you cannot possibly know anything about him, I should think. He has been in foreign service since his boyhood, and came over with General—— Bah! I never can remember names; should not have remembered *his*, but that it struck me as being the same as this child's. He seemed very anxious, too, about Irish affairs; first time he had been in these countries for many years.'

Even Margaret's strong interest respecting Evelyn's sight was for a few minutes overwhelmed by her desire to hear something more about the 'handsome young fellow,' who, she was certain, must be 'Masther Garrett.'

'I can't help thinking,' she said, after a pause—'I can't help thinking, plase yer honour, that he's yon darlint's father.'

'Much too young for that; he cannot be more than four or five-and-twenty.'

'Plase yer honour, he was *all as one** as a boy when she was

* The same.

born, and the Garretts were always young-looking of their age. I'd give the eyes out of my head to see him, plase yer honour.'

'My good woman,' said the matter-of-fact Englishman, 'that would be impossible: if your eyes were out, you could not see him. But I do not think it can be he.' His personal beauty seemed to have made a great impression upon the doctor, for he added immediately afterwards, 'He certainly is a remarkably fine fellow, and appeared much amused and pleased by the attention which sundry ladies paid him.'

'That's natural enough to all Irishmen; indeed, I believe, to men of all countries,' said Margaret; 'and small blame to them, if the ladies forget themselves so far as to pay gentlemen attintion. But did ye hear his Christian name, sir?'

'Not hear it—but I have a note of his somewhere, a line I received yesterday—a question about the utility of a particular glass, which he wants to give to some old soldier.'

'That can be no other than himself. Oh, for the love of God, try and find it, sir!' exclaimed Margaret. 'Do, yer honour; it might be the saving of my life, the saving of the child; nothing can make you know what a scrap of his writin' would be to me.'

'That is, my good woman, supposing it is his writing,' replied the gentleman, as with great good-nature he tossed over various letters and papers. 'Here it is: no; that is not it.' Picture to yourself the keen anxiety of Margaret's blue eyes, the trembling of her whole frame, the torrent of hope that burst upon her, the shivering dread lest it might not be 'Masther Garrett,' the reproaches she heaped in her own mind upon the oculist for being tardy and awkward—imagine all this, and then hear the doctor, after unfolding a note, and casting his eye down the page, say, 'Yes—here it is at last—GARRETT O'DWYER!'

PART THE THIRD.

'Gone!—did you say gone?—really gone!'—were the frequently repeated exclamations of an Irishwoman at the door of the *then* fashionable hotel in Bond Street. 'Gone! for good and all!—gone intirely! Ah, thin, for the love of God, tell me when he went, and where he's gone to.'

'Take your Irish howl out of this,' answered a fat waiter; 'we don't want rebels here.'

'I don't care what you call me *now*,' said the poor woman; 'but from this I will not stir until I hear some news of my Masther Garrett.'

'What does she say?' inquired half-a-dozen voices at once.

'Don't make game of her,' interrupted a respectable-looking servant out of livery. 'Don't you see the poor woman's in tears?'

'Ah, thin, sir, good luck to ye; ye've a *live* heart in yer bosom.

And can you tell me anything at all of the young gentleman, Masther Garrett O'Dwyer?'

'If you mean Mr O'Dwyer who was here with a foreign count yesterday, he is gone.'

'To where, sir?'

'That, my good woman, I cannot tell you; but I believe it was time he went.'

'Quite,' added the first speaker significantly.

'You do not mean to say he did anything to disgrace his name!' inquired Margaret, looking round her proudly.

'Oh no!—only fine feathers make fine birds. He's bound up part and parcel with the Romish powers abroad—the Pope himself, or maybe Bonaparte; he liked to read the Irish papers; and I can't think what our government is about, to let foreigners of any country among us eating our roast beef and plumpudding: it's unconstitutional. Keep them out, I say—keep them out;' and the fat waiter flourished his napkin, and passed, with a consequential air, from the conference.

'If I had only seen him for one minute!' exclaimed the poor nurse; 'just heard his voice—got one word of speaking with him! Oh, sir, sir; are you sure he's gone?'

'As fast as four posters could take him.'

'And where'll I get his direction, will you be plased to tell me?' inquired the nurse with admirable simplicity.

'That I really do not know. There are persons about who say that he was obliged to quit by an order from government.'

'See that now!' said Margaret, while a species of pride, purely Irish, lit up her face—'see that now! Bedad, thin, it's little throuble the government would take about him if he wasn't a person of consequence.'

The man smiled, and *the follower of the family*, after a few more useless inquiries, turned away to tell her troubles to 'the doctor,' and indulge in the belief that it must have been *her* Garrett O'Dwyer 'who had given, like many of his name, a power of throuble to the great English government.'

Imagine everything that was affectionate in Margaret's conduct towards Evelyn during the time she was subjected to the oculist's experiments—imagine the hours of tender watchfulness—imagine the days of intense and often *hard* labour—imagine, amid it all, the deep anxiety with which her heart yearned for news of her brother and his family—imagine her unsparing, unceasing care—imagine a hundredfold more than I can tell of the privations she endured, and, above all, the torturing suspense as to whether or not her darling would or would not receive the blessing of sight; and then picture, if you can, her perfect and entire satisfaction at finding the grand object of her life realised—the child of her affections gifted, as it were, with sight—restored to that unspeakable blessing—the eyes of the young patient, now full of meaning, beaming upon her in the full lustre of youth and love—questioning, as it were, her features, and then forcing her to speak, that she might hear she was not deceived, and that it was really her own, *own* nurse she looked upon. Days and days, and weeks and weeks, of prayer and almost speechless anxiety passed before this long-looked-for end was accomplished. And when Margaret's high and grateful spirit had sufficiently rejoiced therein—when her heart had, as it were, in some degree emptied itself of rejoicing, the care for the future made her continually exclaim, in her own mind, ' Ah, thin, it isn't ungrateful I am to the Almighty God for restoring her, the delight of my soul! to the sight of her blessed eyes! But my heart aches to hear news of home; if we go back, they say we'll be murdered; the trouble *is in the counthry still*, and sure that's no news. And if I could only hear from my brother, and of Masther Garrett, why, Margaret Sheil, you'd be a happy woman. But I must wait, God help me, patiently. The doctor (God be good to him!) says he has some news in store for me. I must own this is a beautiful country for earning money; only, the worst of it is, it *goes* as fast, not to say faster, than it comes. If I had only time to make myself known to Masther Garrett, that he might have carried with him the knowledge that his child was well and living, it would have comforted him when far, far away from the sound of his natural language!'

Margaret Sheil little knew how the cares, the ambitions, the projects of this busy world sap and undermine the finest and best affections of our nature. We imagine that our feelings of love and tenderness for our kind remain the same: we fancy that years roll on, and find us, when we *do* pause, exactly what *we were*. Alas! no fallacy is greater than this. The springs of love have become choked by the foul weeds of worldliness.

Garrett O'Dwyer had been compelled to abandon his child and the stiffened corpse of his mother on that well-remembered night, from finding that his connection with the disturbers of his country was discovered by those who would have been glad to see him sacrificed; for, young as he was, there was a wild and fiery zeal about him, which promised much that was daring: in the great game of life he had everything to gain, and nothing to lose.

From what I have already said, no one will imagine Garrett O'Dwyer one of those who would labour patiently and earnestly in a homely or even exalted calling: he would trust all to a *coup de main;* and if that failed, lose all power of exertion until something else was struck, like fire from flint, to arouse his energies. The frame, hardened in youth by mountain pastime, is not likely to shrink from personal exertion when acts of daring are necessary to effect an object; and the mind takes its bent from the habit of body, when it has not been directed to any particular exercise calculated to call forth its thinking rather than its feeling powers. One or two successful strokes of fortune threw Garrett O'Dwyer, in his foreign exile, amongst those who saw at that time enough in the character of the Irish disturbances to stimulate their own ambition. He did not depart without some 'mystic lines,' signifying his ancient descent and his future desires. He was the very fellow to rise in foreign service; and those were times when the soldier of yesterday was the general of to-day. Garrett had abundance of fierce courage; he was brave, earnest, gay, fond of pleasure, cunning, and gifted with rare powers of pleasing. When first he crossed the sea that separated him from his all—his child —he felt as every young Irishman would have felt—most keenly. On the night of his departure, he tore a tuft of fern from the crumbling walls of his ancestral home, and placing it next his heart, swore, in presence of the silent stars, that he would return and win back those halls to be his own. He passed the lonely and deserted graveyard, where the dock and the seedy nettle triumphed over

'The Blakes and O'Donnels'

of bygone years; he threw himself into the long strong grass that waved in the night-wind over the remains of his careless father; and when his overwrought feelings found relief in violent tears, he repeated on his knees the few prayers taught him by his mother and Margaret, and, with a heart full of wild yet generous and ennobling sympathies, the last of his race departed from his 'Fatherland.'

With a new country came new excitements. For the first year, he was, as Irishmen generally are *during the first year of exile*, a red-hot patriot: he talked of, and, to do him justice, *felt* strongly for, his country. But he had entered foreign service; and the remembrance of Erin, of his indulgent mother, his once madly-loved Moyna, his infant daughter, became rubbed out, as it were, by the friction of stirring events. At first he had wished that the child might live, 'to be the comfort of his declining years;' then, as he grew older and more prosperous, he never thought he could decline; and at last he arrived, somehow or other, at the conclusion that, deprived of maternal nutriment, the child must have died. Those who have not watched the rise, progress, and decay of human feelings, will be inclined to call Garrett O'Dwyer—a monster; those who have, will call him—a man!

Years rolled on, bringing prosperity on their wings; and it was no wonder that Garrett O'Dwyer was spoiled like the rest of his sex, whose strength and beauty is rather of the body than the mind. No wonder that Garrett was greatly injured by admiration and success. How much would poor Margaret have been disappointed—disappointed, though perhaps proud, to find 'Masther

Garrett' a brave officer, in the confidence of the official whom he accompanied to England!—a soldier, polished as much as a soldier ought to be—a man of much penetration and brilliancy of character, but lacking those natural affections which may be considered the core of an Irish heart. Irresistibly drawn by some long dormant sympathies to the details of the fatal turmoil of ninety-eight, he read, as the waiter had stated, the Irish papers with avidity; he could not look over the progress of the disturbances amongst his native mountains, without longing to join in the strife he was once sworn to. Still, it was not the policy of his adopted country to interfere at that time; and the morning his faithful nurse had sought him, he had promptly departed, for reasons unconnected with Ireland, and with which my tale of Margaret's fidelity has nothing to do.

The news that, according to Margaret's phraseology, the doctor 'had' for her was certainly romantic: a lady wished to adopt little Evelyn, on certain conditions, which Margaret was to hear from herself; and accordingly, at the appointed time, she took the child to one of the old suburban houses, and soon found herself in the presence of an elderly gentlewoman, who had frequently passed her when she waited in the hall of the benevolent oculist. Evelyn was not present at the meeting, but left in another room. Her nurse related the little girl's history, suppressing only her belief that her father had been so recently in London, from a cunning peculiarly Irish, which whispered that the lady might not be so ready to do her service if she thought it probable that her father ever would return. The lady's name was Langham. Bereaved of her own children, she had long struggled with that loneliness of heart which is always a bitter trial for woman to endure; she believed this friendless girl would be something whereon she could expend her affection and her benevolence; and after enumerating, rather ostentatiously, the benefits that she proposed to confer on Evelyn O'Dwyer, she added, 'You perceive I remove the burden of the child from you altogether; I adopt her as my own; and I think it would be better if you were not to see her at all; if she were to see you constantly, it would recall her old feelings and associations.'

The Irish nurse looked for a moment abstracted and confused; the possibility of her being denied access to Evelyn had never before occurred to her. So astounded was she by Mrs Langham's words, that she suffered her to enlarge upon the benefits that would arise from this sacrifice, which she considered in that one-sided way which people are apt to do when chiefly thinking of their own feelings. At last, moving steadily towards the lady, she fixed her piercing eyes upon her, and said, simply and honestly, but in a tone of the deepest pathos, 'Ah, thin, ma'am, is it for parting us ye'd be?'

'You must understand, my good woman, that I want to bring her up with the feelings and manners of a gentlewoman.'

'I wish the Almighty would but give ye the power to look into the heart of that blessed child, and there ye'd see, my lady, stamped upon her very soul, the honour, the feelings, ay, and the pride too, that belong to a gentlewoman—yes, and though the world don't think it, to many not born so. I had her, before she was twenty-four hours, *a weeping babe of a weeping land*. I promised her father to purtect her. I kept my oath to *him, and God*. I have watched over her, prayed for *her*, that had no sin, instead of trying to lessen my own heavy load of that same, God help me! —kept all knowledge of bad from her, because I wanted her to be like the angels in heart as well as in body. I have done all this, and more: I would not marry where my own weak woman's heart had settled for years, because of the duty I owed the family. When I saw a chance of restoring her precious sight, I left name and home, kith and kin and country, to see justice done to her. I have loved her, and honoured her. Never let her think me her equal, but her servant. And now you *would turn me from her!* Ah, thin, lady dear, I heard tell onct of a bird that laid eggs of goold; I'm not going to say what sort of a bird she was—but goold they war for certain, as I heard tell, full of goold. But sure, she had no sooner laid the egg, than she trampled it under her foot to nothing. If the egg had not been spoilt, my lady, it would have been worth anything. But what good was it?—soiled and destroyed intirely. Ah, ma'am, it's a pity to mar what's made, as the thunderboult said when it thought of the oak it had riven, just to show its strength.'

Now, the lady liked the child, and there certainly was much kindness in her heart; but it is not every one who can distinguish the difference between rusticity and vulgarity. A woman of such self-sacrificing and disinterested feelings as Margaret, *could* not—no matter how poor or low-born she might be—communicate mean or paltry feelings to others, because they never had place in her own bosom—they were not inherent in her nature. But Mrs Langham, like too many others, had acquired the habit of considering poverty and vice as synonymous. She felt, however, the natural eloquence and power of Margaret's appeal: it was new, and apt; and, above all, it came fully and freshly from her heart. But the lady thought she would try her a little further; her arguments, however, were feeble, for NATURE was against them. *The follower of the family* had been father, mother, home, country, *all*, to the child, which was in reality the creature of her bounty, but which she believed it was her duty not only to *serve*, but to *slave* for, to the end of her days.

'It's no good, my lady—God bless you, you mean it all for the best—I see the advantage, ma'am—let her live with you; I'll not stand in her light for that—let her be to you as your own child; *your* goodness will have earned that duty from her—tacke her, my lady (not that she's ignorant), all kinds of things (only her eyes, God help her, are still weakly, and don't let them be worn out)—let her be yours, heart and soul. I never thought her love could keep the same for me, when she got among her own class like. I learnt that lesson long ago of a little King Charles's puppy that my poor misthress had (the heavens be her bed!), that when onct it was fully reared by a turnspit baste that let it share the milk of her own pup, turned away from the kitchen to the parlour, and would even set its teeth and *girn* at the poor ould brute that sometimes thrust its nose into *the company quarters*, out of good-nature to look afther it. *Mine* will never do *that*,' she added, wiping her eyes. 'But I'm deeply grateful she should keep with those who can put her in her own station; and I'll be no burthen on them or her. I'll earn my own living, as I do now. But to say that I'm not to give her to her father, if I should ever find him—to say I'm not to see her of a Sunday—that I'm not to watch the light increasing in her eyes, that, *through God and his agents, I unclouded*—not sometimes to hear the voice that's the only music my heart danced to for years'—— She could not continue, but turned away her face and wept bitterly. Mrs Langham, too, felt more than she acknowledged. 'I have only spoken of myself,' said Margaret at last, 'but let Miss Evelyn spake for herself.'

She opened the door and called: the little girl bounded in like a fawn, and then paused to look shyly around at the fine pictures and rich things, and, above all, at an exquisite painting of the Virgin with the infant Christ, which Mrs Langham, being a Roman Catholic, treasured for a double reason. The light fell from the window upon her beautiful head, and before Margaret spoke, she turned with a smile towards 'the lady'—a smile of admiration, which was returned.

'Evelyn—*Miss* Evelyn, *avourneen*, do you see that good lady, that has often spoke kind to ye, darlint?'

'I do.'

'Could ye love her, *a-cushla!*'

'Ah, then, I could—I *do*, nurse!'

'Maybe as well as me?'

The child's laugh was momentary music, but it was a laugh of derision—and she twined her nurse's arm round her neck.

'But you'd try, darlint? She's a good lady—quite a lady, my bird alone!'

'*And so am I,*' said the little O'Dwyer.

Mrs Langham observed her proud look; it augured well for her project. The nurse continued, '*Avourneen*, this lady is very kind, very good; she wishes to take you to be her child, to tache you to play the fine music, and behave like a lady, and live in this beautiful room, and drive in a coach!'

'Live in this room! drive in a coach! play music!' repeated the child in ecstasy, her bashfulness conquered by delight. 'Oh! WE shall be so happy!'

'Not WE, *avourneen*, but *you*.'

'Shan't you like it? Oh, dear nurse, you can't mean not to like it!'

'But you are to leave me—not to see me any more—all these beautiful things to be yours to live among—but no mammy nurse.'

'Let us go,' said the child, seizing her nurse's hand between both hers, and rushing to the door—'let us go; *this is a bad place to stay in!*'

* * * * *

It is almost needless to say that nature triumphed. Margaret positively refused to become an inmate of Mrs Langham's house, but laboured in various humble callings, repaid most richly for her self-denial by the continued affection and improvement of Evelyn O'Dwyer. Nor did her energies or affections slumber over one object. Her inquiries respecting Garrett were continually renewed, though continually unsuccessful. At length her curiosity as to the fate of her brother's family was wrought almost to insanity by a letter from the priest of her parish, written several months after the troubled waters of the rebellion had been quelled for the time being.

'The place is changed for the bad entirely,' he wrote. 'Margaret, my poor woman, yer brother and the little girls are not in it now; he was drawn in, *with more of the boys*, to the plot of the Scrimmage; and when the game was up, why, a parcel of them gathered what they could, and left for the new world: there's not the shadow of a Sheil upon their own mountains now. News has come of their safe and happy landing—God be praised for that same! And to be sure, by all accounts, it's a fine place; but the parish is lonely without the faces of them I christened, whose arms I hoped would have borne their ould priest to his grave. The last word he said to me was, "Father Mullins," says he, "when you get the opportunity, tell *her*, my sister Margaret, that luck and her left us together; but say that my blessing is with her and Miss Evelyn day and night. Born and brought up for more than two hundred years under the lords of the soil, the natural heritors, the great O'Dwyers! she did her duty in doing her best for poor Masther Garrett's child. It was hard to part with my sister, the woman that had both head and heart!—but she did her duty, according to the good ould fashion which lost our great-great-grandfather his life with great glory, and put his name and part of his effigy upon the tombstone of the ould lord in the abbey church, whose gray towers and green ivy is to the fore among the hills of ould Ireland still!—a thought that will rise up our hearts among strangers, and make us think of ourselves, and what our people were before us, when we're in the land of strangers. You'll soon know where I'll be, Father Mullins," says he; "and if the Blessed Evelyn gets her sight—or if she does not, it's all one, as far as I'm concerned; and it'll go very hard with me if I can't make out a home for her—and a welcome, and me and mine proud to sarve her—*as becomes the followers of the family.*"

The letter contained more local news, and the name of him whom that poor faithful woman had loved during her life—loved, though forsaken, because she would not trust to any beyond her 'own people' the fealty which she conceived due to an O'Dwyer.

My picture is not too highly coloured. The intensity of affection—the most intense of all the passions of woman—was in this instance united to the clannish pride which in those days was more universal than it is now. We are growing too wise to love without receiving some advantage in return—we must inquire why, and know wherefore. Among the far mountains, by the sides of the distant lakes, and in the bosoms of the deep valleys, there are still such to be met with; but never was there one more faithful than Margaret Sheil. Still, she had many heart-yearnings after her *own* people and her *own* land. She was established in what *she* called 'the way of trade,' at the corner of Cheyne Walk, Chelsea. Mrs Langham lived in one of those stately old mansions facing the Thames; and Margaret, after much patient endurance, adding penny to penny, had taken a little room in one of those poor houses which, as in the Italian towns, crouch at the curbstones of right noble dwellings. This room opened below the pavement, but its window was a little above it; and at this window might be seen a dozen at least of good oranges; three or four lemons laid along the inner ledge, flanked on either side with pottles either empty or full of strawberries; cherries tied in 'hap'orths' on a peeled sally-stick; sundry cabbage and lettuce plants; long red radishes and little nuby white ones; interspersed with gingerbread, and the nameless sundries of a small greengrocer, in a small way; while within, Margaret, ever active and ever clean, washed, or starched, or knit, or did any and everything in the world she could get to do. This industry had its reward: she frequently saw 'Miss Evelyn' walk past with Mrs Langham, to enjoy beneath those old trees the breeze from the river; and she never did pass without leaving her friend for a moment, to fling her arms round Margaret's neck, call her 'dear darling mammy nurse,' and whisper any little bit of half-childish half-girlish news she thought would please her. Margaret perceived that 'the lady' was somewhat jealous of this love, but she had the good sense not to mind it. She *saw* her darling in the enjoyment of positive good—she knew she loved her—she went to see her occasionally in the fine house, and was sometimes, on a Sunday evening, when Mrs Langham took her afternoon nap, permitted to walk with her in the long, stiff, stately garden at the back of the house; and there she could talk of Ireland, the name of which set her young heart beating.

'Love it; my darlint, love it ever! But my wo is, *avourneen*, that you *war dark* when you war in it, and can't tell the differ betwixt the two counthries. The first time ye saw (to remember) the blessed light was in the doctor's study; he's a fine man, to be sure, and a good one, God bless him; but his house had a quare look. Och hone! if you had but seen how green the grass is, and how blue the mountains, and how clear the sky, I'd be satisfied. But, Evelyn, darling, I have no right to be saying "satisfied:" such a cowld word, after the great blessing the Almighty poured upon you—that's what I ought to think of, and you too, *a-lanna-machree!* And the blessing that always followed ye, poor, weeping, dawshy craythur that ye war, the first time ye war given as new sight to my own eyes! Oh, thin, but the ways of the Almighty are wonderful by sea and land! Oh, thin, dear! as ye could not *see*, does yer mind ever turn to the *sounds* of yer own counthry?'

'Yes,' replied the girl; 'oh yes! Often I sit under that old mulberry-tree, and look through its leaves up to the sky; but the music of the lark does not come *falling upon my eyes from the clouds*, as I used to fancy it did when we were at home and I was blind. Do you mind, mammy nurse, how I used to know the birds by their notes; and do you remember how I followed the whistle of the plover?'

'Do I!—oh, but you war the weary child without any fear! And how we all looked afther ye, and no good, until I found ye asleep on the very edge of a bog-hole, that would have swallowed ould Cromwell and all his troopers, if he had only had the luck to fall into it! There ye war, *laughing in the sun's face*, and ye asleep, and one turn would have finished ye! My brother (he had great faith in such things) said it was the slip of hazel ye held in yer hand that saved ye. But I always thought the Almighty put His *two eyes in care over the blind.*'

'Nurse, whenever Mrs Langham gives me praise, *then I wish my father heard it.*'

'The Lord will give ye yer heart's wish yet, *a-chora-machree* —trust in Him. Sure, though I never thought to see Masther Garrett's child depindent on any one, still, sure it's wonderful intirely the luck ye've had: it's like an ould story, so it is.'

'And all through you, dear mammy nurse; through you!' said Evelyn—and she said truly.

Margaret never suffered more than three months to elapse without making inquiry at the oculist's if news had been heard of 'Masther Garrett;' so steady was she in this matter, that 'as persevering as Margaret Sheil' passed into a proverb, and the little *old* Irishwoman—*old*, as she was called by the very young of the family—was a constant querist on the usual subject.

At last came the peace—frail as it turned out to be—of 1802. Margaret's regular habits became confused; she absolutely confounded apples with pears, and two of her neighbours complained that her eggs were musty. She did nothing but borrow and read newspapers, write letters, and instead of being satisfied with a quarterly visit to the oculist, visited him twice, or at least once, a week. She was seen more frequently hovering round the Bond Street hotels than returning from Covent Garden market with her 'greenery;' and truly the gossips thought Margaret was taking leave of her senses. With her usual wisdom and kindness, she did not suggest to Evelyn the possibility of her father visiting England at this period, though it was the engrossing feeling of her own existence. She could not rest by day, nor sleep at night, for the thought that 'Masther Garrett's' voice sounded in her ear, exclaiming, 'Margaret, where is my child?' The oculist, proud of 'Evelyn's eyes,' admiring the admirable fidelity of the Irish nurse, and constantly applied to by her for news of 'Masther Garrett,' was himself stirred up to make inquiries that otherwise he would not have thought of. But though foreigners poured into England almost as rapidly as English poured out of it, still 'he came not.' Each morning Margaret arose with hope, each night sickened with despair. Yet still she wandered in and about the city, peering into every carriage that passed, and inquiring at the hotels, where her rebuffs were many, 'what strangers had arrived in town?' No peasant in the world bears a rebuff so well as an Irish one, even if the sting enters their heart; and that *they feel* it, the quick blood mantling to their cheeks is sure to tell. Still, they either take it meekly, or wing it back to the giver, armed either with a jest or a blessing. The Irish nurse was too earnest to jest, nor was she ever profuse of words, so she took the rebukes meekly, as she never failed to repeat the offence in a day or two. The loungers about the hotel doors were sure to be addressed with, 'I humbly ax yer pardon, but is there such a one here as a gentleman, one Mr, or, it may be, Captain, Colonel, or Count Garrett O'Dwyer?'

'Are you his mother?'

'Is it me!—oh, *wisha*, no!—nothing but *a follower of the family*, that wants to hear tell of him.'

'Why, you asked here last week.'

'Sure I know I did, sir; he wasn't in it then; the more reason he'd be in it now.'

'Go to the d—l!—there's no such person here.'

'Thank ye, sir. I'll just take the liberty to come again in a day or two.'

'You need not trouble yourself.'

'No trouble in life, sir, thanking you for your consideration; and if it was, I shouldn't find it so. Good morning, sir.' And she would turn her patient face towards another hotel, to meet with, it might be, even a more rough reception.

One evening Margaret returned weary and dispirited. The few customers her industry and attention had secured had fallen off, for she was not at home to attend to their small wants. Her oranges had become shrivelled, and her lemons mouldy; she turned them over, sighed, and sat down to look out upon the noble Thames, that glided on, a sheet of molten gold; for the sun was setting in all its glory. She peeped through the trunks of the tall trees, and thought how black and harsh the wooden arches, and crosses, and beams of the old bridge looked; and then the splash of oars from a very gay wherry that was nearing the landing smote upon her ear; and then the strains of a song, certainly not English, which was concluded by a laughing sort of chorus; and that, as the gay boat was moored at the landing, was followed by what seemed a half-English, half-foreign conversation. This aroused Margaret, and fatigued as she was, she went out, 'just,' as she often said in after-times, 'to see if any of them might be Masther Garrett.' They had left their boat to inspect the coffee-house rendered so famous by the wits of a past age, the famous Don Saltero's; which has 'degenerated' in the present day, but still exists; and Margaret, having satisfied her curiosity, was about to turn away, when the accent of one of the gentlemen, a tall, florid, mustachoed man, fixed her to the spot. A residence abroad seems to rivet an Irishman's brogue, and certainly *his* was ripe and racy.

'It's beautiful, certainly,' he said, with reference to the river; 'but somehow, I always miss the mountains. I suppose it is from being used to them when I was a boy.'

'Ah! thin,' exclaimed Margaret, rushing forward more like a maniac than a sane woman, and completely losing the gentle, staid manner for which she was so remarkable, and speaking with fearful rapidity—'ah! thin, ye think of the Slieve-brui, the Gra-na-goul, the—the—— But no, no—Masther Garrett, *avick*—ye think ye do—I know it's yourself that's in it—yer mother's smile —the eyes of yer poor father—the heavens be his bed!—— Ye think—OF THAT NIGHT—yer dead wife—the corpse of yer mother —of the child—the babe—the jewel—that ye left in the heart of Margaret Sheil—you—you—oh God! I shall die—before I give her back!' And utterly overthrown by the outbreak of feelings which had been cherished, and treasured, and concealed for years, the *follower of the family* sank at the feet of Garrett O'Dwyer.

The scene was so startling, that the cheerful party became silent.

Nature tugged at the soldier's heart. He would not, if he could, refute her statement. All the past, which had been but the dream of his boyhood, came back upon him; and man of the world though he was, he leant against a tree, totally overpowered, while others attended to and revived poor Margaret. No feeling of ridicule could be attached to the scene: it was too strong, too earnest, for anything but sympathy. Startling and improbable as it sounded, no one who heard doubted its perfect truth. With the instinctive delicacy, I will not say of refined minds, but of human nature, his companions retreated; when Margaret, restored to herself, was enabled to suppress her emotions, and mutter to herself, while holding 'Masther Garrett's' hand within her own, 'It's no drame—I'm awake—my eyes are open—God bless us! the marcy of the Lord is great! But ye must come with me—I cannot tell ye here;' and never casting a thought upon the rank and station of the exiled but prosperous Irishman, she clung to, while she conducted him to her humble home. And there, without imagining for a moment that she was recording a tale of as great and exalted faithfulness as was ever performed by woman, she told her history, and the history of Evelyn O'Dwyer.

How was it that, even while she spoke, the impulse of that man's heart beat slower and more slow—that a record which, when first I heard it, moved even me to tears, fell upon the father's heart rather as a tale of sorrow than of joy?—how that, instead of the yearnings of a father's soul towards his child, sprang up the selfish calculation of what he should do with her?—of what Madame O'Dwyer, his young, rich, and imperious wife, would say on his return abroad, to a young and beautiful rival in the shape of his daughter? Nay, if she were only a third part as beautiful as described by Margaret, what domestic discomfort would it not create!

The *follower of the family* did not understand the cause of his silence. He was ashamed to confess his thoughts; for we are always ashamed to confess unworthy thoughts in the presence of the virtuous. And the hero of two 'forlorn hopes,' the star of many a brilliant saloon, felt his unworthiness, his moral insignificance, in the presence of that poor, uninstructed, but noble-hearted and high-souled woman: his brave, bold eye could not encounter the holy affection, the bright truth, that rendered hers sunny as the first look-out of the unsullied morning.

'And now, Masther Garrett dear,' she said, 'and now, Masther Garrett, *avick machree* (but I suppose you've no Irish now), and it's Colonel, or General at laste, or maybe My Lord, I ought to be calling ye—*ye bird of my bosom!*—come till I give ye back yer own beautiful child, that will be a blessing, and an honour, and a glory to ye! Oh, stay till ye see her—that's all—and sure I am it will kill the dear kind lady she's with to part with her; for she always said ye'd never come back, sir; but I said ye would—and her eyes, God be thanked! as clear as a kitten's—and will raise yer heart with the tune of St Patrick's day, played by her long white fingers on the piano! Think of that, Masther—I mean General, dear— And—but sure it's all like a play—I knew the glory would be in the end.'

'Stay, Margaret,' he said; 'I shall of course be delighted to see this girl, my daughter; but—you must be aware, deeply grateful as I am for your fidelity—that—in short—it *is* rather an awkward business for a young man like me to have a child of that age. The troubles in my poor country—never hearing of you—I thought the child dead; and, in short, I am married, have one child, a boy, and I never told my wife I had been a father.'

'Never told her ye were married before!' said Margaret. 'Oh, thin, honey, why didn't ye? Poor Moyna wasn't your equal *till ye made her so; and ye owed respect to the memory of a heart that loved ye to death.*'

Master Garrett became confused, but at last replied, 'As to the marriage, it was the couple-beggar who—— But it was hardly —a—do not look at me so intently, Margaret. You know I was a boy—a mere boy, not more than nineteen—a foolish boy.'

'Now, God stop me from saying the word that's struggling in my throat!' exclaimed Margaret Sheil, and her figure appeared to grow into dignity. 'You said you war a foolish boy—I had it on my tongue to say a cursed one. But I can't, Masther Garrett, I can't, though you desarve it. Many's the sleep ye had in these arms—I had the last breath of yer mother—almost the first breath of yer child. I cannot say you are cursed—but, oh! to think of putting a shame on her! Oh, Masther Garrett, it was the cowld, cowld world that spoke, and not the descendant of him whom my great-great-grandfather died to save! I see ye didn't mane it— ye'—— She paused suddenly, and then added in a lower tone of voice, 'Hush! the Lord is about us—he *has* a hand in us all! I hear her step coming down the street—I'd hear it among the tramp of forty horses—it wouldn't crush a grasshopper—it's light and swift as a swallow's wing! She's here!' And truly Evelyn O'Dwyer lifted the latch, and stood a vision of beauty before her astonished father, whom she did not see at first, for the door opened into the room, and he was in some degree concealed behind it.

'Nurse, we want you; I got leave to come for you myself. How warm it is!' she added, throwing back her bonnet, when her hair fell in rich masses over her shoulders. 'Nurse! my mammy nurse! how odd you look! Do speak! Are you ill, darling nurse? Have you any bad news? What ails you?'

Margaret flung to the door, and (for she was unable to speak) seized Evelyn's hand, and placed it in her father's; then falling on her knees, she muttered a few inarticulate words of thankful-

K

ness to God; adding, as she rose, 'That's yer father, Miss Evelyn; his heart is in the hands of the Almighty. Wont ye let me hear ye own her as yer true *lawful* child? Oh, Masther Garrett, I gained the light of those eyes for ye, that they might beam the child's welcome to her only parent. I gained that blessing for ye, *through the help of God!* And now I don't ask ye to take her, or provide for her—the Almighty has done that; but I ask ye, in honour to those who look down upon us now, in a strange land, from the blessed gates of heaven—I ask you, to let me hear you own her as your lawful child!'

Garrett O'Dwyer could not resist this appeal; he pressed his weeping daughter to his bosom, and Margaret heard what she desired. Great indeed was her happiness.

* * * * *

The First Consul did not suffer the peace to continue, and Garrett O'Dwyer left England almost as suddenly as he had done before. The *follower of the family* manifested no regret at his departure. He made her many handsome presents, and gave an abundance of jewels to his child, who remained with the lady that might be considered her adopted mother. A gloomy shadow always passed over Margaret's face when *Count* O'Dwyer's name was mentioned. One thing was somewhat remarkable:— She refused to marry her old, gray-headed lover, who followed her to London, 'because,' she said, ' there was no telling how a man might change.' She never went to her brother, or to Ireland, though she always talked of doing both.

Evelyn is now the mother of many beautiful children; and Margaret, a little, bent, cheerful, though rather silent, blue-eyed, old woman, is still—a FOLLOWER OF THE FAMILY.

REDDY RYLAND;

SHOWING HOW 'THE SHINE' WAS TAKEN OUT OF HIM.

LAUGHING, loving, rollicking, rousing, fighting, tearing, dancing, singing, good-natured Reddy! of all the kind-hearted, light-hearted, gay-hearted fellows that ever whirled a shillala at a fight (*when he could not help it,* for Reddy declared that otherwise he never fought), or *covered the buckle** at a fair, Reddy Ryland was the king! His very face was a jest-book. His eyes, though wild and blue, were not as mischievous as mirthful; his full, flexible mouth was surrounded by folds and dimples, where wit and humour rested at all times and all seasons. His hat sat in a most knowing manner

---

* A favourite Irish step (not known in quadrilles).

upon the full rich curls of his brown hair; his gay-coloured silk neckerchief was tied so loosely round his throat, that if it were possible he had ever seen a picture of Byron, folk would have said he was imitating the lordly poet; his figure was that of a lithe and graceful mountaineer—his voice the very echo of mirth and joy; and his name for ten miles round his mother's dwelling (Reddy was resolved it should not be considered *his* until after her death) was sure to excite either a smile or a blessing, perhaps both. With all this, Reddy was careful of the main chance—a good farmer in a small way, and a prosperous one; read Martin Doyle and Captain Blackyer; understood green crops, and stall-fed his cow; had really brewed his own beer twice, and it only turned sour *once;* talked of joining the Temperance Society—though I need not add, that if Reddy had been fond of 'the drop,' he would not have been the prosperous fellow he was. Here, then, was an Irish peasant free from the common faults of his countrymen; he seldom procrastinated; was sober, honest, truthful, diligent, and, to use the phrase which his mother applied to him at least ten times a day, 'was as good a son as ever raised his head beneath the canopy of heaven.' What, then, can I have to say about Reddy Ryland, more than to give honour due to his good qualities? If this be all, my task is nearly done; for the language of praise, I am told, is used sparingly by the prudent; people in an ordinary way tire amazingly over the record of their neighbours' virtues. It is very delightful to feel their good effects—to enjoy the advantages arising therefrom; but we do not like to hear them lauded what we call too highly; it is a sort of implied censure on our own imperfections that we do not relish; consequently, we are by many degrees too anxious to pick out faults, and thrust our tongues therein, as children do their fingers into small rents, to make them larger. The rent, the faulty spot in Reddy's character, was unfortunately large enough for all the tongues in the country to wag through; and let no one suppose that his popularity prevented many a bitter animadversion upon his imperfection; his particular friends never praised him without exclaiming, 'Ah, thin, sure he *is* a darlint; sorra a one like him in the counthry; and sure it's an angel he'd be *all out,* but *for that fault he has.*' It certainly is marvellous how our intimates discover and publish our faults, oiling their observations with 'what a pity!' Reddy's fault was, in a word, a superabundance of conceit—real *personal* vanity. When he was a little boy, he used to dress his hair in every tub of water that came in his way; and when he grew up 'a slip of a boy,' his first pocket-money purchased—a looking-glass.

Reddy was intolerably vain; he thought himself the handsomest 'boy' in the barony; and more than that, he had the impudence to declare that no woman could refuse him! I must confess that the country girls had, if not sown, cultivated this vanity to a very considerable extent; they paid him a great deal too much attention, which is anything but good for men in general; and the consequence was, that Reddy considered himself very much as a sort of Irish grand sultan, who had nothing to do but throw his handkerchief upon the favoured fair one; and be she who she might, she would rejoice to become his bride!

'Ah, thin, Reddy dear!' exclaimed his mother one Sunday morning, when Reddy had, even in her opinion, taken a very long time to dress for mass—'ah, thin, Reddy dear, what ails the shoes?'

'Mother, dear, it's *boots* that's in it; and I'm thinking they'll wrinkle on the instep.'

'Well, dear, why are you faulting them so? Sure they're mighty slim and purty to look at; and the only wonder I have, is how ye ever got yer feet into them. Oh, thin, what would your father say to see ye turning out on the road in single soles, without so much as a sparable in the heel. Oh, my! why, thin, Reddy, *you have* a mighty purty fut, God bless it!'

'Well, mother, it's nate, I don't deny it,' he answered, elevating his foot, and viewing it in every position; 'I never *go out on the floor** without seeing the notice that's taken of it, especially in heel-and-toe; that's the step to show the shape to advantage— whoop!'

And Reddy cut a caper, while his mother said, 'Aisy, Reddy; it's time enough to begin that sort of *divarshin* afther mass. That's a mighty purty handkerchief ye've got about yer neck, dear; they do be saying you don't close up your throat because it's so handsome; ye always had a mighty clane† skin.'

Reddy showed his teeth at the compliment.

'Darling boy, your hair is a thrifle too long; I'll cut it the morrow morning if you like.'

'Mother,' answered Reddy, somewhat indignantly, 'ye may dock all the children in the parish, but ye shan't *massacree* my curls any more. Ye spoilt me intirely last fair-day.'

'Well, dear,' answered the mother, who was perfectly conscious of her son's weakness, though she encouraged it, 'there's the bowl dish I always put on yer father's head when I cut his hair, that I might trim it all round, even; one would have thought the dish made on his head, it fitted so beautiful: that was when first we war married; but, bedad! after a fair or a faction fight, the knocks would grow up, and grow out, and push it up—I always allowed for them in the cutting—and he never said—not he (the heavens be his bed!), "Nell, it's not to my liking." He was as handsome to the full as you, Reddy, *avick!* but never took as much pride out of himself as you do. Now, don't put a frown upon *your joy of a face* to your ould mother, my son. The times

* Dance.   † Fair.

are changed now, and the young men think more of themselves than they used—times and fashions do change, *agra!* Sure I mind the misthress at the big house riding to church on a pillion behind the coachman, in a green Joseph, a goold watch as big as your fist, and a beautiful beaver and feathers—jog jump! jog jump! all along the road. And then of a week-day, my darlint; to see her up before the maids in the morning at daybreak, and rowling out the pasthry for company, and clearing jelly!—that was her glory. And now, why, the ladies rides in coaches, and leaves word with the maids to get up, and orders the pasthry, and faults the jelly, *avick machree!* There's not the heartiness in the counthry of the good ould times; we're fading from sunbames into moonbames: *that's* what ails us!'

'Am *I* a moonbame, mother?' inquired the son with an insinuating look.

'A moonbame, *avick!* Ah, thin, no; that you aint. You're a flash-o'-lightning boy—oh! that's what you are. And if you do take a taste of pride out of yerself, *who* has a betther right, and all the counthry putting it into you?'

Reddy perfectly agreed with his mother; and after giving her a hearty kiss, as it was yet too early for second, and too late for first prayers, he thought he would open his heart to her, as he had long intended to do.

'Ah, thin, mother darlint, will ye listen to us for a few minutes, and give us yer advice, which we want at this present time intirely, ye see?'

'Why, thin, I will, to be sure, and pray the Lord to put sense into me for that same; for a mother's counsel comes oftener from the heart than from the head. What is it, *avick?*'

'How ould was my father whin he married?'

'Why, thin, not all out twenty-one.'

'And I'm twenty-five next Martinmas, plase God. Mother, that's a shame.'

'That the Lord has given you so many years, is it?' said the widow, with great *naïveté.*

'Dear! how innocent ye are all of a suddent, mother! No, but that I didn't do as my father did before me.'

'Ah, thin, no one can reproach ye with that same, *avourneen;* not many a fair in the counthry but knows the face and figure of Reddy Ryland to be the same as his father's—and sorry a purty girl that ye haven't made love to, ever since you counted—— Oh, my grief! why, Reddy, you made love to purty Peggy Garvey before you war turned thirteen—*that* was kind father for ye, anyway.'

'Mother, now lave off make-believing *innocence;* sure ye know very well what I mane is—it is time I was —married!'

His mother gave a very admirable start of astonishment, and, after a pause, said, 'Well! it's natural, and so—why!—sure my

darling boy has only to ax and have, only to pick the counthry!
Ah, thin, Reddy, why don't ye make up yer mind to Ellen
Rossiter? It's her people, every one of them, that has the warm
house and the warm heart.'

'Mother, I've nothing to say aginst the girl, only I'd be affeard
her head would set the house a-fire. Now, mother, that's enough.
I never could abide red hair.'

'It's only auburn, my son; and sure, after a few years, it will
be the colour of mine—white like the first snow; beauty's but
skin deep, though its memory is pleasant when it does fade.
Well, there, I'm done; I'll say no more about her. What do ye
think of Miss Kitty Blakeney?'

'She's short, mother; all out too short, mother.'

'*Let her stand on her purse*, Reddy dear,' replied the mother;
'let her stand on *that*, and she'll be even with Squire Baine's tall
poplar tree! Maybe Miss Kitty hasn't a purse! Oh, thin, it's
yerself that's hard to be plased; I'll say no more about her,
though it's yellow goold she'd give ye to ate, if she had ye.
Well, maybe Mary Murphy is long enough to plase ye?'

'The *stalking voragah!* She *is* long enough, but her family's
not long. I must have *blood, bone,* and *beauty,* and that's the
thruth, and I'll never marry without it, never throw myself away
—that's what I wont do. I'll show the counthry what a wife
ought to be. I'll not marry a girl, to be ashamed of her people.
I'll not marry a poplar nor a furze-bush. I'll not marry for
money, nor all out pride, nor all out love, only a little of both.
I'd like a girl, ye see, that would be proud of her husband, particularly when we'd be both in our Sunday clothes. I'll never
marry a girl that hasn't sunshine in every bit of her face.'

'And in her timper too, I hope; a good timper is a cordial to
man's heart. It's the nurse for sorrow—the medicine for sickness—the *wine at a poor man's table.* Whatever ye do, *avick,*
watch the timper.'

'I don't think,' said Reddy, looking at himself in the glass that
hung from a nail in the dresser—'I don't think any woman could
be ill-timpered with me.'

'The heavens never shone on a better boy, that's thrue; but for
all that, some women is mighty inganious. But, Reddy, don't
marry a girl that's altogether without money; it's a mighty *savery*
thing in a house; but don't marry altogether for it.'

'Trust me, mother dear; but is there no one else you can
think of?'

'Sorra one, unless it be the Flower of Loughgully, and'——

'Don't name *her,* mother dear, if you plase,' said Reddy, turning away his face. 'I'll not deny that I thought onct a dale of
Kathleen O'Brien; a great dale; but nobody ever thought as
much of her as she did of herself, and so '——

'She didn't dare refuse *you?*' observed Mrs Ryland indignantly.

'No, no, not *that;* but *she* laughed at *me;* and—I wonder at ye, mother, to name the Flower of Loughgully to me. Ye just did it to get a rise out of me, that's all; but don't do it again, mother. I'll show *her,* before a month is over her raven hair, that she bands so neat—before another month has made us all nearer to eternity, I'll show her the sort of wife Reddy Ryland can get. I'll'—— He paused, overcome by contending feelings to which his mother had no clue; and then, while she thought over his words, he added, with his usual gaiety of manner, 'I've made up my mind to go to Kilkenny next week, where I've heard of one from my cousin to suit me; and maybe I wont bring ye a daughter, mother! There's not a girl in this country fit for *that,* mother,' and he looked, *not* at his mother, but at himself; 'not one. And now God be with ye! I've made up my mind to be married, and now I've tould you. I'll punish the hearts of the girls—of *the* girl, anyway, that—— But God be with ye, mother; I must not lose mass;' and off he bounded, leaving his mother to recall and cogitate over the old adage of 'the more haste, the worse speed.'

'If,' said she, 'after all, he should marry out of spite to the Flower of Loughgully, what might come of it! I named her last, to see if he would speak of her, but he did not; and yet I'm sure his heart turned to her above all others, though he'd never *give in* to her, nor she to him—she has such a spirit! And sometimes I think I make too much of my boy, but I can't help it. His face, so handsome, so like his father's; and his voice, when he calls me in the morning, or blesses me at night—I often think my own darlint is with me again! Pray the Almighty,' said the widow, after a long pause, and clasping her hands—'pray the Almighty that, after having had the pick of the counthry, *he don't take the crooked stick at last!*'

Now, it so happened that the widow Ryland did everything in her power to prevent her son's visit to Kilkenny; but she had not accustomed him to contradiction, and he would go, and he did go; and the neighbours said Reddy Ryland was gone to Kilkenny to bring home a wife; and when Kathleen O'Brien, the Flower of Loughgully, heard *that,* she wept bitterly, for she had calculated on the influence of her own beauty over the heart of her lover, having altogether forgotten how completely he was absorbed in the contemplation of his own perfections. A woman never can have much power over a vain man.

Three weeks elapsed, and Reddy returned to his home, and his foot and eye were both heavy; the elasticity had departed from the one, and the brightness from the other. His mother pressed him to her bosom, and his neighbours crowded to welcome his arrival. Many a hand was extended; and 'sure we'll have some fun now ye're come back,' said one. 'Ah, thin, it was a quare wake Andy Macgillicuddy had, poor man; the pipes weren't half smoked, and the dancing not worth a farthing, 'cause *you* warn't in it,' said another. 'Sure ye never saw a gayer boy than yerself, Reddy, since ye left it,' exclaimed a third. 'Well, he's with us again anyhow. But, Reddy, *where's* the Kilkenny lady you war to bring to show us the fashions?' inquired a fourth.

Reddy laughed, and turned off the question, and called for some whisky to treat his friends. His mother observed he made his punch double its usual strength; and, as she said afterwards, an '*impression*' came over her heart '*like the hand o' death,*' for she saw something was wrong, and she sat looking at her son with tears in her eyes; even when their friends were gone, she had not courage to ask him if he was married; but Reddy walked to the table after he had shut the door, and filling out a great glass of whisky, drank it off, and then said, 'Mother, wish me joy. Joy, joy, mother! I'm married!'

'Oh, Reddy, it isn't possible that's true—without ever consulting yer mother, or letting her see yer choice!'

'It's as true, mother—as bad luck.'

'Oh, Reddy, my own son, has she "*the blood*" you talked about! Is she of an ancient family all out?'

'Mother,' answered Reddy, after a pause, 'it's not aisy to get everything.'

'Oh wisha! if ye'd thought of that before, ye need not have gone to Kilkenny for a wife. Well, I daresay she's a fine figure of a woman. She has *bone* anyhow?'

'None to spare,' said the hard-to-be-pleased gentleman; 'however, she's my wife.'

'And a beauty?' added the mother; 'I'm sure, sartin sure, she has beauty?'

'The devil as much as would fit on the top of a grasshopper's toe,' replied her son impetuously.

'Not blood, nor bone, nor beauty! Well, maybe she has better materials than any of them to make a good wife. She was your cousin's recommending, and he knew how much you wanted a girl to set a pattern to the counthry.'

'She was *not* my cousin's recommending, mother; but somehow she's a very town-bred woman, and took a wonderful liking to me.'

'A good edication's a fine thing,' said Mrs Ryland, almost weeping; for, like all the Irish, she laid great value on the qualities Reddy had confessed she did *not* possess; but she was a gentlehearted woman, and desired, in her simple wisdom, to make the best of everything—no bad wisdom either.

'It is, mother,' sighed the bridegroom.

'But what has she besides the edication, Reddy?' inquired his mother, seeing that her beloved son sat moodily with his hands clasped resting on the table, and his chin fixed upon them. 'What has she besides the edication?'

'*Two small children*,' was Reddy's reply.

'Oh, Reddy, Reddy, is that the end of ye?' exclaimed his distracted mother; 'you, the pride of the county—the beauty of the parish—that might have had the pick of the whole county for a wife!—you, who was thought so much of, and who thought so much of yerself!'

'You're right, mother!' interrupted Reddy; '*that last did it.* If it hadn't been for that, I might have been content with—— But no matter—it's all over now. She was a widow, mother; *and I was so sure not to be caught by a widow*, that I took no heed. I persuaded her to stop half way, and that I'd take the car for her.'

'And the children,' added his mother. 'And the same car can take me out of this! *two* widows are too much for any man's house. Oh, Reddy, Reddy, to think of this! to think of this! how you war taken in! How was it?'

But Reddy would not tell; the affair was a mystery. His old mother was broken-hearted; she refused to remain in his house, though somewhat comforted by the information that the bride was rich, though *red-haired;* and at last, unable to withstand the strong intreaties of her son, she agreed to receive her before she departed. The next day was one of mingled curiosity and lamentation amongst the female population of the neighbourhood, while the men agreed, with something like satisfaction, that 'the shine' was now taken out of handsome, loving, rousing, fighting, dancing, singing, good-natured Reddy Ryland. If 'the shine,' as they called it, was taken out of Reddy by the mere 'report,' how much more was he either to be pitied or exulted over when the bride made her appearance! His poor mother could not support it. Of all the crooked sticks, she was the most crooked that had ever been seen. How the married men laughed, and talked of bachelors' wives; and how the young men tittered, and the young girls peeped from under their hoods at the broad, bold, ruddy-faced—— Was *that* his choice indeed? No sunshine in her face; and such a. tongue! In less than two months, everybody sympathised with the young farmer: his vanity was punished. He was fading into a shadow, and certainly his feelings were not soothed by an incident, which is nothing to tell, but a great deal to feel. He met Kathleen O'Brien one morning at the turn of a particular lane, where he had often met her before. She did not recognise him at first, but his voice. 'Kathleen; we may be friends, Kathleen— you *will not laugh at me now*—it was *that* did it, Kathleen—*that:* my pride could not bear it; but I'm punished. I've had the fall which they say follows pride. Wont you spake? Sure the whole counthry sees " the shine is taken out of Reddy Ryland." Wont

ye bid God bless me? I've need of a blessing, Kathleen. I own
I did it to vex ye. Wont ye forgive me?'

Kathleen, the Flower of Loughgully, could not speak the forgiveness that came to her lips, but turned away from her old
lover to hide her tears.

Unvirtuous love, if love it may be called, is almost unknown
in Irish peasant life. Reddy was glad no one had seen him
speak to Kathleen; he loved her fame quite as much as he had
once loved herself.

Mrs Reddy was, every one knew, a regular virago. What she
had been, people only guessed; but she said her husband had
been drowned at sea.

No wealth had been added to Reddy's store—*that* was very
evident; and things appeared going to ruin—the old story where
there is no affection—when suddenly a stranger stood at the
threshold of Reddy Ryland's house, and inquired for his wife.

'She's within, honest man,' said the young farmer.

'But you're not Reddy Ryland?' said the traveller.

'I *was*,' was the reply.

'But I heard he was a fine, slashing, handsome, rollicking
boy,' persisted the stranger, who looked and spoke like a sailor.

'I wish to God I had never heard it,' observed Reddy.

'Well, certainly Poll would take the shine out of anything,
from a new shilling upwards, if *you* are the Reddy Ryland I
heard tell of,' persisted the man, looking at him from head to
foot.

'And who are you?' inquired Reddy.

'Who am I? Why, I'm Poll's husband; and don't be afraid—
all I want is my children. I'll make you a present of her, and
welcome. She thought me dead; and, by the powers! such a
lass as that deserves credit!'

'For what?' inquired the delighted Reddy.

'For having the art, d'ye see, to catch two such beautiful boys
as our two selves.'

Reddy Ryland was in no degree disposed to accept the present
so liberally offered. He was both laughed at and congratulated
by his neighbours. His mother returned, but he never allowed
her to utter a word in his praise. 'I'll never heed a flattering
tongue again,' he would say; 'I've had enough of *that*.'

A little longer, and Kathleen herself took pity on him. And
again he returned to his former self: in every respect but one he
was exactly the same. He confessed that 'the widow,' as he
always called her, had got at his *weak side*, flattered his vanity,
and thus accomplished her purpose. 'The shine,' in truth, was
'taken out of him,' but the substance remained; and Reddy
Ryland, a handsome Irish peasant, is at this moment a *rara avis*
—a vain man cured!

THE CROCK OF GOLD.

In the county of Wexford, and in a nook which, fifty years ago, was completely apart from the ordinary route of travellers, are situated the Seven Castles of Clonmines. An arm of the sea, called 'The Scar,' separates them from the parish of Bannow. In my childhood they were to me objects of deep interest: I had no playmate, no companion; and when my relatives went on friendly visitings in the neighbourhood, they would take me with them; it being a fixed principle that I was never to be left to the care of servants. One of our best and dearest friends dwelt in a house called Barristown, nearly opposite those fine old ruins; and happy indeed was I when the carriage was ordered to prepare for a drive thither. It was inhabited at that period by a very aged lady and her youngest son, an old bachelor; her granddaughter also lived with them, a young lady of most amiable mind and manners.

Sally H——, though a young woman when I was born, was, nevertheless, my playfellow, my adviser, my friend; and proud was I, as a little girl, to have a tall lady for my companion. She would pet me, and scold me, and reason with me, and tell me stories. She had such mild soft eyes, so gentle a voice, and a certain degree of refinement in her manners—the result, perhaps, of delicate health—that now, through the vista of years, I revert to her as one of the sweetest and fairest of my memories. She used to say I would forget her when I came to England; a prophecy that always made me weep. But she did me injustice: I never did forget her, nor the double violets she used to drop over the pew, on entering church, into my lap; nor the delight I felt when placed on her side-saddle, her long fair arm holding me in my seat; dear, kind creature! When the world has been only a little hard with us, how sweetly comes the remembrance of kindness bestowed on our youth! It seems as if there never had been kindness like unto that; and we wonder how the world is changed—grown chill, and cold, and estranged. And we love to shut our eyes upon all things present, and live over again, with the dear ones of the olden time, our young and thoughtless years! But this is worse than idle; we are with the present, and of the present.

When last I drove by old Barristown it looked grim and gray, shut in with its own loneliness—nothing about it telling of existence, except the rooks that cawed above the one tall ivied tower, where the old lady slept and died. It looked gray and sad—and well it might; for those who made it ring again with hospitality were all—all—in their silent graves. It frowned at the sunshine like a thing that would not be comforted. I was glad to send my thoughts and my gaze across the waters to the ruins of the Seven Castles of Clonmines, and they looked, as they had always done to me, landmarks of mystery, and full of the deepest and most solemn interest. Time, which had destroyed the charm of the more modern structure, had only added a few more ivy wreaths to the old castles. I could hardly discern even if they had crumbled nearer to the earth, for the ivy, with the solicitude of the truest friendship, concealed all defects, and laboured to keep the mouldering stones together. Very, very beautiful the old castles looked, lying in the vale of the Scar, covering a considerable extent of the greenest meadow-land it is possible to imagine, and leading the mind back to the olden time, when wassail and superstition celebrated their alternate orgies within those walls. A bridge beyond the castles, called 'Wellington Bridge,' crosses the arm of the sea I have already mentioned, and facilitates communication between the secluded neighbourhood of Bannow, and Ross, and Waterford. Before the bridge was built, those who wished to get to the opposite side were obliged to wait till the tide was out, and cross at the ford. The country girls proceeding to Ballyhack to sell their eggs used to take off their shoes and stockings, and wade across, carrying their marketing on their heads; if the tide ran strong, they would link hands and cross in numbers. And I remember but one or two accidents; though, since they have got the bridge, crossing the ford is spoken of as a barbarism—I should say, since they have got the *road* to the bridge; for, be it known, that the bridge was finished three years before the road was made. But things are better ordered now.

The morning was fine, and leaving Barristown and its host of memories, I thought I should like a ramble round the Seven Castles, and in a short time I was scrambling among the ruins with little Daniel Muckleroy for my guide—the guide being far more ignorant of the locale than myself, yet *too Irish* to suffer his ignorance to appear.

'Dan, do you know who built these castles?'

Dan (a little perplexed), 'Myself can't say *exactly* how ould they are, but some a hundred thousand years anyway!'

'But who built them?'

'Oliver Crom'ell, my lady.'

'And who destroyed them, Dan?'

'Bedad, ma'am, it was Oliver Crom'ell.'

'What! did he build them up and pull them down?'

'Bedad, my lady, I'll go bail he did that same; for ye see, my lady, he had *a bad heart to the counthry*, and could never let well alone.'

This attributing of all things bad to the great Cromwell is

universal throughout Ireland. Dan's mode of reasoning was by no means singular, strange as it must sound to English ears.

'You think he was a bad fellow, Dan?'

'The Lord be between us and harrum, my lady! he was the devil himself! My great-grandfather see him onct, and a bad light he was to him, and his, and us, and every foot o' land he could lay his eye, let alone his hoof on. Oh, bedad! he was all out the worst sight ever came across ould Ireland, or *I* needn't be standing before yer ladyship in *the skin of my feet*.'

Dan's winding up of his country's distress by such a picture was quite in keeping, but it was so odd, that I turned away to prevent his seeing me smile; and at the moment I perceived one of the most remarkable figures I ever saw. A tall thin man, bent nearly double, but still looking very tall and spectre-like, was creeping round a buttress of the nearest tower; one thin bony hand grasped a massive ivy bough, which wound like a huge serpent up the gray wall, and he supported himself on something between the narrow spade they use for digging potatoes and a pick-axe. The handle was long enough to be used as a leaping pole, and the end furnished with an iron cross, upon which he leant. It appeared to me that, without such support, he could not walk, and yet he moved, or rather shuffled along, with considerable rapidity. His coat was long and gray, patched with many colours; and a bag, originally made of sacking, was slung across his back by a leathern belt, from which depended more than one string of 'holy beads,' and a multitude of shreds of different-coloured cloths, several rabbit skins, and one or two skins of birds of prey. He wore no stockings, but his shoes were bound on, sandal fashion, with knotted cords crossed more than half way up his legs. His hair was thin, and white as snow, receding from a high narrow forehead, which a phrenologist would at once pronounce as proud and dreamy. He wore no hat, but a cowl of gray cloth fell behind, and in bad weather he could protect his head from the pelting of the storm by drawing it forward. Indeed his head was a model of ancient beauty, rising so nobly above his cowering figure; and the pure white hair was well thrown out by the dark-green ivy, which formed an appropriate background to the solitary wanderer. His features looked worn and attenuated, but their extreme sharpness proceeded from the thinness of the face. His eyebrows were long and bushy, and his eyes gray, restless, and piercing. He paused, and bowed his head —for all of the peasant class are courteous—and manifested no desire either to retreat or advance.

'God save you, Daddy Whelan, sir!' said little Muckleroy; adding, under his breath, 'he'll root the ould towers themselves up some of these days.'

'God save ye kindly! Who's spaking to me?' answered and inquired the old man.

'A lady from England, and little Dan Muckleroy, Anty Muckleroy's grandson,' was the reply.

'A lady from England!' repeated the old man, relinquishing his grasp of the ivy bough; and, after a moment, he smoothed down his white hair, drew his cowl a little over his head, and advancing close to where I stood, crossed his hands on the top of his singular staff, and gazing with his glittering eyes in my face, inquired, in a low mysterious tone of voice, '*Had ye a drame?*'

It is quite impossible to describe the eagerness of the old man's manner: his mouth open, as if panting for intelligence; his eyes —the word I have used is the only one that can convey an idea of their expression — *glittering* with a wildness that almost amounted to insanity: the very grasp in which he held his staff showed how anxious he was for my answer.

'Had I a dream?—yes, many.'

'Ay, lady, many; but about—about—*the crock of goold*—about *that*, lady dear? Was it a *drame* that brought ye here?—what else could bring a laughing-eyed lady among ruins and dry bones! The *crock of goold*, lady, did ye drame of *that?*—if ye did, send little Dan away; he doesn't know the secret. I do—the witch hazel, and the holy *drop*—I have 'em all—I'll find it.'

'Then why have you not found it for yourself?' I asked.

The brightness of his eyes faded; the lids dropped; the very muscles of his hands relaxed; the excitement was over for the moment; he passed his hand across his brow, and repeated, 'Why haven't I?—why haven't I? I hadn't the luck yet: I lie down under the light of the new moon, but I don't *drame:* I never dreamt but the onct; but that was enough. I saw it—I had it—the crock in these two hands—the goold rolling like the waves of the sea at my feet: that was a drame! Have you dreamt such, lady; have ye? I know the charrum—the witch hazel, the holy drop, the first tear of the new moon!' and he repeated again and again the same words, his eyes glittering, his excitement increasing.

'Daddy Whelan,' said my attendant imp, 'have ye tried under the flat gray stone down by the water? Granny dreamt onct that there was a crock of goold there.'

'I don't know—I forget—maybe I did—maybe I didn't I find *my marks* in many a green hillock, and under many an ould tower; but I have not found the *crock of goold yet*. You'll never find it by yourself, lady. So, if ye *had a drame*, tell me: we'll find it together, we'll divide it together.'

It was in vain I assured Daddy Whelan I had not dreamed a dream. Had it not been that little Dan hit upon a new spot where to direct his attention, the old treasure-seeker would have still insisted that I too must have dreamed of a *crock of gold*.

I watched him stealing away amid the ruins, and then sat down on a bench of soft green moss to recall the story my old friend Sally had told me, in my childish days, about the old man I had seen so unexpectedly for the first time, but of whom I had so often heard.

'Never,' she said, 'build your hopes of future well-doing upon chance, but rather upon industry, whether of the head or of the hands; both have it in their power to win independence, though they do it in a different way. My uncle knew two young men in the gentleman's county—the county Kilkenny—of the name of Whelan, Roger and Michael. They were left a large tract of land by their father, which was divided equally between them. It was in parts wild and uncultivated, but it was all he had to give, except his blessing; and the blessing of a parent gladdens a good child's heart. Roger, the eldest, was a wild, dreamy fellow; and instead of setting steadily to work to mend matters and improve his farm, he was always talking of the "luck" some people had, and how hard it was to be obliged to labour on bad land. It was in vain that Michael told him it was worse to have no land to labour on; he idled and complained. His brother worked night and day, at first with little success, but time helps industry; and what was really owing to industry, Roger said was owing to luck. "If," said Roger to Michael one sunny Sunday evening, when, after walking round and round, and through, and about, the old ruins of Jerpoint Abbey—"if I could only find a *crock of goold*, I'd be a made man. I'd have as fine a hunter as Squire Nixon, and such lashings of whisky and fresh cod and oysters for every Friday in and out of Lent. Abel Ryan found one, and why shouldn't I?" While he spoke, he kept poking, poking with his stick among the stones of the mouldering archway, beneath which they, the brothers, stood; and as he did so, it chanced that he dislodged a stone, and in a crevice, a sort of hole between the stones, he discovered several old silver coins. This astonished one brother, and elated the other, whose wish that he *might* find a crock of gold was fast strengthening into the idea that he *should* find one. It was in vain that Michael reasoned with Roger, and urged him to take the new-found treasure to the landlord, whose property, according to the law of the land, it most undoubtedly was. Roger laughed at his scruples, and kept the coin; but though he had the money, he did not exactly know how to dispose of it. The sum was far too small to take him abroad, and he feared to show it at home, for the news would have flown like wildfire, and the castle be either rooted up or thrown down by those who would have expected to be as fortunate as Roger Whelan. Soon after this occurred, the time arrived for planting seed potatoes. Michael had got his ready, and hinted to his brother that the season was passing, and his ground remained unoccupied.

"How do you think," was the treasure-seeker's reply, "that I can be able to spend my time digging thick clay, when I am, as you, and you only know, night after night, through and through the ruins of ould Jerpoint? Don't I know the red goold *is* in it? And how do you think I can give my mind to such work as *that*, when *I know* what's before me?" It was no use talking to the infatuated man. "Give me," he continued, "the bit and the sup, and a good coat to my back, a new spade and pick-axe; suffer me to go and to come, and I'll give you my share of the land, the dirty barren soil that it is: stockings and croppings, just as it is, take it, and welcome."

"Well," answered Michael, "I will manage it, Roger, till you come to your senses; and then, I'm thinking, you'll be glad enough to get it back."

'Roger Whelan,' continued my friend, 'was a fine handsome fellow, tall and comely, and was at the time very much in love with a very pretty girl, who had a good deal of money; but her parents found out that Roger was always out at nights. The country was, as it generally is, in an unquiet state; and despite Michael's assurances to the contrary, Mary Morgan's "people" believed that Roger was in some way connected with the disturbers of the public peace, at the very time when, to do him justice, he disturbed nought but the wild rabbits, the bats, owls, rooks, and wild birds that sheltered amid the ruins of Jerpoint. Neither Roger nor Michael would tell why Roger was from home at nights; and after some hesitation, and a few tears, Mary relinquished her handsome lover for a short, steady, little husband, who lived to be a rich citizen of the city of Waterford. "Never mind," said the discarded lover; "she'll be sorry for it yet, when she hears Mister Roger Whelan, Esq. talked of, and hears the bay of my hounds on the hills, and sees my carriage overrunning all the pigs on the quay of Waterford: then, maybe, she'll be sorry for changing her mind." The forgetfulness of his fair one, however, preyed upon his spirits; and having gone into Kilkenny, he was tempted to change one or two of his precious coins; and after having drunk the worth of his money in whisky, he was imprudent enough to boast that he had many more of the same "curiosities" at home. The landlord, seeing that the coins were unlike any he had ever seen before, took them to a "knowing man," a little crabbed body, who lived near the church-gate of Saint Xanis, and was as near an approach to a dealer in curiosities as could be supposed to exist in an Irish country town, where the great of those days spent *more* than their spare money in show and claret, and the small had never any money to spare.

Still the old man existed; and when *he* purchased the coins from the whisky dealer, something seemed to occur to him, which he did not communicate to any one; but finding it was still early in the day, he set out to walk to a gentleman who resided about five miles from Kilkenny, on the Ross road. To him he showed the coins; and much to poor Michael's horror, Roger Whelan was arrested at the end of the week, on the accusation of having stolen these coins from that very gentleman's house. About a fortnight before the unfortunate treasure-seeker found them among the stones of Jerpoint Abbey, the house had been beset by some Whitefeet, or Peep-of-day Boys, or whatever they chose to call themselves, seeking for arms, and professing to take nothing else—a profession they generally adhered to. But one of them had doubtless been tempted by the glitter of a drawer of coins and medals in a bureau, which they had broken open to get at some curious Spanish pistols the gentleman was known to possess. After having obtained possession thereof, he doubtless did not know how to dispose of them, and secreted them in the ruin, where Roger unfortunately discovered them.

'I confess my opinion is, that the law in those days was administered in a very one-sided manner; but I must at the same time admit that circumstantial evidence was strongly against poor Roger: he had acquired for himself the character of an idle wandering fellow, and the only one to support his story was Michael; but the counsel for the crown said, "What brother was there who would not say as much for another brother?"

"Plase yer honour," answered Michael, "he is my brother, poor boy; and though he's forenint me, where I never thought he'd be, and the first of his family that ever *stud* in sich disgrace, and though I'd sell the coat off my back, and *the flesh after it*, if that would save him, still I'd not tell a lie, and by so doing sell my soul to the devil. Gintlemen counsellors, you're *used to it*, but *I'm not:* he has tould the blessed truth. Treasure-seeking he was, that's sartin, whin, with a bit of a stick—the very one that stud his friend many a turn, yet, like many friends, betrayed him at the last—poked out the unnatural pieces of money, bad luck to them! and if he had taken my advice, and just carried them to the landlord, there would have been no more about it, only maybe the right made out. Look, gintlemen, I can say no more than this: look round at me, Roger, *avick*, the born picture of our blessed father, the boy that lay with myself many and many a night and day upon the bosom of our own mother; look at me, my own heart-brother, and hear me pray on my knees that curses by day and night may fall, hot, heavy, black, and bitter, on yer head, if you knew anything about the dirty money until that minute when, unknowst to yerself, ye let the light of day shine on the treasure, and thought yer fortune made." To this his brother replied with a deep and sincere "AMEN!" Many in the court wept, for all who knew, respected Michael, and considered Roger as an "innocent boy, who would never do any harm to any one *but himself*." Poor Roger, however, was sentenced to seven years' transportation, to which was added the information, that the law showed great mercy in not sentencing him to death.

"God bless you, Michael," said Roger, when he embraced his brother for the last time; "all the counthry knows I'm innocent; and who can tell but I may find *the crock of goold yet*, when all's said and done? The money *was* hid there anyway."

"If ever," said Michael to his wife, when he returned home—"if ever poor Roger comes back to ould Ireland, it will be to go treasure-hunting; his brain is struck with it, as indeed every brain is when it takes a foolish notion that reason can't conquer."

'Five years had passed, and the only matter connected with the brothers worth recording was, that the man who *really* took the old money from the gentleman's bureau, having wound up his misdeeds by the crime of murder, was discovered; and when about to suffer, confessed his sorrow that a "dacent boy's son, Roger Whelan by name, should have been turned out of the country for his fault." This was a joyful hearing to all Michael Whelan's friends, and they were many: his conduct had won him the approbation of rich and poor; and it long had been evident, that if Roger failed to *find a crock of gold*, it was equally certain that Michael would soon *make* one, as everything prospered that he undertook. The ignorant said *he had great luck*—the wise that he *had great industry.*

'The news of Roger's pardon, and consequent permission to return home, spread through the country; but long before there was a possibility of a ship reaching Botany Bay, a tall, worn, spectral-looking man presented himself beneath Michael's roof, and was soon pressed to the arms of the whole family.

"My own dear brother!" said the true-hearted Michael, "you are indeed returned; and now *your* farm is worth the having; it is stocked, and cropped, and thriving: we will work together, and live together. But how is it you are so quickly returned?"

"Don't laugh at me, Michael," was the reply; "but I had *one drame*, which I never shall rest till I work out: it kept up my heart for three long years of slavery, and I'd often pray to drame it again, but I never did. I dreamt I was in Ireland, standing by cross roads that divided some ould ruins into four halves, and milk came pouring down one road, and water down another, and a swarm of bees flying down another, and a herd of cattle driving down the last; and as I stood, a voice said, 'Seek, and have;' and I thought I made with my hands a trough like, where the milk and water mixed like whisky and water, and the bees hung over it, and the cattle drank of it; and I could tell the place if I saw it. And behould, I worked, worked at the hollow; and all of a sudden I raised up a *crock of goold* between these hands; and as I did so, the red, red goold fell at my feet, like the waters of the wide ocean for plenty: and through all manner of dangers I made my way back to Ireland on the sly; and for the last three months I've been disguised like a bocher, or a natural, seeking through the ruins of ould Ireland for the *crock of goold*—but *I haven't found it yet.*"

"Nor never will," said Michael. "Let me read the dream for you. Didn't your hands make the trough, and did not milk and water rest there, and cattle rest there, and honey rest there! and are not they the fruits of labour? And out of that trough came the crock of goold; and so it will—out of the labour of your hands. That is the only *crock of goold* the Whelans will ever find, depend upon it."

'This interpretation did not, however, suit the treasure-seeker: on all other subjects he was sane enough; but nothing could change his desire to *find*, instead of labour for, wealth. And yet his brother told my uncle he *does* labour, and labour hard. He risked much in venturing to Ireland before he knew that his innocence had been declared. But he did not care: his whole ideas were in the *crock of gold*. There is not a part of Ireland that he will not travel to, spend night after night burrowing in the earth like a wild animal, no matter what the weather is, or what the season; and the first question he asks of every stranger he meets is, " *Had ye a drame?*"'

This was one of the tales my gentle friend told me with a desire to correct my fondness for castle-building; which is indeed even now one of my faults. She enlarged upon the utility of Michael's course of life, and pointed out how totally lost to himself and to society poor Roger was. 'He comes here sometimes, and asks my grandmother's leave to inspect our castle; a permission we never refuse, upon condition that he does not meddle with the foundation. He makes his appearance once every three years, spending some time at Dunbrody Abbey, some time at Clonmines, a night here, another at Danes Castle, another at Coolhull at Duncormuck; and so getting into the barony of Forth, which is full of old castles, he travels by day, and digs by night; but he has not yet found his crock of gold.'

How well I remembered the evening when, sitting on my friend's knee in the great bow-window of the drawing-room at Barristown, she told me that story! The Castles of Clonmines had flung their shadows on the water, and the evening was as calm and silent as the grave. I remember asking her to send me word when next the old treasure-seeker came to the neighbourhood, that I might see him, only at a little distance; and I also remember her saying that 'he might never come again, for that exposure to all weathers had brought on premature old age, and he seemed ill and worn the last time he was there.'

Alas! dear Sally had departed long, long ago to a better world; and I, after residing many years in another land, had, by one of those curiously-turned romances of real life that laugh at fiction, encountered the treasure-seeker upon the very spot where, years ago, I knew he loved to linger and explore—the very old man whom my poor friend had supposed too worn and ill to return again! Indeed I had been so certain of his death, that I had never thought of inquiring about him. I know not how long I might have remained among the ruins, musing over the story I have recorded, and recalling the looks and voice of her who told me many such tales, had not my little busy companion, Daniel Muckleroy, begged 'my honour's' pardon, but 'would I be plased to tell him which I liked best—travelling by night or by day, or in rain or sunshine?' This recalled me to a sense of the rapidity with which time had passed, and I became aware that the evening approached. I had hoped the sun would have set over the castles with the red, red glory I had so often witnessed, bestowing his radiant benediction with all his brightness: but no; the clouds were gray and heavy, the whistle of the plover was more frequent than usual, and a moaning came from the not-far-off ocean—a sound perfectly distinct from the roaring that accompanies the progress of the storm-king, or the loud ripple that beats music to the breeze; it was a *moaning*—those who know the sea understand what I mean—a heaving, as if the mighty waters groaned *inwardly* at the approach of a tempest.

'The clouds have *gathered* above our heads, ma'am, and ye haven't noticed them; and there was a *broch* about the moon last night; and early as it is, sorra a crow, the craythur, that hasn't come home; and since ye seemed so *struck*, my lady, with Daddy Whelan, if ye'll just be plased to step here, you'll see him in his *iliment* intirely.'

I walked on to where the boy stood, and I was pleased when, looking earnestly in my face, he added, 'Daddy's of *dacent* people, ma'am; and *sure you wouldn't laugh at him!* He's as innocent as a baby, only *touched* in the head with the throuble he had onct, and the fancy of a crock of goold.' There was warm feeling round the heart of that wild Irish boy, *though he was standing in the skin of his feet.*

Roger Whelan was preparing for a stormy night, and the prospect seemed to have imbued the old man with new life: he had fastened his cowl more closely round his head, and was seated on the gray stone my guide had pointed out; his curious staff placed upon his knees, his elbows resting upon it, and his attention divided between the arrangement of a piece of candle in an old lantern which I had not before perceived, and the course of the clouds, that were, without any apparent wind, careering above our heads. I advanced nearer, but he did not heed me.

'My lady,' whispered little Daniel, 'he's dug round and round that stone a thousand times, but the neighbours fill up the marks; his brother, Misther Michael, has come to live in this county, and likes to keep the Daddy, as we call him, near at hand. He wouldn't stay in the place if he found his own marks, but go to break fresh ground: granny says he's more easily desaved than he used to be.'

Suddenly a shivering flash of lightning ran amid the clouds, and a few drops of rain warned me to take shelter under a ruined arch close to the gray stone upon which the treasure-seeker was seated.

'Daddy, sir,' said Dan, 'come in the shelter; it's bad for ould bones to get cowld.'

The old man turned his face suddenly towards the smiling child, and holding forth a long arm-bone, which was fastened beneath the shreds to his singular belt, and was polished as ivory, he exclaimed, '*This* doesn't feel the cowld; it has been stript these hundred years and more. I had dug the whole night, and the thunder howling, and the lightning, not laughing like the *weeny* flash that passed us now, but dancing mad with divilment through the heavens and over the earth. It was in Adair I was rooting—rooting—for *the crock of goold*, inside the proud lord's walls, and he thinking none like me could get at his hid treasure. And I saw the handle, the handle of the crock, *forenint* me, in the hole, and I made a plunge and seized it. I knew it *was* the handle; and I was so wild wid joy, that I forgot myself, and shouted, and heard the shout repeated as loud again by some of the *achoes*, and muttered over by others according to their fancy. And I knew I had done wrong to spake; but I held fast; and, ah! ah! I pulled, and *it* pulled; but I held fast, and tore this up—*this!* Do ye understand it!—the spirit that had owned the goold, *had power* afther I shouted. So he *kept* his *crock of goold*, but *I* got his arm-bone! That was my best chance: I never can have such a chance except when they,' and he pointed downwards, and spoke in a lower tone, 'when *they* get *tarryfied* with the thunder: then's my best chance; and I shall have it to-night—if I had but *a drame*. Are you sure you had not a drame, lady?' he added, peering at me as he had done before.

I asked him if he remembered his friends at Barristown, for I was anxious to ascertain if his mind wandered on all subjects.

'Ay, well!' he replied, and his voice changed again: 'God be good to them!—the warm welcome, the open house, the ould Lady Queen of the Castle! *she* often dramed for me: and her son—the flower of the gentry—and the fair young lady: I brought a white rose-tree from Woodstock, and set it on her grave, though *she* would never try to drame for me! Poor thing, she did not believe in drames; *but she knows the truth of them now!* It's a quare world, and everything in it. What is it from first to last but a drame, leading by visions to eternity! Sure, in our own short time, the people are gone from Barristown like a drame! and yet they *war* in it onct; and so with the money in my *crock of goold!* Sure afther *that*, what can ye say agin' the drames? Isn't all life a drame? There's another flash o' lightning! *I love to read my drame-book by flashes o' lightning!* And I love it at sea—the fire and the wather sporting wild sport together! Ah, thin, if ye hadn't a drame, lady, whin will ye go out of this, for ye're *throubling* the earth! Don't ye hear how the thunder growls?'

'May I not wait till the storm is over, Daddy?' I inquired, not without some apprehension, for the old man's features were assuming a troubled aspect, though my little guide did not seem alarmed.

'Oh, *agra!* yes; a lady and a stranger; only the sooner the better, unless ye could sleep, *and tell me yer drame.* God help me,' he added shiveringly, for the wind had risen, and was rattling amid the ruins and the ivy; 'God help me! *I shall soon be little more than a drame myself.*'

It is impossible to convey an idea of the sadness of the tone with which he uttered this prophecy. They were the last words he spoke to me. The storm was short-lived; and though I bade him good-day, he would not answer me: the boy said he was vexed the '*tunder*' was over. Be that as it may, I heard the click-click of his sharpening the end of his axe, as if determined on his singular purpose.

Poor Roger Whelan! one of my last-received letters from Ireland contained this passage: 'I have just left the prosperous and contented dwelling of Michael Whelan; he is a very old man, full to the brim of the happy years of an industrious life, though just now much grieved by the death of his wandering brother, "the Treasure-Seeker;" for despite his eccentric obstinacy, which, as he advanced in years, deepened, in my opinion, into positive madness, he loved him tenderly. Roger's end was as remarkable as his life. He had been occupied, as usual, one stormy night in the old churchyard of Bannow; and the storm he so delighted in but too faithfully assisted the excavation he had made. A portion of the north wall gave way, and buried the picturesque old man beneath its ruin.'

Poor dreamer! he had left his brother's house under the strong excitement of a new vision, and his end was in keeping with his life. The prosperity arising from the industry of the one brother, and the comfortless life and tragical end of the other, form the best commentary upon the most feasible means of obtaining a *Crock of Gold.*

THE WRECKER,

A SEA-SIDE STORY.

'HANNAH, I have tould you three times to go to bed,' said Pierce Murphy to a slight delicate-looking young woman, who, notwithstanding the command, continued to knit the stocking she had nearly finished, while bending over the embers of a turf fire.

'Well, father, I'm going;' but still she remained.

Pierce Murphy was a tall muscular man, with rugged, yet keen features, and shaggy hair, that fell in great profusion over a high determined-looking forehead: after having spoken, he walked backward and forward under the rafters of his kitchen, but occasionally paused to look out through a window upon the night. It is worthy of observation that this window was singularly constructed; Pierce, tall as he was, could not reach it without standing on a stool for the purpose, and then his eyes were only on a level with the lower pane.

'Holy saints!' he muttered to himself, 'there's a flash! Well, that *is* something like.'

The girl who had been knitting started to her feet, terrified at the loud thunder-peal which shook their long narrow cottage, and frightened the poultry that were roosting at the far end of the kitchen on the high rafter so completely, that two of them tumbled down, and ran towards her as if for protection, while the old cock shook his feathers, and chuck-chuck'd something by way of caution to his more alarmed companions.

'What a night, father!' she exclaimed; 'I should think there could be no chance of their running in in such a night as this.'

'Stuff!' answered the man; 'women always talk like fools. What are they to do? If they have come as far down as where we think, they must put in, or tack about for sea-room, which they can't do, because the wind is right in their teeth, or be seized in the morning by the revenue cutter! There's another blast! Go to bed, go to bed—that's a good girl—go to bed.'

And he pressed his forehead close to the glass, which, contrary to the practice in Irish cabins, was perfectly whole, and free from dust.

'I'll be as quiet as a lamb, father, but do let me stop up with ye; if I went to bed, sorra a wink would come on my eye. Sure, what's in the differ if I wake here or in the crib within!'

Her father's thoughts seemed to have taken another direction, for he made no reply to her request; but after gazing intently through the glass for some minutes, he turned abruptly to the door, which opened on the same side as the window, directly towards the sea, and attempted to look forth. It was, however, but an attempt: the wind rushed in with such terrific violence, that the turf ashes were blown about in every direction, and it required all his strength, assisted by his daughter's exertions, to force back and bar the entrance. It will seem strange to those who know what Irish cabins by the sea-side generally are, to talk of 'a bar' to the door. A latch, above which a hole is sometimes bored to permit the twine to pass through, so that the latch may be lifted by the stranger or the friend, both alike sure of a welcome; or a rusty lock, where want of use has engendered rust—these are common enough. Pierce Murphy's cabin door was not only furnished with two bolts, but was as sound and substantial a door as any one need desire to have, even in the neighbourhood of London, where, if you do not lock your doors, and bar your doors, and bolt your doors, you cannot rest secure from danger. Both the door and the long, low, narrow cottage of Pierce Murphy were substantial, and certainly the liability to such storms would seem to render it necessary that they should be so. Pierce, however, had more than one reason for having a strong door and a strong bolt to his dwelling, which stood boldly forward on a toppling cliff, near Point Forlorn; the foundation had been formed of the blue slaty stones, large enough to be called rocks, so general along the coast: these were cemented with stiff yellow clay, and the remainder of the walls was composed of smaller fragments of the same kind of stone; the rafters were, despite all superstitions, of driftwood; the ribs of many a noble ship having been destined to support the thatch of Pierce Murphy's cabin. Murphy's professed occupation was fishing; indeed I may say it was his *real* employment when he had no other. He was one whom danger never daunted; in his little smack he braved all weathers; and when he *did* send fish to Wexford market, it was always the finest there. The kitchen of his dwelling was hung with the implements of his ostensible calling, though many did not fail to remark that Pierce's nets were generally dry, except when the coast-guard was on the alert; and coast-guards at the period to which my tale refers were not as active as they are now; they also wondered at the stability of his door and his high-up window: but Pierce said the place was lonely; that he was often out at nights fishing; and that his old woman was 'timid of being alone' during the long winter's evening.

This 'old woman' was comparatively an old woman when he married her, and had been bedridden many years. The fruit of the marriage was one boy: the young woman whom he called daughter, and who evinced towards him all the duty and affection of a child, was the wife—it might be widow—of Luke Murphy, his only and beloved son.

'Now,' exclaimed Hannah, glancing at him from beneath her

dark eyelashes, when they had really succeeded in fastening the door, 'what would you have done if I had been in bed? Bedad, father, the wind would have had the betther of ye!'

Pierce Murphy looked down upon the gentle earnest face of the pale girl, who had spoken in the half-jesting half-serious tone of one who does not exactly know how the words will be received, and there was both ire and pride in the expression of his countenance.

'The wind have the betther of me—of ME! The wind never crossed the Atlantic, let alone St George's Channel, that would have the betther of me,' he answered proudly.

'Oh, father dear, take care. God be betwixt us and harm! But sure my poor Luke used to call the breezes and winds the Almighty's breath.'

'And why should you mention *him* to *me* now?' exclaimed the impetuous man. 'What put him in your head! I say,' he repeated, in a voice loud as the tempest, as the trembling creature shrank away without replying, '*what* put Luke in yer head now?'

A shrill unearthly sort of laugh rang from one of the two small bedrooms that were partitioned at the farthest end off the kitchen, and a voice feeble and sharp replied, 'And that shows that Pierce Murphy is the same fool as ever, to ask a young wife what puts her husband in her head—to ask fond Hannah Gowry what puts her lawful husband (may the Lord's care be about him day and night!)—to ask *her* what puts her husband, Luke Murphy, in her head! Oh, Pierce, *agra!* is it now ye have to *larn* that the head and the heart of a young Irishwoman are one? What put Luke in her head! Bedad, that's quare! ah, ah!'—— And the old bedridden woman went on laughing and muttering to herself in a way that showed her intellects were not clear. Pierce swore at her while commanding her silence, but she did not heed him; accustomed to his rough words and rough usage, perhaps she did not understand his meaning.

'Bedad, ye're a nice lad, Pierce Murphy,' she continued half distinctly, and, fortunately for herself and Hannah, the smuggler did not hear above half she said. 'Ye turn *the Almighty's blessing,* yer own flesh and blood, into a curse; the *gra* boy! just married too; and in for it, so deep, that if he didn't make a *vartue* of necessity, the law would have sent him abroad free of expince. My beautiful boy! but never heed *that,* he'll soon be back now— his pardon's granted; my blessing be about Hannah for that same; didn't she work it out for him, with her perseverance and her sweet ways—and he'll soon be back, he'll soon be back; and thin, Pierce, my boy, Pierce, slashing Pierce Murphy, ye're book sworn, so ye are, to turn out all rats—all rats; hush—hush —every rat—when my boy comes home.'

'I tell ye what,' said Pierce, swearing a dreadful oath, 'I tell ye what it is, Hannah: if you don't find some way of stopping that ould woman's tongue, *I will*—not even her being the mother of my son, your husband, will save her—do ye understand me? The ould hag gets worse and worse;' and the smuggler spoke these words in the stern under-tone of a resolved and desperate man, hissing them through his teeth, while his fingers grappled convulsively, as if he did, in imagination, what he threatened.

Hannah had glanced at him before; now she looked fixedly, if not firmly, in his face; and ere she had spoken a sentence, the crimson that had mounted to her cheek faded into a death-like paleness.

'You have a right to remember, Pierce Murphy, that if the poor ould senseless creature is what she is, it is *your doing*. Whin she took you first, she had full and plinty. She trusted it all to you; and where is it?'

'Hannah!' exclaimed Pierce, astonished at her boldness.

'Let me alone, thin, with your hints, father; I don't think ye mane half what ye say—I know ye don't. Ye could not be Luke's father if ye did. But while I've a heart to feel, I'll feel for her; while I've a hand to work, I'll work for ye both, *as I have done*. Oh, father! let me love ye *both*, for the sake of HIM, my own heart's core! Oh! how could ye be so cruel as to ax what put him in my head! My thought by day and drame by night!'—and she burst into tears.

Pierce did not repeat his brutal language, reckless as he had grown from long habit and bad associates; he was touched by the truth and faithfulness of the young creature who gazed on him so mournfully. He muttered a few words; and then dashing his elbow against a half door in the wall, which the nicest eye could not have discerned, he disappeared down a narrow subterraneous passage, which led through the cliff to the strand below his dwelling. The memory of the oldest dwellers on that sea-coast could not carry them back as to when the cave was formed that extended upwards, and which Pierce and his associates had continued. Some said 'It was always so!' others said it was the work of men even more daring than its present possessors. The cave appeared to all, but those initiated into its mysteries, precisely as it had always been; but Pierce Murphy, more than fifteen years before the occurrence of the incident I am about to relate, had, with the assistance of two or three companions, hollowed a passage as far as the roof of the cavern, which might be about ten or twelve feet above the rugged stones that formed its flooring. It was wonderful how well the opening was concealed; and the rocky roofing was of itself so uneven and commonplace, that though the revenue officers, as I have said, not by any means as active *then* as they are now, though perfectly well aware that smuggling, if not more fearful crimes, was carried on in that immediate neighbourhood, could not form an idea how the business was managed. Indeed they were sometimes found to be too well satisfied with the proscribed article, to care much for its distribution, though it is a well-known fact that a revenue officer was never yet really trusted by a smuggler.

When Pierce descended, the young woman sat down by the fire, which she had replenished with fresh turf, and wept long and bitterly; it was sad to hear the voice of one so young and fair, and with an expression of so much innocence in her countenance, harmonising with the moaning into which the madness of the storm had for a time subsided.

'Hannah, *avourneen!*' inquired the half-demented woman from the little room—' Hannah, *avourneen!* is there any fresh throuble on ye, my comfort?'

'No, mother; go to sleep.'

'There's no use, darlint. Is there any noise about the hearthstone, my jewel?'

'No, mother.'

'I thought I heard the ticking of the death-watch; the only clock that ever strikes here.'

'I didn't hear it, mother.'

'Hannah, how long is it since there was a winding-sheet on the candle?'

'I don't know, mother; but sure the last time Father Gandy was in it, he tould ye not to be minding such foolishness; that the Almighty would be above giving a hint about sich a thing as death out of a bit of candle-grease; and that a poor little insect—which he says the watch is—could have no knowledge of life and death, only keeps minding its own business in the warm places.'

'Ah, ah!' laughed the crone; 'and sure he's a fine man, and said more than that when he was about it.'

'Ay, mother, both priest and minister say good enough, if we'd only heed it. God help us, he did say a dale of what was true, and so did Misther Burrows—Heaven bless them both!—about the sin of breaking the law, which was both bad and dangerous: and what was worse, about the curse of sinful people, which sich doings bring about a poor man's house; and the evil courses sich lead to, the swearing and the drinking; and the fear o' God, put all on one side for the lucre of gain; and the end that comes of it all—transportation and shame, or maybe death. Oh, it's a cruel wicked way; and how poor Luke, though brought up in it, ever turned to it, so fine and honourable as he was, I do not know. I little thought how it was when I married him!'

'And would that have hindered ye, if ye had known it?' inquired the old woman.

'I don't know, I'm not thinking it would; for all the throuble I've had on his account seems to draw my heart closer to him;

he is more to me now than ever he was; and when he's with me again, we'll go to some furrin part, and work in the honesty that will bring peace.'

'Ah, ah, ah!' laughed the old woman; 'I shall be dead before that; but the worms will have no feast, for I'm only skin and bone, skin and bone;' and she laughed again the laugh that made poor Hannah's flesh creep; and then continued—' Luke, *a-lanna*, never *took* to it, though you don't know, for reason ye didn't come to us for good and all till he was on the point of going; but he never *took* to it. Sure if a man's in a whirlpool, he doesn't take to it, though he is drowned in it. And Misther Burrows said all that agin the smuggling. Ah! he *said* all that agin the smuggling, did he? and yet I'll go bail he took the hot drop of the hot stuff afore he left; that's no way to instruct the poor whin they're in the sin, and have the temptation to go on in it; the example must go with the lesson to do good; the poor have the comfort, and not the strong principle, and yet they'd take away the one, and not give them the other!—that's quare—that has no *sinse* in it—no more than ould Margaret Murphy.'

'Go to sleep, mother dear,' said Hannah.

'Will you pray for me the while?' inquired the old woman earnestly, and there was sorrow in the tone of her voice. 'I can sleep if you pray for me, *avourneen*.'

Hannah replied she would, and knelt down for the purpose; but nothing could keep Margaret Murphy quiet.

'Lave off, Hannah, and come sit by me,' she said; and accordingly the gentle girl—who was so unsuited for such scenes, and who had quitted 'her own people,' in a more inland part of the country, simply that she might take care of her husband's mother, to prove her love for him—left off in the middle of an 'ave,' and seated herself by the bedside of the strange woman, whose former mode of life, before she became Pierce Murphy's wife, was unknown to her neighbours, though various had been the rumours in circulation on the subject.

Margaret Murphy seemed worn more by the perpetual restless anxiety she could not quell than by age; her bright, wild, blue eye was never calm, and her lean, colourless lips were in perpetual motion. She was subject to occasional fits of insanity, but her memory was at all times distinct, and her reason frequently clear; her observations were keen and sarcastic; and whatever of affection lingered round her woman's heart, was for her son. Hannah she regarded as a part of him, and the tenderness evinced towards her by the kind young woman was the only balm her heart tasted. Margaret was in reality the daughter of a gentleman in a distant neighbourhood; the *natural* daughter, and consequently treated in an unnatural manner. She had a better sort of education until she was thirteen or fourteen; her father then married, and she was put forth with her degraded mother to endure as best she might the contempt which follows the parent's sin. Of all the crimes which man in a civilised state of society is guilty of—and there are many of which the law can take no hold—there is none equal to this; none so black in its depravity; none so injurious in its consequences to the moral dignity of society. What her after-career was, for many years, remains a mystery. She fell, it was believed, into sin herself; for the dwellers in the neighbourhood never spoke of her without saying, 'God break hard fortune before every one's child;' a Christian and beautiful prayer, to which each kindly heart must say Amen! 'Hard fortune,' however, seemed the poor woman's 'rock a-head' all her life. When she did marry, there was little doubt that she wedded Pierce for the sake of being made 'an honest woman,' and he took her because of the possession of a scanty store of that ill-gotten gold which melts away, and leaves nothing behind but its poisoned memory.

Still, when Hannah, seated by her bedside, looked into her worn and wrinkled features, she felt how lonely would be her own fate if that poor half-wild woman were to die. She was the mother of her beloved husband, and that formed a strong link in her affections.

Again the storm whirled on without; the winds did not howl more furiously than the waters; both raged together; and the din of elements became more fearful than ever. So loud, indeed, was the tumult, that the thunder over the cliffs, which at any other time would have seemed to shake them to their foundations, formed now only a part of the troubled whole. The only distinctive feature during this storm was the lightning, which flashed and forked throughout the dwelling like a thing instinct with life.

'It's dancing, jewel,' said Margaret; 'dancing mad it is with joy, because of the mischief that will come upon those that walk the wathers before morning. There's another blast of the ould one's bellows! Hannah, pray, in the core of your own heart pray, *avourneen*, for the walkers of the wathers. God bless you, girl!' she added suddenly, while darting her quick glittering eye over the calm clear face of her daughter-in-law; 'God bless you! sure it's a mercy to have anything near such a wretch as me that puts one in mind there is a heaven upon earth, where there's innocence. But pray, Hannah, jewel; pray—pray—only don't lave me.'

If Hannah had been even more inclined than she was to pray, she could not have done so, for her mother-in-law continued to mutter and give voice to various exclamations and broken ideas that were in ill-keeping with prayer. Suddenly the secret door through which Pierce Murphy had descended to the beach opened, and a tall active-looking smuggler, by name Andrew Furlong, proceeded to a cupboard; and taking out a quantity of tow and other combustibles, asked Hannah why she was not gone to bed, and commenced forming something which appeared like a very long and massive torch.

'Any sign of the boat, Andy?' inquired Hannah.

'None; and there's some of *the lobsters* we hear beyond the Point, so we can't make the right signal, and the waves are dashing like mad in there. It's as dark as pitch, and even if she had a light (which, ov coorse, she wouldn't), we could not get a glimpse ov her, good or bad, bedad! The weather is as contrary as yerself,' he added in a low voice; 'there's hardly half ov ye left, fretting yer heart and soul afther one ye'll never see again.'

'A blisther on yer heart for that speech,' exclaimed the old woman, who, despite his effort to lower his voice, had heard the whisper—'a blisther on yer heart for that same, Andrew Furlong. Haven't ye wickedness enough on hand by sea and land, but ye must thry to take from my lone boy the only thing he has left in the wide world—his young wife's love? Ah! yer reign 'll not be long when he's in it! ye must harry the salt sea then on another tack.'

The young smuggler muttered a curse, and after finishing one torch, commenced another.

'Ah, thin,' inquired Hannah, 'what do ye want of another; sure the lanthern from the window is as good as any, and they'——

Andrew Furlong interrupted her. 'Haven't I tould ye that *the lobsters* are at the other side the Point; and would it be sense, do you think, to have light *here*, to bring them to our own hiding-place? Sure we must strike a light lower down; it's to warn them off we want, not to get them in.'

'But one red flare is the warning light,' persisted Hannah; 'and what do you want of two?'

'Suppose one goes out? there's hardly a glimmer will stand such a wind.'

'One will stand it as well as another; besides, I know ye shelter yer lights.'

'If ye're so knowledgeable, maybe you'll lend me a hand at melting a drop of pitch to make them burn stronger; we'll be ruined intirely if the boat comes in—betther it should go to the bottom.'

'Oh, my God!' she exclaimed, 'how can you say so? and the poor craythurs on boord ov her! But, Andy, is it going to make another ye are?'

'Three torches!' said the old woman, who had risen from her bed without Hannah having given her any assistance, or even perceived her intention, and stood now by their side with no other covering than her cloak, which she grappled rather than folded round her. 'Three! is it three ye're about! Then it's well ye know that the boat is far enough away; three had never anything to do with a smuggler's sign; it isn't *the boat* ye're thinking of. Hannah, are ye a fool to suppose it's a boat they're minding! No, no; it's a false light they're afther, to 'tice some unfortunate ship into the very jaws of death, that's it;' and having so said, she seized the small vessel in which Hannah, unconscious of the real design, had melted the pitch, and before Andrew had time to prevent it, she had flung the contents upon the embers of the fire. In an instant there was a blaze that illumined the cottage, and glared fiercely on the old woman's spectral figure, the pallid and anxious features of her daughter-in-law, and the excited and strongly-marked countenance of the reever.

'Answer for it to yer masther,' he said sneeringly. 'If ye must know the truth, and I don't see the use o' screening it, there *is* a ship close in-shore; and what's more, no earthly power could get her out. What does it matther to the craythurs aboord whether they're dashed to pieces here or lower down? though it'll matther to us. Sorra take the woman—just look at her! Sure I didn't make the storm! Ye might just as well say it's a sin to burn the branch the wind tears from the tree.'

'Pierce Murphy swore me an oath that never, never, never, while grass grew or wather ran—never, while the sea was salt, and the moon bright—never would he resort to that, afther— afther what *we both know*. Ough my grief! the smuggling's bad enough, brought sorrow enough on us; but the curse of drowning men, the laugh, and the jibe, and the jeer of the walking spirits who rise up from the rocks and sands, and cold sea beds, all green and slimy, their shrouds of sea-weed—there—I see them now—and now!'

So terrific were her gestures, in a great degree the workings of insanity, so bright her eyes, so haggard her features, while she stood like a resurrection before Hannah and Andrew, that even Andrew, bold villain though he was, forgot his task in the momentary terror she inspired. Visions of the past crowded to her heated brain; she had depended on her husband's promise—adhered to, as she believed, for some years—that he never again would link himself with wreckers. She did not know, poor miserable woman, how hard it is to overcome a tendency to great crime, while smaller ones are continually practised without reproof or remorse; but the agonising memories that rushed upon her, when she saw the well-known preparation for decoy lights, were too much for her shattered senses, and she conjured up the most horrid visions from the depths of the ocean, the roarings of which mingled with the wind that beat around the cabin.

After an instant's pause, Andrew seized his 'corpse candles,' and had nearly gained the secret passage, when Hannah sprang after him—'Ye would not go heavy with my curse!' she exclaimed. 'Andy, Andy, think first on what ye're afther!—drawing them to their doom, whin they think they are gaining a harbour from the raging seas; think if ye had a brother, a father, on board that ship; think what *that* would be. Oh, can ye have the heart to see the vessel beat to pieces on these rocks—the poor, poor mangled bodies! Oh, blessed Virgin!' she added, falling on her knees, 'look down and save the helpless crew—save us all from this great sin!'

'Let me go, Hannah: yer keeping me here is no good. Pierce Murphy, yer own father-in-law, has decoyed them already—only you could not hear wid the wind; her guns have fired, and '—— Before his sentence was finished, the boom of a gun, sudden and abrupt, shot, as it were, through the storm; it was echoed by a frightful scream from the old woman, who stood beating the air with her hands, and uttering imprecations too horrid to repeat. Hannah ran to her side, not, however, before she had heard the voice of her father-in-law shouting up the cavity to Andrew Furlong to hasten down.

The poor young woman at any other time would have sunk under the conflicting feelings, tortures I should rather say, of that desperate hour, had it not been that the deplorable state of Margaret obliged her to act rather than think or feel.

Smuggling is unhappily considered, even by some of the best of the Irish peasantry, as a venial offence, and they catch at every excuse for a crime which furnishes them at a cheap rate with the liquid fire that distils poison through their veins; they totally overlook the demoralising effect of what is contrary to law, inasmuch as it immediately forces even a man with comparatively good intentions into the most depraved society. But though my poor countryfolk find a too ready excuse for smuggling, I never knew them make excuse for 'wrecking;' their national hospitality rises against it, and the crime is always referred to with a shudder, even by those who would make no scruple of committing other equally lawless crimes. Bad as Pierce Murphy had been, bad as he still was, he never systematically practised this base sin, but his associates and his depraved habits in other respects led to it; and the conviction that the doomed ship was too far in-shore to escape on that fearful night, that she must go to pieces somewhere, led to the argument, 'she may as well come in here as go elsewhere;' and instead of devising means to save his fellow-creatures from so wretched an end, he plotted with the elements to destroy, by imitating in a particular way the light of the nearest lighthouse; thus luring the ship to the very rocks which groaned for her destruction, when, having lost their bearings, they believed they were avoiding danger.

'Did I not tell you of the winding-sheet and the death-watch?'

screamed the old woman; 'but my curse will be on him for this, and the curse of a broken oath: think of that, Hannah. And there's another gun nearer the shore,' she added, 'much nearer the shore, on the rocks.' She paused a moment, and then added, with a calmness of manner that astonished Hannah, accustomed though she was to her fitful changes, 'And now the Lord have mercy on their souls! for nothing can save 'em. Help me to bed, girl, *asthore*, for the strength has left me intirely.' It would then have been a mercy to poor Hannah if the wind had continued to battle with the waves; but after the discharge of the last gun, the wind lulled, and the sea rolled and roared in proud mastery, save when the thunder gave token that the lightning had glared over land and sea. Hannah, after a pause, finding that her mother-in-law continued quiet, placed a chair beneath the window I have before-mentioned, opened the casement, and looked out over the troubled waters. It was more like the mad riot of a fearful dream than reality; and accustomed though she had been to sea storms, this seemed the most terrible she had ever witnessed. To say that the waves were mountains high, gives no idea of their awful appearance. Far out from land, the huge black billows, frowning and dark, heaved themselves to the heavens, as if the mysterious world beneath, disturbed by some mighty earthquake, flung up the heavy waters, rebelling against their pressure. Exactly opposite to where she stood, the moon (then at its full) shone palely out from between the rifted clouds, that rolled back from its path. Pale, stern, and supernatural, it gleamed, like the unclosed eye of the dead (deriving its light from *without*, instead of *within*), over the mighty tumult; while the forked lightning glared upon and amid its fierce playfellows, showing their darkness the more terrible by its surpassing brightness. As the waves neared the rocks, they reared themselves high, and more high, until their inky crests, maddened by opposition, broke into snowy and sparkling masses of glittering driftlike foam, and upon those the lightning showed like living fire—now tossing its brilliancy aloft, now beautiful in its destruction, tipping the foam with magic light, and then twisting like a fiery serpent in the very jaws of death! A little to the right of the cabin, where Hannah well knew the rocks were most fearful, a dark mass seemed fixed amid the spray. As if the very lightning of heaven determined to show the worst, a broad mass of light fell upon the devoted ship: short as was its duration, Hannah screamed with agony at its revealments. The shrouds were thickened by despairing wretches, who clung to them as their last frail hope; the stern of the vessel, high in air, was covered with human beings; nay, more, she saw them struggling in the water, dashed into mangled masses against the murderous rocks. Although all was again darkness, she covered her eyes with her hands, and so suddenly still did the tumult become, that she distinctly heard Pierce Murphy's voice calling to his comrades. With the quick and sudden impulse of her countrywomen, she could have fallen on her knees and cursed—WHOM! Her husband's father! There was no touch of humanity in the tone of his cruel voice; it arose on the night-wind like the fierce growl of a tiger over his prey.

She looked again. Now God have mercy on their souls! The ship had split asunder; one half was hurled with a mighty crash higher on the rocks, the other dispersed amid the boiling bubble of the stormy deep. Bright masses of lightning continued to illumine the frightful scene; horrible as it was, poor Hannah continued to look down upon it, though her face and hair were drenched with the salt spray. At length the idea occurred to her that she would brave the storm below, and perhaps she might save some sailor from the jaws of death; and then the memory of her own beloved one rushed with its full tide of tenderness into her woman's heart; her eye rested for a moment (as, dashing the water from her face with the tresses of her long hair, which the wind had flung over her shoulders) on the sea, and strongly illumined by a flash of lightning, she saw, or fancied she saw, for it is difficult to believe that a mortal eye could have distinguished an object so distinctly at that distance—still Hannah thought she saw upturned towards her, amid the foam, the face of her young husband, Luke Murphy!

She sprang, rather than ran, down the secret passage, and along the shore. Pierce Murphy (for the morning was breaking) seeing her flying like a sea-mew through the haze and mist of the sea spray, seized her by the arm, and roughly demanded what she wanted; her words were few, but they were enough to paralyse the avowed smuggler—the secret wrecker. She called him *his son's murderer*. She declared she had seen that dear, that well-remembered face rise upon the surface of the water. Her father-in-law, as I have said, was paralysed at her words, but he believed them to be the dream of a distempered brain; he called to one of his companions to bear her up the cliff, for the scene was awful. The mangled remains of more than one body, still quivering with life, had been washed in, mutilated by the rocks, or crushed by the cargo that the wreckers were dragging on shore, heedless of the cries and supplications for help of the drowning crew. Her screams rose above the echoes and the sound of the watery tumult. She would not leave the beach; and the wicked, always superstitious, trembled at her incoherent words—at her wild shrieks; trembled even amid their thirst for such unlawful, such unholy plunder. Through the mist, amid the dawning light, and down the steep but beaten path leading from the cliffs to the shore, several of the coast-guard were seen descending, and this rendered Pierce more furious, as his prospect of booty decreased.

'Away, mad fool!' he exclaimed, as with eyes straining from their sockets Hannah opened her arms to every advancing wave, as if she expected it to yield her husband to her embrace.

'Take her away, will ye?—she lies,' said Pierce.

'No, no; I do not—I do not,' she exclaimed wildly. 'See—see—see—he comes—he'—— And with the effort of a despairing woman, she threw herself farther into the white surf, which had run up on the sands, bearing another victim to the land.

The story is well remembered to this day—it is this: that Hannah *clasped her husband's body*, and was dragged back to the shore with it. Pierce Murphy, fully awake to the fact that he had been the means of the destruction of his own son, who, full of hope and joy, was on his return to his young wife and his native land, could only gaze on the fruits of his wickedness—no one can tell with what feelings, for he imparted them to none. His companions in sin quickly recognised the once gay, light-hearted youth; but Hannah would suffer none to approach her. She dragged the body under shelter of a rock, and sitting down with frightful calmness, drew it across her knees, resting the mangled head upon her bosom, and enfolding all that she loved on earth, as a mother enfolds her child. She did not heed the oozing blood, the broken bones, nor the cold chill of the dead, but parted the streaming hair from the brow, and kissed and murmured over it words of such tenderness, that the wreckers and the coast-guard—the one forgetful of their plunder, or personal safety, if their share in the destruction should be discovered, the other neglectful of their duty, but all strong fearless men, accustomed to death and terror—looked on with tears at that sad picture of mute and maniac agony. Gentle as she was with the poor senseless clay, she would not, even when the sun was high in the heavens, and the receding tide showed how fearful the destruction had been, suffer any one to approach her. Several of the crew were saved, and their testimony was of such a nature, that Pierce (who made no attempt to escape) was seized and conveyed to Wexford jail. As the evening drew on, it was determined to remove Hannah from the body by force. To shield her from the sun's heat, which burst forth as if to contrast the power of light with the power of darkness, one of her neighbours had thrown her cloak over the broken-hearted woman and her burden: the same kind hand removed it when the parish priest declared she must not be longer left with the corpse. Alas! there was nothing living to separate—to put apart from the dead. The heart which had beat so warmly within that gentle bosom was broken! * * *

To the great horror of the country, Pierce Murphy destroyed himself in prison—a crime never anticipated in Ireland, because of such rare occurrence.

Margaret, the old woman, wandered for many a day—months, years—throughout the neighbourhood, a confirmed maniac; her bodily strength seemed to return when her faculties were totally destroyed; but she has now long been dead.

'To see how the innocent suffer for the guilty, and how one crime leads to another,' observed a country girl to her companion after hearing this sad tale.

'True for ye, *aileen;* and sure it's a great pity people don't think of that in time.'

'IT'S ONLY MY TIME.'

'PADDY—Paddy Blake—Paddy, I say,' called out Mr Manvers, seeing that Paddy Blake had left his long, heavy, narrow spade standing upright in the side of a *ditch* he was making to keep his neighbour's giddy young colt out of his potato garden, and having so done, commenced pulling his 'big coat' over his brawny shoulders. 'Paddy Blake,' repeated Mr Manvers, 'where are you going to?'

'Is it where I'm going to, sir? Bedad, thin, I'm just going over to Castle Connel wid a bit of a message for Mary Tomlins.'

'And why cannot Mary Tomlins go herself?'

'Oh, she's busy, she says, at the squire's.'

'Well, and you *were* busy at your ditch.'

'Ay, yer honour, but that's *my own;* and poor Mary would lose her eightpence if she broke her day's work, and it's a good step to Castle Connel.'

'Paddy Blake, how many children has Mary Tomlins?'

'Oh, thin, throth, I'm ashamed, sir, ye'd ask sich a question. Is it my sister's slip ov a girl? Childre! bedad, she hasn't made up her mind to a bachelor yet.'

'And how many children have you, Paddy Blake?'

'Why, thin, the Lord forgive me—I was going to say I had more than was good of 'em, and that would have been a lie, for they're all clane-skinned, wholesome, good-hearted childre, as ever broke a poor man's bread or cheered his heart wid their innocent ways. Let me count,' and he held up his great thick red fingers. 'I've five—Jim and Larry—no, Kathleen's next to Jim—thin Larry—thin—bedad, I don't rightly know whether Tommy or Lanty is next to Larry; but oh, I remimber now—

Tommy and Lanty came together. Twins, the heavens look down on us! in the hard season too—and thin Shelah.'

'But,' said Mr Manvers, 'you said *five*, and now you have counted six; I suppose you count twins as one!'

Paddy laughed, scratched his head, and replied, 'Bedad, yer honour, as far as the eating and the drinking goes they are two; thin—I'm all out together, for there's another besides Shelah, the darlint! Yer honour must have the wife to reckon the childre if ye want to know their number—there's a houseful of 'em anyway.'

'Oh,' said Mr Manvers, 'I only inquired because I wished to ascertain whether *you* or Mary Tomlins could best afford to waste a day.'

'Sure, sir, as to *that*—poor girl! if she went to Castle Connel, haven't I tould yer honour she'd break her day, and lose her *eightpence?*'

'And if *you* go to Castle Connel, and break *your* day, what will you lose?'

'Lose! nothing, sir.'

'Oh yes, you will!'

'Not a ha'porth, plase yer honour—*sure it's only my time.*'

'And is not your time worth a halfpenny, Paddy Blake?'

'Sorra a halfpenny I can get for it these bad times,' replied the ready-witted Paddy, 'fixing' his coat more firmly on his person by shrugging his shoulders.

'Suppose you finish that fence,' said Mr Manvers; 'is not *that* worth something?'

'Finish the fence, sir! the ditch you mane. If I don't finish the ditch, that baste of a coult, to say nothing of the pigs, will be all over, and indeed I may say *under*, every paytee we have to depind on for the winter; that coult has done me more than two pounds' worth of damage through the hole in the ditch, while I was seeing after Jerry Deasy's bit of business at Carrigagunnel.'

'Then charge Jerry Deasy, or whatever his name is, two pounds for your time.'

Paddy Blake looked exceedingly perplexed, and after staring at Mr Manvers as long as he could with propriety, he inquired, 'What did ye say, sir?'

'Charge Mr Deasy two pounds for the colt's damage, or rather for the time you were occupied in his service, instead of mending the ditch.'

'Lord, sir! is it a *tame nagur* you'd be afther making me! *Sure it was only my time.*'

'And pray, what property has a poor man but his time? What property has any man not born to fortune but his time?'

'It's a mighty poor fortune,' replied Paddy, shaking up the handful of straw that kept the sun out of the crown of his hat in summer, and the rain out of it in winter, and which at all times was seen peeping out of the holes of his hat.

'It is a noble fortune, *if put out to proper interest*,' observed Mr Manvers. An Irishman is quick of understanding, and Paddy replied, '*Irish* interest is *mighty small*, plase yer honour!'

'Granted; but though sixpence is not as good as a shilling, it is better than nothing; better for you to earn sixpence than nothing, my good friend.'

'Tare and ages, haven't I just tould yer honour it's I don't know how many weeks since I earned the value of a *traneen!*'

'Then you have been idle all that time!'

'Well, I must say, it's yerself that's the provoking gintleman! D'ye think I sat down in the midst of my small starving childre to sing ballads? Bedad, I looked afther my paytees, and put in the cabbage plants the coult ate—the devil give him the good of it! Not that I'd wish any harm to a neighbour's baste, only it's a poor case to think that instead of the beautiful *heads* I reckoned on, we'll be put off wid nothing but *sprouts*. And sure I plased the o'oman too, in her fancy of what they've put in her head—green mate for the cow.'

'Well, and suppose you had not so occupied your time, when you wanted potatoes, and cabbages, and green meat for the cow,' said Mr Manvers, 'you would have been obliged to purchase it?'

'Is it buy it ye mane? Ah, thin, ye're a mighty pleasant gintleman; where would a poor craythur like me get the money?'

'Now,' said the gentleman, 'Paddy Blake, I have you. If you save money, you make money; if you employ your time in doing what would cost money, you save money; and yet it *is only your time* put out to interest, as it were, that returns you the profits of its industry. Do you understand me?'

'Oh! I see what yer honour's driving at fast enough,' answered Paddy Blake. 'But now, isn't it a poor case to see a *boy* like me, able and willing to work, that can't earn a penny! The o'oman and the childre could manage the bit o' land well enough, and if I had work, I could do as clever and dacent as any boy in the counthry.'

'Much better than you do, undoubtedly; and it is a shame—a sin—a disgrace—to see so much unreclaimed land in Ireland, *and to think that a few thousands expended in employing the peasantry would reclaim it,* and give abundant blessings to the poor, in the way of employment and food. It *is* a shame; but, Paddy,' added Mr Manvers, 'remember what I said, that a shilling is better than sixpence; so, if you have not got the shilling, the sixpence is better than nothing. You can obtain no sale *for your time*, but you can *occupy* it yourself, and it behoves you to do so more industriously because of your difficulties. You can bestow additional care on your little half acre, or acre, or whatever it is, and make it produce better. A man with a small plot of land, *if he understands the value of time*, can, as I have already said, put it out to good interest. As long as the Almighty leaves the poor Irishman his health, and he is not rack-rented, it is marvellous what he can effect in a small way by industry—patient and steady industry, and attention to time—provided,' continued Mr Manvers smiling, 'he does not neglect the days of sunshine, and, leaving his little bit of ground unfenced, go scampering over the country, attending to the business of others, consoling himself when the night comes, and his work is still undone, with the exclamation, *Sure it was only my time!*'

'And, sir, would you never have us do a hand's turn for a neighbour?'

'Indeed I would. I have never loved Ireland so well as when I have seen a group of warm-hearted Paddys'——

'They're a large family, sir,' said Blake, smiling in his turn.

'Yes, and a fine one too, for I have seen them assemble by dozens to build a widow's house, to cut a neighbour's turf, to stack a neighbour's corn: to assist those who need assistance is one of the great and guiding principles of Irish life; God bless them for it!' added the Englishman, with a warmth that brought tears into the gray laughing eyes of Paddy Blake; 'but that is altogether different from the habit they have of acting upon the saying, "*Sure it's only my time.*" Why, *time*—time, with its innumerable uses—time IS THE ONLY FREEHOLD MAN RECEIVES DIRECT FROM THE ALMIGHTY. I would not have you abstain from assisting a neighbour *because* it occupied your *time*, but I would have you, as the father of a family, consider whether you can spare your time from *that* necessary to their support, and if you did give it, I would have you understand that if you devoted a whole day, you bestowed a shilling, if a half day, sixpence. You need not hurt your friend's feelings by this calculation, but your duty to your family requires you to make it. You Irishmen, rich and poor, do not set sufficient value on your time; your gentry never care how long they keep a poor person waiting, when they could give him an answer at once; and when I tell them of it, they reply, "*Oh, sure it is only his time;* he may as well wait; he has nothing particular to do." But *why* has he not? Why don't *you* either give him work, pay him in a fair proportion for his time, or teach him how to employ it? Above all, set him a good example.'

'That's it, sir!' replied Blake, much pleased at the course Mr Manvers's observations had now taken, and glad to escape from them himself. 'That's it! they'll keep us waiting and waiting, dancing and dancing afther them, and the *half* gintry altogether expecting twice as much *attintion* as the *whole;* and if we complain, which the heavens above knows we seldom do, we get as much abuse as would cover the railroad from Dublin to Dunleary.'

Mr Manvers looked, and felt sorry, for he knew there was a great deal of truth in this; but he also knew, that if the Irish peasant *felt his own value*, understood and managed his time, and by so doing became independent (for a poor man can be as independent as a rich one, if he manages properly), he could stand as erect, and complain of an injury with as great a certainty of redress, as an Englishman. I wish I may live long enough to see the Irish peasant understand his own value; his doing so will make him a better man and a better subject.

'Things are better for you than they used to be,' observed Mr Manvers; 'your children receive education if you choose to permit it; you are taught, or with your natural quickness you can learn without teaching, an improved system of farming; you can make your bit of ground produce three times as much as it did in former days. Prizes are given by Agricultural Societies to those who do best; Loan Societies* are established; a poor man can have (to him) the large sum of three or five pounds, and return it by *regular* weekly instalments of a few pence; but Paddy, these good things would produce good *seven*-fold, if you knew the *value of time*, and regulated your employments according to that value. Suppose, now, you go to Castle Connel, you leave that fence in so unprotected a state, that the colt or the pigs will be into the garden before you return.'

'The o'oman would mind them, now she's aware of it,' returned Paddy.

'To do which, she must leave her spinning.'

'Well, thin, Jim, he's not at the school this afternoon; he can keep them out as well as me, only he's as wild as a young hawk.'

'And cannot he do your niece Mary's message?'

'God bless yer honour! ye've a long head, so you have; think of my not thinking of that; he can do the message as well as me, and betther, for he's lighter footed. And as this is Sathurday, he'll be home from school, and 'll have a half-holiday.'

'His time,' said the steadfast Englishman, 'is of less value than yours; only such a journey will help to wear out his shoes.'

Paddy Blake laughed. 'Oh! no, God bless you, sir, whinever he's going a walk, he takes off the shoes; that is, *whin he has 'em*, which he hasn't had this two months back, though he soon will, plase God, from the school, yer honour. He has a power and all

---

* I was greatly pleased to see one of those set on foot by Browne Clayton, Esq., near New Ross, and close to the unfortunate barn of Scullabogue. At that time, the autumn of 1838, it worked well, and in that spot was a beautiful type of Christianity—returning good for evil.

of *good marks;* they count for something, and he'll have the price of a pair of brogues out of them one of these days.'

'There!' exclaimed the Englishman exultingly—'there! it is *only his time*, properly employed, that can win him not only education, but reward for diligence! Oh, Paddy Blake, I wish I had you in England for twelve months.'

'I'll be happy to gratify or accommodate yer honour by any means in my power,' said Paddy slyly, while taking off his coat to resume his work.

'Very good, Paddy; I should like to show you what a fine family estate TIME is to the whole population. As I told you before, *it is the only freehold that man has direct from the Almighty,* and ought not to be neglected. They know how to employ the phrase " it's only my time!" in a very different manner to what you do. " How," I inquired of a tradesman'——

'A what, plase yer honour?' interrupted Paddy.

'A tradesman. "How is it that I left you a poor workman, and find you a prospering dealer!—had you a fortune left you?"'

'"No, sir," he answered; "*I had only my time.*"'

'But sure he had the trade anyway,' observed Paddy Blake; 'and that was something.'

'Nothing, unless he had applied *his time* to gain it. You cannot swallow a trade as you can food; you must *take time* to learn it. One of my own labourers has managed, by industry, by carefulness, by never misapplying, but always properly applying, his time, to take a small farm.'

'Ah, sir!' said poor Paddy, shaking his head, ' in England I've heard tell the landlord builds the house, and the tenant gets his bit of ground, be it much or little, in good condition; he is not expected to lay out money on it at all, only keep it as he gets it; and, above all, my o'oman heard tell at the big house that there's a *Labourers' Friend Society* in England to look afther the *cottchers.* Oh, if the Lord would put it into some kind Christian's heart to do the same thing here, wouldn't it be a fine thing?'

'So it would,' said the benevolent gentleman; 'and I assure you there is a great deal of kind feeling towards the Irish peasantry abroad in England.'

'You may well say *abroad*, sir,' chimed in Paddy; 'it's so far *abroad*, that it will be long before it *comes home* to us anyway.'

'Now, Paddy Blake, do *not* be ungrateful; it is *not* an Irishman's failing. Your country is improving.'

'It is, sir.'

'Your condition is improving; I do not mean *your individual* condition, because as yet you do not manage your time as well as you might, nor have you as much employment as you ought to have; but your national condition is improved, and there is a school for your children, there is'——

'I know, yer honour; we are better off, on the whole, than our fathers war; I'll not deny it.'

'And will be still better; the constant communication between Ireland and England is of great advantage; the prices you obtain for your eggs, butter, and small merchandise in that way is much increased; you are more thought of; and if English capitalists can once be convinced, as I am, that they can live amongst you without danger, and you will resolve to make the best use of *time* and its advantages, why, please God, in a few more years you will be as you ought to be, as the great bulk of the English gentry desire to see you—as remarkable for your prosperity as you are for your ability.'

'Many thanks to yer honour; I'll go to the ditch now and send the boy to Castle Connel; he'll be back in less than no time. And sure, now I think of it, all Mary wanted of Katty Donovan (that's the o'oman at Castle Connel) was the loan of a "beatle."'

'A what?' inquired the Englishman; 'a beetle! What can she want of a beetle?—one would think she could catch them in plenty.'

'Oh, plase yer honour, it's a *beatle;* a thing for beating linen— beatling it in the wather; washing it clane, you know; thrashing the dirt out of it. Sure enough it *was* making little of my time to send me for that—great logs o' wood lying about the door, and Jim Brady the carpenter would make her one for a pinny or tupence, or for nothing; for sure the wood is there, and *it would be only his*—— But I ax yer honour's pardon; I'll sind word to her to have some sinse, and get Jim Brady to make her a beatle of her own, and give *him a pinny for his time;* will *that* do, sir? And, look now, *does* yer honour see that coult in the far field jist watching till my back's turned that he may begin his *gammocks* agin—thim animals are mighty knowing, like Andy Murphy's pig.'

'And what of it?' inquired Mr Manvers.

'It was so knowing, yer honour, it would root the paytees out of the ground, and settle the earth afther that, so that if ye war on yer oath, ye couldn't tell where it had been. But there's my poor o'oman, sir, wants to show you her spinning; and she'll plase ye if I don't, for though she hasn't much raison in her, she makes *much of her time.*'

Mrs Blake was a thrifty Irishwoman. When thrift and industry go hand in hand, they can remove mountains. She had not missed a word of the dialogue I have just recorded, and anticipating 'the English gentleman's visit,' had set her 'little place' in order, and succeeded in getting two out of three of the younger children's faces washed. She dusted the best chair in the house with the corner of her apron, and invited Mr Manvers to be seated. She showed the effects of her industry with evident pride. 'She had little time for spinning,' she said, 'except when the childre were asleep, but she blessed the Almighty he had shown her the value of time, and but for *that*, God knows they'd be bad off; not but Paddy was a good husband—"sorra a betther ever broke the world's bread"—but he was too soft in himself intirely; too good-hearted; not a fault had he in the world but *that* one. Sure she thanked God it was no other, for sure every man must have some fault. He did a dale with *his time*, when he was let alone; but the neighbours knew how *easygoing*, what a *knock-softly* he was, and played on him. He'd be sure to mend, now that his honour had took such pains to show him the rights of it, God bless him! Time was a fine thing, now that she had it set *afore* her; it was wonderful to see how it changed everything, and while it took the beauty from the cheek, put wisdom into the head.' She hoped also 'it increased the fear o' God in the heart. Sure time was one of the Almighty's miracles.' She would pray 'to the Lord to forgive her for having thrown away so much of it, whin his honour had so clearly proved to any one of common sinse that mate, drink, and clothing could be got out of it! She'd set Kathleen to card flax tomorrow afther school hours, and sure that would save *her own time*, for while the little girl was carding, she could be spinning—and tache little Shelah to knit over-hours: supposing she only began with garters, it was something. Sure that *would save her time*, and blind Abel would tache the twins to make baskets; that would turn a penny: and the two big boys could gather rushes and switches. And more she would do; and—sure—God look down upon his honour!—she would strive to hinder any one belonging to her from saying or thinking, "*Sure's it's only my time!*"'

GOING TO LAW.

PART THE FIRST.

Showing how John Leahy, commonly called Johnny the Giant, *would* go to law.

'WELL, well, John Leahy, will you just stick to the one point, and before you take an oath, explain to me what you want to swear to?'

John Leahy, a tall muscular Irishman, stood before the gentleman who put this question (a good-natured magistrate, Mr Richard Russel, who resided for the shooting and hunting season on his estate called Russel Court, not quite three miles from the ancient city of Limerick); John Leahy stood before the fox-hunting but most peace-loving magistrate, his long gray frieze coat thrown back from his ample chest, his green neckerchief, so loosely tied, that the brawny muscles of his neck, heaving and swelling with the impetuosity that sent the red blood rushing to his face, were fully seen; while that face, so powerful, and yet generally so pleasing in its expression, was wrought into painful distortion by exceeding wrath; his nostrils were distended, like those of a war-horse scenting the battle from afar; his large gray eyes were absolutely flashing; his mouth was not only closed, but clenched. And so firmly did he grasp his shillala, in a 'fist' that would have served Vulcan as a sledge-hammer, that his fingers had become perfectly white from the exertion. He had removed his hat upon entering the magistrate's breakfast-room, but in his eagerness had crushed 'the bran new beaver' into a most unnatural shape.

Mr Russel was so accustomed to these vehement displays of temper, or whatever they may be called, that he proceeded very quietly to finish his breakfast, regardless of the half-open door, through which five or six anxious faces were seen poking one over the other—all friends and allies of Johnny Leahy's; and regardless also of the widely-opened window that was only between five and six feet above the level of the lawn—for every now and then a head popped up, and then as quickly disappeared, betraying anxiety to ascertain what was going on within.

John Leahy remained silent after Mr Russel had put his question, not for want of words, but literally because he could not speak, from the quantity and quality of those that rose to his lips, and well-nigh choked his utterance. Mr Russel repeated the question.

'Well, now, let me understand what it is you want to swear!' At last out it came, like a thunderbolt from the angry heavens—

'*Anything, anything, by the blessed book! for satisfaction!*'

'Oh!' said the magistrate, upon whom the admission had no effect—'oh! it is, I suppose, the old story about the quarter of an acre; anything particularly new?'

'If yer honour will be plased to hear me, and listen to *raison*, I'll put the rights of it before you at onct; and there's my mother, poor ould craythur, without, and two or three more neighbours, and it's ourselves that have been waiting on yer honour since break of day, and got into the house, hoping favour from yer honour, seeing you ought to lane towards *ould* residenters, that have a natural claim on the gintry.'

'Haven't I often told you,' interrupted the magistrate peevishly, 'that all this has nothing to do with the justice of the case? Where is Abel Carr?'

'Oh, the little bla'guard (saving yer honour's presence), it's without he is. He thought to make his way in, but I didn't want yer honour to be put in a passion with his lies—the thief of the world!—so I jist made bould to draw the boult of the hall door.'

'Draw the bolt of my house against your neighbour, who has as good a right to justice as yourself!' Mr Russel rang the bell after so saying, and John Leahy, not aware that he had done what was exceedingly improper, exclaimed, 'As good a right to justice as me? Oh, mother honey, hear to that! You who lived under his honour's father and grandfather a'most before the world was a world, hear to his honour saying that Abel Carr, the circumvinter, the depopulating vagabon, the fella' who could never count back to his grandfather, the half-withered little leprehawn, that's growed up like a musharoon under our noses, the little insinuating bla'guard, stealing my beautiful strame of spring wather, turning it away from my meadow, and laying claim to as beautiful a half acre of bog—not only axing the right of turbary, but wanting the half acre, to the very foundation of the earth—only jist, mother honey, think of his honour's saying that that *scum o' the earth* has as good a right to justice as *me*—his father, his grandfather, his *great-grandfather's* tenant's son, John Leahy!'

'His honour manes no such thing,' said Mrs Leahy, advancing into the room by a series of curtsies—'his honour means no sich thing as *that*, I'll go bail!—not he indeed. Let *me* spake, and I'll lay it out afore him like print. We're ould tenants, yer honour; and setting a case, that yer honour will give Peggy's husband, that *is* to be—but I'm not at that yet. Ye see it come altogether of that vagabon threat of Abby Carr's wife before she was married—she wanted Peggy's bachelor for her own, and the turf bog that isn't big enough for a'——

At this moment, and just as Mr Russel was going to desire Mrs Leahy either to come to the point at once, or to hold her tongue—neither of which, experience might have taught him, she would do—the servant forced his way through the crowd at the door to answer the bell.

'Unbolt the hall door,' said the magistrate—'unbolt the hall door directly, and call to Abel Carr to come in.'

'It's not naided—many thanks to yer honour all the same. It's not naided by any manner o' manes,' exclaimed a squeaking voice from the open window. 'I'm here, yer honour's worship, to the confusion of my inimies, and the establishment of law and justice. I'm here, yer honour!'

And truly, astride on the window seat, one leg in and the other out of the window, flourishing his hat above his shaggy crop of yellow hair, was Abel Carr, forming in voice, manner, and appearance, a singular and ludicrous contrast to the Herculean Irishman who complained of his 'innovations.' Any one with the commonest observation could perceive, that though Abel was but a pigmy to his giant foe, yet the full broad forehead—the blue, cold, almost *cruel* eye that twinkled beneath the overhanging brows of the little man—the firm, inflexible mouth, that could close in its thoughts as if with the seal of death—any one, I say, could see that Abel 'had a head,' while John Leahy's powerful frame was only surmounted by a handsome 'animal development.' Strong passions, rash, daring, were stamped upon a high but narrow brow, over which his rich brown hair curled in profusion. I beg the English reader to understand, that a few years ago no man ever went near a magistrate without being accompanied, at all events to the hall steps, by a tribe of 'friends,' who either had, or fancied they had, something to do with the affair in question; while others followed because they had nothing to do: thus two contending factions have frequently met, and not unfrequently 'done battle' upon a magistrate's lawn. This has occurred within my own memory: they are better behaved now-a-days, and would wait, at all events, until beyond the entrance gate. Having said so much, it can be easily imagined that when Abel Carr's 'friends' saw him waving his hat triumphantly, they set up a yell of delight and defiance, while 'John the Giaunt,' as he was called, made a plunge towards the window, which caused the worthy Mr Russel to spring from his chair, and to declare, heading his declaration with an oath that would have shaken into atoms the whole bench of Middlesex magistrates, that 'if they did not keep the peace, he would give them forty-eight hours in Limerick jail.'

'Axing yer honour's worship's pardon,' observed Abel Carr, speaking with great rapidity in a thin shrill voice, bringing his other leg into the room, and edging round so as to interpose the worthy magistrate's person between himself and his foe—'axing yer honour's pardon, it's *you* ought to be sint there, or pay a fine— that is, if the swearing of a *justice of pace* is as sinful as the swearing of a poor man, which in coorse it is not; if it was, yer honour's worship wouldn't have rapped out sich a one as that, yer honour!'

The scene was curious. The room was hung round with sporting prints, of various dates and orders of merit. Above the long narrow glass which surmounted the old black marble chimneypiece, were suspended a couple of fowlingpieces, crossed above a couple of swords; and each side of the glass was garnished by what I should call a horse pistol—I mean a large determined pistol, done up with bright steel; not one of the finikin gilt-edged little gentlemen which I see in London, seeming only fit for Cupids to shoot with, but a sturdy, blood-thirsty-looking fellow. Not even a good-tempered magistrate in that fire-eating county Limerick would consider himself quite safe without firearms in his sitting-room. And the wild group outside, backed by the distant mountains, while the noble Shannon, that most boisterous yet most gracious of rivers, foamed and fretted as it dashed over its native rocks in the foreground—always confirming my imagination in the belief that the county Limerick, rich in the bounties of overflowing nature, is still an awkward place in which to pitch a tent, and play at Arcadians. Within the magistrate's room the scene was as wild as without; the furniture seemed well fitted to bear the knocking about of careless guests; the shaggy wolfdog and the sleek pointer were stretched with a couple of superannuated fox-hounds upon the ample hearth.

John Leahy seemed as though the concentrated anger of half a century had exaggerated his features and agitated his entire frame. If looks could have destroyed, Abel Carr would have been annihilated; but he had crept round with the stealth of a cat and the crawl of a reptile behind Mr Russel's chair. Mrs Leahy's figure and face were a study; the hood of her genuine Irish cloak had fallen from the rich and abundant lace that garnished her lawn cap; her withered arms were thrown forward in the attitude of intreaty, and her features expressed both rage and anxiety. Those of 'Johnny the Giaunt's' friends, who had remained in some degree outside the breakfast-room, had entered when Abel Carr made his descent; and a little in advance of the rude group was Alice Leahy, the plaintiff's wife, as lovely a specimen of fair Irish beauty as ever spun at a wheel or plaited a hat. Alice's fair hair was banded beneath a cap of finer texture than that of her mother-in-law; her cloak was of bright scarlet, and a little girl of five or six years old clung to it so as to draw it more than half towards her, leaving somewhat exposed the womanly symmetry of her mother's perfect form, which otherwise would have been quite concealed. There was no bitterness, no revenge, no strong passion written on that gentle woman's face. The one expression was interest in her husband, towards whom her eyes were directed; while the child looked with evident terror up to her mother, and then, as if reassured by her gentleness, advanced a little more into the room; not, however, loosing her hold of the cloak.

Her clear and lovely features were perfect, and hallowed by an expression of the most heavenly purity: it was next to impossible not to wonder who she was, and how she came there; and this feeling would have been increased, if her cheeks had been as pale as they were in general; but the agitation of the scene had called into them a rose-like colour. Irish gentlemen, polished as they are when mingling with those in their own sphere of life, are by no means gracious to their inferiors. There are some exceptions, to be sure, but Mr Russel was not one; and yet he bowed to Alice; not the leering bow of a fox-hunter, but the respectful salutation which is man's natural tribute to beauty and virtue. He even asked her to sit down, but she gathered her cloak gracefully round her, and shrinking, as it were, within its folds, drew back her little girl, who had renewed an acquaintance with one of the dogs,* which licked her little fat hands, moving his tail with great dignity, as if to intimate that he did the little maid an honour.

'Stand back every one of ye!' said John to his faction. 'Have ye no manners?—no more manners than to dar to come without invitation into his honour's own room? I'm ashamed of ye, I am, to *dar* to come into his honour's place. Stand back, I say, and show that little carroty-headed *spalpeen* a patthern of gen-til-ity: if we are strong in our cause, boys, let us be marciful! Now, yer honour, now that that Omadawn has got his dirty mane-spirited *soul* into your prisince, I should like to tell him a piece of my mind.'

'You can do *that* at any other time quite as well,' observed the magistrate.

'Only if I had yer honour's glory for a witness.'

'I tell ye what,' said Mr Russel sternly, 'you, John Leahy, commonly called Johnny the Giant, and you, Abel Carr, commonly called Aby the Goldfinch, if you exchange either words or blows within the precincts of my house or domain, I'll commit you both for forty-eight hours to the body of Limerick jail; and what will be worse, I'll confine you both in the same cell, where you may eat each other, like the Kilkenny cats, and a good riddance the country will have of a pair of fools—who are eternally GOING TO LAW.'

'Oh, my Lud A'mighty!' exclaimed the old woman, 'did any body ever hear the like o' that! His honour a *justice o' pace*, and to see him set agin the law!'

'It is because I am a justice of "*pace*," as you call it, that I *do* my best to prevent my tenants from going to law. Why, you people can never enter into a lawsuit without committing assault and battery upon each other during its progress, so as to create half-a-dozen actions out of one. You bring ruin and degradation upon yourselves, and frequently, too frequently, disgrace the records of your country by murder!'

'Oh, bedad, yer honour!' said the Giant, 'ye may make yer mind aisy as to *him:* sorra take me if I'd dirty my fingers with such a *grassnauge*† as Abel Carr. The only way I can touch him, sir, is with the arm of the law; and by the holy'——

'Stop now—gently,' said Mr Russel; 'no swearing. But if you can come to the point at once, I will hear you, and little Abel shall afterwards tell *his* story; and I must say Aby comes more quickly to the point than you do.'

---

* In Ireland a sporting landlord sends out his young dogs ' to be nursed ' at the farm-houses; and I have seen many recognitions between the peasants and dogs, which, however, I believe the huntsman does not approve of.
† Hedgehog.

'Aisy for him!' muttered old Mrs Leahy; 'he's been at a point all his life—the point of the gallows!'

Mr Russel had resumed his seat with the air of a man determined to be patient; 'the Goldfinch' had watched with cat-like observance the words and gestures of the whole company; he now folded his arms, and seemed resolved upon patience also, only saying in a whining tone, 'I'm a fair-daling, fair-maning little man, yer honour, wishing to earn a bit of bread for myself, my wife, and five little childre, and never quarrelling with any one except for what's *my own*, yer honour!'

'Hear to that, Father of Justice!' exclaimed the Giant. 'But yer honour sees how paceable I am—(oh, you false-hearted little leprehawn!)—I'm as aisy as a cow in clover—(I'm not done nor begun wid ye yet). There now, I'll tell ye all—I'll begin at onct at the beginning.'

'Ay, do!' groaned the magistrate.

'Well, sir, my great-grandfather's new *lase* is dated, as I daresay yer honour knows, 1722—a ninety-nine years' lase it was— which yer honour had the goodness to renew for three lives and thirty-one years. Sure we're bound to take good care of yer honour, for your own life and Masther Arthur's are first of the three.* Well'——

'Good heavens!' exclaimed the gentleman, 'I've heard that twenty times, and all about the half acre of bog which Abel Carr says is on his land, and you say is on yours; and I have besought you over and over again, if you could not agree as to who had a right to it, just quietly to divide it.'

'Is it give up me right!' exclaimed John Leahy indignantly; and flinging down his hat and shillala, he dropped suddenly upon his knees, snatched the Prayer-book from off the table, pressed it to his lips, and began, 'I, John Leahy, will never cease by day or by night, at home or abroad, rich or poor, houseful or homeless, to have the law, or my vengeance out'——

Before he could proceed farther with his fearful oath, the hand of his beautiful wife was pressed upon his lips. To rush forward, sink upon her knees by his side, encircle his neck with her arm, and close his lips as I have described, was but the work of an instant. 'You shan't swear like that,' she exclaimed, 'and I to the fore. You shan't indeed, John *asthore*. *Cor-a-ma-chree!* you wouldn't break the heart of yer poor Ally, John, darlint? Sure it isn't for you to demane yourself like a poor ignorant craythur that knows no better, only flying in the face of the Almighty with an oath, as if you hadn't the courage of a man, John, in your own brave breast, to keep your promise without that. Sure if the law and the justice is on our side, darlint, isn't that enough? Let

* Landlords in Ireland frequently use the precaution of having their own lives in 'the lase.'

them take oaths and swear that won't be believed without,' she added proudly, while her husband rose with her, half ashamed of his impetuosity. 'Let *them* swear whose word is lighter than the down of a thistle in a high wind, but John Leahy's word is the word of an honest man: tell his honour ye'll have yer rights, and keep them!—though, God knows,' she added, while her voice faltered, 'God knows his honour's advice was best—it's better to divide what one has, than'—— She saw the keen eye of the Goldfinch fixed upon her, and she paused; then curtseying to Mr Russel, she added mildly, 'I ask yer honour's pardon, but I couldn't help it. He's my husband—and—— But I hope yer honour will excuse me; I know yer honour does not like swearing no more than me, if I may make bould to say so.'

'Well, plase yer honour,' said John, 'I only mane that while I've a shilling in my pocket, a coat on my back, or a straw in my thatch, *I'll have the law;* and if yer honour *(whom I'd rather trouble by day or by night*—on account of the respect I have for yer honour, and me and mine having done so for the last hundred years *and more*—than any other magistrate in the county)— but if yer honour wont listen to raison, and see me righted, and punish that desaver, that has never had the courage to *open his face* since he came into yer honour's house, why, I'll go to Limerick—I'll put myself under the care of 'Torney Botherum. If I starve, I'll have justice; if I die, I'll have *law!*'

'And the devil give ye good of it,' squeaked out the Goldfinch. 'Now, if yer honour's glory will listen to me—see that now! if he'll give up the half acre, that, according to a covenant in my Uncle Tom's will, was to be mine if his Aunt Biddy on the mother's side died without childre—which she did, poor unhappy ould craythur'——

'What's that he says?' interrupted the old woman, setting her 'talons' in order. 'What's that he says about my Aunt Biddy?'

'Whisht!' interposed the Giant; 'I'm aisy now—jist give him rope enough, and he'll hang himself. Go on, if it's plasing to ye, Misther Abel Carr—sir, if you plase!'

'I'd scorn to talk to you, you unedicated bogtrotther!' quoth the Goldfinch.

'Who do you call unedicated!' returned Leahy; '*I* did not get *my* larning off the pack-saddle of a broken-down exciseman, nor in the office of a dirty 'torney.'

'Shame on you both!' interposed the magistrate; 'and you, Abel Carr, stick, if it be possible for an Irishman to stick, to the one point; do so, in God's name, and say what you propose.'

'He has tould yer honour, I suppose, about the strame? Ye understand, it runs through my ground before it comes to his, little as it is; and it was my convanyance to make a ditch across the dawshy strame'——

'He owns to that, yer honour—hear to that; he owns to making the ditch,' said the Giant.

'To be sure I do! Sure I've a right to make a ditch on my own land; but this man, as soon as my ditch is finished—in the night-time or day-time, it's all one to him—shovels it down again.'

'And you thought to take a dirty advantage of me whin my foot slipt, and smother me in it,' added Mr Leahy.

'Oh, Heavenly Father!' exclaimed the tiny red-headed man, 'listen to that; and me trying to get him out, and he so tossicated with the liquor, that *his breath crossing a sunbame would have set the heavens in a blaze;* the Lord above purtect us from drunkards!'

It required all Mr Russel's influence to prevent John Leahy (who might really be called a sober man) from seizing and annihilating the provoking little farmer. The quarrellers had tormented Mr Russel touching this half-acre business at least twenty times, and always with the same result; asking his advice, and following their own. It is odd enough that a people so fond of breaking the law, should be so fond of going to law, and generally end by being dissatisfied with the law's result, and then take it into their own hands. An Englishman, if he is insulted, walks off as quietly to a police-office as if he were going to a funeral, makes his charge, and is, generally speaking, well satisfied with the result. He does not do as a huge Wexford farmer, Jasper Corish by name, once did. 'How have you managed with Lawrence Costello?' he was asked one day.

'Why,' said Jasper, 'I took the law of him first, and then I bate him just within an inch of his life.'

'And what followed?'

'Bedad! he took the law of *me* thin, and I was cast.'

'Well?'

'Why, thin, *I bate him again.*' And for this, Jasper added, 'he was murdered intirely, for he was bound over to keep the pace for two years, *and was losing the use of his limbs for want of practice.*' It is impossible not to laugh at Jasper's perseverance and pugnacity, but it is too true that we often laugh where reflection would make us weep. Whoever would check the spirit of litigation which fills the pockets of the Irish pettifogging attorneys who dwell in county towns, on fair and market days, with crown and half-crown fees, would do almost as much towards the salvation of Ireland as he who checks the progress of intemperance.

Mr Russel knew perfectly well that in cunning Abel Carr was as much an overmatch for John Leahy, as John Leahy was in bodily strength for Abel Carr. He knew that Leahy had embroiled himself for the last year with the crafty Abel, and yet Abel was, in the sight of the country, getting the advantage of his opponent at every hand's turn; working him out of his land not only on this but on other occasions. It was neither Abel's interest nor his intention to suffer any matter pending between them to be clearly understood. He was the sort of person who would bear a beating for the sake of the damages; and Mr Russel knowing this, was anxious that, while he yielded him the freeborn right of answering his accuser, that accuser should hold his tongue, for Abel was proud of his knowledge, proud of 'his law;' and the magistrate knew that, as John himself said, 'if he had rope enough given, he would hang himself.' But this giving of rope was what, with all his knowledge, John would not do, and so he foiled the magistrate's kind intention.

John called Abel Carr 'the artfullest thief under heaven,' and yet he met him, as it were, open-mouthed. He knew he had spent all his early days in the chicanery of an attorney's office, yet he ran into law with him with as much avidity as if he had been coursing a hare.

After much stormy discussion—for at every second sentence Mr Russel was obliged to interpose his authority—the magistrate came to the conclusion that, in addition to the disputed half acre, the Giant charged the Goldfinch with turning a stream he had no right to turn, and for an assault; and the Goldfinch avowed his right to turn the stream, and denied the assault; and upon this there were half-a-dozen of the clan Giant ready to swear it had been made, and half-a-dozen of the clan Goldfinch ready to swear it had not been made. And this tangled net of bog, and stream, and battle was crossed and recrossed by several webs of minor but not less perplexing import: how Aby Carr's brother Mike had laid a plan of abduction, in which Alice's sister Anne was to have been the victim; how John's brother's boat on the Shannon had a hole knocked through its side by Aby's sister's son; how—— But I shall never get to the end of my story at this rate. The worthy magistrate saw it was impossible to unravel their mysteries; the best advice, to make it up amongst themselves, they would not take; and so Mr Russel, his whole morning wasted (but as he was an Irish country gentleman, *that*, in his estimation, did not signify very much), desired them all to go about their business, and trouble him no more. And Abel Carr, well pleased, said he would never have troubled his honour but for the necessity there was of clearing his character to so good a 'gintleman.' And John Leahy declared there was no use in going to a landlord, and a magistrate, who had no 'laning towards an ould residenter,' but that he'd 'take the law of the leprehawn, if it left him a beggar on the face of the earth.' And it was piteous to see the expression of agony that passed over Alice Leahy's face as she glanced from her husband to her child.

And now how were the contending factions to disperse? The

women of both begged that his honour's glory would prevent the spilling of blood, and keep one set prisoners till the other was gone. But Mr Russel, by a skilful manœuvre, despatched the Giant's friends by the stable entrance, and those of Abel Carr through the hall door, and finished his morning by arranging, in a more satisfactory manner, some trifling disputes amongst some of his humbler neighbours, who had the good sense *not to go to law*.

But his trials for the day were not over. Neither an Englishman nor an Irishman likes to be disturbed immediately after dinner; yet Mr Russel had not finished his second tumbler, when the servant said Mrs Leahy wanted to speak a word with his honour, and would not keep him a minute.

'Is it the young or the old one?' inquired the magistrate. The servant said 'it was Alice,' and Mr Russel said she must be shown up immediately; and the two young ladies nearly quarrelled as to who had the best right to place a chair for the farmer's sweet wife: a legal question, which papa decided by declaring *both* had the right—the eldest, because she was the eldest, and the youngest, because she was the youngest. As soon as this point was settled, Mrs Leahy was introduced. She sat down, for her trembling limbs appeared scarcely able to sustain her weight; but after resting a few moments, she rose, curtsied, and advanced to the table, upon which she placed her fingers, as if fearful that, unsupported, she could *not* stand; she then, in the low soft tones of suppressed feeling, apologised for her intrusion, and commenced in the earnest language of a warm but untutored heart to ask counsel of Mr Russel, and state her fears and anxieties.

'Plase yer honour, and you, ma'am, who knew me before I knew myself, and you, young ladies, growing up before my eyes in beauty, garden roses that ye are, my husband is gone over to Pether Pendergrast, and the ould woman along with him; and the child—the only blossom left us—asleep, the Lord look down on her! and so I thought I'd make bould to come over and open my mind, on account of the notion John has in his head of going to law. Ye see, yer honour, Pether Pendergrast pushes him on to it; and his mother, living so long on the land, poor woman, it's no wonder she should take on about every blade of grass, and think a dale of every green shamrock that springs from the sod. It's as good as four years since the first notion took him about law. Yer honour minds the fair that time, and how he was brought in about a bit of a dispute; well, everything went so much to his mind then, sir, that he unfortunately took a liking to the law; and little Aby Carr urged on his claims to this weary bit of bog, and my trouble is, that through the half acre we shall be broke altogether.'

'How do you mean?' inquired Mr Russel; 'my agent has said nothing of your husband's being in arrear.'

'Thank God he's not *that*, sir,' replied Alice almost proudly. 'We paid the agent up, sir, though some of the cattle, the brindled cow I reared from a calf with my own hand—the same age as little Peggy she was—went with the rest to make up the last gale.'

'I should have been told this,' said Mr Russel, who, though a magistrate when present, was generally *an absent* Irishman, and knew but little of his estate except during the hunting season.

'I don't complain of that, yer honour; there's no use crying afther the snow that fell last year; but I *do* complain of the money that goes in law, and, above all, of the time spent about it for nothing. Never a cause in the coort-house of Limerick that comes on, but he's off to hear tried, saying if it does not do him good one time, it may another; and then, yer honour, his people and neighbours, knowing his way, get round him, and he treats them, and '——

'This is very bad indeed,' said Mr Russel, for poor Alice's emotion overcame her.

'This is very sad; I thought John was an excellent husband,' said Mrs Russel.

'A good husband!—Oh, thin, the Lord guide and purtect him, that he is, and always was—never an unkind word did he give me; but for all that, he's a man, and will take his own way, though when he gets into any little distress, he's sure to bemoan himself, and say if he had took my advice he'd not have had that trouble; but sure he does the same thing over again the next minute. There's many idle, bad-minded persons going that don't care a mite what comes of any one, so their own turn's served; and it goes to my heart to see such as my husband put upon by some, and tormented by others, who have nothing betther than him—*but cunning*. I can see through Aby Carr. If my husband gave up that half acre quiet and aisy, it would break his heart. He knows he has a hould over it, and it's just a bare bone of contention. As long as he keeps him in contention about that and the little strame of water—that's good for nothing in the world but the wild birds of the air to drink of—he knows that he must fall into trouble, because he neglects his farming that he does understand, for the law which he does *not* understand, thank the Almighty! I'd sooner see him—dear as he is, and wrapt up within my heart ever since I heard the first sound of his voice, as the misthress remembers me, a little *colleen* at my mother's door—I'd sooner see him dead—I think I would— than the mean bad thing the law turns many an honest man to.'

'You are quite right; but what can I do more than advise him against this going to law which he is so fond of?' inquired Mr Russel. 'I never knew a rich man take to law, that he was not made much poorer by it, nor a poor man, that he was not ruined.'

'Well,' said the wife, with a look of beautiful resignation, 'if it must be so, it must, that's all; I'll do my best to prevent it; but if it comes, why, *the worst will be over*—the grace of God is above us all. I'll never reproach him by word or look, and I'll work with him and for him, and for the *bird of my bosom*—work for them—or '—— She could not say BEG; the word was stayed in her throat, and instead, she added, '*Travel* with them to the grave.'

'Not while we have a house on our estate to shelter you,' said Mrs Russel kindly.

'May the great God bless you for that!' murmured Alice through her tears. The prayer came warm and pure from her heart, and as such was registered in heaven.

'But a poor woman like me,' she resumed, endeavouring to smile, 'has no right to be troubling the quality with her troubles. Yer honour understands that there isn't a *jackeen** 'torney in the town that hasn't given him half-a-crown, or five shillings, or maybe seven-and-sixpence worth, of bad advice, either upon this or something else, and called it law; and now he has the notion of going to 'Torney Botherum, who, they say, any day is as good as a counsellor, only he wont do any law, not open his lips, under ten shillings to the poorest; and though his tongue is as glib as an eel, it'll tell no law till he has the bit of yellow goold; and he wont let me go with him, because his people say I tell all, but he takes his mother and one or two more. Now, the 'torney, if he was as great a lawyer as King Solomon, would never make out the rights of it from John; and to get rid of the trouble of thinking, he'll maybe give an encouraging answer, and that will be worse than ever. So I had a thought, if yer honour, who knows the 'torney so well, would be so good as to give him an idea of how it really was, maybe HE might get him to give up the weary bit of bog without risking all we have in a lawsuit, for men of my husband's temper *will often take an advice from a stranger that they would not listen to from their own people.*'

Mr Russel could not help admiring the wisdom of Alice Leahy, it was so simply and modestly spoken, and yet replete with the difficult knowledge of human nature—that knowledge which books cannot teach.

'Well,' he said, 'I will call upon my friend Botherum the first thing to-morrow morning, but you must explain to me exactly how it is. I have heard the half-acre affair six times at least, without being much the wiser.' Alice did so, and increased the astonishment of the worthy lady and gentleman by her clearness

* Petty, low, sharp, cunning, pettifogging.

and perspicuity. Mr Russel renewed his promise of being with the attorney the first thing in the morning; and as she was about to withdraw, he put to her an experimental question—'Mrs Leahy, are you quite right to do this without your husband's knowledge?'

'If yer honour had a relation gone mad, wouldn't you strive to hinder him from doing any harm to himself or another?'

He replied, 'But my tenant, your husband, is not mad surely?'

'Plase yer honour, I do not think any man going to law can be in his senses.'

'What a sensible as well as a beautiful woman that is!' observed the magistrate, as Alice curtsied herself out of the room.

'So she is, my dear,' answered his wife. 'Do you remember what she said about the obstinacy of all men, and being obliged to regret afterwards that they did not follow their wives' advice?'

'Humph!' said the magistrate. And here we conclude the first part of our story.

PART THE SECOND.
Showing what John Leahy, commonly called 'Johnny the Giant,' got by going to law.

A fine bright sunny morning beamed upon the ancient city of Limerick; the principal street, which in the afternoon is crowded by the far-famed 'Limerick lasses,' was comparatively deserted; the shopmen were removing the shutters with an 'I can't help it' sort of air, gossipping and staring, instead of getting their work done as fast as possible; even the beggars looked as if they considered it too early in the day to begin business, and a stranger would have imagined the juvenile population to treble in amount that of any other city in the world. I never elsewhere saw so many children as I have seen in Limerick; they seem to spring up the areas, out of the pavement, as you walk along—rosy, roistering, laughing, quarrelling, coaxing, begging young vagabonds, ragged and happy. I heard an English lady say she was convinced that every birth in Limerick was a contribution of twins to the world; and truly this appears the only way of accounting for the superabundant supply. A number of these urchins were rushing and screaming after a gentleman who cantered carelessly down George's Street; and when he stopped at a brown door with blue mouldings, in the centre of which figured a large brass plate, bearing the inscription, 'Mr Cummins Botherum, attorney at law,' the high-bred animal was surrounded by a regiment of young rogues, each intreating 'his honour' to let him 'hould the beauty.'

'I'm Pat Mullins, sir; sure you knew my father before his

throuble, yer honour; I'd go to the world's *ind* to sarve yer honour.'

'I'm Jimmy Dowlan, sir; my great-grandfather, sir, was born on yer honour's estate.'

'God send yer honour safe out of the lawyer's house, *and soon !*' exclaimed a third.

'Yer honour's glory always lets Billy the Play hould Diddler whin ye're to the fore yerself,' shouted a fourth.

'Ah, thin, it's me that has the best right to hould the baste, *and thank yer honour for your* generosity afther,' said a long-legged lanky fifth.

'Why so, my man?' inquired Mr Russel, as he nodded to Mr Botherum's servant, who came peeping up the area to see who was there.

'Because yer honour was imposed on, and sent my poor innocent father for three months to the stone jug!' 'Hear that!' said another, 'and his father the heart's blood of a thief.' This caused a diversion in Mr Russel's favour, as the son of the gentleman in the stone jug immediately struck the evil-spoken youth, and a row ensued, which the magistrate did not deem it necessary to interfere with.

Attorneys generally look as if they suffered from a curvature of the spine; there is a sort of bodily and mental crookedness about them, the result of professional experience, that is anything but pleasant; they are fond of putting leading questions, and giving evasive answers; their eyes are sharp and cunning, from a habitual peering into the purses of their clients; cruel eyes they have, *that never wink at human misery.* Nothing could ever induce me to think well of an attorney, *as an attorney;* but I have known two or three men calling themselves so, whose honest natures scorned the cupidity of the profession: such, though *in* it, are not *of* it, and deserve tenfold honours for overcoming their temptations.

Mr Botherum was too much of a wag to be a regular rogue; he understood and enjoyed the rich panorama of Irish life which the exercise of his profession brought before him; he had a small income independent of his business; his wants were not many, for he was an old bachelor, whose notions of luxury might be comprised in two words—claret and whisky: *he* did not suffer from a curvature of the spine; but then, to be sure, his spine was a very short one, and when Mr Russel entered his room, he presented the appearance, rolled up as he was in a whitish cotton dressing-gown, of a large India-rubber ball. His breakfast-table was a curiosity: upon one corner of it stood a wig-block, and on it a yellowish little scratch wig, much too small for the attorney's 'bullet-shaped' head; this he always declared to be an advantage, as he could put it down behind after dinner, leaving the *top of his head to cool*, as it was apt to get hot after the fourth or fifth tumbler; razors, eggs, egg-shells, toast, dog-collars, shaving and hat brushes, all in most admired disorder; there was a volume of 'Burn's Justice' half under the tea-tray, as Mr Botherum would have said, to keep it aisy; for the breakfast-table answered a double purpose; it was a slanting desk, backed by a queer old book-case containing a few volumes of law, and *all* the volumes of Smollett, Fielding, and Richardson, together with the poetry of Swift.

''Pon my honour, Misther Magistrate, as we say,' he exclaimed, 'I'm proud of the visit—mighty proud. I hope Mistress Russel and the young ladies are well. Sit down, and have something to *ate;* riding's hungry work these keen mornings. You won't— well, then, a drop of something to drink; strong waters to keep the gout off yer stomach, upon medical principles, eh? Not a member of the Temperance; though, between you and me, *and the wall*, Mr Russel, temperance up, law down! A sober man makes few quarrels, eh, Mr Russel? A fine contributor to our pockets is strong drink. I submit the question to my superior. A drop of the mountain dew?—pure!—never saw the shadow of an exciseman.'

'You forget,' said Mr Russel, pushing the bottle from him with a good-humoured smile, 'that I'm a magistrate.'

''Pon my honour, yes; I paid you the compliment to forget you had anything to do with the law. Ah, ah! but I hope *you* have nothing to do with it at present—no post obits or mortgages? I congratulate you. I live by the law one way or other; that is the reason I don't like to share it with my friends—ah, ah!'

'You are in capital spirits, Botherum.'

'I oughtn't to be,' he said, pulling off his green nightcap, that looked like the little sprout on the top of a huge Swedish turnip, and replacing it by *the* wig—I ought not to be—I lost *nine* clients in one morning last week.'

'Indeed!—how was that?'

'Seven transported, and two hanged! It was all up with them, and I had only one consolation—they deserved it long ago.'

'Have you much business on hands now?'

'Plenty!—there's always plenty of law, active and passive, in a distressed country; the worse the times, the more busy the law. There are half a score of fellows waiting for me now in the back yard and office.'

'I will state my business, then, at once,' said the magistrate; and at the word 'business' the attorney-at-law pulled down his wig over both ears, put on his spectacles, placed his little fat hands on his knees, and looked Mr Russel steadily in the face.

Mr Russel proceeded—'There is a poor man in my neighbourhood, John Leahy'——

'Leahy *versus* Carr,' interrupted Mr Botherum.

'The same,' replied the magistrate. 'He has not been here yet, has he? How did you know?'

'Retained for the defendant, if it goes into court. But that doesn't hinder me from hearing your story, or his either, for the matter of that. Both sides of the question, that's fair.'

'John Leahy says,' continued Mr Russel, 'that the half acre of bog is his by right of some will or other, which I daresay he will show you by and by. He also says that the stream Abel Carr turned, he had no right to turn; and there was a row in consequence of his shovelling down Abel's ditch.'

'My dear sir,' said Mr Botherum, 'don't trouble yourself to tell me anything about it. Leahy is between the horns of a dilemma; he is wrong, I assure you, with regard to the half acre; but if he gave *that* up quietly (the last thing Abel Carr would like), Aby (he'd be worth any money to a process-server or an exciseman) has his crux ready about the *strame*, and then enough to warrant an action *on either side* for assault and battery. He knows John Leahy's weak point, and he'll work on that weakness till he ruins Leahy. Sir, the love of going to law is an insanity; it is like the eye of the what-you-call-it snake, that fixes its piercer, and opens its mouth; the little craythurs of birds see the destruction before 'em, and *know it;* they see one, two, and three, go down the *baste's* throat, and yet they follow after. I've observed Johnny the Giant for many a day. First of all, I think he got into the court-house as evidence, and wanted to show he understood law— a bad sign, for the law is a thing hardly ever got under by an educated man, but an unlettered one has no chance. Then he got up some little matter of his own, and placed himself under the care of two or three beggarly practitioners, who bleed as zealously for a shilling as a sovereign; and Aby Carr discerned the *wakeness*, and is likely to profit largely by it. Nevertheless, if I can do anything, I will. Only tell me what you wish me to do.'

'Simply this: John Leahy is resolved to have the best advice in Limerick, and considering 'Torney Botherum the most capable of giving it, he intends consulting you this morning. Now I want you to endeavour to convince him that his case is hopeless; that the only way to save himself from ruin is to give up the half acre; and place such a picture of the law's uncertainty before him, that he will return home a wiser man. You surely can make out a few desperate cases, where ruin and law have meant one and the same thing? You can invent'——

'My dear sir,' interrupted the attorney, 'there is no need to invent anything; to *you*, as a friend, between us *and the wall*, I may say that when a man goes wantonly to law, I know he will go to ruin. I have had five-and-thirty years' experience of it, and I never knew a little law with such as Johnny the Giant that did not bring great ruin. He gets into it, and he can't get out; bit after bit of his land melts away to meet its expenses; he hopes in the very teeth of despair, till the roof is swept off his house, and he turns forth a homeless beggar to starve. A man of an open nature has no chance with such a quiet keen fellow as Aby. Why, he had the impudence to try to cheat me. Fancy! a clod-hopping, bog-trotting fellow trying to cheat *me*. I never take less than a half-guinea fee, and first he comes—" Misther Botherum, sir, I wanted to ax yer honour a question."

" Lay down your half guinea, and I'll answer it."

" It isn't *law*, plase yer honour, only a question. Sure it isn't the likes o' me would be trying to get law out of yer honour without paying for it. Now, the question, sir, is only "——

" Talk away, my good man, as long as you like, but I'll make you no answer until you put down your half guinea." Now, Mr Russel, seeing he was foiled on that tack, he takes another.

" Oh, thin, yer honour has great knowledge, but it isn't for the likes of me to purtind to set up with the quality; yer honour 'ill take five shillings from poor Aby Carr, who finds it hard to get that same," and he pulls out five shillings. " Yer honour will hear my question now."

" Yes, but not answer it. If you don't put down the half guinea, you get no opinion of mine."

" Well, I declare, before the Almighty, I haven't it *on me*, sir, in the world; but here is Michael Macavoy, and anyway he'll go bail for the other five "——

" And sixpence."

" Well, barring your honour's beautiful complexion, it's a *nagur* I'd call ye. Mick, will ye answer to his honour for five-and-sixpence?"

" To be sure I will," says Mick.

" Here, then, put it down on paper," I said, knowing their tricks.

" I have no larning, yer honour; I'm no scholar; I can't write."

" Make your mark then."

" Oh, sir, if my word wont do, I'll have nothing to say to it."

' Abel Carr twinkles his cunning eyes for a moment, and then, seeing I perfectly understand my customer, he pulls out five shillings more, and lays *them* down.

" Sixpence more, Mister Carr."

'Out comes the sixpence with a groan, and a muttered exclamation of "God help us! the craythurs at home must go barefoot for this."

" And now," said I, "*before* I answer your question, I must ask you how you dared to call the Almighty to witness a falsehood?"

"I didn't do such a thing, sir; sure I hadn't a half guinea on me, bad luck to the one; *I didn't say I hadn't change for it!*"

'Now,' said Mr Botherum, 'that's Abel Carr; and for him your bold-faced, honest-hearted, thick-headed John Leahy is no match; it's like pitching a horse against a rattlesnake—the poison will bring him to the earth.'

'But he may be persuaded—he may be turned,' said Mr Russel.

'Rely on me, I'll do my best; but you'll see what the result will be. He has been edged on hitherto by those reptiles of the court-house who live by *putrid law;* who don't care how poor the man, so they get the spoil; who are the means, one way or other, of driving hundreds to the road, or out of the country; who set men fighting about *traneens;* they are nothing, one would think, in the scale of society, but they are *filthy pebbles in the wheel of justice,* that impede its course. He comes full of the *rights* of his case; I *convince* him that he is wrong, and yet he wont believe me; he immediately thinks I have a *motive* in not agreeing with him; he hears that Abel Carr has been with me; I advise him *not* to go to law; he commences his address with "knowing how yer honour loves justice," and he concludes the interview, thinking I am either a knave or a fool! My dear sir, *agree* with a man, he thinks you a miracle of wisdom; *differ* from him, and he turns away with the opinion that you are astonishingly overrated;' and the shrewd attorney pulled down his wig with considerable vehemence.

'You will do your best to put him off this matter,' said Mr Russel, rising, 'for we are deeply interested about him and his; and as (if the differences are arranged) you will be a loser, I can only say I shall be happy to make it up by placing any little matters I may have in your hands at the next assizes.' The attorney bowed low.

'Sir,' he answered, 'when such men as you go to law, the result is easily anticipated; there is much beautiful practice in a gentleman's lawsuit.'

'Leading pretty much to the same result, I fancy,' observed the county magistrate, who had smarted more than once. 'My poor friend Leahy is likely to be sacrificed by a pitchfork; I should be despatched by a well-tempered Toledo: there is not much difference in the end. But use your best exertions, however, to get this madness out of Leahy's head, and, believe me, it shall not be forgotten.'

'Rely on my doing my best. I will treat him delicately,' answered the attorney; 'not let him see what I intend at first—rush with him into it at first, and, if possible, rush with him out of it at the last—though I am not sanguine. Carr let drop a hint that he was like all law-lovers, in difficulties already.'

'Those I can manage for him,' said his landlord, 'if he does not plunge deeper.'

'What sort of a wife has he?' inquired the attorney.

'One of the best and most superior women I ever knew for her station.'

'Fond of law?'

'No.'

'Is he fond of her?'

'Very!'

'That makes my hope less,' said Botherum. 'If a good and superior woman can't manage a husband who loves her, there is little hope, I fear, for me.'

The attorney was right.

More than two years had elapsed since the conversation I have related took place. Mr Russel had spent the last six months on the continent, and Mr Botherum continued his ordinary course, sidling from his office to the court-house of the good city of Limerick, and from the court-house back again, just as usual; popping his little head up and down as he went along, and saluting his familiars with a 'How de do, Jack?' 'Good-morrow, Tom,' 'How are you, Bill?' 'God save ye, Harry,' 'Mend ye, Ned,' and so on; while to his superior clients he moved his hat, or kissed gallantly the tips of his three little fat fingers. The world prospered with him, and he with the world. How far he was able to influence the conduct of Mr Russel's law-loving tenant, will be immediately seen.

John Leahy was a wrong-headed man, a man who drove forward without reflecting on consequences; but he was both honest and kind. I hope those who read this story will remember that his great fault was obstinacy; that he would not, in reality, wrong his neighbour; and that, when he exclaimed before Mr Russel, upon being asked what he would swear to, 'Anything at all for satisfaction,' he neither meant to perjure himself nor to injure even Abel Carr. He used strong language, it is true, but only what Irishmen use when over-excited; he meant he would have law—*and he had it.*

Much bustle and confusion were evident in the immediate vicinity of a well-built farm-house, that, well built and substantial though it was, seemed to have known better days; the windows were broken; the thatch evinced no marks of care; it was brown and uneven; the corn-stands in the rick-yard had no piles of the golden grain upon their exposed crossings. Such a farm should have been able to muster five or six fine cows. There was but one, a miserable rough-coated thing, though of the Ayrshire breed. There were two or three pigs standing or grubbing about, but they were thin, neither fit for living nor dying. The only vigilant-looking animal at liberty about the door was a stern stiff dog, evidently aged, but not less inclined to live and die in the service of his puppyhood, for he shadowed the footsteps of a slight pallid little girl, who would have been called very beautiful if her cheek had been graced by the hue of health. Regardless of the people who passed backwards and forwards, she rambled first into the garden, which, like the rest of the farm, betrayed tokens of great neglect. She pulled a rosebud from one tree, a degenerate pink from a clump that trailed the ground, a sprig of thyme, and a few other simple flowers that might have been called 'wild;' and stopping before some empty bee-stands, tears gathered within the transparent lids of her large gray eyes, and then rolled down her cheeks. The poor dog looked meekly and affectionately in the pale child's face; he did not wag his tail, for his features, if I may venture so to call them, expressed a perfect understanding of and sympathy with her sorrows; and at last he seated himself by her side, and placed his rough paw gently on the little arms that were crossed one over the other beneath her throbbing bosom.

'Let me alone, Bran, good fellow; let me alone; let poor little Ally alone. Why should you care for her? Sure she's going away from ye, poor Bran!'

The animal, as if comprehending her words, stood erect on his hind-legs, and commenced licking her cheek. 'It's no use,' she continued, flinging her arms round his neck—'it's no use, Bran; the farm is gone, and the house is gone, and poor ould granny is in her grave, and we're going away from Ireland for ever; but I can't part ye, Bran—oh, I can't part ye, ye poor dumb baste, that minded me many a day, and looked afther me, and played with me! Ye'll come with me, Bran—wont you? You wont let me go without you, ye ould darlint of a dog! Maybe,' she added, with that quick transition of feeling which is one of the many blessings of childhood—'maybe we'd be happy yet, and find as green fields as these, where, as mother says, "*there'll be no law to tempt father to ruin again.*" Oh, Bran, oh can ye tell yer poor Ally what ruin is? It seems something that's all over us, and about us. Wag yer tail, Bran, honey, *and don't look in my face with yer breaking heart.* Oh doggy, doggy, sure it's something anyway to have the father, and the mother, and poor Bran left to little Ally Leahy!'

The girl returned the caresses of the poor dog with interest, but nothing could animate him, or oblige him to express anything like joy; he hung his head, though his eyes were restless and vigilant; he did not like the bustle and the strangers; his tail, which it was his habit to keep in a perpetual yet quiet motion, was slouched between his legs, as he followed the footsteps of his young mistress, who looked back at him every moment, repeating over and over again the same wail. 'Bran, *a-cushla*, we shall never see that ould tree again.' 'Bran, *a-cushla*, we are done with the race across the meadow.' 'Bran, *a-cushla*, no more blackberries 'll grow for us on the fairy wreath.' 'Bran, *a-cushla*, bid everything good-by, for if ye come with us, you'll never see *any* of them more!' And so the little simple affectionate child wandered on and on, and over the fields and about the garden, taking leave of every bush and 'bohreen,' and talking to her silent friend, who sympathised in her afflictions.

Within, there was sorrow more loud; for the fact was, that utter ruin had overtaken one it had long pursued—the law-loving John Leahy. There was nothing peculiar in his case; it is on a par with thousands that have occurred with the same result. It was to be anticipated that he would scorn the advice of Mr Botherum, however skilfully it might have been bestowed. When his poor wife met him at ' the turn of the road,' where she was in the habit of watching for him, she hoped a far different termination to his visit; but when he dismounted, and after having thrown the bridle over his arm, declared ' he really thought the half of the counthry *war* mad to go dancing afther that 'Torney Botherum, that hadn't by a cart-load as much law in him as Mr Garrett, the long 'torney of Mullinabeg,' Alice Leahy thought she would have fallen to the earth: her hopes were extinguished; she foresaw the ruin that soon made rapid strides towards their home. Leahy was, as they call it, ' cast ' in three successive actions with Abel Carr. One misfortune led to another. Nothing could exceed the energy and activity of Alice Leahy as long as her strength remained. But broken spirits induced broken health; everything about her changed, except her temper, which was greatly tried during her husband's absence; his mother was as eager as her son for 'law,' for having, as she expressed it, 'her rights,' and was perpetually upbraiding Alice with ' want of spirit.' Poor Alice bore it all, and every one wondered how she could. Leahy seemed like a man in a perpetual fever; the bright moonlight and the long heavy starless nights found him alike wakeful; and whenever Alice, with gentle firmness, would endeavour to draw his attention to his domestic wants—to the necessity that must always exist for a perpetual and regular outlay, if a farm is expected to yield its fruits in due season—he would throw far from him every industrious thought, and angrily revert to the necessity for money to carry on 'the law,' which, *he said*, would preserve his property and get him justice. At last, bit by bit, the land

' His forefathers tilled '

was parted with to feed the harpies who fatten on the misery of human kind, until at length the agent considered it to be *his* duty to save what remained for the benefit of the absent landlord. Had Mr Russel been in Ireland at the time, he would doubtless have softened this last trial; but he was in England, or France, or somewhere far away, and requiring all the rents, which had now been long unpaid.

When heavy distress comes upon a man, unless his mind be very highly strung, he will yield to the dangerous and evil advice which, in better times, and with happier feelings, he would have spurned. John Leahy was not strong-minded, and his poor wife's most bitter trial was to see him gradually drawn into the vortex of the discontented. Of such, who so abound in the neighbourhood of Limerick, he was acquainted with many; and Alice's observations led to the belief, that unless he emigrated, he would become a worn-out and morally ruined man—that his life would be the last sacrifice to ' the law.' This idea haunted her by day and night; and she resolved that whenever the remnants of their property were seized, the emigration often hinted at, often debated, should take place. The arrival of what she knew *must come*, and that soon, was communicated by the entrance of two of 'the neighbours' while she was dressing her child. 'The agent's caretaker,' they said, ' and two or three more with him, were coming; John Leahy must guess for what, but they would stand by their " ould comrade" to the last; they'd never see him wronged; there were many more of the same mind, to whom he had only to lift up his finger.'

John Leahy turned pale as death at this information, but took down and prepared to load an old gun, which, rusty though it seemed, was quite able to do mischief. One of the men ran to secure the pigs in their sty, and the other showed *he* had not come unarmed.

Little Alice screamed, and clung to her trembling mother. For an instant that mother's brow, cheek, throat, were suffused with crimson; she then became white and rigid like a corpse; and her husband, forgetting all but the love of his youth, caught her to his bosom.

'Let 'em do what they like !' he exclaimed, dashing down the gun—' let 'em do what they like, *now she is dead*.'

'No—no—no: only wait till the breath comes back,' murmured Alice—' wait;' and gulping down some water, she summoned her mental strength, which was great, to aid the little that remained of bodily power. ' John Leahy,' she said, grasping her husband's arm, and looking in his eyes with the pure and earnest intensity of wedded love—' John Leahy, across that door, now twelve years ago, I came a young bride, a young loving bride, resting my whole heart, and, maybe, too much of the safety of my soul, on you. I have borne you five childre, of which this was the first, and God willed should be the last; the rest are in heaven! Don't look so, John Leahy; have a mite more patience, till my heart beats easier, and I'll go on.'

Several of the neighbours now crowded in at the door, although the 'distrainers for rent' were not, nor could not be, in sight for nearly half an hour; but the news had spread, and the people are ever ready at a rescue. Several of the young men had stout sticks, and the women, whose most acceptable service in the sight of Heaven is that of being peacemakers on earth, had their aprons full of stones. Seeing Alice half kneeling at her husband's feet, while he endeavoured to raise her again to his bosom, they withdrew, and remained outside ready for action. 'And now, John,' she said, 'let me ask you how often I have been wanting in love or duty to you during them years!'

'Never!' he exclaimed passionately; 'never onct, if this hour, as it maybe, is my last—never, never ONCT.'

'The past is past; ye can't think but that this place, these walls, that little bed where I watched the dying, as I had done the living, hours of our babys are all in my heart; but, John Leahy, the memory of *that*, and everything else, is all we'll have left of it to take to a foreign land, and'——

'Stop, Alice—stay; inside these walls I was born; inside these walls I will die; and let him who dares to put me out take what he'll get!'

'Hurra!' exclaimed the man (James Thurles by name) who had brought the news; 'I knew Johnny the Giant had blood in him yet, for all that the law drew out; I knew *that*. Shout, boys and girls, shout! we'll not have a straw of his thatch touched.'

The Giant's eyes glittered, and he seized the gun again, but his wife grasped his arm. 'Hear me for the last time, John,' she exclaimed—'hear me. Suppose you war left by the landlord in this house, with so little land, with no money, with not so much as the price for seed potatoes, everything going to rack and ruin, what would you have?—what good would it do you? You've neither means nor money to keep us from starving; all we had is gone—gone—in the law! and you would end all by breaking the law, and trying to keep *what isn't your own*.'

'What do you mane by that?' exclaimed John fiercely; '*not my own*—these walls not my own?'

'Not now, when you can't pay for them,' she answered calmly.

'Blessed Father!' he said, 'and is it *you* that send the reproach to my heart?—is it *you* that but just this minute tould me what you war, to show you'd be so no longer?—is it come to this wid ye? But that 'll only make me worse. What have I now to care for?'

'Yer character, John. The worst any could say of ye was, that you war too fond of law!—but if ye keep yer landlord from his own share, who then can say John Leahy's an honest man? The land is his; we cannot pay for it; he never was hard upon us when we tried to pay; but in spite of his advice, look what you did yourself. Look, John: I have a friend who will give us enough to take us away from the ould place in dacency—enough to take us to another land. No one can say then this was a rogue's house. In another land we can live and work. What matters our poverty there?—no one will be to the fore to remember our riches. John, *agra!* the landlord bore with us long; he saw the farm going to destruction, and he wasn't like many another, wishful to turn out old residenthers for new. John, *avourneen!* remember, in this bitther time of trial, remember that the landlord stuck to us longer than we stuck to him.'

'*Me*—you mane me!' interrupted the Giant sulkily.

'Then let it stand so,' she said, 'and still you know it's the truth. John, rouse up the pride of an honest heart! We may hould out for two or three months, but in the end *we must quit*. We saw *that* before you owned to it the other night. Do not let blood be spilt when you can hinder it. This isn't like a hard landlord,' she repeated, gaining strength from justice. 'I tell ye, John, I've turned everything over in my own mind; it can't be helped; give up at onct, bravely. It is bravo to resign like a man.'

'I can't part the counthry, Alice; it's no use talking; I can't part the counthry,' he said, looking round and speaking through his clenched teeth. 'I did what you wanted three days ago. I made every inquiry as you wished, but I can't part the counthry—the fields, *the sod* I was born on, or the people!'

'And why should you?' exclaimed James; 'aint we all ready to stand by ye to the last? Sorra a windfall of the law shall set foot in it while we stand here.'

Alice took no notice of these words, but looking at her husband tenderly, and pressing his hand between hers, she replied, 'And do you think that *I* do not love the counthry?—wouldn't I lay my life down for it? I don't want to lave it because we're prospering in it, but because we should burthen it, like too many others. I love it as much as you, and if you *will* stay, let it be still in peace and honesty. Make no resistance.'

'Stay!' he said. 'What! stay to see this very house, maybe, the property of Abel Carr! I'd—I'd——'

'Let us go then; I have more to lave behind than you,' said his wife.

'The bones of all belonging to me are in the ould churchyard,' he answered, much softened; 'but where will mine rest?'

'With mine,' was the reply. 'But, John, I lave my brothers, my sister, my ould mother, and she I never can see afther we go. They will hear her last prayer, receive her last blessing; and

though you know how I love her, I am content to be far away
from her at the last moment, *to be with you. My* counthry is where
you are, John. My'——

'We can see them crossing the near hill,' interrupted James;
'don't be tramped in the briars, John Leahy; we'll all stand by
ye.'

The Giant's powerful frame quivered like that of a girl in
an ague fit. Strong as he was, he trembled, not from fear, but
emotion.

'But for the landlord's claim, it would go to such as Abel Carr,'
whispered Alice wisely.

'You are right, Alice,' replied her husband. 'I own it; and
now all's gone, I take yer advice. Hide me somewhere,' said the
heart-broken man; 'somewhere that I can't see or hear 'em : let
'em have possession; and then, when all's gone—— Oh, Alice,
Alice!' he added, as staggering into the bedroom, he fell on his
face upon the bed—'oh, Alice, to think it should come to this!
—I onct so proud, so independent, so high in myself! Thank
the neighbours. But, my God! I cannot let it go—I must'——

'Ally, come here,' said Mrs Leahy to her child—'Ally, come
here, and keep with yer father; tell him you will live or die with
him, beg with him; put yer arms round him, Ally; say the prayer
I taught ye; I've strength for it all, John, darlint. May the Almighty
bless you!—your peaceableness has given me strength;
I'm able for it all, if you'll keep quiet. My husband will be an
example to the whole counthry; all will see what he is now; they
thought him a disturber of the law—they will find their mistake.'
She closed the door, paused a moment, and then, as if afraid of a
sudden outbreak, turned the key upon it, and removed the gun.
'Kind neighbours, and dear friends,' she said, advancing to the
open door, 'my husband and I are for ever obliged to ye for yer
kindness; we shall soon be far away from ye, but we shall never
forget ye ; we know that the agent is acting for the best, in doing
his duty for his employer. Boys and girls, just is just, and its
fitter he should have it than such as ye all know who. We thank
ye kindly, but intreat that a finger may not be raised in defiance
of those that are coming. We take ye to witness, kind friends,
that we offer no opposition; we have no one to blame but ourselves—not
even the law my husband thought long ago to get the
betther off; for its nature is to take advantage where it can, and
we can't expect anything to go against nature. Thank ye kindly,
Mrs Doolan, but let the stones go; a woman's best arms are a
prayer and a blessing, and you'll all give us those before we lave
ye.' There was something so different from anything the kind-hearted
but wrong-headed people expected in all this—something
so brave in a weak, delicate-looking woman stifling her feelings,
and resolving to give up everything because it was just to do so,

particularly when (according to the opinions of their defenders) they might have repelled the invaders, and fought it out—there was something so unusual in the dignified bearing of the still beautiful Alice, that even Mrs Doolan let the stones she had gathered slide out of her apron on one side, as if ashamed of her intention, while the men still persisted in their intreaties to let them have one fight for her anyway before she'd quit them for good and all. They also (as the distrainers were now at the gate) called loudly to John Leahy to come out; but the heart-broken man heard them not, overcome as much by the reason and eloquence of his wife, as by the pent-up but most powerful feelings of his nature.

Ashamed—ruined—the innocent caresses of his child wrought his heart to agony; and pressing the little creature to his bosom, he gave way to those desperate sobs which storm the frame of a strong man, but seldom, perhaps never, more than once in a whole lifetime. John Leahy, stimulated by bad advisers, had refused on more than one occasion to yield possession to the agent, with whom, indeed, he had never been on good terms. If Mr Russel had been in Ireland, though he could not prevail on him to abandon law, he would have preserved his influence over him, and *that* would have prevented much that was painful. As the men advanced, they perfectly understood they were engaged in a service of danger, and were greatly astonished when Mrs Leahy advanced to the gate and said they might enter. The peasantry could hardly be prevailed on to depart; they clamoured to see the poor farmer; but his wife's presence of mind, and the power which conscious integrity invariably gives to those who otherwise would be powerless, carried her through as trying a scene as it ever fell to the lot of woman to endure. She told them he would thank them to-morrow; the women clung to and embraced her, saying she was fitter for heaven than earth; the men—while they cursed their disappointment, and insulted the distrainers as much as their kindly dread of hurting Alice's feelings permitted—declared she was an angel, and called down blessings on her head; and the necessary officer of the law, a strong but well 'battered' specimen of human nature, who had received and returned many a sound drubbing, removed his hat, and waited to think over what was the mildest way of performing his duty. When she had seen the last of their faction depart, when the strong necessity for exertion was over, her woman's heart fainted as it had done before; and one of the men, not so accustomed to scenes of misery as the others, departed without intimating his intention to his companions, to tell the agent how peaceably they had obtained possession, and of the extraordinary conduct of Alice. 'It was the finest example set to the counthry,' he said, 'for years; and surely his honour would be as mild as he could, considering.'

Alice found her husband in a state of stupor, and sent her child into the open air, where, poor little maid! she had held such long converse with her dog. Never did distrainers perform their duty with such tardy steps; and the agent, with the trust which Alice Leahy's noble conduct merited, sent word to those he employed, that if they pleased they might remain there for a few days. Leahy went through the form of giving up his house with a stolid frame, and an eye moveless, and almost rayless. His wife saw, and trembled, for she knew that with a violent temper this appearance was far more dangerous than rage. He then quitted his dwelling, and sat down beneath the shadow of an old tree that grew on the opposite side of the road, and which many a time he had climbed in his childhood. He steadily refused to accept the agent's offer. It was a frightful proof of the growth of evil, for his obstinacy seemed to have returned fourfold. He sat down on a wide flat stone, and insisted upon Alice sitting at one side and his child at the other; he would suffer none other to approach him, and spurned the poor dog even, that crouched to his feet—spurned it away more than once; but the animal still returned, and at last softened his sternness by licking away the tears that dropped from his child's eyes on his own hand.

The evening drew towards its close, and the warm kind-hearted people, who have no ungenerous faults, crowded round John and his wife. They brought them share of their provisions—invited them to enter their dwellings—endeavoured to reason with John, who remained fixed as if by a spell, his eyes red from the intensity of the gaze which he fixed upon his cottage. Finding that he was immovable, they endeavoured to persuade Alice to leave him and take some repose; but she was too true-hearted for that; and when the child was induced to quit his side, he felt about as a blind man in search of his staff, until Alice deemed it right to recall her. The neighbours hung a blanket over their heads, to save them from the night dew; and at last his head fell on his wife's bosom, and he slept.

Little Alice had been long asleep, but the wife and mother could obtain no repose. She recalled the days of their early love—the days of their prosperity—the intreaties she had used to avert the consequences of litigation—the hardness and perverseness of her husband, who would go through anything 'for satisfaction.' The crisis had arrived, a crisis rendered still more painful by the obstinacy of him who at that time was as an oak resting on a reed for support. Although her brothers had promised her the means necessary for emigration, yet the future was as dark as the night-clouds that lowered above their heads. The moon broke through the obscurity, and its beams fell upon her husband's face; she could see huge drops of moisture, the heat-drops of the fevered brain, standing on his brow: he had been the cause of her affliction, the cause of their mutual ruin. She knew it well; and yet in the first beatings of maiden love, in the deep earnestness of matronly duty and devotion, not even when she took her first-born from her bosom to place it in its father's arms, not even *then* did she love him so devotedly as at that moment. This knowledge made her draw her husband more closely to her heart, and bless God that had still left her two treasures. She closed her eyes in thankfulness and prayer, and might have slumbered; but a low sullen growl from Bran arrested her attention. She looked down at the dog, and saw his eyes were turned in the direction of a little dell on the right-hand side; she looked along the line, and discovered at first a palish light, succeeded by a red glare; then spiral tongues of fire ran into the air, and a wild haloo came on the breeze; then the fire brightened, then quenched; then the dull heavy smoke showed like a funeral pall above the light below. She felt her heart sink within her; she could not be mistaken as to the direction of the fire; and she suddenly remembered the words, uttered by one of her neighbours when he saw her resolve to have no disturbance at the farm, 'that they'd have revenge somehow.' She traced the direction of the flames, and well knew that the fire was the burning of Abel Carr's house. Ripe for mischief, and not content to leave all to the wisdom of HIM who returns the poisoned chalice to the poisoner, some desperate spirits had resolved to 'punish' Abel Carr; and their 'punishing' would indeed have added to the annals of crime and violence which disgrace the country, but for the interference of the horse-police; they arrived hardly in time to save the life of the wicked man, who had so continually provoked the evil spirit of litigation which dwelt in the Giant's bosom.

The agitation of Alice was extreme, yet she did not dare to awake her husband. The glare of light was fading, when a voice from behind the tree I have mentioned whispered, 'We've hot the right nail on the head now, Mrs Leahy, anyway.' But the words were hardly spoken when a couple of the horse-patrol were heard gallopping along the road; they drew up opposite to where the little party sheltered. The close of that sad day saw Alice Leahy arrested with her husband on suspicion of having originated the fire.

They might have charged John Leahy with any crime they pleased; for before the following morning had thoroughly dispelled the shades of night, the unhappy man was enduring the frenzy of a brain fever. Nothing could exceed the interest created throughout the country by this event. Mr Botherum himself stept out of his usual practice on the occasion, and declared, 'that so convinced was he of the incapability of Alice Leahy's concealing, much less perpetrating, such a crime—so convinced was he that though John Leahy might have committed a breach of the law in defending his own house, nothing could have induced him to do the cowardly deed of an incendiary—that he would, if it came to a trial, undertake their defence without professional fee or reward. Irish interest once excited, is not satisfied with lip service; the neighbourhood was in a state of fermentation during the few hours the Leahys were incarcerated; the peasantry gloried in the bare idea of effecting a rescue; but it was not needed. There was no evidence against them; the state of the poor fevered man spoke for itself; and when Alice and her unconscious husband were discharged, she, while supporting his head on the car sent to convey them to 'a neighbour's house,' observed, in the thankful spirit of a true Christian, 'that there was no evil but had good in it. Sure it was a blessing he wasn't right in himself to feel the disgrace such a suspicion would bring on him.' Her excellent spirit was not weary of well-doing; she nursed him through that fearful malady with untiring fortitude; she refused to accept the agent's offer, and return till he was recovered to their old home. 'It would be only breaking her heart intirely,' she said, 'to go back to and then leave it, which she must do, for they had no means to keep it on;' and though she did not say so, she knew that Mr Russel himself could not afford, even if he had the inclination, to let them have such a house rent free; besides, she remembered that, owing to her husband's love for law, persisting so obstinately in his course against his landlord's well-founded opinion, he had completely worn out his patience, and that he must feel as if a firebrand were quenched when 'Johnny the Giant' left the country. Nor would she accept shelter in any of the cottages of her neighbours. The Irish peasantry have suffered so desperately from fever, that they stand in great awe of infection, though it seldom makes them forget the rites of hospitality. Many offered their humble homes, and desired to give 'the place' up to her altogether. 'Sure the weather, God be praised! was beautiful, barring the drop of rain that never harmed Ireland; and it would do them good to know that the poor man had all they had to give.'

Alice Leahy made her husband's bed in a farmer's barn, and watched him there until it pleased God he was able to lift up his heart in thankfulness for his recovery. Tears—calm, gentle, refreshing tears—trickled down his pallid cheeks, when he recognised the loving face of his wife bending over his pallet; and though he had not strength to speak, she saw that he knew her—knew his child—knew even poor Bran, who looked with his sad earnest eyes into his master's countenance. She had disposed of the articles of furniture, which Mr Russel, informed of the facts, had ordered to be returned to her, so as to meet his observation on his recovering his consciousness; and he closed his eyes in refreshing slumbers, without apparently reverting to their changed circumstances. Abel Carr, though he knew his unfortunate opponent had nothing more to lose, would have caused him to be arrested for the last law expenses if he had dared; but there are few instances on record where the hearts of both rich and poor so completely united in admiration of the enduring virtue of a simple unpretending woman as in the case of Alice Leahy. The poor revelled in the idea that Abel was not only beggared in reputation but in pocket; and those who wished well to their country, took every opportunity of pointing out to those who were fond of going to law, the curious fact of two men, the vanquished and the vanquisher, on the verge of starvation. But for his wife's admirable conduct, Leahy, with many fine natural qualities, would in all human probability have suffered the penalty which awaits crime; and Abel Carr's success, independently of the losses he too had suffered by paying 'costs,' was sacrificed by the fury of those who, whatever their motive might have been, had no right to judge and execute judgment.

It was a fine summer evening, and John Leahy's health was comparatively restored; the next day he was to leave for ever the land of his fathers. Alice and their child accompanied him midway up a mountain which commanded a view so extensive, that the farm which had once been his seemed but as a patch of very small extent; he shaded his eyes with his hand so as to intercept the rays of the setting sun, and enable him to take a farewell look of all he had known so long and loved so well. Neither husband nor wife spoke, but they both wept bitterly. The sun set gloriously; they waited until he had sunk in the not far distant ocean that was to bear them to another land; and then, while the whistle of the plover and the low of the kine were yet upon the air, they descended together, little Alice and Bran lingering behind—Alice to gather wild flowers, and seek for a four-leaved shamrock that was to bring her luck in 'furrin parts,' and Bran to sniff at every rabbit hole that was not concealed beneath the prickly furze.

'Alice,' said John to his wife, when they were turning into the *bohreen* leading to their place of rest for the night—'Alice, if it had not been for the generosity of your brothers and your friends, I should not have had wherewith to begin life again in another land—and I find you war right; I could not have borne with it here.'

'The Lord above is very good!' she answered, though sobbing bitterly.

'Look!' he exclaimed, 'if I hear you cry that way, it will break my heart. I know it is my fault—my crime—my—— If you cannot go without tears and sobs like these, we will remain, although I work as a day labourer.'

'They will be the last,' she said meekly. 'I have bid my mother farewell; and she, John, *she* said I did right; she said she was proud of me; and sure *that* is a proud hearing for a child from a parent's lips. You shall not have to reproach *me* with the weakness again.'

'*Me* reproach *you* with weakness!' he replied. 'No, Alice. Even this morning when you were putting in the box the bits o' things that we had for years, and that the goodness of Mr Russel left us, yer eyes war dry, and even cheerful, and I wondered at yer strength. I couldn't put up my tools myself. And now, Alice, setting a case that you war not strong-hearted, where would I be?'

'We shall be happy together wherever we are,' she said.

'Plase God!' replied her husband. 'But, Ally, betwixt ourselves, if I was beginning life again, I'd go to law altogether in a different way to what I ever did before.'

'Oh, John!' exclaimed his wife, pained but not surprised at his mind still being clogged by the old leaven, and too thoroughly acquainted with the windings of the human heart to expect the habit of a life to be overcome—'oh, John, sure you've taken your Bible oath to me to bear even death before you'd go to law!'

'Ay,' he replied, 'and for your sake so I would; and you're right, Alice, darlint. Warm blessing of my heart! you are right; and to-morrow, plase God, the neighbours who will set us on our way, when they see a man onct so prosperous obligated to quit his native counthry, reduced so, that but for charity'——

'Hardly charity, John,' said his delicate-minded wife. '*Not* charity, sure; the generosity of our own *people** maybe is *bounty*, but not *charity*, John; though even if it was,' she added in a more subdued tone, 'betther than us have wanted it and had it, and but for it my heart would never warm to Ireland as I know it will to the last hour of my days. The Lord of heaven, who knows the beating of my heart, and the prayers of my soul, look down upon it!—bless it with peace!—increase its power!—turn its enemies into friends!—make it wise as it is fruitful, and prudent as it is brave! Oh, *lanna machree*, ould Ireland! what keeps yer green hills down and yer people poor? Isn't it the mistakes of the law? But, as I was saying, John, my heart would never warm to Ireland as it now does, if I thought they'd hould their hand back from a fellow-creature in want. And so, John, darlint, call it *charity* if you like; I wont fault the word a second time.'

'I'll tell them,' resumed John Leahy, 'when they see a prosperous man reduced to begging, and forced into exile, I'll tell them *that's what he got by going to law!*'

* Irish relations.

'UNION IS STRENGTH.'

'UNITED IRISHMEN!'—the phrase will startle many who think, and think rightly, that I am no politician; though, as far as zeal *for*, and love *of*, country goes, I hope I am a patriot. With *political united Irishmen* I have nothing to do; my object is simply to show how much Irishmen *could* do if they were united—how much they lose by not being united. 'Union is strength,' said old Dicky Delany—unconsciously quoting the memorable expression of a mighty mind—when lecturing his five sons on their unfortunate propensity of all pulling different ways. 'Union is strength,' repeated the old man—and he was right.

I would have every Irishman, rich and poor, both in and out of his country, read and ponder over the fable of the bundle of sticks, and remember that though it is easy enough to break *one*, it is impossible to do so *when they are combined*. It has always seemed to me a strange contradiction in the Irish character that they, who are so kindly to each other in their own land, should be anything but kindly to each other in the land of strangers. In Ireland, they assemble together to assist in building a house, in getting in harvest, in digging potatoes, in cutting and bringing home turf; they do it right cheerfully; and, according to the happy and merry maxim that 'many hands make light work,' so does such labour pass off pleasantly; but this generosity of feeling is almost confined to the peasantry, and they lose it in a great degree when they emigrate.

Take an example:—In our village is a baker, a Scotchman; he employs three men, two of whom were Scotch, the third an Englishman. One of these men was much respected by the gentry; he had been a long time in Mr Macneil's employment; at last we missed him, and inquired where he was gone.

'Oh, he's awa',' replied Macneil; 'he's awa' to Wimbleton to a business o' his ain; he was as steady a lad as ever drew a batch of bread, and saved mair than you could ha'e thought possible; and having a mind to marry, he spoke to me about it; and though I shall *miss him for mony a lang day, yet we maun help each other* —and I lent him a trifle, forby his savings, to begin on.'

Another of our tradesmen is Charley Murphy, the butcher, a native of Dublin; *he* deemed it necessary to apologise one day for employing *an Irishman* as his foreman. He's of *very decent people* in the county Longford,' said Charley, 'or he would not be here.'

'Is he a good butcher?'

'Oh, never a better between this and Dublin.'

The foreman was also a well-conducted steady young man; being an Irishman, he was civil and obliging of course, and much liked by his master's customers. Suddenly, however, there arose a schism between him and his employer, and the young man applied to a friend of ours, a very peace-loving magistrate, to take an oath that his master owed him some money and would not pay him. Our friend said that was an illegal course of proceeding, that he must take out a summons; but being anxious to prevent litigation, he thought he might as well send for Charley Murphy, and endeavour to adjust the difference.

'If your honour plases,' said the foreman, 'I have *slaved* late and early for this man for *next to half* what he'd have to pay any other man in the world. And now, when I've an opportunity of bettering myself, he says *I'm striving to cut his throat behind his back*, gives me no peace, nor will he pay me the thrifle of wages, which, small as it is, would help to set me up in the world.'

'He's behaved like a traitor, that he has,' was the reply; 'with his winning ways he has got the inside of the houses of all my customers, and has the assurance to ask me to lend him money to help to set him up.'

'And if you *had* lent me a thrifle,' answered the young Irishman, 'it would have been nothing so very wonderful. I didn't want to try my luck at all in this neighbourhood. See what Macneil did for his countryman. But,' he added, 'it's true enough what they say here, that no Irishman ever helps another, *barring it is down the hill.*'

'Suppose,' suggested my friend, 'you were to arrange it thus: if it is not convenient to you, Murphy, to pay this demand, give this young fellow a share in your business; you are countrymen, and ought to help each other. There are frequent instances amongst the English and Scotch of this sort of arrangement: one partner brings youth and zeal as a set-off against the money and connection which his older but less active partner has to offer. What say you?'

'I say, plase your honour,' replied the foreman hastily, 'I'd sooner beg my bread than be *behoulden* to him. Let him pay me my wages; that's all I'll ask.'

'I don't owe you any wages; and I've had enough of you already; and more than that, you're *the last Irishman I'll have any call to.* I'll keep clear of my countrymen in future; for when they find one of themselves a little up in the world, they'll try to pull him down, and hardly give a "thank ye" for all you can do.'

Our worthy friend cited the Scotch baker as an example of how much people even in small trade might do for each other by being united; he urged that it was our duty to assist each other, and used every argument in his power to dissuade them from 'going to law;' but in vain. Charley Murphy entered into a long story as explanation about board and lodging, and weekly money, and a feather bed, and new blue sleeves and apron, and the grinding of a knife and steel, which detail caused his foreman to exclaim against his meanness. One offered to take an oath that *this* was the case, and the other that *that* was the case; and at last the magistrate was obliged to tell them that they had better go to Queen Square to settle the business. To Queen Square they accordingly went; and the magistrate decided that the wages were due, and ought to be paid; and paid they were, though, having run on for a considerable time, to get together the amount caused Charley Murphy to run in debt; for the young foreman, irritated by his master's conduct, would grant no time. But this was not all; Charley had a daughter, and this daughter and the young foreman had become strongly attached to each other. At first Charley Murphy used to laugh at this young love, but afterwards refused his consent. The daughter, English born, had more of English wilfulness than Irish yielding in her disposition, and married without his consent. This was certainly an imprudent step, as little by little they fell into poverty; and Charley Murphy confessed, when too late, that if he had assisted his countryman at the commencement, if he had behaved justly, if they had remained together *like the bundle of sticks*, he would not have been left in his old age without his pretty daughter to keep his books, or a hale hearty son-in-law to attend to their mutual business. As it was, the young people migrated to Australia; while the baker's daughter, who with her father's consent married the Scotchman, is able to drive over in their own comfortable cart on Sundays to see Macneil, whose national and most praiseworthy consideration for his own countryman secured his 'Jessie' in the end a comfortable home and a good husband.

'I *hate* the Scotch,' exclaimed a hot-headed Irish friend of mine the other day, 'they are so "*clannish*."' I could not help asking him if he did not think a little of the same quality would wonderfully improve his own countrymen. This young man is now doing very well in the world, and I hope felt too much the bitter loneliness of an Irishman in London, to be cold without a reason to those of his own land who come hither to seek their fortunes. The prejudice in England for a length of time was cruelly great against my countrymen. When a handsome young Irishman got into English society, I have seen the chaperons draw more closely to their charges, and while they looked icebergs and daggers at the good-humoured face of the somewhat forward youth, whisper the young ladies to 'beware, for an Irish adventurer had entered the charmed circle.' I do not attempt to deny the young man made the most of his handsome face, and 'blarneyed' to the best of his ability; but English, ay, and Scotch men too, do the same thing; and if they do not succeed as well as the Irishman, it is only because they lack ability, not inclination. I do not mean for a moment to defend the unprin-

cipled adventurer of any country; but I do sincerely rejoice that
the English have discovered that imposition is not by any means
the necessary attendant on an Irish face or an Irish tongue. But
to the answer to my question.

'Indeed and you are right,' he said. 'When I was coming to
London, I bothered the very life out of every one I knew in Dublin to give me letters of introduction to *all* the Irish *they* knew in
the *great* city. I did not care so much for letters to the English,
like a fool as I was, for I was not aware then that when once
you are known by the English, your hold upon their friendship is
as firm as the rock of Cashel; and so I thought my fortune
was made when I had secured introductions to several Irish
leaders. Well, I left a card and a letter at one house, and received a note saying that really the influx of young Irish gentlemen seeking employment was so great, that he had, however painful to his feelings, been *obliged* to decline receiving introductions
at all. Several asked me to dinner: others to "tea and turn out."
The member for our town, who had made fierce love to my aunt,
and spoken of my uncle as "his talented and distinguished countryman" *during* the election, by some strange chance was never
at home when I called, as I well knew, for I heard him tell the
servant so himself. One fellow gave me an introduction to his
friend in the city, and I afterwards found out that he clearly said,
though he wished me well, he would not be *answerable* for me, as
I was *Irish*. Another could not introduce me to his partner, who
had the management of his business, because *he had a family of
daughters*. Certainly, out of about five-and-twenty, I found one
whose warm manners sprang from his warm heart, and he made
up for the rest, though I was on the *shaughran* for months and
months before I could earn as much as would afford me a dinner.
Now, it is not more than eighteen months ago since a Scotch lad,
Alexander Fergusson, came up from Aberdeen with letters to
only two or three Scottish manufacturers; why, in less than a
week he was provided for; every Scottish house in the city was
applied to, till a suitable situation was found him. *I doubt if they
asked him half as often to dinner as my countrymen invited me;* but
they provided for him, and quickly—they are so *clannish*.'

'If they were less so,' I said, 'I should not esteem them as
highly as I do. I confess that I think *clannishness*, as you call it, the
root of much noble action. If every country provided for those
of its own who need provision, we should have no distress. There
is something in the everlasting affection the Scotch bear each
other that elevates them in my esteem almost beyond the inhabitants of all other countries. I have seldom known a Scotchman
whom I did not respect; and I wish, with all my heart, that the
Irish were as united by the magic of the sound of "native land."
In this should be sunk all political differences—all religious ani-

mosities. There is no country in the world that has sent forth finer soldiers, better sailors, firmer patriots, more eloquent statesmen. *Single-handed*, an Irishman conquers. *Singly* triumphant in art and literature, what might they not have accomplished long ere this for the good of their ill-used country, if they had only been *united*—only known the inestimable value of domestic and social union — only remembered that a house divided against itself *cannot* stand—and also kept in mind poor old Dick Delany's quotation which the practice of ages has proved true, that "UNION IS STRENGTH!"

FAMILY UNION.

It is strange how, amid all the changes and chances of life, the recollection of, and affection for, the scenes of childhood remain unaltered. More brilliant and beautiful prospects open upon us; we climb higher mountains, traverse more expansive seas, look over deeper and wider valleys, yet our affections are with the homes of our youth. I believe this feeling to be more intense when early days have been spent in the seclusion of the country; the eye is not then distracted by a continued varying of objects; there is leisure to number the heart's pulsations; feelings have time to take root, to spring up, to grow and strengthen; there is, day by day, a converse with nature, a communion with God; sounds, and sights, and miracles; nature's moving miracles by sea and land stamp their impress on the mind; and yet city memories are frequently as strong, though altogether different—inferior I had almost called them.

The love and remembrance of place of birth form the strongest and most enduring of human affections, for it is associated in feeling with scenes of infancy and recollections of early attachments and sympathies. Let me go where I will, or write upon whatever subject I may, I find my heart turning to the home of my childhood. All natural and happy thoughts are wound up with it: if I think of the ocean, the billows that laved the beach of our little bay roll before me; of trees, those that shadowed my childhood's path seem to wave above my head; of music, the peal of the old organ that stood in the hall, and was generally played during the twilight of the summer evenings, swells upon mine ear. And when I want to illustrate a subject, what numbers of characters and topics crowd upon me—all drawn from the same source! A sea-side neighbourhood, with its fleet of fishing-boats, has abundance of new incident to add to the stock always on hand in an extensive parish. Unless the heart is shut against the sympathies *of its own kind*, there *is* nothing, there *can* be nothing, approaching to dulness in a country neighbourhood. To me, it is the town that is as a 'howling wilderness;' the thousands that crowd its streets, and upon whose faces you look without meeting one answering glance, tell you that you are alone in the vast universe of human beings. Oh how bitterly I felt this when first we came to reside in London! How earnestly did I long, again and again, for the air and freedom, the freshness and the friendliness of those warm-hearted peasants who, for the love they bore my kindred, never met me without a blessing! How sweetly does the remembrance of these wayside prayers come upon me!—a remembrance which I would not exchange for the loudest public praise that ever echoed to human ears. And does not all this prove the depth and earnestness of early associations, the strength of early affections? And ought it not to teach a lesson to parents, as to the necessity of seeing that the first objects presented to the young should be well chosen with reference to the future? Does it not prove how very needful it is to *know*, in the strictest sense of the term, the character of those who associate with youth, that so no impressions of an injurious kind should be communicated at a time when they are certain to be retained! But I am digressing—creeping into a topic towards which my heart and mind are always turned—when, in fact, I ought to be occupied in portraying the difference which existed between the bringing up of 'Easy Jack Cummins' and 'Hard Tom Hartigan'— two men as different as can well be imagined, and yet both deserving the epithet of 'good-hearted fellows.'

Easy Jack's father was also an easy Jack. His landlord could do nothing with him. Although the rage for improvement was not by any means what it is now, still the landlord wished to improve; but Easy Jack—I cannot say the *first*, for the race is coeval with Irish existence—but Easy Jack the elder had no taste that way.

'Jack—is Jack at home?' he inquired one morning.

'No, yer honour,' said his wife, rubbing the dirt into her face with her dirty *praskeen*.

'Yes, daddy's down below,' screamed one urchin. 'No, daddy's up above,' shouted another. 'He's gone to the mill,' said a third. 'He's asleep in the room,' said a fourth. And *that* was generally the truth. Easy Jack Cummins *senior* loved his ease, and all his children pulled different ways. At last the landlord succeeded in forcing Jack to break cover; and after sundry reproofs on the score of idleness, and touching the necessity for truth, 'Jack,' said the landlord, 'if you will unite with Andy Mullins and Roger Dacey, they will assist in draining the three acre which is divided amongst you; and instead of its being nothing but a marsh for more than half the year, it will be a most useful piece of ground.'

'Maybe your honour would be thinking of raising the rint on us thin?' said the fellow, looking shrewdly into his landlord's face.

'No,' he answered; 'on the contrary, I will forgive you all a year's rent.'

'God bless yer honour! that's mighty good of you. Well, sir, I'll see about it, and spake to Andy and Roger.'

The landlord, however, from past experience, still doubting, said all he could to urge Jack to *combine* with others in what would have been a mutual service, and to impress upon his mind that where there is not sufficient power in individual exertion, nothing aids a cause but combination. A month passed over without anything having been done to the field, and again the landlord visited his tenant.

'Well, Jack, how is it that the field is in such a state?'

'The wather is it, yer honour? Sure that's the way it always was. I believe Ireland bates all the counthries on the face of the earth for wather, plase yer honour.'

'But you told me you were going to join Andy and Roger in draining the field?'

'Well, I put it to yer honour, what call have I to their share of the land? And sure if I drain my piece, it's theirs will have the good of it.'

'And if they drain theirs, yours will have the good of it.'

'Well, that's thrue; but sure, yer honour, my father left it the way it was in his time, and my mother always found it mighty convanient for rearing young ducks and blaiching flax, and I'll let it alone *till the boys grow up*, and then maybe we'll do it ourselves.'

But the children grew up with the same indifference to the wisdom of mutual assistance; and the field, at least Jack's part of it, was a literal slough the last time I saw it. Easy Jack the first had hoped to make his eldest son a farming labourer like himself: but no; he would be a shoemaker, and a shoemaker he was.

When the poor resist all plans for mutual assistance, their power weakens with each succeeding generation, and Jack Cummins the shoemaker is worse off than Jack Cummins who would not help to drain the farm. I shall revert to him again, but must now show the difference in the bringing up of 'Hard Tom;' indeed in this also the son was the counterpart of the father.

Old Tom was the first of his race who manifested a decided character. What he desired to do he would do well, and it seemed marvellous what he accomplished by judicious combination both abroad and at home. He had not even the advantage of possessing an acre of ground; but whenever others wanted help, it was sure to be given, and in the most judicious manner.

He brought up his children to help each other, both because it was necessary, and because it was right; and whenever any little work for the public good, as well as his own individual benefit, was going forward, old Tom Hartigan's head, and old Tom Hartigan's hand, which were both of the strongest, were sure to be ready on the instant. Nothing could be more opposite than the theory and practice of these two men, and I must now show the fate of their descendants. 'Easy Jack Cummins' the second would, as I have said, be a shoemaker, and he had brought up his children, or rather nature had brought them up, to run wild about the country, to the destruction of every well-built ditch, every furze fence, every tree, every bird's nest, in the parish. Never were such a wild and wilful set as the young Jack Cumminses; if you heard a huge long-backed pig squealing at the top of its voice, and discovered two or three children mounted thereon, shouting and hurraing louder than the pig itself, be sure they were some of the Jack Cumminses; if the young quicks in your hedge were converted into firewood, the Jack Cumminses were truly to blame; if a riot ensued, which enticed the old and the young to take part in the 'shindy,' the Jack Cumminses were surely the ringleaders. At first they were merry, rosy, wild, laughing rogues; they then grew into troublesome daring boys, and wilful slatternly girls. One would *not* dig the potatoes; another would *not* bind the shoes; another would *not* be a shoemaker, but would be a wheelwright; and because there was no money to make him so, he would not do anything required of him. Another would go to sea; another would do nothing but follow blind Beesom the fiddler, and dance jigs. The whole family pulled different ways; and the consequence was, that *Easy* Jack Cummins, and his no less *easy* wife, were obliged, as long as they were able, to pay for the assistance in their business which their children could have rendered them, if they had been, like the bundle of sticks, *united;* but as Jack's neighbour, Thomas Hartigan, said—and his good father had not only taught him to read, but placed one or two good books in his way—'Easy Jack Cummins *brought the sticks together, but had not strength to tie them up.*' This is often, particularly in Ireland, a grievous parental fault; they suffer their children to run wild; they do not consider that the strongest and best lessons can be taught in almost infancy, when the mind will receive any impression, and retain it. Easy Jack used to say, 'Ah, thin, let the little fellow have his own way; *sure he has no sense.*' But the 'little fellow,' when he had sense, was so accustomed to have his own way, that he would *not* give it up. Now this was the case with all the little fellows, and 'female fellows;' all in Easy Jack's household pulled, as I have said, different ways; all but one, and that poor boy was nearly an idiot—'a natural,' as he was poetically called by his neighbours, who also designated him 'Black Barney,' on account of the darkness of his complexion. While his brothers and sisters wearied their parents' hearts by wildness and neglect, 'Black Barney's' lustreless but affectionate eyes were the light of his father's house, his inarticulate voice the music which gladdened his mother's heart. He gloried in a shoemaker's apron, and would brandish an awl as if it were a sword; he would wax the ends for his father, and card tow for his mother; and though he could not speak distinctly, he could sing snatches of old ballads; and sing he would, in rain or sunshine, all the same, and dance uncouthly, but still it was dancing. He would even undertake to chastise his brothers and sisters when they would not work; and if his father seemed worn out with his endeavours to support his careless family, the poor idiot wrung his hands, and tears coursed each other down his 'lubber' cheeks. Poor creature, he possessed just sufficient intelligence to know what is wrong, but not enough to render him useful to his fellow-beings.

The misapplication of intellect incurs far greater penalty and blame than its absence; the reckless progeny of Easy Jack Cummins—which, if united by the bands of love and industry, could have scared poverty from the door—were scattered away, and two of the sons only returned to their native cottage when they wanted money or food. The old man's connexions dropped off one by one; there was no *uniting* principle there; and the last time I saw the old shoemaker, he had been to Thomas Hartigan's mill to beg a little meal for his wife, who was dying. Black Barney was rolling along the road before his father like a huge hedgehog—now singing one of his old songs, then weeping bitterly for *hunger*, and, as he said, '*nurning* that God had made his broders widout a heart.'

Look now at the other picture: thank God, if there is shade, there is also sunshine in this world. Tom Hartigan, the second, is a fine specimen of the chief stick of the bundle, round which all the little sticks are tied.

Tom—and I regret to say there were not a few of his neighbours who called him *Hard* Tom, a cognomen he acquired from his prudence, a virtue which Irishmen in his day held in sovereign contempt—Hard Tom began life just in the same way that Easy Jack Cummins did, but with a far different example; Tom ground at another man's mill, while Jack worked another man's leather; but in process of time one achieved the dignity of his own last and cabin, and the other rented a windmill. What a picturesque old mill it was! perched on the top of the hill of Graige, and commanding a view which is often, even now, spread out before me in my midnight dreams; the well-cultivated grounds and rich plantations of the old manor-house sloping to the edge of the brimming ocean; the house itself, with its gables and high chimneys; the bay beyond—the bay where the waters of my own blue sea were ever to me a source of serious yet unspeakable joy; the tower of Hook on its promontory, and nearer still the ruined church of Bannow; for the inland view, there was the bleak black stormy mountain of Forth, rearing its rocks into the very clouds. How fresh and invigorating was the breeze upon that mountain! How fresh that which swept our own hill! How often have I climbed to the old mill on a summer morning and counted the ships, whose silver sails showed like petrels upon the waves, and wondered when I, too, should be in a vessel on my way to my mother's country, to that rich and learned England, where I was often told I must go, to study and become steady!

The old mill, if it had been tenanted by any but Tom Hartigan, would have gone to destruction long before; but Tom patched and plastered and kept together its old stones with marvellous affection; and his wife, once when a storm tore the sail to tatters, absolutely mended the rent with her red Sunday petticoat, rather than the mill should stand still, and walked to Waterford to purchase the necessary material for new sails herself. I think the mountain air Tom breathed invigorated his independent and industrious mind tenfold. Tom and Anty began by being the most united couple in the parish.

'How you do slave yourself!' observed Mrs Easy Jack Cummins to Anty one evening, when the young families of both were increasing, as she strayed up the hill from the moor. 'How you do slave yourself and that *dawshy* child, keeping it winnowing! Sure it can do no good?'

'Yes,' replied Anty, 'it can; it *learns* to work, to divide the chaff from the *whate*—in which there is wisdom—when we work; and if poor people are not united in labour, they can't get on.'

'Well,' said Mrs Easy Jack, 'your husband must make enough to keep you all without such slaving. *Mine* does; and anyhow, I did'nt marry to *keep* my husband.'

'*I* did not marry to *keep* my husband,' was the sensible reply, 'but I married to *help* him. Sure we are one in the sight of God and man; and though the hands don't do the work of the head, nor the feet the work of the hands, yet they can all work together for *the same purpose;* and if two heads are better than one, surely two pair of hands are better than one; even the poor can get over a *dale* of hardship *if they are united.*'

'But where's the good of *slaving?*'

'Work is pleasure,' answered Anty Hartigan, 'if a body has a mind to make it so. Sure it's the greatest pleasure in life to me to help Tom, the craythur! If he works hard, wouldn't it be a sin for me to be idle? And as to the child'——

'The idea,' interrupted Mrs Easy Jack Cummins—'the idea of buying a sieve, a morsel of a sieve, for such a baby as that to winnow with! Sure *that* was throwing away a day's earning?'

'But the child couldn't be at my foot all day doing nothing; and if he wasn't doing good, he'd be doing harm; *and one day's earning is well spent to lay the foundation of an industrious life, plase God!*' replied Anty; adding, 'How do you keep your young ones quiet?'

'I don't look to do it.* Sure the world will be hard enough on 'em by and by; it's the least they may have their fling a bit now. I didn't marry to slave,' she repeated.

'Where there's love,' said Anty, pushing back her hair from her heated brow, 'there may be labour, but no slavery; the being *united* in the work is itself a blessing.'

'Setting a case, you didn't love Tom, and he didn't love you, what would you do?'

'Ah, *bathershin!*' laughed the young wife; then added, 'But in earnest, if I didn't, *that* would not put me past my marriage agreement; I should work all the same, though it would be with a heavy heart instead of a light one; and if he didn't love me, why,' her voice faltered—'why, I'd try to help him twice as much, just to *get back his love;* sure that would be both right and wise, for the *comfort of doing my duty would be the only comfort I'd have left*. And now, Mrs Cummins, *avourneen*, don't take it ill of me if I tell you what my mother told me, not exactly to fret or contradict a young child, but to *turn its mind to useful employment;* to rule it by love, *but to rule;* or by and by the little craythur that lay on your bosom may stab yer heart. Above all, keep children *employed;* it keeps them together *like the bundle of sticks,* and then they are sure to prosper.' That Mrs Cummins did not heed this admirable advice I have already shown; and the contrast between the two families, as their respective children grew up, was great indeed.

The miller's cottage was like a bee's nest: two sons helped in the mill; the girls winnowed, and made and mended; the others were always employed as best suited their age and knowledge; and though labour in that part of the country is badly paid, according to the rate of English remuneration, yet provisions were at that time, and still are, cheap. Tom Hartigan began life poor; he will die rich. To use his own words, 'Single-handed, I might have struggled on like my neighbours, if my wife had not helped me. We began by being *really united*, and finding the power that it gave us, we taught the children the advantages we felt. If little Bat (that was the youngest) wanted to make a toy-boat, Nelly would stitch the sails, Jem fit the cordage, Terry splice the timbers, and *all* would help to set it afloat; and then I'd say, "See, now, how quick that was done, because you war *united;* if Nelly refused to stitch the sails, Jem to fix the cordage, and

---

* Try to do it.

Terry to splice the timbers, Bat, honey, how long would it be before you'd have had your ship afloat?" Though that's but a play toy, the lesson is the same through life. Thank God! the mill has never wanted grist; and now I'm a farming miller, I grind a dale of corn that my boys have thrashed and sown, and my girls have reaped and bound; and there's a warm corner for the poor natural, Black Barney, whose family are scattered like chaff before the wind.' And my belief is, that if Irishmen *were united*, at home and abroad, they'd carry the world before them. So the heavens above look down, with the sunny beams of encouragement, on *United Irishmen!*

GOING TO SERVICE.

'THERE'S many have done it before; and let people say what they like, and however disagreeable it may be, it's no disgrace,' said Mrs Mulvany, the shopkeeper's wife in the little town of Ballycastle, or, according to its original designation, Ballycaushlawn. 'It's no disgrace, Mary Cassidy, and so don't cry, dear. If you are not comfortable after a while, you can come to me. Remember there's "A time for everything, and everything in time;" "A place for everything, and everything in its place;" "Dust the corners," as my poor mistress used to say (she was English, as well as myself, Mary)—"dust the corners, and the middle will dust itself;" "Never leave till to-morrow what ought to be done to-day;" "A stitch in time saves nine;" "Keep on doing, and you will soon be done;" "Keep a civil tongue in your head, and your head will keep you;" always remember "Time and tide wait for no man." Why, Mary, girl! if my husband, Terence Mulvany, had minded my advice, where he has single pounds now, he'd have dozens in his purse; but he's an Irishman, Mary, and they're very affectionate in their way, yet very, very thoughtless. But for all that,' added the good woman, leaning her large red arms on a counter that was as clean as hard rubbing could make it, 'for all *that*, I would not exchange my Terence for any other husband, no matter what his country.'

Mrs Mulvany was a bustling, industrious woman. Many people are bustling who are not industrious, but she was both; and she was kind-hearted withal, though her kindness did not take the form it usually takes in Ireland. Her hospitality was not reckless; she would place enough before her husband's guests, but not a great deal too much. Provisions are cheap in her neighbourhood, but she did not conceive that their being so justified her in any species of extravagance; she considered their abundance an especial blessing, not to be wasted. She did not think that prevailing on persons to eat or drink more than they liked, more than did them good, was a proof of either kindness or generosity; she loved her husband dearly; she worked with him, thought for him, saved for him; but she also remonstrated with him, when, instead of minding his business, he would borrow a pointer, and use, or endeavour to use, the old gun as a fowling-piece. She steadily refused her sanction to card-playing in all its branches, as being an unchristian and unthrifty amusement; and when, having taken a 'stiff tumbler' of punch, Terence would express his desire to have another, or, if not another, half a one, or 'only a little drop of sperits in the cowld wather, *just to kill the insects*,' Mrs Mulvany would lay firm, if not violent hands on the ugly green bottle, put it into the cupboard, lock it up, and consign the key to her capacious pocket: this was when there was nobody by. She had good sense enough, if Terence filled his glass too often when a neighbour dropped in, to hold her tongue *until* he was gone; or if Terence had really taken too much, to keep it qniet till the next morning; then, indeed, her husband received a lecture, long or short, mild or strong, according to circumstances.

Men generally listen to reason when suffering from a bad headache produced by indiscretion, and Terence knew his wife was right; besides, her entire conduct in her own homely way convinced him that his interests were hers, and that the desire of her life was to see him well and happy. To be sure she wanted him to be happy in her way rather than his own, and was not as yielding, not as subservient, as Irish wives generally are; consequently the young idling men, who would have enjoyed their hot punch and feasting at Terence Mulvany's expense but for his wife's carefulness, were apt to say 'that she kept his nose to the grinding-stone.' Nevertheless the worthy shopkeeper grew fat, looked happy, and prospered.

And what has all this to do with 'going to service!' you inquire. I will tell you. Mary Cassidy, the pretty interesting-looking girl who stood in Mrs Mulvany's shop, had in a great degree been brought up under her eye, and improved by her counsel. She had within the previous six months lost her uncle, or rather her mother's uncle (for poor Mary was an orphan), an amiable-hearted, gentle-minded old man, a friar, who had been educated in France, and who was both polished and tolerant. Mary was only sixteen, and her great-uncle's death had deprived her of bread; indeed, during the last four years of his life his mind had faltered, and to the kindness of his neighbours he was principally indebted for the few comforts he required. Mrs Mulvany, as she declared, loved the girl 'as if she were her own;' but, contrary to the usual Irish practice, she had sent those of her own children whose assistance was not required in the shop to service long before. They had gone cheerfully, because they had been brought up with that intention; their mother's well-known diligence and industry had secured them good situations in the best families, and it was not in Mrs Mulvany's bustling nature to understand poor Mary's feelings. Mary had occupied a dangerous position; she was above the lower class, and greatly below the higher; the poor called her 'Miss,' the shopkeepers 'Mary.' She had received a little education; enough to begin upon, and enough to make her desire more, but not enough to raise her above the rank of an ordinary English servant. This she hardly believed could be the case, though Mrs Mulvany had told her so. She had no near relation in the world; but the Irish world is not a cold one. All who knew sympathised with her, except Mrs Mulvany, who declared she was in luck to get what was as good as an English place, to go where she'd have fresh meat once a day, regular meals, a good bed, and a mistress who 'would have her work done properly.'

Mary Cassidy silently agreed with every word uttered by her active and disinterested friend; she then as silently stole into the parlour behind the shop, and from that into the little garden, where she shed many bitter tears at the prospect of 'going to service.' Mrs Mulvany supplied her with all she deemed necessary for English servitude; and as she was going as housemaid, under the lady's-maid, there was every reason to suppose she would learn well and quickly. She was, however, to spend a few days after she left Ballycaushlawn at the house of a country gentleman, a sort of person midway between a farmer and a squire—a very dangerous position for any one to occupy. The gentleman's wife was a distant relative of poor Mary's, and as in Ireland 'poverty' does not often 'part good company,' she was not ashamed of her fourth cousin, though she was foolish enough to lament her going to *sarvice*. Here it was Mary's fate to witness the reverse of all the maxims inculcated by Mrs Mulvany's kind advice. There was no settled time for any one duty; everything was conducted by the rule of 'hurry scurry;' consequently when night came, at least half the work was laid to the account of the following day, which thus became overburdened. The kitchen was a scene of most desperate confusion; instead of the noggins and jugs being hung in regular lines along the dresser, they were laid down when done with on the floor, 'that the cat, the craythur, might finish the sup of milk,' or 'the chickens pick the last of the stirabout,' or 'Rover, the baste, lick the end of it.' There they remained until they were wanted, when all was perplexity to get them ready. The dust was never disturbed from the corners of their parlour, or from behind the tables and chairs;

consequently every breath of air that entered the room set it whirling over 'the greenest spot' that had received *the promise of a sweeping.*

Mary discovered in the morning, while commencing her breakfast, that the milk had not been properly strained before it was set for cream to make butter; consequently the cow hairs stuck round that compound like a *cheveau-de-frise.* Mary could not eat.

'Indeed and it is very troublesome they are,' said the lady, picking out the offenders one by one, and laying them on the breakfast cloth, which bore tokens of being 'used to it.' 'It's mighty troublesome they are; and while I think of it, I'll just speak about it to Nelly. Ring the bell, Mary.'

Mary tried; the bell was mute.

'Well, call then, dear; tongues were made before bells; but anyway, if Jerry had strengthened the crank when I told him with a bit of wire, we needn't be made hoarse with calling, or lame with tramping after those blind and stupid sarvants; now we must have the bellhanger, I suppose, *when we can get him.*'

'A stitch in time saves nine,' thought Mary Cassidy as Nelly entered.

'Nelly, the hairs prevent our eating the butter,' said the 'misthress' with the greatest composure.

'Bad luck and bad manners to 'em for that same,' replied Nelly, leaning her shoulder against the door-post, and running her finger backwards and forwards across the back of the nearest chair, so as to form a meandering figure in the dust.

'Nelly, it's your fault.'

'Bedad! I'm as clear from it as if I had just risen from the priest's knee, God bless him! My *faut,* agra! Bedad! misthress, it's the *faut* of the strainer, that's gone into *smithereens* ever since yerself, ma'am, took it to bate paes in.'

'Devil take the peas!' chimed in the husband. 'Sure milk vessels should be kept to themselves; I had the taste of split peas off the butter for a month.'

'Ay!' said Nelly, making a very long slide with her finger in the dust—' ay, and last market-day, Pether, Sandy Pether, the *graboy,* lost the sale of the butther through one of Andy Muckle's jokes—may the devil choke him wid the next, I pray! He said it was cows' hair he was bringing to market instead of cows' butter.'

'Still, Nelly, that is your fault,' said her mistress in a more angry tone.

'See that row! Bedad! ma'am, *I thought ye'd say so!* Sure ye could not expect me to hinder the strainer of wearing, and the paes, and'——

'Don't dare to talk to me of the peas!' exclaimed the good

woman, angry that *her* fault should be exposed; 'could you not have mended the strainer?'

'It's a-past mending now.'

'But at first?'

'Oh! at *fust*! Sure it was only a *dawshy* hole at *fust;* and Miss Nancy used to take the world's delight in seeing the *kitling* put her paw through it. The hole did no *harrum at the fust going off, as we used to lift the strainer on one side.*'

'If Mrs Mulvany heard this,' thought Mary, 'how she would storm!' and ventured immediately to suggest that, until a new strainer could be purchased, a piece of coarse linen should be sewn round the wood. She would do it with pleasure herself, 'as it was a pity to lose the sale of the butter.'

'Oh, very well,' said Nelly, rather piqued than pleased; 'miss might do it to be sure, if the misthress liked. The *butther* had the hairs in it many a day, and the misthress took it aisy enough; and as to the sale of the *butther*, the laugh was agin Pether in the market. But to be sure some people, especially those reared by half English, such as Mrs Mulvany, was mighty nice;' and Nelly flounced away, her mistress talking loudly of the 'dirt of the sarvants,' quite forgetting that she had set the example, if example was needed, of carelessness, by corrupting the milk-strainer by the impurity of other matter.

Dinner was ordered at four that day, and as poor Mary was wandering about, observing, without knowing it, how different everything was from the thrift and care manifested in Mrs Mulvany's dwelling, two of the children came running to tell her that 'Peenawn the piper was outside the backdoor playing " Rattle her down the Hill," the hunter's jig, and that Nelly and Molly, and little Jemmy, war dancing a double jig.' Mary thought it must be near the hour of dinner; as she passed the clock she looked up; *it was not going* (a sure sign of a mismanaged house); but in the kitchen, the ducks, suspended by a string of twisted worsted before a fire, roaring like a burning mountain, were at a dead stop, while a dog was licking round and round the edge of a huge cracked dish that did duty as a dripping-pan, as the *cook* (!) had not been able to find time 'to rid' the baked potatoes out of the proper dripping-pan, though they had been nearly consumed by the picking of chickens and the licking of animals, to whom the kitchen was free ground; and over this kitchen there was no presiding genius, as the cook had fled at the sound of the pipes to turn her foot in a jig, leaving the dinner to dress itself.

Mary drove away the dog, and turned the ducks, seeing there was no chance of the servants 'keeping on doing, and consequently being soon done;' but the servants regarded her care with scorn, and held her labour in contempt. 'Indeed they war not going to lose their step of a dance for nothing; the dinner would be time enough. *Masther nor misthress was never ready to the minute; why should they bother then?*—it wasn't every day they heard the pipes.'

If Mary had known enough to understand the full force of the observation, 'master nor mistress was never ready at the minute,' she would have understood how necessary the practice of punctuality is to enforce its observance. The slovenly habits of this house did Mary Cassidy infinite service, for she had a sufficient quantity of good taste to perceive they were such as to mar everything like comfort and economy.

Five months elapsed after she went to Mrs Singleton's before she wrote the following letter to Mrs Mulvany:—

'MY DEAR FRIEND—for so you have ever proved yourself to be to a poor friendless girl—and you will therefore, I am sure, let me call you so—I am doing, thanks to your advice, very well indeed, and, I may say, give great satisfaction; and if it warn't for Mary Dacey, the lady's-maid, I should be as happy as if I wasn't at service at all; everything is regular as the clock, and my mistress so particular. "You are a good girl," says she to me one morning; "Mary Cassidy, you are a very good girl; I have examined all the corners, and find them well dusted." "Ma'am," says I, making a dutiful answer, "Mrs Mulvany told me to sweep the corners, and the middle would sweep itself," and that pleased her very much, and she said I was a nice clean girl. But what puts betwixt me and my rest entirely is Mary Dacey. Oh, Mrs Mulvany, if it wasn't for Mary Dacey, there wouldn't be a happier girl betwixt this and the Bay of Dublin than myself! Now, you see, the mistress asked me when I came if I had any *followers*, and I felt my cheeks burn up like a coal of fire, for *you* know I never encouraged but the one, and he went to sea before my poor uncle (the heavens be his bed!) died; but he did not go without *breaking the ring* which hangs about my neck at this minute, though, even if he is alive, maybe it's too proud he'd be to think of a poor servant, though he'd regard a priest's niece. However, I said, and I trembling alive with the shame, "None at the present time, ma'am," for you told me to speak the truth.

"At this *present* time!" she repeated; "then you *hope* to have!"

"If it's pleasing to God and yourself, ma'am," I answered, curtseying; "for," I added, "I broke the ring with one that's beyant seas, and that *I'm afraid will never trouble yer honour about me.*"

'Now, Mrs Mulvany, was there anything to laugh at in that! Sure I *was* in fear, and *am* in fears, that I may never see him again! But the mistress laughed outright, and then said, "Well, I am sure you have told the truth, and if you continue to do so, we shall have no reason to repent Mrs Mulvany's recommendation. But, Mary, the reason I asked was, that if you *had* a lover, I would find out who and what he was, and if he was steady and well-conducted, never object to your seeing him occasionally *in my house*, though I do not permit young girls to meet young men *out* of my house. It is perfectly natural," she said, "that you and every other young woman in due time should wish to be settled; and as I hope to be not only a mistress but a friend to you, and to all who serve me, I wish to know whom *you* know, that I may be able to advise you for the best, and reward you for good conduct. Always tell me the truth, frankly and simply as you have done now, and I will always be your friend."

'I'm sure they talked of my *little token* in the parlour, for Miss Annette looked very slyly out of her blue eyes at me the next morning, and asked me if I wore nothing about my neck but my "*handkercher*." But was not that very good entirely of the mistress? Now, I never was used to lying; but look, after those words of hers, Mrs Mulvany, honey, I'd suffer myself to be cut into sparables before I'd tell her a word of lie; and that's what's ruining me with Mary Dacey—the lies I mean. Oh, Mrs Mulvany, the contrariness of Mary goes *beyant* the beyands—it's shocking, so it is. There's an old henwife in it—a little put-together of a woman; and she gave out that all the young pullets were cocks, and the old hens past laying, so there never was any fresh eggs for breakfast. Moreover, she let a goose-plucker into the goosery at night, on condition that she was only to take half the feathers off the poor innocent birds. As this was done on the sly, even I did not know it, and the plucker was going on with the brutal work, until one old gander, which, I daresay, was up to the mischief, went bang through the window, and never set foot on the ground until he flew right under the mistress's window, and then the cackling he made woke the dog, that woke the mistress, and she wakes the master, and rings the servants' bell. Up I bounced, and, to my astonishment, Mary was not in her bed. I ran down to the mistress, and, "Cassidy," she says—the quality think a surname grander than a Christian one I suppose—"Cassidy," she says, "there's a light in the goosery; go and see what's the matter, and tell Dacey to come to me."

'Well, I went down, and the gander kept on roaring a thousand murders; and when I got out, there was the plucker and the hen-wife, one on a *boss*, the other on a *creepy*, plucking for the dear life at an old goose, and half the flock shivering in a corner, and Mary Dacey with a dirty pack of cards in her hand, that had been reading her fortune.*

"Go back," says the old goose-plucker, "and say there was a cat or a weazel among the geese."

---

* The custom of plucking geese is carried to a shameful extent in Ireland; men, and we feel shame to add, women, go about with huge bags to stuff the feathers in, and pay generally twopence or threepence each to the farmers and cotters' wives for permission to strip the poor bird as close as they please.

"I'll tell no untruth," I answered; "and the master saw the light, besides the gander!"

"I wish the devil had him!—and I'll give him something will make him stiffer in the wings soon!" says the henwife.

"Mistress asked for you," I said, wondering at their craft, and addressing my words to Mary.

"Tell her I'm very bad entirely with the toothache," she said, "and that I can't get out of bed."

"I tell you what," I replied, "you, Anty Mullowny, have no right to sell the birds' feathers *unknownst* to the mistress."

"She wont sell them herself, so I do no harm," she said.

"They are not yours," says I.

"Praich to the skylarks, priest's niece!" she answers.

"Mary," I said to the lady's-maid, "for the love of God, and the sake of your character, run in at once; I can tell no lie for you or any one else; I must say if I am asked, and tell the truth."

"Oh dear, how mighty righteous we are of a suddent!" exclaimed Mary. "But do go your own way; make tales, and carry tales, and see what you'll get by it. I don't care."

"Mary, remember what Don't Care came to," I answered. "And as to *making* tales, you know I never did that; but certainly I will not see my master and mistress plundered without informing them of it."

"It does not take a penny out of their pocket," said the plucker, while the old hen-woman shook her fist in my face, and the lady's-maid dropped me a *sneer* of a curtsey.

'Well, Mrs Mulvany, I don't know how it would have ended, had they not seen, from the light of a candle he carried, the master himself picking his steps through the sludge of the yard, on account of the drain of the duck-pond being going to be repaired; and the moment Mary Dacey saw the flare of the candle, she turned white as a silver penny.

"I'm done," she says, "I'm done for ever, if the master catches me here!" "We're all done," says the goose-plucker, shaking a whirl of feathers from her that looked like a snow-storm; "we're all done!" And as she said the word, old Anty bundled herself into where a goose, poor thing, was sitting on her eggs, and like lightning she puts herself down on the eggs, and takes the goose in her lap, drawing her head down, for she is but a mite of a woman; the goose-plucker stood her ground, but Mary Dacey fell on her knees to me.

"Oh, Mary, *avourneen*," she said, "just stand here that I may creep down behind you, which will get the master to pass me over. Do—now do. *For the sake of your uncle's soul,* don't tell on a *poor motherless girl* like yerself; I'll burn the cards, and never do wrong again." Well, Mrs Mulvany, I did let her do as she desired; and maybe when the master came in, wasn't he in a towering passion entirely; for being a gentleman mighty used to his own way, he didn't like being disturbed; and then every minute he opened his mouth to spake, the *flaff* of the down got into his throat, and then he was dancing mad entirely; and the goose herself, poor thing, got unaisy about her eggs, as good raison she had; and after turning the plucker out, and she on her knees to his honour, "Mary," he says to me, "that goose is distressed at something; I hope they haven't poisoned as well as plucked them;" and while he walked over to the far corner with the light to see what ailed the bird, Mary Dacey slipt out, and my heart grew lighter then, for I thought she'd mend for good.

'And indeed I could not help laughing, for the master, angry as he was, did the same thing as he pulled Anty of the eggs; and when the poor goose found them broke, she got into her tantrums, and raised a regular rebellion among the other geese, so that old Jerry the gander, *which had sold the pass** on the goose-plucker, came tottering home; and the upshot of it all was, that, in spite of a thousand lies, and as many curses, old Anty was sent off the next morning, and two more, who certainly deserved it, with her; but they did not tell upon Mary Dacey, which at the time I thought very good of them entirely. But now this is my trouble.

'I believe Mary's heart softened; but not only must the heart *soften* with sorrow, but *harden* against future sin; if it does not, the sorrow does no good. Well, Mary promised me, if I did not *let on*, that she'd change, and give up the card-playing, which, as you told me, brings not only temptation with it, but a hard and heavy curse wherever it is encouraged; and she seemed mighty *study* and good entirely, until one morning I thought I saw the old goose-plucker in the far shrubbery waiting under a tree. Now my poor uncle used to say it was through such as her that servants so often got into trouble; for they maraud through the country, sometimes pulling feathers, sometimes with a basket of hardware, or a pack of soft goods, tempting the foolish girls with finery unfit for them, and taking payment in meal, or corn, or apples, or anything the girls are tempted to take unknownst from their employer or their parents: this is worst of all; and she was so surely on the watch, that I watched her, and by and by I saw Mary Dacey go to her and give her something *blue*, but what, I can't say. Well, I met Mary at the turn, and she running home for the dear life. She grew red and pale when she saw me. "Where have you been?" I says. "Down the grove for a mouthful of fresh air," she says. "The air is fine and fresh here, Mary," I says; "glory be to God for it!" "Maybe I had a bachelor to meet down there!" she says, laughing it off.

"Maybe, Mary," said I, "you went to meet the goose-plucker."

* Given information.

'Well, what staggered me was, she swore such an oath she never set eyes on her since that night; and when I reproached her with her wickedness, and said I *knew* she was there, she turned on me with the greatest abuse, called me a spy, and said I might be an informer if I liked; that if she did not see the gooseplucker whenever she sent for her, she would tell the mistress, by a synonymous letter, all I had to do with them before.

'Oh! Mrs Mulvany, what am I to do? The woman is often about the house, and neither master nor mistress knows it. Mary meets her, I know she does, constantly; and master said the first person who encouraged her about the house should lose their place; and what he says *he'll* do. I know she's after no good, and I tell the cook so, and she says the same; but she says also, it's not your business, nor mine; and if you tell on Mary, she's an *orphin*, and can have no character if she's turned away for comrading with that old fortune-telling woman, that's the curse of the neighbourhood.' [The letter continued to repeat her anxiety as to what she ought to do, and her fears as to whether or not Mary took anything of value, and her dread of making enemies, and all the various fears and feelings which a well-meaning mind, that nevertheless wants strength, is likely to urge, both to itself and others, as an excuse for not doing at once what it is a duty to do.]

When Mrs Mulvany read the letter, she first called to her youngest daughter to be ready to take charge of the shop, as she was going from home for maybe a couple of days. She then asked her husband if she might have 'the sorrel swinger,' as demurely as if she wished him to believe that he really had some command over his stable. And then she ordered 'Jem' to saddle the horse, and put on the big pillion and his best 'top-coat,' as she wanted him to look decent. After she had made these arrangements to her perfect satisfaction, she commenced dressing herself in her best, and commented aloud on the contents of the letter as she did so. 'That's the way the world gets worse instead of better, and good, honest, industrious servants suspected, because of the bad ones that have gone before them. It's all through the want of a proper feeling for the great principle of truth; that's what it is; confounding the character of an *informer*—who tells lies, and if he does tell truth, does it for a reward—with that of the *truth-teller*, who cherishes truth for the love of God, and whose duty it is to prevent evil. "What is she to do?" Why, if Mary Dacey wont take her warnings, it is *her* duty, as a servant and a Christian, to tell her mistress. My poor child! she'll get into trouble, that she will! But I *don't* care a rush for the whole set of them! I'll just give my own Mary's letter into her mistress's hand, plain and above-board. "Anonymus letter!"—he who writes an anonymus letter is a knave, he who *believes* it, a fool.

Oh that servants should be so base as to see their employer robbed, and say "it is not their business!" As if it is not everybody's business to prevent robbery—as if we should not speak truth! Oh if plain-speaking was minded, how seldom we should meet rogues, for they would know that every honest eye was as a watch-tower over the inroads of roguery! To think now that she'd be led by the cook! But that's the way: if one servant does not exactly corrupt another, she saps the foundation of good principles. Mary Dacey, an orphin indeed! Good reason she should be more careful, after all the warnings too; and why should she *have* a character, if she does not deserve it? The idea of letting fraud be practised, because, if it was known, the person who cheats and robs will not have a character!—the person, too, who gives bread, who spends money in his own country instead of going abroad. That little minx, my own Mary, she *ought* to have known better; but she *is* young, poor child! However, I'll set it all to rights; I don't care for any of them.'

And having so decreed, she strapped on her riding skirt, put on a warm shawl, surmounted her handsome lace-cap by a black beaver hat, which boasted the ornament of a steel buckle; and after her husband had lifted her on the pillion, and the 'sorrel swinger' was fairly off at his usual hard, high trot, Mr Mulvany was heard to declare that his wife ' grew *heavier* and *handsomer* every day of her life.'

She had not proceeded far, when she saw strolling towards her the goose-plucker, who was well known to every one in the country.

'Got anything good and cheap?' she inquired, as the old rogue looked up at her with an expression of cunning and fear, for rogues had an instinctive dread of Mrs Mulvany.

'Oh, ma'am, there's no good in telling you; for you wont let a poor body come within a mile of ye, much less show ye anything.'

'Well, I'm taking a turn perhaps,' said the shopkeeper; 'so hand up yer basket till I have a look.' There were threads and tapes, and ribbons and laces, and little looking-glasses that libelled the human face divine, and the usual assemblage of odds and ends; but Mrs Mulvany knew, from the weight of the basket, that it contained more than it appeared to do.

'How long is it,' inquired Mrs Mulvany, 'since you were at Castle Hazard? How long since you saw my little pet Mary Cassidy?'

A change, too perceptible not to be at once noted by the quick-witted Mrs Mulvany, passed over the goose-plucker's face; and in a tone of mingled anxiety and anger she exclaimed, ' *Yarra wisha!* ma'am, give me my basket; sure it's well enough I knew ye didn't want to buy anything.'

'*Here's* a remnant rolled up of *blue* satin,' persisted her tormentor; 'what will ye take for that?—or where in the world did ye find such satin?'

'What's that to you?' she replied tartly. 'Give me back my goods, and don't be stopping a poor traveller on her way.'

'I'm not stopping you,' replied Mrs Mulvany, who remembered that Mary had said in her letter she thought what the lady's-maid had given the goose-plucker was *blue*. This determined her on a singular course of proceeding.

'What's yer basket worth?'

'Myself can't tell.'

'Did you give ten shillings for what's in it?'

'Where would a poor craythur like me get ten shillings?'

'There's ten-and-sixpence for it then,' said Mrs Mulvany quickly, throwing her half a guinea. 'There's ten-and-sixpence for it. Will that do? Go on, Jerry; ye heard her say it wasn't worth ten shillings.'

The goose-plucker stood with staring eyes, looking after the rapidly-trotting horse of Mrs Mulvany, while Jerry, delighted at his mother's frolic, turned round grinning most gloriously, and waving his *clan-alpin* in adieu to the outwitted rogue. But suddenly gathering up her energies, the goose-plucker set off screaming after the horse and its riders, while Mrs Mulvany, having discovered that the basket had a false bottom, sat coolly examining its contents.

When she arrived at Castle Hazard, Mrs Mulvany had good reason to rejoice at her promptness. She found that Mary Dacey had got up a well-arranged plan to destroy Mary Cassidy's character. Several things had been missed by the lady of the house, and the charge of robbery laid both directly and indirectly upon the priest's niece. Mary Cassidy was in tears; but protesting innocence is not proving it.

Mary Dacey was wicked enough to say she'd take her oath that she *saw* the blue satin, which was one of the things her mistress missed, in Mary Cassidy's possession. It so happened that Mrs Mulvany arrived at the very moment the examination was going on in the parlour, and she said at once, 'Mary, let your boxes be searched.' This was done; while the poor girl protested her innocence, and saw, when it was too late, that *truth cannot be compromised with safety to our own honour*.

'Oh, Mary Dacey!' she exclaimed, 'how could you treat me so, when you knew right well what I saved you from?'

This led to the inquiry what she had saved her from? And then came a daring appeal from the young sinner. She turned to her master, and asked him if it could have been possible that she was in the goose-house the night he entered without his seeing her?

This boldness in lying almost paralysed Mary Cassidy, and her master was compelled to confess he did not think it could.

'How often,' continued the artful girl, 'have I found money, madam, that you lost, and brought it you?—this was not the act of a rogue, was it?'

Her mistress was obliged to admit the fact; and the feelings of their fellow-servants not in the plot wavered from the priest's niece to the lady's-maid.

Mrs Mulvany kept her purchase all this time concealed beneath the shadow of her riding-skirt; then suddenly producing it, she said, 'Mary Dacey, do you know this basket?'

'It's mighty like—a—a—basket,' she stammered.

'Whose basket?' inquired Mrs Mulvany, fixing her sharp keen eyes on her.

'Why, I don't know; sure I can't tell; how should I know?'

'Do you know this blue satin—this lace—this fine scent-box?' And she continued drawing forth a curious assemblage of things, peculations not only from Castle Hazard, but other houses. How frightful is vice at any age, but in the young it is awful!

'Well!' exclaimed the hardened girl, 'now I *do* look at the basket, it's mighty like Nanny the goose-plucker's; the creature has been about the house, and of coorse Mary turned the ready penny with her!'

Just as she had so said, Mrs Mulvany observed the goose-plucker advancing down the avenue at a much more rapid pace than she could have conceived possible, her blue cloak flying behind, and her progress marked by the escape of sundry feathers that floated away upon the breeze.

She observed that Mary Dacey changed colour, but Mary Cassidy wept as before.

'I have one favour to ask, madam,' said Mary's friend, advancing to the lady who had been so wrought upon by this bad girl. 'Will you permit ME, and *me* only, to have a word with that woman before she enters here?' and Mrs Mulvany pointed to the advancing enemy.

This request was granted. Mary Dacey at first intreated and expostulated, saying Mrs Mulvany and the goose-plucker would sell her *betwixt* them; but in vain. And when the woman entered the room with Mrs Mulvany, the girl saw that the truth would be known, for the goose-plucker imagined it was known already. Still the love of lying, aided by the natural quickness of a clever but corrupt nature, swayed them both. The goose-plucker's evidence was most cautiously given; and it was marvellous how she acted upon the hint of Mary Dacey's eye.

'Why, not two minutes ago,' said Mrs Mulvany, 'you admitted that Mary Dacey gave you those things to purchase your silence, as you and the hen-wife determined to tell all you knew, and get her out of her place if she did not give you all she could.'

'Ah!' said the old wretch, assuming the most simple expression of countenance, 'you bothered me, so you did, betwixt the two Marys—it was Mary Cassidy I meant!'

Mrs Mulvany looked—but no matter how she looked; the goose-plucker had confessed all to her, yet now seemed determined to turn that all to the ruin of an innocent girl.

'Here's a letter of Mary Dacey's, directed to Ben Tomlines, and that's her sweetheart, I know,' exclaimed one of the children, who had been rummaging over the pedler's basket with childish delight.

Then, indeed, the lady's-maid saw her plot was discovered—then she knew all was over, for the letter, which the goose-plucker had engaged to convey to her lover (one of the worst fellows in Clonmel, and that is saying a great deal), exulted, in very strange orthography, over the success of her scheme to turn the priest's niece out of her place; it evinced how impossible it is for bad people to appropriate proper motives to the most virtuous actions, for it contained these remarkable words—'*She has not done me any harm yet, but I'm sure she will, for she has the power.*' The ingratitude of this wicked girl speaks for itself; but I hope it is unnecessary to make any observation on Mary Cassidy's culpable weakness, which brought all this trouble upon herself. When she saw that her fellow-servant persisted in a course which was decidedly at variance with her employers' interests—a *course* which she had *moral proof* was dishonest—she should have said so. She should have told her mistress; and any servant who does not, *becomes the accomplice of thieves.*

Mrs Mulvany remained all that evening at Castle Hazard; and Mary, after seeing the folly of her ways, was reinstated in her mistress's favour, while those who deserved it lost both place and character.

'I have heard,' said the poor girl before bidding her friend goodnight—'I have heard—from—*you know who*. In the midst of my trouble the letter came; he knows all; and what do you think he says? That he's got promoted, and is in the rank of a gentleman. A gentleman at sea!—and when I came to that, my heart sank. But a little farther on—here, you can read it yourself—he says that he will be home, and we shall be m—a—. There, dear Mrs Mulvany, *you* can read the word, and he does not think the worse of me FOR GOING TO SERVICE.'

DEBT AND DANGER.

'But I tell ye I must have it, Lanty.'

' Well, but, masther, honey, wont ye listen to raison ?'

' What has reason to do with the matter?'

'True for ye, Masther D'Arcy,' replied Lanty Lurgan with peculiar emphasis.

'Mind, then, that I hear no more about reason; but tell Murphy I'll pay him for the horse.'

' *Whin*, Masther D'Arcy ?'

'When it's convenient.'

Lanty Lurgan shook his head.

'Hear me!' exclaimed the young squire, looking himself as angry as his good-natured handsome face would permit. 'Lanty, you're not worth the toss of a bad halfpenny to a fellow.'

'Maybe *not*,' said Lanty.

'You've no management in you.'

' Not now, sure enough, Masther D'Arcy,' was Lanty's reply.

' What do you mean by " not now?"' inquired his master.

'Just, thin, because there's nothing left me to manage,' said Lanty, having, before he made this declaration, taken the precaution to get at a sufficient distance from his irritable young master, to prevent any personal chastisement for his frankness, to which he had a particular dislike.

D'Arcy O'Rourke seized the bootjack that stood near him, and was in the act of flinging it at his old retainer as he half stood half crouched behind a high-backed chair; but apparently struck by some cheerful reminiscence, he suddenly burst out into laughter. 'Come out of your hiding-hole, old boy,' he exclaimed; 'come along; I did you injustice, for no half-ruined vagabond in or out of Ireland had ever a more faithful follower.'

'*I was born to it*,' said the old man pathetically, while at the same time his eyes beamed tenderly on the thoughtless creature, whom, as a child, he had often carried in his arms; and pausing, he added, 'God bless you, Masther D'Arcy; but whin ye smile, I think it's yer father stands *forenint** me.'

'I wish to God he was alive now!' observed the young man earnestly; 'he could advise me.'

'He was always a fine hand at that,' said the servant. 'A mighty fine hand he was at the talking always; but, poor dear gentleman, he never practised what he *praiched*. Many's the time I've heard him tell that same Murphy's father, that wont let yer honour have the horse, " Remimber, Mike, to keep out of DEBT; for wherever there's debt, there's DANGER."'

* Opposite.

'Agh!' said the young squire; 'so he really refused you the horse, did he?'

'Bedad! he did, sir.'

'Lanty, did you say anything to him about a bill at four or six months?'

'Plase your honour I did.'

'And what did the rascal say to that?'

'Plase ye, Masther D'Arcy, he said it was no good, for the last you gave him has been renewed six times, and the horse is all he has to depind on for his rint.'

'He lies!' exclaimed the young squire rising; 'it was only renewed three—no, four times.'

The old servant shook his head.

'I tell you, Lanty, it was but four times. Look—once, of course.'

'Ov coorse, that's only in raison,' observed Lanty.

'Well, the second time was when that infernal scoundrel the wine-merchant made me pay for the pipe of claret that was drunk before I was born.'

'A vagabon thrick; for sure him and his brother and his wife and childre had always three months' pleasure anyway for intherest (though it was always added on to every fresh acciptance), and the run of the house, and shooting and fishing in the *presarves*, which, God be good to yer honour's father! war *common* to the counthry as long as they gave fair play and liberty to the foxes. Oh but those war the times, whin the brush was dipped in claret, and the young sportsmen baptised before you could say Jack Robinson!—anyway, he was the heart's blood of a scoundrel, to put an ould friend's son to throuble for sich a thrifle.'

'Well, that was twice,' said the squire, when Lanty had brought his reminiscence to a close. 'A third time'——

'Whin yer honour was in keeping,' said the old servant, seeing his master at fault.

'Ay, I remember that; that was decent of Murphy, for I was in trouble then, and he would not press me. I should have remembered *that*, Lanty,' added the young squire, with one of those just impulses which spring up in every human breast; it may be to be instantly uprooted, or it may be to flourish. But with such as D'Arcy O'Rourke, the most common end is suffocation, from the pressure of other impulses of a more agreeable kind. 'I should have remembered that, Lanty,' he repeated; 'and when I did not, you should have told me of it.'

'Plase yer honour, it's hard to get spaking with ye; whin throuble's plinty, why, thin, ye toss it away, though the best way is to look into it. *A bit of common paper often thickens into a parchment for want of attintion.*'

'Well said, old boy. The fourth time'——

'The fourth time ye pledged yer honour ye'd take it up that day three months!'

The colour deepened on the young man's cheek. 'Well, well; there, never mind; I suppose, as usual, *he* is right and *I* am wrong.'

'The fifth time, Masther D'Arcy,' persisted the old servant, heedless of his master's peevishness—'the fifth time, ye may remimber, ye had the money ready, but *you broke into it* to save James Sturgon of the Forge from ruin. Don't you *mind ?**—his wife and the childre war turned out, and the things begun *canting*,† whin you saved them; and sure the hape of blessings you got for that same through the counthry has reached the heavens long ago. Even Murphy himself said, "Well, Masther D'Arcy has the heart of an Irish king in his bussum anyway, though he did take *my* money to do it with."'

'His money! What did the fellow mean by that!'

'Why,' answered Lanty with Irish sophistry, 'he had but yer bills, sir, till the *fifth*, but *thin* he had yer honour.'

'I tell you what,' said the squire, with the sad and most pernicious principle which the dangerous wit of a Sheridan stamped into an English saying—'I tell you what, Justice is a hobbling beldame, which, for the life of me, I cannot get to keep pace with Generosity.'

'More's the pity,' said Lanty, not understanding fully his master's meaning—'more's the pity, for Murphy had *depinded* that turn entirely upon yer honour, *and has never been the man he was since,* which is the raison of his refusing the horse. And by the same token the sixth time he was disappointed, his mother and wife war down in the fever, and '——

'Lanty,' interrupted the young man almost fiercely—'Lanty, you are an old fool, and say things on purpose to torture me. Haven't I enough without *that?* Have I ever a pound in my pocket? Do I ever know when I may or may not be arrested! Ah!' he added, clenching his teeth, and striking the table with his fist, while the words hissed from between his lips—'ah! do I not know, that if some sudden mercy does not take me out of the world, and quickly too—if I do not break my neck, or die by the bullet of a—a—a—*friend*, I shall rot in a jail! And *that* would be better than living as I do—in debt and danger!'

'My poor boy,' muttered the old servant, 'my own fine darlint.' Then, in a louder tone, he added, 'My darlint young gentleman, you take this more to the heart than you ought. Sure yer grandfather, and great-grandfather, to say nothing of yer father, war always in the height of throuble; but from all we heard, they did not *take on* like yer honour. Why, whinever the sheriff rode

* Remember.   † 'Cant,' Irish—*auction.*

down to O'Rourke's for to see after an execution, it's the height of good usage he'd get, till he was made *blind drunk*, and then *spirited* away until the assizes war over.'

Young O'Rourke smiled.

'You're showing yer beautiful teeth at my *bothering* the lawwords, as yer honour's pro-gen-ni-tors and ancestors bothered the law,' continued the old servant; 'but they managed to get the betther of it, or keep it aisy. And when they didn't, why, they had plinty of divarshin to keep the throuble off.'

'Rather to fix it on,' observed the young squire musingly. 'Surely, if they had been provident, commonly careful over an estate, which, according to the old saying, an eagle's eye could not compass, though she looked from the highest mountain in Ireland—had they been commonly careful, I should not now be as I am.'

'Maybe not just now,' said the old retainer. 'But ye see, Masther D'Arcy, they never denied themselves any humour they had.'

'More shame for them,' observed the almost landless heir.

'Thin, masther, honey,' said the servant, once more getting beyond his master's reach, 'just put the horse out of yer head, and begin at the denying, for the other plan, somehow, doesn't thrive.'

'You old ——— ! But, no; Lanty, come out of yer hole, my old friend. The spirit is down in me to-day, Lanty Lurgan; and any man might insult me who pleased.'

'Thin, by St Patrick!' exclaimed the servant with true Irish zest, 'I'll knock Murphy's brains out, and take the horse for yer honour.'

This violent outbreak and strong language roused the squire into a hearty laugh; but the boisterous mirth soon subsided, as it does—or more frequently changes into bitterness—when we have assisted at the formation of our own troubles.

A massive table of carved oak, that would have driven half the curiosity venders and collectors mad, was covered, or rather heaped, with parchments, dog-collars, writs, new snaffle-bits, account-books, whips, spurs, letters opened and unopened, and various specimens of minerals. The pictures were covered with dust, as indeed was everything in the room, and spiders mingled their tracery with the rich mouldings of the ceiling. The young man sat in the chair which his ancestors had filled for many generations; and as if to render his position easy, as contrasted with the state of his mind, he put one foot upon one side of the grate, and the other on the other, and looked into the mouldering cavities where the fire had been. There is no one object that conjures up so much misery to my fancy as the remnants of the once blazing fire, round which, on the previous night, gay faces had assembled. There lay the dark, grim masses, ruins of a mimic Hecla, frowning over the white and crumbling ashes that every breath of wind scatters round the cheerless chamber, even as man's hopes and speculations are dispersed—we know not how. It is easy enough to nurse real sorrow or sad imaginings by such a scene: the glare, the warmth, is gone; the mysterious power (dwelling within the bowels of the earth upon which we tread, applied by the ingenuity of ingenious man to his own purpose) is quenched; but like all revolutions, all changes, whether great or small, there is something from which the giant THOUGHT can spring—though it would be difficult to say whether D'Arcy *thought* or *mused*. All who observe the action of the mind have observed the difference. It was evident to his old servant that his young master endured much mental trouble, for he changed colour repeatedly; his lips quivered, and his fingers closed more than once convulsively upon the palms of his hands.

Lanty Lurgan was one of a class of Irish servants who, however privileged, never intrude. He could not bear to leave his young master, as he would himself have expressed it, 'alone wid the throuble,' but he had too much good taste to appear to watch his excitement; he therefore busied himself at the 'far corner,' 'settling a place for the pet pups, the craythurs, that would be more natural in the kennel, only *it's fallen in*.' And addressing a long confidential and apparently interesting conversation to their mother, an aged but beautiful long-eared spaniel called 'Chloe,' which, having had the luck to lose one eye, was entirely consigned to her maternal duties, ever and anon both servant and spaniel directed a sidelong glance towards their master, and then, as if by mutual consent, looked at each other. At last, having taken up and examined each pup half-a-dozen times at least, Lanty betook himself to a deep bay window, his privileged seat time out of mind; for Lanty was a little lame, and had been by common consent the right hand of three generations; he was therefore, I say, *privileged;* so down he sat, took 'the Farriers' Friend' out of the pocket of his blue frieze coat; the round spectacles without ends, which he first wiped with his cotton handkerchief, and then *polished* on his sleeve, were next extracted from between the leaves; his little greenish wig pulled carefully over his grizzled hair; and thus 'settled,' he held his book open on his raised knee, having crossed one leg over the other for the purpose. To say Lanty read would be untrue; he could spell over words, and knew 'the Farriers' Friend' from beginning to end, it had been so often read to him. But in the present instance he did not even attempt to read; the book was certainly before him, but his eyes looked *over* his spectacles, and *at* his young master. The room and its occupants would have formed a mournful picture. There was the singularly handsome noble-looking man, seeming to all appearance more young than he really was, bowed down by the pressure of circumstances which he had then no means to alter, and which he had assisted in accumulating, without thinking of consequences, that now weighed him to the very earth. His fine features were shaded by his hand from that light which he did not wish to witness his struggles, and yet their action was sufficiently marked by the convulsive efforts he made to restrain his feelings, which, though evanescent, were powerful in the extreme. The chamber, with its mingled furniture of the shreds and patches of old nobility, and the positive misery of the present, was in itself sadness; and the old servant, lingering like the last leaf of autumn on a blasted tree, was another link to bind the heart to the sufferer, whose misfortunes originated in the errors of his ancestors. Stung by some sudden remembrance more bitter than the last, D'Arcy sprang to his feet, and encountered the gaze of his humble friend.

'And you too—you watching me! I suppose you are bribed by my *good friend* the *sheriff*, or my kind friend Mr Driscoll the attorney, or by Jack Mullins the dog-man, or the jockey of Ferns, Benjy Roden, or'—— Then, with a fearful oath, he added, 'But I'll be watched by none of you, Mister Lanty Lurgan; you shall not win your pocket full of silver, and your bottle full of whisky, by *watching*, and then betraying me. I'll betray myself; I'll give myself up at once, and let the fag end of what was once the principality of the D'Arcy and the O'Rourke go to —— for ought I care. Only mind this, old man, I'll not be watched.' While D'Arcy paced the room, Lanty, letting the book fall to the ground, stood up as firmly as his lameness would permit, and, almost petrified, gazed more intently than before upon his master, repeating, as a consolation to himself, under his breath, 'He doesn't mane it, he didn't mane it; sure I know that he doesn't mane it.'

'What are you muttering for?' stormed the impetuous young man again. 'I tell you I wont be watched. I—tell—you—I—wont—be—watched. Do you hear?'

'God knows I do, Masther D'Arcy; but how can I help it? Didn't I watch yer father from the first minute he made a *horse* of the big *dog* Bran, until I shouted for his coming of age, and joined the cry at his funeral? And didn't I watch you, God bless you! though you have scalded the heart in the ould man's breast with raw and bitther words?—didn't I watch you in long-clothes, and out of long-clothes? Didn't I button on yer first jacket?—tache ye to load a pistol?—and drink a glass of whisky, before ye war ten years ould, to the face of the Lord-Lieftenant whin he paid yer honour's father the visit—and didn't his lordship say he never see the like of it before? Didn't I go with ye to college, for fear you wouldn't be comfortable? Have I ever left you, by day or night, sleeping or waking? Oh! Masther D'Arcy, haven't I been thrue to ye?—to be sure, I could not help *that*—and been fond of ye?—but I could not help *that* either! Ye may kill your poor ould slave if you like, Masther D'Arcy, honey; but I can't help watching you—I can't indeed. Wife and childre, and all, is gone from me off the face of the earth—all, but the *mighty* blessing, the masther's son. While there's light in my eyes, it will settle on you, Masther D'Arcy; and for no harm, sir—for no harm.' The old man's voice faltered, and he turned to the window weeping. In an instant the rapid current of his young master's feelings turned. Lanty felt the pressure of his hand upon his shoulder, and looked up; there was moisture in his large blue eyes.

'Lanty, forgive me—forgive me. I did not mean it; you can forgive me, can you not? I have no one to speak to here now—no one who understands me; it seems to do me good to vent my feelings—it relieves my heart. If I could only give some of those law fellows a—a—good thrashing, I should be as happy and cheerful as a prince! that I should; but it is cowardly to vent my humours on you.'

'I'd not hear yer inimy say that,' said the old servant smiling; 'but abuse me to dirt, masther, honey, *if it aises yer heart.* I'd stand a bating too, sir, if it would do you any good. What else are ould bones like mine fit for?'

'No more of this, Lanty,' answered his young master. 'I am the wayward son of a wayward race, whose race is almost run. I despise myself, and am despised by others.'

'You are not,' said Lanty.

'No one in the country would give me credit.'

'Oh, that's another thing,' said Lanty; 'but they'd all give yer honour a *welcome.*'

'Old Ireland always gives that.'

'Thrue for yer honour; and whin this present debt and danger is got rid of, things will go on well again.'

'Look at that table,' answered the young man; 'there are debts there that would swallow up half-a-dozen estates like mine.'

'The devil choke 'em!' ejaculated the old servant. Then added, 'And all the fine lawyers, sir, whose selves and opinions we had down here together, whin they ate the last sheep we had, to say nothing'——

'Bah!' interrupted D'Arcy; 'of course they have as many doubles as lawyers could have. But the end is come!'

Lanty had so often heard the son, father, and grandfather say this, that he did not exactly believe it. The country had cried out at intervals that the D'Arcy O'Rourkes were ruined during the last forty years; and so the old man wished to hope in spite of hope, and only said, 'I'm sure, thin, yer honour would die game—keep the bailiffs off to the last!'

'I don't know :—only this, Lanty; it was very bad of me to give a thought to Murphy's horse; I *hate* myself for it. I only wanted it, and, as usual, did not think; and that plan of long credit is always uppermost in a young fellow's mind, when *once he gets used to it:* it's our ruin—CURSE IT! So tell him to keep his horse; and that I hope, when he sells it, he will take ready money, and nothing else. When I look back at the things I have done, the meannesses I have been guilty of, to prop not so much a sinking credit, but an extravagant habit, I feel as if I could shoot myself, or any man who did the same.'

'Eah, bother! what would become of the great families thin!' exclaimed Lanty. 'Sorry a gintleman but knows the *smell* of debt some time or other.'

'And danger!' sighed his master. 'But send Lennard up to me. If I had turned as steadily to these papers when I came of age, three years ago, as I do now! Well—well—send Lennard up; one step towards a new system, Lanty. I *don't want* the horse!—ah!' And then he muttered, as Lanty departed, 'But why should I bother about them *now?* I have nothing to save—all is lost! *Debt and danger!* it was the death-wail of my poor mother —I have nothing to save!'

Opposite to where D'Arcy O'Rourke sat was hung one of those old carved glasses, wreathed around with flowers, Cupids, and bows. Dusty though it was, he could see his own reflection in the spotted and worn surface: there was the high, brave, manly brow, the bright blue eye, the noble form in God's own image; the aspect and bearing of one who, if not born to fortune, could achieve it. Some sudden thought, God's own direct messenger from heaven, struck him at that moment, and he gazed earnestly upon himself. The resolve was made and taken; whether it was kept, the future will tell. This passage occurred in the life of D'Arcy O'Rourke some thirty years now past.

* * * *

The cabin of Phelim Murphy, or, as he would have it called, the *house* of Phelim Murphy, was well built and comfortable for a house of its class. His youngest daughter was engaged in preparing a supper consisting of the usual potful of potatoes, which was slung on the iron crane that found refuge in the huge cavity of the chimney, so as to be on one side of the fire; while over the burning embers was a broad iron griddle, upon which a large thick oaten cake was browning. Moreover, a tea-kettle simmered opposite the potatoes, and the presence of 'the chaney' on a small table would have told any one acquainted with Phelim Murphy's *menáge*, that he and his wife and daughter had gone to market in the neighbouring town that morning, and were expected home to supper in a very short time.

Kathleen, the second daughter, had taken unusual pains with the arrangements; the 'far table' was made ready for the two farm-servants and her brother, but the '*little* table' was prepared for the absent ones, who had doubtless undergone much fatigue. Kathleen having done all that was necessary, sat down on 'the settle,' upon which the old house-dog curled himself round her feet, and she began to hum over an old tune to the metre of a new ballad, until the repose of the room, which would have been stillness itself but for the hissing of the kettle and the chirping of the crickets, lulled her to sleep—the ready sweet repose purchased by labour and an untroubled spirit. Kathleen would, I dare to say, have slept on until her parents' return, had she not been roused from her slumbers by a sharp growl from her friend and companion 'Gruff,' and suddenly starting, she saw Lanty Lurgan, staff in hand, standing before her.

'Oh, Daddy Lanty, how you did frighten me!' she exclaimed. 'Oh how could you? And, my gracious me! if there isn't the cake burnt as black as my Sunday shoe, and the kittle singing away as if nothing had happened! Well!—my! if ever I go to sleep, something bad comes over the house at onct, so there does. But,' she continued, looking into the old man's face—'but Daddy Lanty, what ails ye?—what's on ye, daddy dear? Sit down, sir. And, stay; take a drop of mother's cordial. What's with ye at all at all, daddy?'

The old man gulped down 'the mother's cordial,' whatever it might be, that the kind girl offered, and staggered rather than walked to the settle. 'What's keeping yer father, Kathleen?' he inquired.

'Sorra a bit of me can tell,' answered Kathleen. 'If they had come home whin they said they would, the cake wouldn't have gone to the bad, for he had this griddle mended, and wouldn't let mother get a new one at the big shop till he could pay down for it. I wish he *was* come though, for you seem in throuble, daddy, and I don't like that. Whin did ye hear of the young masther, sir?' she added, coming close up to him; 'and indeed, though you war angry about the horse, sure it's what father could not help. We never can let Mr D'Arcy's throuble out of our mind whin we see the notice for the sale of the lands, and all, posted up on the chapel gate last Sunday was a month. I thought the life would have left my mother; and father, though he never spoke a word, had *heart* sorrow on its account, and could not bear to go near the house, only little Tommy (oh, Daddy Lanty, that *is* the bouldest devil of a child that ever broke a sister's heart with his conthrary ways!)—well, he went off afther flowers or something among the woods, and meets the young masther. Sure he'd threatened to send the dogs afther him many a time, but now he stooped down, poor dear gentleman, and patted his head, and gave him a silver shilling. "Take it," he says, "for ye're the child of an honest man;" and whin Tommy danced home, flourishing his stick and shouting like mad, " Hurra for the O'Rourkes, the ould kings of the counthry for ever!" and tould father, father laid his head down on the table, and I know he cried like a child. But Phelim Crane was here, and says that though the young masther has give up everything, even to the watch in his pocket, he says if he was caught, he could be took and put in the jail—the devil raze it!—on account of one vagabond that has no heart in his breast. Now, Lanty, is that thrue?'

The old man said it was.

'Then thank God he's out of the counthry, though father does lose; but he wouldn't go forward with his claim at the latter end, *and many did the same, hoping the property would hould out to pay the large ones, and the masther get free.* Oh, Lanty! father sets the rights of things so before us, that though Mrs Myers has offered me credit for the pink gingham, and I haven't a *tack* to my back, I wont take it, because of the debt and danger! And, Lanty, I hope the masther did not lave the counthry in anger on account of the horse father refused him; that often is on *my* mind, Lanty, though no one thinks anything is ever the matter with me, I'm so happy. Sure, whin I get the makings of a frock of that gingham, there wont be a happier colleen on Ireland's ground than myself.'

'Poor child! poor child!' sighed the old man; and she could have echoed 'Poor Lanty!'—for when her volubility was somewhat exhausted, and she looked and thought of the change which a few weeks had wrought in his appearance, her large gray eyes filled with tears; and the desire to relieve the sufferings of others, which is as common to the Irish peasant as the air they breathe, came upon Kathleen, and she overwhelmed the old man with questions of ' What will you have?—another drop of mother's cordial, or a tumbler of father's *stiff* whisky punch? Or, sure, Daddy Lanty, I'll wet the *tay* for ye; and the cake is so nice and hot with a bit of fresh butter.' Then, in utter despair at the various shakes of the head that were given in reply to her questions, Kathleen clasped her hands together and exclaimed, 'Thin, oh my grief! is there nothing I can do for ye, Daddy Lanty, jewel, and ye looking so pale and poorly?'

'Nothing, Kathleen, only thank ye kindly. And sure the good man himself will be home in a few minutes anyway, and it's wanting him I am.'

'And the masther, Lanty?' she inquired, lowering her voice; 'have you heard nothing from him?'

'*From him?*' repeated the old man. 'No, nothing.'

'To think of the likes of him being forced to fly the counthry through debt and danger!' ejaculated Kathleen earnestly. 'But it's well it's no worse—if he was caught! Only think of his being put in a prison, like a bird in a cage!—it would break my heart, so it would!'

'God bless you for that word!' said the old man.

'Father *murns* greatly for him,' continued the little maid; 'but he says it's a great lesson to the counthry. And the other day, on the side of the mountain, where they war quarrying stones, my brother set on my father about a venture he meant to get up, and for which he could have borrowed the money aisy. So my father made no answer until he took him up to the very top of the mountain, and then looking far over and away, he asked him to whom the bog and river and land belonged a hundred years ago; and he made answer, to the O'Rourkes and D'Arcys, who married into one; and then he pointed to where the wood had stood, and asked how it had been all levelled, and the birds that inherited it of the Almighty forced to fly *along with the four winds of heaven* to seek another home; and he said it was because of the debts gathered over it: and my father asked again who had the lands now, and my brother said, the stranger and the cunning man. "Ay," went on my father, "and the *money lender;* the *borrower* is banished from the face of the earth," says my father, "but the *lender* is established in his stead. We'll go on as we are," says my father, "not spending all we earn, but laying by all we can, and then putting out *our own* honestly. I well know the danger of debt, and the debt of danger. We'll learn to do without what we can't pay for, and give God thanks we don't owe the value of a brass farthing through the counthry." My father has a saying,' continued the pretty chatterer, 'that debt is like a grain of mustard seed, that springs into a great tree.'

'He's a wise man,' muttered Lanty, who was too much of the old school fully to value the wholesome doctrine—which, moreover, was given at an injudicious time. 'He's a wise man with a bigger head on his shoulders than a heart in his bussum, and that's what I don't like.'

'That's not thrue all out,' hastily replied Kathleen. 'My father's head and heart are much of a size, thank God, and that's the blessing! And sure, if he could have sarved the young master he would.'

'Ay, ay, when sarvice is not needed; there's many say that,' muttered the old servant.

'I don't know what's come to ye,' exclaimed the girl, bursting into tears; 'but I'd take the bit out of my own mouth to give to him, and so would all my people, Lanty, in spite of yer bad words.'

'Would you though?' said Lanty. '*Do it then;* the young heart is not *desateful* like the ould. The masther isn't fled the counthry; Kathleen, *he could not fly;* he was seized with the sickness, and I hid him away from the vagabones that would have laid him in his grave before this, if they had had their way. He was so beleaguered, he could not get off. But, *avourneen,* you'd pity him from yer heart. The spirit is so high in him, that he'd die before he'd let any one—I mane any of his own sort— know where he is, or how he is: and he's wanting the little nourishments, which, God help us, his mother, and grandmother, and great-grandmother, and every mother he ever had in the world, bestowed upon all belonging to them in the counthry. *Sure they ever and always considered the poor their own people.* Yet he's made a resolution not to go on trust for anything; though we're expecting money every day from an uncle he has, that's a general in foreign service, to get him out of the counthry whin the suspicion is over, and the coast clear, and he able: and, Kathleen, what I wanted to tell yer father was, that I'm afeard his bitther foe, Jack Cronan of Limerick, suspects he's not gone, from seeing me about, and is watching me when I go up towards the Black Abbey. Now, though yer father's hard, he's honest; and as the poor masther never settled that ould thrifle of a bill about the last horses and things, that was renewed so often, why, those mane-hearted vagabones would think he was like themselves, and never suspect he was doing Masther D'Arcy a good turn. So I was thinking that you, I mane yer father, would maybe'——

'Take him all we have on our bare knees, watch him, and *tind* him, and save him, and get him out of the hands of his inimies at last, God be praised!' exclaimed the generous-hearted girl. 'Oh, Lanty, I'll forgive you all you said. To be sure we'll put a blind on the law; and sure enough it's my father will manage everything, and you only did him justice. But you said something about his wanting; shall I take him *mother's cordial*, and the *tay*, and the cake, and everything in the house at onct! No one would suspect *me*, you know, Lanty; only, in God's name, where in the Black Abbey could you have put him away?'

'I'll give you the tokens, *avourneen*, whin yer father comes in; I could have got what he wanted, only for the waywardness he shows. And, besides, I *know I'm watched.*'

Not many minutes after this disclosure, the farmer, his wife, and eldest daughter returned; and it would have been a lesson worth remembering to those who argue on the selfishness of human nature, to have witnessed the zeal displayed by those humble but warm-hearted people in the cause of one who had injured them, but whose injuries were forgotten the moment his real situation was known. This is no fable, invented by the author to bear out a theory. I have known innumerable instances where, stimulated partly by the clannish feeling towards their landlords, and partly by the natural generosity of their characters, the peasant-Irish have completely sacrificed themselves to benefit those who had injured them in a *pecuniary point of view—which is the last injury they would dream of resenting.* In Ireland, they do not value money as we do in England, and his want of punctuality in the discharge of pecuniary engagements is injurious to himself and to all with whom he is connected. But Murphy's conduct was the more noble, because his habits had been at variance with those of his landlord.

'I thought you'd do the right thing,' said old Lanty, while tears trickled down his cheeks. 'There are many have the heart as good towards the masther, and maybe *softer;* but there's none have so much sinse.'

It was arranged that Lanty should lie by for a couple of days, and that either Murphy or his daughters should convey what was necessary to the Black Abbey for the poor sufferer.

The country had not yet done talking of his imprudence, misfortunes, and rapid disappearance from amongst them. They could understand his extravagance and carelessness; but if they had known, they could hardly have comprehended, the sensitiveness and pride that would, independently of the circumstances which left no alternative between voluntary or jail confinement, have compelled D'Arcy to hide what he considered a dishonoured head in the depths of the grave, sooner than have it seen by his old associates. The storm had been even more desperate than he anticipated; and agitation brought on fever, which his humble friend had truly designated as '*the* sickness.' To the services of poor old Lanty D'Arcy O'Rourke had an undoubted right; but he saw his old friend sinking under exertions which were likely to destroy him rapidly. The only thing those of his obdurate creditors could obtain by detaining him in prison was revenge; and this, as I *have* said, for debt, found no echo in the generality of Irish hearts. Many were the instructions Lanty gave Murphy as to what he was to say and do when he visited 'the masther:' that night his directions were particular indeed: one thing only he did not feel it necessary to recommend—perfect silence; he knew they would die sooner than betray their trust.

That night Murphy took down his gun, and being amply provided with all things necessary, which his wife and daughters prepared with unusual care, departed on his mission. The good woman would not call her husband back for fear of 'turning his luck,' but she ran after to whisper in his ear 'that he was to remimber it was one of the *rale* ould stock he was going to, and to be very particular in his manners, especially *now,* as the dear gintleman was in sore throuble.' This was in unison with the farmer's own opinion, and he was somewhat offended at the caution which his own generous feelings, clad in coarser garments, told him was unnecessary.

Many visions floated before him as he climbed the rocky acclivity leading to the Black Abbey. The footpath was wild and tangled. First of all he had to ford through a portion of that peculiarly Irish morass that adheres to the mountain side, then to spring from crag to crag, until having attained the highest point commanding a view of the ivied ruins, which lay peacefully in a little dell sunk between two hills, he paused to consider what he should say. Murphy's salutation to friend or foe, to superior or inferior, would have been ready without thought, but D'Arcy was a combination of all at once. The national fealty to his landlord that had been, was combated with the severe loss and degradation he had endured from his reckless habits and broken promises. D'Arcy was vastly his superior in birth and education, but the upright and honest spirit, the firm purpose and taintless word of a freeborn man, assured the brave tiller of the soil that those high moral qualities elevate the peasant, while their abuse degrades the peer. He stood alone under the canopy of heaven; the pale stars were 'dreaming their path through the sky,' the rabbits were gambolling in the moonlight, and the hoot of the owl ascended from the little valley, mingled with the honest bark of the distant dog. Murphy paused to consider what he should say. He knew what the ardent and fiery temper of the young man had been, and he had a shrewd suspicion that it would rebel against, not yield to, circumstances. He almost wished he had suffered his wife to come; she would certainly do nothing wrong. While these ideas were passing through his mind with what may well be called the 'rapidity of thought,' he fancied he heard some one breathing near him, and turning suddenly round, he saw the shadow of a man reflected on an opposite rock. He called out 'Who goes there?' and seeing the shadow retreat, levelled his musket, declaring he would fire if there was no reply. It advanced, and the next moment Murphy saw it was the very person old Lanty had named as being on the watch for him. After the recognition had taken place, Cronan asked what brought him on the mountain, which Murphy answered in the true Irish fashion by asking another question, what brought him there? and Cronan, in reply, thinking he had secured an ally, told him his suspicions, that, instead of having fled the country, he really believed the young squire was 'on his keeping' somewhere, for he had certainly observed Lanty 'prowling' where he never prowled before: he declared his intention of watching while he had a leg to stand on, and having his revenge at the last. Murphy knew well that expostulation would be vain, and contradiction worse.

'Indeed!' he answered; 'well, ould Lanty has been on the prowl, like, but more like an ould bird whose young has desarted the nest than anything else. I'm going to the ould abbey with some things my wife has prepared for a poor craythur that's lying in the fever there like a dog in a ditch.'

'Cross o' Criest about us!' exclaimed Cronan, blessing himself hastily; 'you don't mean that you are going down to the abbey with things—walking straight into the jaws of death! Surely it's not mad you are?'

'Oh, I've a charm against it,' answered Murphy laughing; 'that's what I have. If you've any idea of Mr O'Rourke's being on "his keeping" here, you'd better come down with me and see.'

'May the holy saints be about me!' answered the other; 'I've been through every inch of the place alone this evening, and could not see a thing but the bat, the beetle, and crawling craythurs. I'm sure you must be out in saying any living thing is there, barring such-like, for I walked it through and through.'

'War you in it yesterday?' inquired Murphy.

'No,' said Cronan; 'I was not; for I had no suspicion of what I told you till yesterday, and I don't like having any call to such places. But, God bless us! sure even to nab him, I'd not go near *the sickness*, and it so mortal bad through the counthry.'

'Well, the poor craythur my woman had the pity on was there yesterday anyhow, Mr Cronan; and you may depind on it, if she wasn't alive there to-day, she's lying dead among the bones, or briers, or fallen into some half grave.'

'Don't go on! don't go on!' ejaculated the coward, trembling. 'I tell you there's nothing living there; and sure afther death it's more taking than before. Don't go on!'

'Oh, I'd have no business home without knowing the rights of it,' persisted Murphy; 'and if you think at all about the young squire'——

'To the devil with him!' he exclaimed. '' I've caught my death maybe, as well as lost my money, through him and his. May the heavy and bitther curse of'—— Bang went Murphy's gun ere the curse could be pronounced. 'You'd frighten the soul out of any one!' said the man. 'What did you fire for?'

'To waste my powder, it appears,' replied the farmer, calmly reloading, 'for I've missed the rabbit.'

'Good-night,' said the other, hastening off in an opposite direction. 'You've no sinse to thrust yourself into the jaws of death, as I tould you before. I'll go see afther ould Lanty, for I suppose he'll be on the right tack. I traced him twice in this direction, and thought it must be here—but it couldn't. I wish I could hinder ye from going. Well, good-night.'

'I stopt the curse that time anyhow,' thought the farmer, as he observed the man's receding figure. 'I'm glad I stopt the curse! I hate curses; they hang over the innocent like a raven over a lamb, and are heavy and bitther above the guilty. But I can hardly blame him; he credited beyant his strength—credited in depindence, and was desaved: it's hard to bear. But the suffering brought by such as the poor squire is often worst where it's not seen, and makes no noise. A gentleman breaks his word with a poor tradesman, the poor tradesman cannot keep *his* with those who supply him with leather, or cloth, or groceries, or let it be what it may: he is charged more and more for everything he wants—he cannot sell as others do, who have ready money or unsoiled credit to go to market with—he grows dispirited, and thinks, work as he may, he cannot keep his head above water— he sinks and sinks, ruined, to his grave, amid a starving family— and all through the want of forethought or punctuality on the part of the gintry, who little imagine that the five pound or three pound to the poor man who humbly asks for his "little bill," is of more consequence to *him* than if a rich trader dunned boldly for so many hundreds. I wonder are great folks as thoughtless in every country?' he said aloud, while proceeding to his destination; 'I hope not. Anyhow, I knew he'd run ten mile from *the sickness*. He's fairly off now, and I am free. Ay, let him go watch ould Lanty, who is *'cute* enough to send him on a wrong scent.'

Lanty had secreted his master in a small square underground chamber, not exactly a vault, nor yet a room; the air was admitted through a loophole at one side, on a level with the roof; it had been used formerly as a sort of restingplace for those who carried the coffins of the O'Rourkes to their last home; and two large stones, that occupied the whole of one side, marked the entrance to the vault of D'Arcy's ancestors. It had been inhabited for many years by a 'holy man,' who, after performing his penance of fasts and seclusion, disappeared from the country altogether about a year before the young squire's ruin. The entrance was then closed, as a child playing about the abbey had fallen in, and been seriously injured. The very existence of such a place of refuge was unknown to Cronan, who, be it remembered, was not an inhabitant of the neighbourhood.

When Murphy entered, he could only discover at first a heap of old tapestry laid along three high-backed chairs, which Lanty had so arranged, as to form a sort of couch for the sufferer; and the words, 'At last, at last you are come!' were succeeded by a feeble movement; and while Murphy struck a light by the aid of his gun-flint, D'Arcy managed to raise himself on one elbow, and gaze wildly on his visitor, whom he now perceived was not Lanty.

'Don't come near me!' he exclaimed—'don't come near me! I know you now; but I'll never be taken alive; I've sworn it. I have lain all day watching these stones, and wondering if they would open for me. But don't come near me, Murphy. I suppose you *rode* here, eh? Well, some have horses, but others have none—but others have none!' he repeated wildly; while the farmer, overpowered by the sight, as he afterwards said, 'of the brave flower of the counthry cut down and blasted,' stood perfectly powerless opposite to him, the candle flaring against the walls, and giving just sufficient light to enable D'Arcy, when a little more cool, to observe the mingling of agony and pity depicted in his face, while tears coursed each other rapidly down his manly checks. The young squire then became alarmed for Lanty, and eagerly inquired if he had caught the fever, which gave Murphy an opportunity of explaining all in a few words. At first the young man was silent; but true generosity is infectious; it is a sort of signal-light, which, when lit up in one bosom, will communicate to the next, without any seeming contact. And weak as an infant from disease, faint for want of sustenance, utterly and completely exhausted, the last of his race sobbed like a sick baby on the shoulder of the kind-hearted Murphy. 'I wish it was my wife was in it,' said the farmer; 'I'm mighty unhandy about yer honour, so I am; and sure she shall come and tind yer honour, if you will let her.'

'Don't "honour" me, Murphy,' said D'Arcy sadly; 'I've no state left now.'

'Ough, what matter!' he answered; 'the state may go, but the honour lives in a man's own breast. I'd uphould it through the counthry, that it's *alive* there anyhow; *and, plase God, whin yer honour is out of the fangs of the fever, and the hands of yer inimies,* ye'll prove it. Give an honest man time to get through his throubles, and he'll prove he's honest—I'm sure of that.'

'God bless you, Murphy!—God bless you!' he murmured. It was astonishing how, in a couple of hours, Murphy improved the aspect of the place. Lanty had brought some old carpeting and matting there by stealth, which had been thrown away as valueless, and by it's aid the worthy farmer concealed the entrance to the vault, and managed to make a more comfortable couch. He kindled a fire, and contrived to keep it burning all night, despite the smoke, which, as the night was calm, escaped through the rugged entrance. The fire enabled him to supply his patient with warm tea during the watching hours. At times D'Arcy's mind wandered; but in general he was tolerably calm, though most anxious about his old servant. He talked to Murphy about the future, and his resolve to starve rather than go in debt—a resolution which the farmer declared would make a greater man of him than ever. And when the morning came, and Murphy was obliged to depart, the young squire experienced the benefit that is easier felt than explained, and which always succeeds a conversation with a person of strong mind, no matter how unlearned.

'I did not deserve this from you,' said D'Arcy; 'I did not think you would give it. Lanty knew you better than I did.'

'He had a betther right, sir, being one of ourselves. *It isn't the likes of you, in general, that understands the hearts of the poor.*

But sure, sir, dear, I have the honour of *sarving* you, and that's a rich reward for me.'

It is rarely that one of Murphy's countrymen is so right-judging, rarely that he would be able to separate the giving the horse on credit to the young squire from the personal service rendered gratuitously, but the straightforward honest man had, as he well said, his reward; and while I give him due praise for his warmth and wisdom, I must remember that D'Arcy endured much; for to accept most generous service from one he had injured, was deeply humiliating to the tried and wounded spirit. Proud also by inheritance—a pride that had been both trampled on and goaded—if D'Arcy O'Rourke had been of a common mind, he would have taken refuge in his pride, gathered himself up therein, as in a mantle, and cultivated the idea that being a lord of the soil gave him right over 'his people,' as I have heard them called, forgetting that the real law of landlord and tenant is an interchange of services, one having the gold coin which he exchanges for its value in silver, or it may be brass, yet still receiving the value. But D'Arcy's mind was not of a common or coarse order; he had persisted in the errors of his *caste* from habit, and a desire to keep up the dignity of his family, little dreaming that the man who runs in debt beyond his ability to pay, surrenders his peace of mind, and prostrates his dignity under the feet of his creditor. When awoke fully to a sense of his situation, his resolve was boldly and bravely taken; and though the nature of the cure was so severe that the patient might sink beneath its operation, still, if he survived, he did so in the genuine pride of conscious strength, in the enjoyment of that mental health which enables a man to look steadily forward to a given end, that end being HONOUR, the HONOUR of an honest man—the HONOUR from whose star a ray of glory expands on every side.

In the meantime, the report that 'a travelling woman was ill of the fever in the Black Abbey, and that Murphy of the hill and his wife were able to see afther her without danger, on account of the charrum,' was industriously circulated, and obtained easy belief in a credulous district. Lanty, though suffering from severe illness, like the poor bird in the story managed to decoy the intruder from the cherished nest, and had the satisfaction of knowing that Cronan believed 'the masther,' if still in the country, was secreted some five miles off. This was all they desired, except, indeed, the recovery of the poor sufferer, which the undeviating attention of Murphy and his family accelerated. To Mrs Murphy's great relief, she discovered on her first visit that the young man had not been suffering from *the sickness*, but from a fearful derangement of the nervous system, amounting almost to insanity—a nervous intermittent sort of fever. '"Brain sickness" is not catching anyhow!' she said joyfully to her husband. 'I'm thinking that first of all to have it, honey dear, people must have brain; and you know,' she added, smiling at her husband, 'none of the Murphys have enough to *let loose* for that.'

'Every kindness you show me,' said D'Arcy, when he was sufficiently recovered to move about his narrow chamber—'every kindness you show me is like a dagger in my heart. I did not deserve it.' He was always inquiring what was said of him throughout the country, and when it was likely he could leave it. It was interesting to observe what able tacticians both Murphy and his wife became, simply by the teaching of a kind heart. They let him know all that would be pleasant for him to hear, and avoided all that was contrary. At last they took advantage of the darkness of a summer night, and removed him to their own cottage, where the change of air and the additional comforts tended greatly to accelerate his recovery; but still he remained the shadow, the very shadow, of his former self—so worn, so weak, that he was literally unable to raise his cup of gruel to his own lips. They made his bed in 'the loft,' which was above the kitchen; and as the boards rested on the thick rafters, and there was no ceiling beneath, D'Arcy O'Rourke heard everything that was said in the house; and to poor Mrs Murphy it seemed as though illness had sharpened his perceptions, for sometimes the neighbours would talk what she did not wish him to hear.

'Did ye hear, Mrs Murphy, that the new people at the big house are going to pull down every cabin on the red slip near the cross-roads? Oh! the throuble must be heavy on the young squire, wherever he is, to think of the suffering he brought on the poor by not taking care of his own.' Or,

'Oh! dear, there's Tom Mulligan of the Forge gone altogether to the bad; he's fled the counthry, and they say his sickly wife, and the four grawls, must *take to the road*.* He was a thriving man in a small way, until the young squire gave him an order for the new iron gates, just whin he came of age; he thought *that* would make him, and *ran in debt for the iron*. Sure, like everything else, they were never paid for.' Or,

'Sad news this morning, Mrs Murphy, ma'am. Mrs Nowlan died last night; she was always mighty tinder about the heart, and her little way of business was destroyed through the goings on at the big house. People, who maybe only wanted an excuse, said they could not pay her, because the squire never paid them. But she's gone now anyhow.'

Mrs Murphy tried all she could to keep these babbling tongues in order. Sometimes she told them to 'spake aisy, for one of the girls was above on the bed sick.' Sometimes she dismissed a neighbour with the information that she 'had a power and all of

* Beg.

work to do;' but though her eldest daughter, and Kathleen, both exerted their ingenuity to the utmost to keep the house quiet, they could not always succeed; and if the subject had not been of such an agonizing nature, D'Arcy must have admired the stratagems put in requisition on his account.

This was bitter schooling. He knew perfectly well that he had inconvenienced and distressed the rich, but he had not imagined that the influence of his own and his family's imprudence had so injured the poor. Those who had heaped blessings on his head as he passed along, and whose faces he knew even as his own, the more gentle and unpretending their complaints were, the more he suffered.

'Ah! sure the poor gintleman could not help it; he'd have paid it if he had it, God help him!' Or,

'They say he's gone beyond seas. Well, betther luck to him wherever he goes. Sure the good drop was in him!—we know that. God break hard fortune before every one's child!' Or,

'Ah! it's not right of us to be so hard upon the poor young gintleman. What else could be expected from the way he was reared. *I'm sure, though we must eat our paytees dry this year through his manes,* I can forgive him; he did not mane it.'

D'Arcy O'Rourke had often inquired why Lanty did not come and see him, and not one of the kind people who laboured so earnestly to minister to his wants could tell him that Lanty was breathing out his last faithful breath in a neighbouring cottage. Various excuses were made, the principal being, that 'Sure he was watching the post for his honour, and when a letther came, he'd bring it'—or, 'He had hurt his foot with a splinter, and could not walk, and the people would be wondering if he was carried to the Murphys.' The old servant had outlived 'his people,' outlived all his affections, save the strongest and dearest. The poor creatures where he was taken ill made up a little bed for him in a shed—that is to say, they gave him their own, and slept themselves on loose straw, for *self has no place in the heart of an Irish peasant.* I remember once hearing a poor cabin-keeper address her son, who had been some time in Dublin, in the following words:—'It's *yerself* ye're thinking of, and I'm ashamed of ye—to deny the poor traveller yer bed! Who'll make *your* bed in heaven, I wonder, if ye don't give to the poor! I never thought I should have had such a son!' Lanty Lurgan's sole comfort during the last days of his existence arose from hearing daily, through the medium of the benevolent Murphys, that the young master was better.

'I know I'm going, Kathleen, *avourneen;* I know I am. If I could only see the letther from his uncle, and look on his sweet face onct more, I'd die aisy; for what's done can't be undone now. The letther will come under cover to me, *for a cloak*, you know; and sure enough if I'm not in the world to receive it, what will he do at all?'

'Don't bother yerself, Lanty, honey—don't; you'll be well enough by and by; ye'll go with the young masther away; keep up yer heart; maybe the letther will come to-day or to-morrow,' replied the weeping Kathleen.

'Yes, *avourneen*, yes; I will be well enough by and by—betther than ever, I know that, praise be to HIS holy name who provides a place where the poor are made rich, and the troubled comforted —I know that! But, Kathleen, though the trees know that the spring will bring them fresh flowers, they keep on the *ould* ones as long as they can—it's nature, child. I *know* I shall see him *hereafter*, but still I want to see him *here*—just onct. I remimber a poor ould setther of his father's, very ould entirely it was, and the baste had lost the use of its hind-legs, and we wanted to end it; but the young masther would not hear of it, and had the ould baste brought up to a little room he had off his own, and, to plase him, I used to tind ould Nero. And, "Lanty," he says to me one morning with his sunbame of a smile, "Lanty, whin ye're an ould man, I'll tind you, my boy, as you have tinded my father's poor dog," he says; and I says, "God bless you, Masther D'Arcy;" and I had hardly said the words, when the baste comes staggering out of the little room, dragging its poor legs afther it, and I saw the dart of death in its two eyes, and I wanted to put him back, but the young masther wouldn't, and the craythur dragged on to its feet, and the masther put down his hand to coax it, like; and Nero put out his ould tongue and licked his hand over and over for more than a minute, then turned up its head with a shiver, and died. And with that Masther D'Arcy took his own forehead betwixt his palms, and I saw the tears drop, drop, dropping on the dead dog. "Let me take it away, D'Arcy, honey," says I, forgetting to "masther" him, for my heart was full; but he would not—only turned the head and closed the eyes of the craythur, as if it was a Christian.

"Masther," says I, after a bit, "will you let me die that way whin my hour comes; and will you do as much for me as you've done for Nero?"

'And he grips me by the hand, and says, "Yes, Lanty, God knows I will, and more." "I only ax as much," I says.' And Lanty added, 'If I could have as much, I'd die happy.'

The next evening, when the Murphys were occupied as usual— some spinning, some knitting, and the men and boys looking to their cattle, or half asleep over the fire—a little child in the neighbourhood entered with the observation, 'There's one without wants ye, Mr Murphy, sur.' Murphy rose and followed his guide, and leaning against a tree that flanked the gable end of the house, was Lanty Lurgan, his greatcoat flung over his shoulders, and his white hair and unshorn beard glittering in the fading light. The good man exclaimed that his visitor was mad; but a smile was his only reply—a smile so grim and ghastly, that it made the farmer start; and then he drew forth a letter, and the words 'It's come at last; just let me see and give it him,' crept from between his lips. The farmer managed to employ or dismiss those not in the secret of D'Arcy's concealment, and then Lanty entered, without any assistance, beneath the hospitable roof.

'Oh, Daddy Lanty!' exclaimed Kathleen, flying towards him; and then, horrified at the expression of his countenance, so deathlike and wretched, she drew back, and observed to her sister, 'That sure there must be something about him not right, for he wint up the ladder to the loft with a noiseless step, and the look of a spirit.' The setting sun was throwing his farewell beams over the landscape, and a light of mingled yellow and red entered the loft through an opening the worthy farmer had 'pulled' in the thatch to admit air and sunshine to the invalid. D'Arcy was seated on his narrow bed reading, or seeming to read, and his countenance, though pale, wore the expression of one who, having gone through the worst, is resolved to exert himself for the best. On seeing Lanty, he started forward to receive him, and though judiciously apprised a few minutes before that the old and faithful servant was very ill, he was quite unprepared for the spectral appearance which, flinging off his hat, almost sank at his feet.

'It's come masther!—it's come!' he muttered, extending the letter to his master. 'Here it is; and *I* brought it, and seen you onct more—*and seen you onct more!* There's money in it, masther, honey, and the coast's clear now, and ye can get clean off, and be a great man. Sure yer young years have hardly blossomed yet! But, masther, honey, *avick!*—and they are a'most my last words—don't forget *ould Ireland*, though the throuble came on ye in it; and ye war too high in yerself to be among your equals, sure ye did not want a humble friend. I'm a'most gone—and the distinctions of life are a'most gone—and all I can say is, it isn't the jewels on the hand that gives the charity we look at, but the *hand itself*. Give me a drink, for God's sake!—I'm choking; and, masther, honey, open yer letter. Sure I've kept ye from doing so long enough! Let me see ye open it!' he continued, while his master's eyes were fixed upon him with an agonizing and intense gaze; 'do—let me see ye open it. Ah! the Lord be praised!—though my own eyes are dim, I see it now—I see it all now! It's me, the poor Lanty Lurgan, yer honour's thinking of, and not yerself—I see that. *Isn't* THAT *life to my heart!* Oh! my joy! Look! I've lived many a day in the height of it—the " debt and danger" I mane—until I thought I was used to it; but it broke the heart in me at last, even I, who was born in it—it's poisoned it is—it ended me; but you'll be out of its reach. I praise the Lord for that! and yet you wont, masther, *machree!*—the *body* will be, but not the *heart*, not the mind. Oh my God!' he added, clasping his withered fingers together until the bones rattled in the loose skin—'oh my God! to think that while so many is dashing, and spinding, and striving for masthery—to think that all that time they are only *haping curses on their own graves!*'

'Oh, Lanty! Lanty!' exclaimed D'Arcy; 'do *you*, too, reproach me?'

The old man started as from a dream, and sinking at his master's feet, clasped his knees, and while looking wildly with his glazed eyes in his face, answered, 'Me! is it I?—me? Oh! may the heavenly powers forgive a dying sinner! Me!—did I?—did I? —'twas a *drame*, maybe, I tould; it *could* be nothing else! It was a *drame*, I'm sure, masther—it was; but you'll forgive me. Reproach *you!* No, masther. Bless—bless—bless you! May all the powers of heaven and earth bless you, my own dear masther!'

D'Arcy, greatly moved, moved even to tears, hung over his faithful servant, and endeavoured to raise him; but in vain: he continued to grasp his knees with the grasp of a dying man.

'Bless you, Masther D'Arcy; open the letter—do, dear. I can't see you now; *there's a mist betwixt us*, but I see yer shadow. I'm here—I feel yer hot tears upon my cheek. Christ be praised, I've my wish! I'm like the ould masther's dog Nero. I'm dying —at—yer—feet—and you've cried—over—Lanty—the ould—dog of the family—and—that's—all!'

It was indeed ALL—the old servant was dead; and D'Arcy O'Rourke lifted up his voice and wept. It seemed as though the grave of all dear things yawned at his feet. The old man had cherished even his faults; he had been his nurse, his playfellow, his friend, his slave. He had hoped to have taken him with him to a foreign land, but the hope had expired!—the warm, true heart had ceased to beat; and for the first time when he, his master, called, there was no reply.

The letter contained a far more liberal supply than D'Arcy expected; and with the increasing and strengthening love of justice which was fast spurning all other thoughts from his mind, the young man forced upon the Murphys ample remuneration for their trouble, and a small sum for several of the poor who had been overwhelmed by the wreck, which, he frankly confessed, the system pursued by his family and himself had created. 'The time will come, if I live, when I will pay ALL,' he added, when preparing to accompany the true-hearted farmer to the nearest seaport, where his uncle had arranged that a vessel was to convey him to his destination.

'I'm sure of it, with the blessing of God,' said Murphy. 'And thin, instead of riding out of the place in the gray of the evening—which, to be sure, is the pleasantest—yer honour will come in broad day *like a flash of lightning* in yer own coach wid four beautiful horses; but ye mustn't get married till ye come back, because a furrin wife might turn yer head from yer own land.'

'Hould yer tongue,' said his wife; 'what do you know about it! *Wouldn't she love the land for his sake?*'

Each had prepared some 'token for his honour'—a pair of lambs'-wool stockings, or a red comforter, or a pair of worsted gloves. 'And now,' said Murphy, when they got to the boat which had been some time in waiting, 'I hope yer honour will accept the *baste* that brought ye down to the wather—it's own brother to Badger—and sure'——

But D'Arcy would not hear of this. He quitted his beautiful country and his friend in a silence more eloquent than words; and the last thing he saw through the clear midnight air of a moonlight night was Murphy kneeling on the shore, while his hands were outstretched towards the receding boat. When he unpacked his little valise, he discovered that *all the money he had given to Murphy for himself was folded in his best silk handkerchief!*

*   *   *   *

Years rolled on. The very old were dead, and those who had been young had grown gray, when it was rumoured about the country that old Murphy was giving money to a great number of people who had suffered distress in consequence of the ruin of the last of the O'Rourkes; a thing which had occurred before some were born, and when others were just beginning to go 'their lone.' Some said he visited the country himself, for that a large headstone was put over a grave that the young had called 'unknown' in the Abbey yard; it was only inscribed, '**To the memory of Lanty Lurgan, a faithful friend.**'

There, however, was the stone; and some said a tall large figure had been seen kneeling by the grave. Be that as it may, old Murphy was called a 'proud old man,' chiefly because he wore a 'goold' watch in his fob like a gentleman, which watch has some letters 'printed' round it, which his children, grandchildren, and great-grandchildren regard with peculiar veneration. It was only a few months ago that he inquired if the gentleman who had purchased the family house, with its more immediate estate, would part with it; which he seems inclined to do, for he also has suffered from the danger of debt.

'There's one wants it,' said Murphy when speaking of it; 'one that's a *rale* hero. There was but one thing ever wrong with him, and in spite of everything, he got over it like a man. He's an honour to the counthry, for his trials have been bitther. He had what might be called TRIALS, which I *could* tell; but I'm grown ould, and have tould so many stories in my time, that though this is every word true, maybe it wouldn't be believed. Only this I'll say to ould and young, rich and poor, bond and free, *Keep clear of* DEBT, *and ye'll keep clear of* DANGER!

THE TENANT-RIGHT.

'Sir, I advocate the tenant-right.'—The Candidate.

'You have a fine time of it among the quality, there's no denying it,' said Mary Connor to her foster-sister, Grace Kenny. 'You have, miss, a fine time of it; and why not? Sure it's your birthright, dear. You have as much right to the carriage as I have to the piggin,' she continued, lifting it up from the ground with a cheerful smile, and poising it upon her head with the grace of a Grecian nymph.

'But, Mary, why do you not come up to the big house and be my own maid? My dear uncle lets me do just as I like. I might have twenty own maids if I wished. Bell will soon go away to be married; so do, Mary, come; surely I have a right to my foster-sister?'

'Every right in life, dear; next to my grandmother.'

'And, Phil——' added the young lady; 'but indeed, Mary, Phil is not worthy of you. My uncle says his land is very bad.'

'His honour could mighty aisy give him better,' replied the maiden; 'but that's nothing against Phil that I can see, though it may be against the land. Still, miss, dear, don't be evenin' Phil or any one else to me. I've plenty of time, and things will mend; it's a long lane that has no turning.'

Miss Kenny bade her foster-sister good-morning.

Mary Connor had a great deal of native grace and dignity in her carriage and manner; she was fully and beautifully formed, and her dark hair and eyes, combined with delicate features, spoke of her southern origin. She was, so to say, more ladylike than Grace—a laughing, mischievous, blue-eyed, round-nosed little person—but whose attractions were pronounced 'surpassing,' under the influence of ten thousand pounds. Not one in possession, and nine in prospective, but ten thousand in actual cash. Grace drove on, humming 'my heart's my own;' while Mary, more thoughtful, walked slowly along the mountain-path that skirted Philip Boyle's farm. She was going for 'spring water' to the hill well; but instead of drawing the water at once when she arrived there, she set the piggin on the wall, and leaning against it, held the gate open with her hand.

'Is it for me you're waiting on the gate, darling?' exclaimed Philip joyfully, while he pressed her to his heart. 'Sure I'd have soon opened it, and you on the other side!'

'I like to meet you here,' she replied frankly and innocently. 'I like to meet you here, in the view of those old grand hills, and beside this well, where so many in old times got the sight of their eyes and the use of their limbs: it must be a holy place for all that to be done in it.'

'I am sure of that, Mary; and, moreover and above, I've a way of thinking every place you are in to be holy.'

'I wonder did Miss Grace ever hear a purtier speech than that in her beautiful drawing-room?' said Mary laughing. 'But, Philip, what I wanted to talk to you about is the bit of land.'

The expression of Philip's face changed in a moment. 'It's sad to say it, Mary; but without help from the landlord, I can make no hand of the farm. I was a fool to take it; nothing but weed and shingle.'

'Can't you get a better? There's lands changing hands now.'

'No; it's as much as life's worth to take the bit of land from a poor man when there's not another bit to be had. It's like taking the breath out of his body. All the murder is about the bit of land, and hundreds upon hundreds of acres lying idle, darling. I don't mean barren rock, and deep bog, and bleak mountain, though something could be done with all of them if the landlords either *would* help or *could* help; but available land, that they can't cultivate themselves, and wont let any one else touch, except at a price they can't pay—creating the misery and starvation they complain of. Look at it one way or the other way, they're bad sort of landlords for a poor fellow to have anything to do with.'

'Miss Grace is very kind,' said Mary; 'she's always after me to go to the big house as her own maid.'

'You'll do no such thing, my Mary,' said her lover. 'Service is honourable and honest. I got rid of all my old ancient pride and prejudice at the Agricultural School; but there's no need for it. My heart's own darling! I'll tell you what you'll do. I've got this blessed day a legacy of a hundred pounds!'

'A real whole hundred pounds!' repeated Mary in a tone of great delight, and blushing; for she guessed what would follow.

'Yes I have; and, darling, I'll *speak to the priest this evening.* I'll give up the farm: better do that than throw good money after what's gone. We'll pack up your grandmother, and go off to America.'

Mary turned pale. She had drawn water from that well ever since she could carry a noggin; she knew every mountain by name; every path, every flower, had a place in her abundant affections.

'Don't you think, Philip,' she said, 'it would be more like an Irishman to stick to your own country, and lay out your money in it, than in a land of strangers?'

'I love every blade of the sod,' he answered, 'God knows it; but as Ireland is managed, it hardly finds graves for the dead, much less food for the living!'

'As much as she is let to do, Philip; but if you, and the likes of you, with life and means, leave her, it's worse she'll get instead of better. There's nothing staying on the next townland but creatures that haven't the passage-money to leave it. It's heaped up alive with beggars it is.'

'And so every spot of the island will be, unless we can have the bit of land at a paying price; unless the landlords here will do like the landlords elsewhere—give *tenant's-right to tenant's labour*, and encourage the willing workman. I tell you how it is: my grandfather had no education; my father only a little; but I have had enough to make me discontented with the law—not so much of the land, but of the land's lord.'

Mary did not understand this, but she knew Philip was a 'fine scholar.' She believed all he said was right; but her affections were with her own country. 'Philip,' she said, 'I will go to Miss Grace, and get her to speak for us—for *you* I mean—and ask him to make an abatement in the rent, and help you to build a slated house. He's one that would always do more for interest than for justice, and if he thought you'd lay out the hundred pounds upon it——'

'You'll be a good farmer's wife, Mary, though you're a bad farmer,' said her lover. 'No, darling, it's no use; the land I've paid two guineas an acre for isn't worth five shillings. If indeed he'd let me, and half-a-dozen like me, the strip he once talked of, that's of no use in life to him but as a cover for game, then I'd be talking to him; but he wont, darling. It's hereafter Mr Kenny, and such as Mr Kenny, will be mourning, when they find the heart's blood, the bone and sinew of the country, has left it, and with nothing to the fore but those who had neither health, nor wealth, nor a good name to carry them where a man can have a fair day's wages for a fair day's work. Let us go, *avourneen deelish*, before poverty draws the marrow out of our bones; before we're wasted by fever or famine; before the carelessness—and it's more carelessness than cruelty that does it—of Mr Kenny makes me have a call to the combination, which I'd be long sorry for afterwards! I've clean hands, now, thank God! of everything going, and a light heart, and strong limbs, and a dear little colleen that will make me a country wherever I go.'

Mary laughed and cried by turns. Philip was esteemed the

handsomest and 'best learned' boy in the parish. She was an orphan girl, with the burthen of an old grandmother, so wise, that in former times she would have been esteemed a witch or a fairy-woman. Certainly Miss Grace was her foster-sister, *that* was a great deal: but Philip might have had any girl he pleased long ago; and yet now, when a hundred pounds were added to his charms, he generously offered to marry her, and take her dear old grandmother with them to the new world.

'The new world!' What an *El Dorado* it was to poor Mary! and what an enormous sum that hundred pounds appeared; what ever should they do with it! The mountains whirled round during her homeward walk, and she hardly knew how to communicate the news to the feeble old woman, who sat within the chimney watching the boiling of the potatoes, and churning an old ditty to the monotonous accompaniment of her wheel. Mary was reproved for her long delay, but she did not mind that. The old dog put his cold nose on her foot, and a pang shot through her heart when she thought what should they do with the dog; but as Philip had so much money, perhaps they could take *him* also to America—that is, supposing they went—which they would be sure not to do, because Mr Kenny would not part with Philip: he would certainly let him have a long lease of a good farm on his own terms: he never could part with Philip. Still, she would tell her grandmother: the old woman heard her to the end.

'Mary, *ma bouchal!*' she said, 'don't be feeding your heart, dear, with false music. Mr Kenny will do no such thing as you think —not he: he takes pride out of his wide domain and his fat cattle rather than out of a comfortable tenantry; and so did his father before him: it's a way the gentry have got of thinking, that it's grand to have a deal of waste land about their houses; and rather than get enough out of it to pay their debts (as they might easy do), they send their natural body-guard to foreign parts, where, I am tould, after much hard work, they are nearly as well off as, if they war well managed, they'd be in their own natural country. This is all well enough for the young; but, jewel Mary! the fox loves his ould earth, and the crow her ould nest. Go with him who loves you, Mary, and who proves his love; but I'll lay *my* bones in my own land, among my own people, beside your sweet mother, Mary, and my own ould husband. I'd just like to rise with them on the last day. I'd be lonely in my coffin, darling, if I wasn't under the same sod. My blessing will be about you all alike; it will come to you over the sea, jewel, every morning, on the first sunbeam, fresh and fasting—your ould granny's blessing! I'll never cross your good-luck, my blessed, blessed child!'

'Do you mind when my mother was dying?' inquired Mary.

'Do I mind the heavy trouble of my own heart!' was the reply.

'"If you wish your mother's blessing to light you into Paradise," she said, "never leave your grandmother." I'm not going to deny what God, who sees my heart, knows that I love the very ground that Philip walks on. I have known him ever since I knew night from day. When I was too little to cross the brook going to school, *his* were the hands that carried me over: he would leave his place, the top of the top form, and hear me my A B C: for all that, my own dear only mother, and for twice as much as that, I'll never, never leave you—I'll do my best to keep Philip here.'

'Stop, Mary, and hear the wisdom of the white head: look at the thing both ways—for your own feelings, and against your own feelings. If you want to see a thing straight, *never sit always on the same side of the car*. I see a deal: the gentry, to put away some of the sin of neglecting their own people, have been setting the country a-fire with education, and now they wonder at its burning; they are giving the young knowledge, without the power to use it, and expect that when a man knows how to earn the bit of meat, and the cut of white bread, and where to earn it, he'll be as well content to stay with them, *on the ould terms*, with the poor potato, and the fever, and the same sort of a right a dog has to his kennel, and a pig to his sty, to repay him for the labour of building what is little else than his own grave. Darling, look, the sense of it is this: such as Squire Kenny want to keep on in the culd way—*but the people have got before them;* and so, to get rid of the bother, they'll let them get out of the country. Don't gainsay, Philip, dear; he'll never be content to go on with Squire Kenny on the ould plan, and like many another, he'll get into trouble if he stays. The ould and the infant will stop in the place; but the law must change for the better, in more ways than one, before Ireland will be the home of the strong-headed, strong-armed, educated peasant! But you're not heeding me, Mary, honey?'

'I'd never forgive myself if, through staying for my sake, he got into any trouble,' said Mary; 'and it's hard to miss the face that smiled over my cradle.'

'Go with him, darling; every girl in the place will mind your ould granny, if it was only for your sake.'

'No, I'll never leave you: but where's the use of fretting; maybe he wont go?'

'Then he ought to go,' said the old woman firmly. 'Squire Kenny is not the right sort of landlord for such as he.'

That evening Mary went up to the big house, and craved audience of the young lady. Grace heard all she had to say with patience and sympathy.

'My uncle told me the other day,' she said, 'that if Philip chose to leave the farm, bad as it is, he could let it immediately at an increased rent.'

'There are some will take land whether they can pay for it or not,' answered Mary; 'but all I wanted to tell his honour is this, that maybe, as Philip was the son of an old tenant, and had improved so much, he'd let him have a few acres of fair land at a fair value. I want him to stop in the country; for indeed if he goes, the squire will lose an improving tenant.'

'And *you* a sweetheart.'

'No, miss, I would not,' replied Mary with her natural simplicity; 'the seas would be between us, to be sure, but we would be all the same, true to each other; and we're both young.'

Miss Grace promised to speak to her uncle, and to present both Philip and Mary to him the next morning, and let them tell their own tale.

Mr Kenny was the type of many of his class. That there are as good landlords in Ireland as in England, is unquestionably true; but, alas! they form the exceptions to the rule! There is no doubt that, though an educated people will exhibit less brute violence than a people uneducated, yet they will be more determined to obtain what their reason teaches them they have a right to possess. Mr Kenny never took into consideration the mental change that had been wrought in more persons than in Philip; nor could he, for the life of him, discover why the people were not as contented as they had been when he was a young man. Thinking this over, as he generally did after dinner, when he had drank a few tumblers of 'stiff punch,' he was not very likely to understand how such alterations were to be comprehended and met.

He was a careless man at all times, and in everything; good-natured and hospitable; always more ready to give a present than to pay a debt. In all things he belonged to the 'old school.'

Grace had been rather unfortunate in her diplomacy. She had lost her temper in the morning, and hardly recovered it during breakfast; but she trusted to Mary. Mary was a great favourite with the old squire, and she hoped her gentle smile would do more for Philip than Philip's eloquence would do for himself.

'So,' said Mr Kenny, 'you want more land, Philip?'

'If your honour would let me two or three acres of the fence farm at the same rate I have the hill ground, I'd work them well together; for I never was a gale behind with the rent for that barren place, where the crows don't think it worth their while to look for worms.'

'And in the fence farm, your honour,' put in Mary, 'my grandmother says there'd be pasture for a cow, or maybe two.'

'That land is worth five pounds an acre if it is worth a farthing,' said the squire; 'and I must get *that* for it if I break it into small holdings.'

'I couldn't pay that for it, sir, at the best of times, and make anything by it to live,' answered Philip. 'I'd like to stop in the country if I could, your honour. If I can't, why, I must go where others have gone before me. I don't want to spend all my life labouring for potatoes and salt, and being as poor at the end as I was at the beginning of my days.'

'As good as you have been glad of that same, Philip; and what can a poor man want more? But I've a regard for you, and for my little friend there, whom it concerns; so, if you like three acres of the fence farm put on to the five on the hill, you can have it all round for three pounds an acre.'

'Is it three pounds an acre, sir, for what every man in the parish knows I have never cleared two for yet? only spent every farthing of the little my uncle the priest left in making it what it is. The day I took on me the three acres, in addition to what my father made, I may say himself, there wasn't a fence that would keep out a bonneen, let alone a pig; not a gate, nor a drain; and I'm sure you might have counted the blades of the two first crops. I hope your honour will think of that before you put another pound on them acres.'

'But haven't I taken two pounds a year off the fence farm?'

'To put it on the other, sir.'

'I don't want to let it,' said Mr Kenny; 'it's only out of regard to you I'd break my land at all. If you don't like my offer, stay as you are: or stop; I'll do this for you—pay me, say two pounds for the eight acres all round.'

Mary's heart beat, and Philip coloured.

'Two pounds for the eight acres all round,' continued Mr Kenny, 'and let the third pound stand over for three years or so, till you're better able to pay it.'

Mary's heart beat on, but Philip's countenance changed. 'Thank your honour,' he answered, 'but that would be getting into debt; yet maybe you'd give me a bit of a memorandum, if I left the place, you'd pay me for what I'd put upon it—a shed, or gates, or pig-sties, or——'

'Whew—w—w!' interrupted the landlord; 'you're getting new-fangled notions with a vengeance! It's the *tenant-right* you're after, is it? If you do not like my offer, stay as you are.'

'I can't do that either, your honour. I can't go on slaving the life out of my four bones for the bare bit I eat. If I hadn't means to go elsewhere, I must do it: if I hadn't education, I must do it; if——'

The landlord interrupted him by sending all species of education to the *bad* place, and cursing him for an ungrateful fellow, for thinking of taking his money away from the sod 'where he was bred, born, and reared.' 'But I do not care a farthing about it for my own sake; give me back the land, and you may go to the ——! I can soon get tenants, and increased rent!'

'Your honour will get tenants enough: there's plenty would

take on the running gale, and be glad to wear out the improvements I have made. I'll be heart-sorry to leave it,' he added, rubbing his hand round the edge of his hat, while poor Mary grew pale; ' but your honour wont lay out a penny with me on it, nor give me the *tenant's-right* over what I do. I've wattled and thatched the house, I've mended the windows, I've fenced the little garden, I've planted trees, I've drained, and manured——'

'And who asked you to do it?' inquired the landlord tauntingly. 'You're newfangled with green crops, and one thing or another, and not content to go on as your father did before you—*plain* and *easy*, honest man.'

' I am not content, sir, sure enough, to go on as my father did before me,' he replied; ' I own to that. I saw him go down as worn and strengthless to his grave at fifty, as a man ought, that had fair-play in the world, at seventy—a fine, hale, hearty man he was, but worn out by hard work and fainting food——'

' And whisky,' added Mr Kenny.

' That had its claw on him too, I'll not deny it, sir: it seemed an easy way for a man to put the trouble off him, and then, like a false friend, it was sure to bring him into more: but that reproach is gone from *us*, sir, thank God! There's none gets drunk at all now, *barring the gentlemen!*'—The bolt was shot, and it was drawn by an impatient and impolitic hand; but, as Philip afterwards said to Mary, he could not stand that reproach to his father from one who never remembered going himself quite sober to bed.

Mary put in her gentle voice, but too late; the crisis had come; angry words followed; Philip threw up the farm. 'In other countries,' he said, ' where a tenant's labour creates a tenant's right, you'd be forced, sir, to pay me back for the stock I leave you on it. Here I can't claim it, and I'd scorn to ask for what I've no call to. I took that land with the intention of giving, as I have done, my strength to it; and there it is, all the better, while I'm all the worse. The cow and the horse both died with me, and yet you'd give me no help; and if it hadn't been for the goodness of God, which sent me help to leave it, I'd have been tied to it in slavery for the rest of my days. If I had had it at a low but increasing rent, I might have made a home of it for myself, and a property for you. I'm clear of it now. You may get those on it who wont leave it as I have done; that's all I can say. I need not tell a gentleman of this country of the bad that's going, of the impossibility there is for him to know who has or has not to do with what is, I own, a disgrace to the people; but I do say, that when a gentleman finds an honest, hard-working man, who is able and willing to do justice to the bit of land, he ought to give him an honest man's hold upon it.'

'Don't vex the master; he's not used to be crossed that way,' whispered Mary.

'Let him go on,' said the angry squire; 'give him rope enough, and he'll soon hang himself!'

'Please God I will not, sir: there's enough said; you'll all wake up some day and see the land left without able-bodied honest men to till it; you'll cry out then in vain for those who have earned, and can keep, land of their own over the seas, to come and help yours to bring forth its fruits. God be with you, sir! I thought to have had some consideration from you, and not be forced to turn my back on my country.'

'Have nothing to do with him, Mary,' said Mr Kenny. 'I know a smart fellow to come in on his place: let him go—a *colleen-das* like you has no call to leave her own country for a sweetheart—let him go!'

Philip became dark with rage. Mary tried to reply, but she could not; she burst into tears, and followed her lover out of the room.

As they descended the brow of the hill, the sunbeams were sporting over the very small farm Philip was about to resign for ever; even the sunshine failed to make it look prosperous. He had really done a great deal to it: it was tolerably fenced and drained, and additional time and additional labour would of course increase its value; but Philip knew that even then it would never be prosperous, nor would what he had done meet with consideration, much less justice. Moreover, he was a peace-loving man, and he feared being drawn into the combinations which have so completely baffled all the investigations of the law.

'It's cruel hard,' sobbed Mary, 'that he wont allow you a penny for what you've done; he'll get a higher rent *from some that will never pay.*'

Mary and Philip were unconscious of the blunder; but they understood the meaning. Mary saw that Philip was suffering; but he brightened his countenance, and talked of the 'hereafter,' urging her to go with him at once, and that he thought her grandmother would accompany them; but she knew better, and reverenced the feeling which caused the old woman to desire to leave her bones in her native land.

All the country cried shame on Mr Kenny. This was the fifth of the 'good ould stock' that he had let leave the place; and who had he got in their stead? That question remained to be answered.

Philip was a good specimen of what an improved education can effect for the Irish peasant. He felt that, however humble his position, as a man, he had a right to exert his strength, mental and bodily, for his own advantage; however much his feelings yearned towards 'the sod,' he knew that his little capital could be more advantageously employed elsewhere; not but that Ireland possessed every advantage that could be had elsewhere; but *free agency* was so completely a sound, and not a reality, that a humble, peace-loving, unslavish man, at all events in *his* district, had no chance of having a firmer hold on the *property he helped to make*, than had others of the property *they helped to mar*. 'Better times,' he was told, were coming; but as in his father's days they had not come, except, indeed, through the door so tardily opened by 'national education,' there was something to his healthy, self-thinking mind, even in this infancy of knowledge, very pleasant and *independent* in the idea that he might yet call a plot of *land*—*land!* that *Alpha and Omega* of Irish ambition— HIS OWN.

There were far-away districts where such an advantage might in a degree be his: but his attachments were localised; they circled round the settlement of 'his own people;' and as Mr Kenny's shortsighted policy refused his honest and liberal offer, the cord was sundered, and he only desired to leave it as soon as possible. Mary was not the only one who regretted this determination on Philip's part. The young man, had he remained, would have found life itself unsafe, if he had not yielded to the influence of self-organized lawmakers; and this reconciled Mary to his departure, hard as it was to part with her betrothed.

'I thought to the last,' she said, 'the masther would come round; but I see he wont now; I see the hardness of his heart. He thinks poverty and misery is our birthright, and that we have no reason to go against it; that's what he thinks. He has looked so long at starvation, that he's grown used to it; and he'd think there'd be something going wrong if he had no beggars on the road.'

'You're book-sworn, Mary,' interrupted her lover—'you're book-sworn to let me know when any change comes to your grandmother. In the sight of God you are my wife, and you mustn't think bad of any little present I send you home, because you'll want it all; and deny yourself nothing, avourneen. I'll wait true and patiently for you, jewel; and hard as the parting is, I'll not deny but I love you all the better for your duty to your parent; besides, I'll have all things settled for you, and maybe come home for you myself. The black poverty can't touch you, Mary; and don't go the path by the hill farm when you go to see Miss Grace; it would only fret you, darling; but set a stout heart to the wind. I'm going out like an honest man; I owe nothing, and I shouldn't be ashamed to look a king in the face.'

This was all very brave, and, what was better, it was very true; but it could not prevent the mingling of many tears; and none flowed more abundantly than those of the poor old grandmother.

'I've seen fine heads laid low, and buried many a one years younger than myself, yet I'm to the fore still, and no good in me, Mary, darling!—only you're such an angel, I should think you wished the grave closed over me: but the great comfort of my life is thinking how we'll all rise together at the last day; and I couldn't leave the sight of the ould churchyard; I could not, avourneen.'

'And I could not leave you, darling grandmother,' was the reply; and after Philip's departure, Mary redoubled her attention to the aged woman, and did more in an hour than she need have done in a day; 'the work,' she said, 'kept the trouble off her heart.'

'Do anything but sing, my darling!' exclaimed her grandmother—'anything but sing! There's a sigh in your voice like the moan of the wind in a fir-tree, which makes me pray to God to hasten my journey, that you may be happy when I am gone.'

'So you are off, Philip, I suppose?' said Mr Kenny, as he met the emigrant on his road to Waterford.

'The young man looked up courageously. 'I am, sir; and for all my hot words, sir, I've a kind heart to you and yours: and if I said anything that my father's son should not have said to your father's son, I hope your honour will overlook it. It did not come from the heart, only from the necessity of the case; that was all, your honour.'

'I believe you,' was the gentleman's reply; 'but if you look at it, Philip, it is rather strange for such as you to take a hundred pounds, as I hear you do, away from your country and your natural protector, to employ it upon you know not what.'

'I know anyhow, sir, that if I stayed, I should employ it on what would never be my own. It's done now, and God be with your honour! See, sir'—and he laid his hand on the shoulder of the beautiful horse Mr Kenny rode—'I may never set eyes on you again; but take care who you let in on the land—promises grow no gold.' His voice faltered; his eyes filled with tears; he took off his hat, and held out his hand to the squire; it was kindly taken. 'I could say a deal more, sir, but you wouldn't heed me; and so take care who you let in on the land; promises grow no gold: and God be with you and Miss Grace!'

'He's a fine fellow to look at,' thought the squire, 'but a disturber—one of *the tenant's-right* men. No good will come of it. No good comes of letting the poor into one's secrets, or taking them out of their place.'

Things seemed to be going on pretty much as usual in the valley where Mary continued to reside with her grandmother, and yet they were changing every day. Many of the cottages in the village were in ruins; and Mary shared her old dog's and her own food with more than one half-starved cat and cur that lingered about the lonely places where they once had friends. The chapel on Sundays was filled; but there were few horses or cars waiting outside, where there used to be numbers, made 'sonsy' for the farmer's wives to ride in, by featherbeds, covered with gaudy quilts. The young men that lounged about the door and against the walls bore no likeness to the 'old stock,' and were careless, scampish-looking fellows, who more frequently handled a musket than a shillala. There were many white-headed old men; but the race of 'strong, young, small-farmers,' who rode a good horse, and wore boots and corduroys, had disappeared. Altogether, there had been a sort of voluntary clearing; if that could be 'voluntary' which was compelled by circumstances and reason.

'Grace,' said Mr Kenny to his niece one morning, more than two years after Philip had left the country—'Grace, dear, I wish you would send for the glazier to put a pane of glass in the library window.'

'You forget, uncle,' replied Grace, 'that there is no glazier in Kennystown since young James Daly went to Canada. What a nice workman he was! He made my fern-house; but it is broken now, and there is no one to mend it.'

'Ha!' exclaimed the squire, 'the fellow wanted increased wages, and got talking of the value of time, so he was not fit for this country. Do you ride to-day?'

'How can I ride, uncle? That horrid new blacksmith, who took Whalan's old forge, has lamed my mare. I am sure I hate those new-comers. I cannot think why you did not encourage those to remain who worked so well. The resources of the country are dried up.'

'Whalan certainly was a capital workman, Grace; and I own I am sorry that the gentry all grumbled when he raised the price of shoeing horses. It had been fixed so long—ever since my grandfather's time—that I did not like a penny a shoe put on: he might have raised it to three-halfpence.'

'Better that,' murmured Grace, 'than have half the horses in the country lamed by a botch, who does not mind his business either. He told my groom to-day he would attend to the mare when he had finished reading the paper. Whalan would never have sent such a message as that.'

'That is certain: those fellows grow so impudent.'

'Those who were born,' answered Grace, 'upon our own land were never so. I do miss the old faces.' Tears were in Grace Kenny's eyes while she spoke.

'You are a fool, child,' said her uncle abruptly; 'they grew discontented, and wanted change.'

'They wanted their rights,' answered Grace firmly; 'they wanted to be paid according to the times—they wanted tenants'-rights. And those new people, with all their fine promises, are far more likely to do us wrong than those who loved the spot whereon they were born; and who, despite all disagreements, would rather leave you than harm you.'

'You are a saucy girl to talk about what you do not understand; go and see if the hoops are put on the vat.'

'They are not,' she replied; 'there is not a cooper within five miles since Naylor went to Sydney; and the carpenter says he cannot see to your vat until he has finished the priest's fence. What a ready obliging fellow Dick Murphy was! He has sent his mother five pounds since he settled in Connecticut. It was a great pity, uncle, you quarrelled with Dick about the new gates.'

'They all grew so conceited, and so extortionate in their demands, that it was impossible to get on with them. I wish the times had remained as they were with all my heart.'

'Wishing wont make them what they were; and I wanted to speak to you, uncle, about the shearers. The two men you got cheap to shear the sheep this year have, I am told, taken almost as much skin as wool from the poor animals. You used to be so proud of your sheep-farming before Murphy went to Australia.'

'Grace, you are enough to drive one mad!'

'I could go on for an hour,' continued the positive girl. 'The dairymaid gave me warning this morning, because, she says, she can have better wages in Cheshire; and my own maid is going to marry the gardener, and go to Pennsylvania. He says you have been unkind to him about some trees. We are all going wrong somehow; I am sure of that.'

'It's all the education, and fine learning, and politics,' said Mr Kenny; 'but that's not the worst of it. Here's a threatening letter about my notice to the rascal who took poor Philip's farm when he quitted it. He has never paid a farthing of rent, and racked to pieces the land that was just coming round.'

'Poor Philip!' repeated Grace: 'you should see his letters to Mary, and then you would not say "poor Philip." He is doing so well; and though things are dear, he says labour of all kind is so highly paid for, that it makes the things twenty per cent. cheaper than they are here! It is quite interesting to see Mary vibrating between the two great affections of her life. And she keeps her grandmother so clean: she carries her in her arms into the sun every morning, as if she were a baby, and attends her with so much tenderness. The old creature has lost the use of her limbs, but her feelings are as acute as ever. "I pray," she said to me, "to the Lord to take me, for I know I'm keeping them asunder. I can't see Mary's tears now, nor hear her sobs, for I'm both blind and deaf; but when she kissed me last night, I felt her cheek was wet, and I feel that she is much thinner than she was. I know her heart is withering away, but I can't help it. If I was fit to go, the Lord would take me."'

'Grace,' said her uncle, 'I have just told you I received a threatening letter, and instead of talking to me about it, you run on concerning a foolish old woman and as foolish a girl.'

'Every one receives threatening letters who ask for rent,' replied Grace carelessly; 'I hear of them wherever I go. If your old people had remained with us——'

But Mr Kenny would hear no more; the theme was ungracious in his ears; he would not see where he had done foolishly; he only knew that he could not get his rents; that there was a combination against him; that those who would pay dared not pay; and that others would not. His nominal rent-roll, increased by the emigration of the old tenants, had almost ceased to be of value; but this did not prevent those (not a few) to whom he owed money insisting upon prompt payment for long, long standing debts. The network of the whole—owing, and being owed—had got into tremendous confusion; and when his paroxysm of temper was over, and Grace saw how miserable the old man looked, she forgot all but him, and endeavoured to divert his anxiety by every means in her power. She saw there was no use in trying to convince him that it was better to receive five shillings than the *promise* of twenty. With a perfect relish for the enjoyment of existence, he did not see any reason why the 'lower orders' should have any enjoyment apart from labour; he could not perceive that the spirit of serfdom, so long in the ascendant, was passing away; and that though there must be grades in society—that, like the steps of a ladder, some must be high, some low—yet none could for the future press upon the other without disorganizing and materially injuring the fitness of the whole. He was irritated because people were not content to be 'as their fathers were before them;' he made grievous laments over 'the good old times,' when claret and whisky were on draught in the gentleman's house; when the master could horsewhip the man, and the man would only twist his shoulders and say, 'God be praised, sir, there's a power of strength in your arm!' when, to live free, any man who had a thousand pounds might 'split it into three halves,' and lend it upon mortgage, and whenever he called for the interest, be certain of two months' hospitality, with fishing and shooting into the bargain. He treasured up the memories of the past, and could not understand why the present generation differed from the last; he was one of those mentally-blind men who would attempt to stem a torrent, not guide its course; he could not see that, whether the past were best or worst, it had vanished; and that however it may be honoured, it is but a memory—at best an example; that living beings have to do with the present, and not with the future; he was, as he often said himself, 'bothered entirely;' he regretted that Philip, and such as Philip, were gone; but he did not see why he should have given them what he considered a premium to remain. His father thought sixpence a day good wages. Capital soldiers had been '*raised*' on potatoes;

then what could they want of better food? As to the fever, why, there always was fever more or less in Ireland: sure it wasn't worse than it had always been. Some people say 'let well alone;' but Squire Kenny acted 'let bad alone.' He could not think but those were insane who broached the *tenant's-right* to anything but labour; he had subscribed to an anti-slavery society once, but never thought of the white slaves he held in thrall at home; never thought of the effects of books, and steamboats, and railways, and newspapers; never bestowed an idea on *progress;* never, I believe, thought that the 'people had mind.' While so many things went on, he stood still.

Of all men, he thought he had no right to receive threatening letters. He was always generous to the poor, so he was; he gave in 'meal and malt;' he gave to the young and strong as well as to the old and feeble, and so encouraged beggary. 'He only asked his own'—'his land was not let higher than other people's'—'he was considerate.' How? He suffered 'the gale' to run on, and then seized on the improved land as a set-off to his debt. Custom, in his particular district, had sanctified this wicked practice into a law. It has passed now; it has gone down, steeped in blood, along with other tyrannies which have been swept away by the glorious thunder-voice of an indignant public; and yet Squire Kenny believed 'he only sought his own.' In the case of the tenant who had succeeded Philip, he had most certainly been badly treated; and his hardness to Philip was no excuse for the new man's delinquency; but so mysteriously are all the links of society twisted together, that one wrong deed is the herald of others. Grace was not only more quick, but more strong-sighted than her uncle: she told him his only plan was to sell the estate; but he replied to this by saying that even if he did, he should still be an 'encumbered beggar!' She sat alone in her chamber, the moonlight shining through the open window —the whole country steeped in that magic light which conceals defects and exaggerates beauties. She had left her uncle with his solicitor, and was companioned by any rather than pleasant fancies; a low tap at the door, and Mary Connor entered. She stood without speaking for more than a minute.

'She's gone from me, Miss Grace! Went away this morning when the sun was brightest, just as a butterfly folds its wings, and dies on a flower! No more than that, miss—gone! Oh, then, I can hardly think it! I went out of the room, in the fancy that maybe she'd come to herself again when I came back; for never did I come into the place that she hadn't the kind word for me, and the wise word, and the good prayer. I ran for the priest, but he could not overtake her: was not that a sorry thing? But his reverence said she was always prepared. She's gone from me! And I think, maybe if I had taken more care of her, she'd have lasted longer. It seems unholy for me even to think of Philip, though she's gone. "*Tell*," she said, and she groping with her hands—" *tell the squire my dream about the man that thought to treat the bull as if it was always a calf, and what it did to him.*" Oh, Miss Grace, she was greatly troubled about you and yours! May the Lord protect you! The good went fair and easy out of the place, but that wont be the way with those that's in it now! If the master distrains, I don't know what might not happen. Let him talk of it, miss, but not do it—at least while he's in the country. Oh to think how those that's gone would have stuck by the ould stock, if they had had only fair-play!' The poor girl's sorrow was relieved by words and tears, and Grace insisted upon her accepting the shelter of their roof until she heard from Philip.

'I wont have you as a servant, Mary, but as a humble friend. When all is over, you must stay with me. Your grandmother will be laid in her people's grave; you have the consolation of knowing that you did your duty. I only hope I may do my duty to my old relative as well as you performed yours.'

Mary went to live with her foster-sister, and Grace frequently derived consolation from the straightforward, right-hearted opinions of Mary Connor. In the country, matters were growing worse instead of better. Mr Kenny became naturally more and more exasperated at the course of conduct pursued by the people. As his difficulties increased, his temper became worse: and he acted upon a system of aggravation and injustice, until he became cruel as well as careless. The country combined against him, and added fuel to the flame; while he attributed every wrong thing to others, not to himself.

Mary, as time passed on, spent a good many anxious hours watching 'the post,' wondering why Philip did not write. Despite her lover's caution, she cast many a glance at the hill farm; the trees Philip planted had been cut down; the gate hung on one hinge; the thatch had not been mended; the pigs had grubbed up the garden; the land, with the exception of the potato field, had returned to its sterility; the man who possessed it was *known* to be the most *actively* dangerous man in the district. But what of that? Who would give evidence against him? Who, if they saw him pocket the pistol with which he committed murder, would inform? He had at one time sought to win Mary's heart: but a woman who really loves, knows how to keep off all suitors but the *one*. There is a protection in devoted love which renders a maiden sacred even to the profligate, and Mary continued an especial object of admiration and interest to the new settlers of Kennystown.

Irritated not only by the open defiance which met him when he demanded a portion of his rents, and driven to the verge of insanity by debts which he could not discharge, the old squire still said he had done nothing foolishly. It was deemed necessary to put bars to shutters that had grown worm-eaten without them; and the carpenter who did it was brought from a distance, under the protection of the police. The pistol took its place at the family table, on the master's right hand; and even in the daytime he did not care to ride much beyond the avenue gate. The light-hearted, cheerful Grace, was changed into a sharp-featured, anxious-looking woman. The interest of her money was all they really had to subsist upon; for, luckily, neither her uncle nor herself could touch the principal until she completed her twenty-fifth year. She performed her duty, and she did not do it grudgingly; but it requires a great deal of patience, as well as purity of intention, to labour in the path of a duty upon which love never shines. It is bad training for a young heart to live with the age it cannot reverence; and circumstances had worn out the kindliness that once distinguished the old squire. Moroseness succeeded good-nature; the house of his ancestors was tumbling about his ears, and he had not wherewith to put it in repair; the new people were openly leagued against him; and those who remained of the old were too feeble or too fearful to 'stand by the old master.'

One evening Mary was slowly descending from 'watching the post;' the lad walked past the road leading to the avenue, and waved his stick, in token that he had nothing to bring. Her steps were slow; the hill farm was mouldering away beneath her eyes; frequently she brushed away the tears with the back of her rough hand; the leaves which an autumn wind whirled from the few stunted trees that remained of the plantations were circling with the dust along her path; the thin stubble was decked with gaudy weeds, like paint on the cheek of withered beauty. There was a chill over the landscape; the rays of the setting sun looked straight and hard, cut into lines of garish light, on the dark sky; the rushes that fringed the pools were brown and discoloured; a group of ragged boys were pelting half-a-dozen newly-plucked miserable geese that had been groping in the mud for food; the rooks were cawing discontentedly on their homeward way; and the village of Kennystown sent up but little cheerful smoke to the heavens.

'It's so changed altogether,' muttered Mary to herself, 'that St Patrick would not know it! And they're fighting about who shall and who shan't go to the National School; and the masther must go the wrong way in that too,' she sighed bitterly, and turned to look again to see perhaps if the post-boy was really out of sight; and as she did, she saw Lawrence Jones, who had taken Philip's farm, running towards her. He made her a sign to stop, but she immediately turned homeward: he overtook her.

'Mary,' he said—'Mary, when did you see your aunt beyant there?'

'Not these three weeks, Lawrence.'

'Well, she's got a heavy fit of sickness. I don't mean *the* sickness—not the fever—but a heavy turn of some kind; and she sent word to you to be sure to be up there this evening. Mind, *this* evening—to-morrow wont do.'

'And why wont to-morrow do? and why didn't whoever she sent come up with the word, and not give it to another?'

'Because he was going for the doctor.'

'Sure it's turning his back on the doctor he'd be if he'd come this way,' said the shrewd Mary.

'Why, girl alive! how sharp you are on us,' was the reply; 'hadn't he to go back after he left the message? And who knows but it's dead she'd be by to-morrow night; so do as you like—only maybe it's a heavy heart you'll have if you don't do my bidding. I've small reason,' he added carelessly, 'to care whether you do or not; only I'm a fool about you still, Mary.'

'And about everything else, or you'd never have that farm in the way it is,' she answered; and then, thinking perhaps she had been 'too sharp,' she added, 'thank you all the same; though my aunt was never much of an aunt to me, I'd be sorry she was to go, and I so near her, without my seeing her once more.'

'You'll go?' said Lawrence anxiously.

'I will,' she replied.

Mary equipped herself for a three miles' walk, and set out; yet more than once her 'heart,' as she called it, misgave her; more than once she paused and turned back; but 'it might be that her *aunt was ill,* and how unkind not to go near her!'

She resumed her path. When within sight of the cottage, through the twilight she saw a woman rolling up some cloth that had been put out to bleach. It was her aunt, who declared that, 'glory be to God! she never was better in her life. What set *her* to inquire, who never looked the same road she was?' Mary told her. 'It's not going back you are without taking bit or sup with your own blood relations?' said the woman; 'sure you wouldn't think of such a thing as that? If you wont stop the night, it's early moon, the road is fine, and the country safe *for such as you.*'

There was something in her aunt's expression in 'for such as you' that struck on Mary's ear like a warning. There was nothing in the words; they conveyed no new information; but they awoke a dormant anxiety; they revived a half-formed dread for those who had protected her in her time of trial: why should Lawrence wish to get her out of the house? She put out a good many leading questions, but her aunt had simply said the truth—the country was safe 'for such as her,' though it might not be safe for others; that was literally all. She ate cheerfully the potatoes and milk set before her with a taunting observation, ' that, to be sure, they were no food for one used to the run of the big house, where there was *lashings* of what wasn't always paid for.'

Mary roused at this sneer, which was unpalatable in proportion to its truth; and without waiting for many more words, she commenced her return. The corncraik was running along the hedges, and the night-owl hooted as she passed the burial-place of her grandmother. It was the first time she had passed the grave without kneeling beside it; but she could not venture among the shadows which imagination conjured up and superstition believed in. Presently she heard the sound of wheels and the fast trotting of a horse. She felt very lonely, but turned down a new road which had been lately made, and led round the base of the hill which the old road crossed. The driver of the car called out to her to know which was the shortest of the two to Kennystown. She made no reply: he repeated the question: there was no answer. Mary attempted to rush to the car, but fainted in the attempt. The man sprung from his seat; he lifted her up; he unfastened her bonnet; in another moment he pressed her to his heart; he called upon her to awake by all the endearing names in the eloquent vocabulary of Irish love—that it was Philip, her own Philip, who called her; that he had come to take her to his new-made home; that they should never more be separated; never—never! It was the sudden feeling of all this, when his voice struck upon her heart, that overpowered her. In a few minutes she was seated by his side, weeping tears of thankfulness and joy. She assured him of a welcome at ' the big-house,' and the horse was urged forward to its utmost speed. The avenue gate was open; the door of the lodge was open also. This startled her at the moment as strange; for of late, at night, the gate had been chained and padlocked. They drove on: the moon was shining forth in the queenliness of her glory; the house was within sight, but what a sight it was! A loud, long, ringing shriek, told of violence and terror; men were struggling on the steps of the hall-door with the old squire; they forced him on his knees, but their intention was for a moment frustrated: a woman, feeble in all but purpose, interposed: she clung around him with twining arms; more than once, in a brief space they were separated, but again she flung herself between him and his murderers.

Philip did not lack courage, but it was Mary who urged the horse forward. Dreading the arrival of the police, the ruffians hurried to perpetrate their crime with increased violence. A clump of trees interposed between Mary and the view she had of the fearful struggle. They saw the light of firearms through the branches, and heard the report of more than one. Faster, faster, they drove to the door, under shelter of the plantations, which in a degree concealed one end of the dwelling. The murderers had disappeared, and Grace was kneeling beside her uncle. It was impossible to tell which of the two was wounded, for Grace's hair and garments were dabbled with crimson.

'I do not know,' she said to Mary with terrible calmness—'I do not know how I am; but I know one of those who fired. I know *one;* and I know you, Philip. Uncle!' she said to the dying man—'uncle, Philip is come back to save you!'

'He cannot save me; but he should not have gone—he should not have gone! I am not fond of newfangled notions; but tell him,' he added, raising his head, though his glazed eyes told how little he could discern—' tell him he shall have the *tenant's-right* if he'll come back—the tenant's-right—if—he'll——' The old man's spirit passed away from the scene of his own mismanagement, and of the atrocity and blindness of those who, suffering more or less from the insufficiency of the law, take revenge in its place as their counsellor and protector, and brand their country in the eyes of the universe as a land that winks at murder, and harbours the assassin.

'I see he is dead!' said poor Grace, as she drew the old white head upon her lap: 'if he had not been dying, he never would have given in to the *tenant's-right;* it's the last thing the old landlords will yield. Oh, if you had been but sooner!' she said to the police, who came crowding up from their station, which was sufficiently near to hear, as indeed they did, the report of the firearms : 'if you had been sooner! I know Lawrence Jones of the uphill farm ; he fired the fatal shot; my poor uncle fell then! You are well revenged, Philip! Do not cry, Mary! No, I will not go in! I will remain where I am with my poor uncle!' and she rested her cheek upon his white hair with a tenderness which those who knew her best thought she had forgotten.

It is one of the beautiful properties of woman's nature that she forgets the bad, and recalls the good, of those whom she has loved 'when they are no more seen;' and in after-times Grace persuaded herself that her uncle was blameless. His was one among many deaths that have occurred from the same cause— murders which admit of no apology, but for which those who know the history of the past misrule and maladministration of the laws do not find it difficult to account. No country can be greatly prosperous, or permanently safe, where justice is not administered with an even hand to rich and poor, high and low : the injustice of the one causes crime in the other.

Philip had been sufficiently long in the new world to look with horror on the conduct of those who concealed the murderer from the grasp of the law, and he found it necessary to hasten his bride's departure from Kennystown. She paused on her journey by the old churchyard, to drop a few tears on the grave of the old master, and to say a last prayer over the green mound which covered the ashes of a beloved parent, to whom she had been so dutiful a child. Nor was she unmindful of the simple superstition of her country: counting amongst her greatest treasures a long tress of Miss Grace Kenny's hair, cut by a new pair of scissors from her head, when the moon was in its first quarter—alas! it was abundantly streaked with gray!—a slip of witch-hazel, a four-leaved shamrock, a sixpence carefully reunited (it had been broken between herself and Philip), and a handful of the mould from the burial-place of her humble ancestors. 'If I die in foreign parts,' she said to her husband, 'this must be buried with me; *but maybe we may return?*'

'Please God,' he said, 'when the TENANT'S-RIGHT IS ESTABLISHED IN THE LAND!'

THE END.

EDINBURGH:
PRINTED BY W. AND R. CHAMBERS.

The List of Titles in the Garland Series

MARIA EDGEWORTH

1. Castle Rackrent *(1800)*
2. An Essay on Irish Bulls *(1802)*
3. Ennui *(1809)*
4. The Absentee *(1812)*
5. Ormond *(1817)*

SYDNEY OWENSON, LADY MORGAN

6. The Wild Irish Girl *(1806)*
7. O'Donnel. A National Tale *(1814)*
8. Florence Macarthy: an Irish Tale *(1818)*
9. The O'Briens and the O'Flahertys *(1817)*
10. Dramatic Sketches from Real Life *(1833)*

CHARLES ROBERT MATURIN

11. The Wild Irish Boy *(1808)*
12. The Milesian Chief *(1812)*
13. Women; or, Pour et Contre: A Tale *(1818)*

Eyre Evans Crowe

14. To-day in Ireland *(1825)*
15. Yesterday in Ireland *(1829)*

John Banim and Michael Banim

16. Tales, by the O'Hara Family *(1825)*
17. The Boyne Water, A Tale, by the O'Hara Family *(1826)*
18. Tales, by the O'Hara Family. Second Series *(1826)*
19. The Croppy. A Tale of 1798 *(1828)*
20. The Anglo-Irish of the Nineteenth Century *(1828)*
21. The Denounced *(1830)*
22. The Ghost-Hunter and his Family *(1833)*
23. The Mayor of Wind-Gap *and* Canvassing *(1835)*
24. The Bit O'Writin' and Other Tales *(1838)*
25. Patrick Joseph Murray, The Life of John Banim, the Irish Novelist *(1857)*

Gerald Griffin

26. Holland-Tide; or, Munster Popular Tales *(1827)*
27. Tales of the Munster Festivals *(1827)*
28. The Collegians *(1829)*

29. The Rivals *and* Tracy's Ambition *(1829)*

30. Tales of My Neighbourhood *(1835)*

31. Talis Qualis; or Tales of the Jury Room *(1842)*

32. DANIEL GRIFFIN, The Life of Gerald Griffin by his Brother, revised edition *(n.d.)*

WILLIAM CARLETON

33. Father Butler. The Lough Dearg Pilgrim *(1829)*

34. Traits and Stories of the Irish Peasantry *(1830)*

35. Traits and Stories of the Irish Peasantry, Second Series *(1833)*

36. Tales of Ireland *(1834)*

37. Fardorougha, the Miser; or, the Convicts of Lisnamona *(1839)*

38. The Fawn of Spring-Vale, The Clarionet, and Other Tales *(1841)*

39. Tales and Sketches Illustrating the Character of the Irish Peasantry *(1845)*

40. Valentine M'Clutchy, The Irish Agent; or, Chronicles of the Castle Cumber Property *(1847)*

41. The Black Prophet: a Tale of the Irish Famine *(1847)*

42. The Emigrants of Ahadarra: A Tale of Irish Life *(1848)*

43. The Tithe Proctor: being a Tale of the Tithe Rebellion in Ireland *(1849)*

44. The Life of William Carleton: Being His Autobiography and Letters; and an Account of his Life and Writings from the Point at which the Autobiography Breaks Off by David O'Donoghue *(1896)*

HARRIET MARTINEAU

45. Ireland *(1832)*

ANNA MARIA HALL

46. Sketches of Irish Character *(1829)*

47. Lights and Shadows of Irish Life *(1838)*

48. The Whiteboy. A Story of Ireland in 1822 *(1845)*

49. Stories of the Irish Peasantry *(1851)*

WILLIAM HAMILTON MAXWELL

50. O'Hara; or 1798 *(1825)*

51. The Fortunes of Hector O'Halloran and his man, Mark Anthony O'Toole *(1843)*

52. Erin-Go-Bragh; or Irish Life Pictures *(1859)*

ANTHONY TROLLOPE

53. The Macdermots of Ballycloran *(1847)*
54. The Kellys and the O'Kellys *(1848)*
55. Castle Richmond *(1860)*
56. An Eye for an Eye *(1879)*
57. The Land-Leaguers *(1883)*

JOSEPH SHERIDAN LE FANU

58. The Purcell Papers with a Memoir by Alfred Perceval Graves *(1880)*
59. The Cock and Anchor: Being a Chronicle of Old Dublin City *(1845)*
60. The House by the Church-Yard *(1863)*

WILLIAM ALLINGHAM

61. Lawrence Bloomfield in Ireland. A Modern Poem *(1864)*

CHARLOTTE RIDDELL (MRS. J.H. RIDDELL)

62. Maxwell Drewitt *(1865)*
63. The Nun's Curse *(1888)*

T. MASON JONES

64. Old Trinity. A Story of Real Life *(1867)*

ANNIE KEARY

65. Castle Daly. The Story of an Irish Home Thirty Years Ago *(1875)*

MAY LAFFAN HARTLEY

66. Hogan, M. P. *(1876)*
67. Flitters, Tatters, and the Counsellor and Other Sketches *(1879)*

CHARLES JOSEPH KICKHAM

68. Knocknagow: or, the Cabins of Tipperary *(1879)*

MARGARET M. BREW

69. The Burtons of Dunroe *(1880)*
70. Chronicles of Castle Cloyne. Pictures of Munster Life *(1885)*

EMILY LAWLESS

71. Hurrish. A Study *(1886)*

72. With Essex in Ireland *(1890)*

73. Grania. The Story of an Island *(1892)*

74. Maelcho. A Sixteenth-Century Narrative *(1894)*

75. Traits and Confidences *(1898)*

WILLIAM O'BRIEN

76. When We Were Boys *(1890)*

ANONYMOUS

77. Priests and People: A No-Rent Romance *(1891)*